MW01489980

HOLLAND ROAD
CAROLINE KELLY

CHARIKLO PRESS

CHARIKLO PRESS

Copyright © 2024 by Caroline Kelly

All rights reserved.

No part of this publication may be reproduced, distributed, or transmitted in any form or by any means, including photocopying, recording, or other electronic or mechanical methods, without the prior written permission of the publisher, except in the case of brief quotations embodied in critical reviews, and certain other noncommercial uses as permitted by U.S. copyright law.

This is a work of fiction. Names, characters, places, and incidents are the product of the author's imagination or are used fictitiously, and any resemblance to actual persons, living or dead, businesses, companies, events, or locales is entirely coincidental.

Cover design by Paige C. Kelly

Character art by Shelby Nicole McFadden

Author photo by Leah Carrere

First edition 2024

ISBN: 979-8-9912517-0-9

To my parents,
Douglas and Laura Kelly,
who always welcome me home

O love,
Open. Show me
My country. Take me home.
—Wendell Berry

GLOSSARY

Squad < Platoon < Company < Battalion < Regiment < Division

Richard's unit: 3rd platoon, Fox Company, 2nd Battalion, 505th Parachute Infantry Regiment, 82nd Airborne Division

Operation Husky: Allied invasion of Sicily

Operation Overlord: Allied invasion of Normandy

Operation Market-Garden: Allied operation in the Netherlands combining Airborne and ground troops

AA = All-Americans, nickname for the 82nd Airborne

Ack-ack = slang for antiaircraft artillery fire

ASE = Armed Services Edition (pocket-sized books sent to servicemen)

Corcorans = lace-up jump boots worn by paratroopers, with their trousers tucked into the top

CO = Commanding Officer

CP = Command Post

DZ = drop zone

ETO = European Theater of Operations

Jump wings = badge worn by qualified parachutists; each combat jump earned a paratrooper a star on his jumpwings

KIA = Killed in Action

LCI = Landing Craft Infantry

MIA = Missing in Action

NCO/Noncom = Non-Commissioned Officer

ODs = "Olive drabs," the fatigues worn by paratroopers

PIR = Parachute Infantry Regiment

POW = Prisoner of War

Repple depple = slang for Replacement Depot

V-E Day = Victory in Europe

V-J Day = Victory over Japan

XO = Executive Officer

PART I

CHARIKLO PRESS

I.

HOMECOMING

23 April 1945

E arly tulips dot the fields out the train window the day I come home. The trees are at the beginning of their bloom, too, puffs of white showing through the greenery. I lean my elbow on the tabletop and watch the fishing villages give way to hills and woods. As the train rolls deeper into the heart of Maine the landscape sinks back into winter, flowers gone, the grass wet and brown from snowmelt. Ducking my head down, I can just make out the mountains in the west and Mt. Katahdin watching over Piscataquis County, where, until three years ago, the whole significance of my life took place.

Someone a few seats back asks the time as the conductor passes collecting tickets for Millinocket. I move my legs restlessly, resisting the urge to tap my fingers on the table. Instead I flip back and forth through the pages of my book—a dime western that a medic in Belgium told me to keep. The old woman across from me glances up and smiles and then returns her eyes to her knitting.

"Going home?" she asks, drawing the needle out and back in.

"Yes. Finally." I smile back and look out the window again.

She tugs the needle through a loop of red yarn. Then she nods at me, or maybe to my uniform, and says, "I hope your folks are proud of you. We're all very grateful, I'm sure."

The letters I wrote my parents from the veterans hospital in New Jersey told them enough so that they wouldn't worry. My stomach feels tighter with every revolution of the train's wheel-axles that bring me closer to home. I close my eyes, thinking of autumn evenings when I'd run to my dad's church in downpours with a raincoat over my head. Once over the threshold I'd shake the water out of my hair and go to a pew in the last row and sit, still dripping as I watched the votive flames quiver. I can almost smell the burned matches and rain that would linger in my nose as I sat, staring at the altar.

I don't realize how much time has passed until I hear the conductor's voice. "Next stop Caspar, five minutes," he announces as he walks down the aisle. No one moves to hand him a ticket except me. He tips his cap to me as he takes it. "Well done, son. Welcome home."

There's no one at the station in Caspar to board the train as it heads north to Aroostook County. I step off the narrow steel ledge with my army duffel over one shoulder and look from one end of the platform to the other. To the east, the tracks stretch through the open fields and then disappear in the dark woods. To the west is Caspar, two church steeples the only buildings tall enough to stand silhouetted against the gray sky.

The high school kid behind the ticket window is cleaning his nails with a toothpick as a local ball game plays on the loudspeaker. He doesn't seem to realize that someone's gotten off, or that the train even stopped.

Just as I'm thinking I'll need to walk home, I hear a whistle.

"Ay-uh, look at what the cat dragged in," a familiar voice calls. "A little rough around the edges, but he'll do, I reckon."

Pulled up in front of the station house, leaning against the rusted white pick-up that should've been salvaged for scrap metal at the start of the war, is my brother. His dark hair blows back in the wind, hands shoved in the pockets of an old plaid jacket that used to be mine.

My heart pounds as I say, "Got any room?"

Laurie smiles. "We'll make some."

Before I can even step off the platform, he runs up the steps and pulls me into a suffocating hug. He says against my shoulder, "I filled up your room with my books, though. Even on your bed. Was it an easy trip? Are you okay—didn't they only release you yesterday?"

I open my mouth to answer and realize I have no idea what to say, even after that whole train ride when I had nothing to do but twiddle my thumbs. I don't know how I could be caught off-guard when I've imagined this day obsessively.

"Yeah, I'm okay," I answer, offering him an easy smile as he pulls out of the hug. "My lungs aren't what the doctors call *fighting fit,* but it's only a matter of time till I'm running with you again."

"I'll hold you to that." Laurie shuffles a bit, looking down the empty tracks. He doesn't quite look at me when he says, "I guess you have a lot of stories to tell, huh?"

"A few, I guess."

Even after three years apart, he's still my brother, and I can tell there's more he won't say. That the stories should be his and would be, if he'd been able to go. Instead his war began and ended with a red *4F* stamp on his personnel file at the recruiting office in Bangor. He never mentioned it in his letters, but I know it crushed him to watch all of us Caspar boys go without him.

"Right, well, you're something of a hometown hero now," he remarks, covering his disenchantment with a grin. "Better watch yourself, or you'll get hoisted on someone's shoulders and paraded around."

I smile and roll my eyes, then look over his shoulder at the truck. "You can still drive this thing? It must be like shifting a tank."

"Hey, it's half yours. Couldn't sell it without your permission."

"Very loyal of you. But how about you take me home?"

"Hell of an idea," Laurie says, slinging his arm across my shoulder. "Time to let Mom get a good look at you. You know she won't let you out of her sight for a couple days."

The wind is rough, and I hold onto my beret to keep it from flying out on the rails. When I go around to the passenger side of the truck, a shaggy head pops up in the seat and barks.

"Hen!" I call, and she stands and stretches her neck out, barking and clawing furiously at the door. Her strangled yowls of excitement turn to purring when I open the door and catch her in my arms, burying my face into the thick ruff of golden fur on her neck.

"She's been following me around all day, must've known something was up," Laurie says as he slides into the driver's seat and turns the key in the ignition. "When I went to leave, she was already sleeping here, just waiting for you."

"Do you remember me, Hen?" I laugh as she licks all over my face and neck.

"Look at her—she still worships you."

Hen crawls happily down into the footwell, sits on my feet, and sniffs the laces of my boots. Laurie talks most of the drive home while I watch the houses go by.

"...don't you think?"

I turn from the window and look at him. "What?"

"I was saying that we should go down to Boothbay and see Nana and Pop soon. They're dying to see you."

"Oh, yeah, of course." I press the back of my hand to my eyes, realizing I didn't hear a word of that.

"Everything okay?" Laurie casts a sidelong glance at me before turning his attention back to the empty road. Caspar's what you call a one-street-light-town.

"Yeah, no, I'm fine, all good."

We continue in silence for a minute. When we turn onto Holland Road and I see our house framed against the cloudy sky and the woods, I draw in my breath. I dreamt of it so many times, waking up on a cot or in a foxhole aching with disappointment, that I feel a little wary seeing it now.

Laurie watches the house, then turns to me. His voice is quiet as he says, "You know, I could drive around the block if you'd rather."

I almost say yes. But then I wonder if once around the block would turn into running away and putting all this off. And I can't do that, not after all it's taken to get here.

"No, let's go on."

"I didn't tell them." Laurie pulls into the driveway, the tires grinding up dust. Hen jumps from the footwell onto my lap and knocks the wind out of me. "About the telegram you sent this morning. Should I have?"

I open the door and Hen hops out, and then I straighten my jacket and adjust the gold paratrooper jump wings pinned on my chest, four stars clustered beneath them. I don't know what to say to my parents. I don't know what to make of the full stop, the stark line cleaving who I was in the war from whatever comes next. It all happened so suddenly after I was wounded. The turn from taking care of others to being taken care of myself.

"No, no, I meant it for you," I answer. "I want to surprise Mom." I swing my legs out and lift the duffel out of the cab, although I could've carried everything I have without it.

"Well, don't go giving her a heart attack or anything like that." Laurie shoves his hands into his jacket pockets as Hen and I come around the side of the truck. "Shit, she's going to kill you for not telling her."

"She'll forgive me," I say a little over confidently. "But she might not forgive you for swearing."

"Guess I've been picking it up from Mattie."

I glance at him. "Mattie's home?"

"Oh, sure." Laurie nods. "Mattie minus one leg. But he's home." After a few seconds he says, "You want to go in?"

I stare at the house. It's a rambling thing, two stories but barely, with a porch wrapping around the sides. Winter winds have beaten up the white siding, and one of the steps into the dead garden is hanging off by a nail. But there are still the rocking chairs on the porch for neighbors to come sit and talk on warm nights, and even all the snow that my dad always mentioned in his letters didn't uproot the twisted little apple tree. Its branches still brush the porch railing.

"Come on." Laurie touches my shoulder. "Let's go in. Then you can go see Dad…"

His voice trails off as the screen door creaks open. Mom comes out onto the porch, wearing a wool sweater over her flour-covered apron. The door bangs shut behind her. She's carrying a sack of birdseed, and kernels fall out of it as she walks down the steps. Her long black hair is pulled up from her neck with probably a hundred pins.

"Where've you been, Laurie? I know I've been on you to fix that step, but you really need to take a hammer to it. Sooner or later someone is going to trip on that nail and hurt themselves, and you don't want—"

"Mom," he says.

She raises her head and sees me in my dress greens with a bag at my feet, standing by the truck as Hen licks me. Then she drops the sack of birdseed in the dirt.

Her arms hold me so tight that at first I can't breathe. Then a burst of pain in my rib cage makes me draw in what breath I do have, and she pulls away enough for me to see her face and the worry in her dark eyes. "Oh, I'm sorry, *yiannaki*—are you okay? Did I hurt you?"

"No, it's okay—I'm okay," I answer, holding my right hand to my ribs on the left, where the stabbing pain begins to recede into an ache.

"Three years," Mom says. She holds both my cheeks in her cold hands and studies me, not bothering to wipe away the tear trailing past her nose. "Look at you, Richard, all grown. Where's my boy gone?"

I don't have time to come up with a half-hearted answer before her expression changes and she smacks me lightly on the back of the head. "What were you thinking, *yiannaki mou?*" She's always been fond of using the Greek diminutive of my middle name, Yiannis, and in doing so makes me feel twelve years old again. "You come all the way from New Jersey today without telling us? Did you not think your mother might want to know you were on your way?"

"Providence, actually, I missed the early train so I got a hotel room last night."

"I guess I should've told you he was coming," Laurie says behind us, "but I wanted you to be surprised."

"No, Laurie, don't try to take the blame for him. Three years and you just strut into the front yard as though you were only down at the post office!"

"I didn't want anyone making a fuss, *μαμά.*" The fragment of Greek, *mama,* sounds so unfamiliar that I almost don't recognize it. I kiss her cheek, and her attempt at harshness falters. She moves just as quickly from admonishment to holding my hands and exclaiming how grown I look, how handsome I am, then less flattering observations such as how thin I've gotten and how tired I must be, tapping my cheekbone to indicate the dark circles under my eyes, I guess.

She leads me to the house as though I might not remember the way. On the porch she says, "What am I going to make? What do you want to eat, *yiannaki?*" Then she pulls my face toward hers and kisses both cheeks. "Oh, Richard. Welcome home."

Laurie holds open the screen door and whistles, and Hen trots up the steps after us into the bright kitchen. As they go inside, I notice the flag hanging in the front window, indicating that this house has a father or son or husband at war. I hesitate in the doorway and stare at the sun-worn cloth. Its scarlet border frames a white box and a blue star. I wonder if they even see it anymore. Maybe it blends in with the old furniture, a symbol so commonplace that its meaning is lost in the dozen others displayed in Caspar front windows. And some of those flags have stars stitched in gold thread. But I never even imagined it, never thought how my absence was just as much a presence, and it unsettles me, to have been here without knowing I was here. To have been remembered, no matter how much that star faded into its surroundings.

"Richard?" Mom pokes her head out. "Coming in?"

"Yes, sorry."

She seats me at the kitchen table, refusing to let me help her do anything. After a quick barrage of questions—interspersed with her touching my arms, my face, my shoulders, repeatedly asking if I'm okay and how do I feel—Laurie tells her to let me just sit for a while.

"Oh, I know. I know. You're right." She chops vegetables with hands she can't keep steady, and she talks without waiting for answers, which is okay because I don't really have any.

The kitchen looks exactly the same as when I left. Those might even be the same bundles of dried herbs hanging by twine on the windowpane above the sink. Other than a couple quick glances, I don't look around. I don't know why but I don't want to see any of it. If Mom and Laurie weren't here, I'd run back out to the porch and breathe in the evening air and not sit surrounded by all the luxuries of everyday life.

Around dusk, with the nightjars swooping, I walk to the church. Our house—the house my grandfather built, where my mom grew up and where my parents met—watches over the corner of Queen and Holland. From our porch, the church bell-tower and its cross peek above the trees. These two places are like the starred points on a map of my life, the constellations from which all the other patterns form.

The clouds clear as the sun sets, tinting the sky rosy in the west over the mountains. Outside the church I stand on the sidewalk for a minute and watch the colors fade. At last I open the big door and step quietly in.

Shadows of candlelight loom on the white wood panels between the plain glass windows. A woman kneels between the pews a few rows back, her hands folded. She doesn't move when a gust of evening wind blows in through the door behind me, but she lifts her head and glances at me when the door creaks closed. I realize it's Mrs. Coldwater, who lives in a brick house on Linden Avenue and whose son James must still be in the Pacific, or she wouldn't be here praying. I think of kneeling too, but I don't know what I would say, and I can't stand the thought of anyone watching me while I pray. Then she slips out, and I'm alone in the sanctuary, feeling the layers of all the years I've spent here.

A voice behind me says, "Richard?"

I turn. He stands backlit in the light of the corridor. He looks so much shorter now than in my imagination—the towering giant of my childhood, presiding over Little League games, high school track meets, over this church itself. In the dusky light, watching one another, I feel an undercurrent of both love and uncertainty, like two riptides at odds.

I've no idea what to say, but that doesn't matter—he'll hug me and we won't need words for that.

Except he doesn't. He takes my hand and grips it tightly, the perennial sign of affection between fathers and sons in New England. My shoulders feel suddenly tense, expecting an embrace that doesn't come, and I glance at our feet, hoping he didn't notice that I started to lean into that hug before he shook my hand.

Hand still tight around mine, he says quietly, "Welcome home, son."

For a few moments neither of us says a word, his eyes on me, mine not quite on him. Then, because I don't know what else to do in place of collapsing into his arms as I'd imagined, I say, "Mom said to be home for supper by seven."

I finally meet his gray eyes as his hand moves to grasp my arm. What a normal way to live a life. Supper on the table at seven—wash your hands—the coffee's on for later. Real coffee, not brewed in an ammo case over a lighter flame at the bottom of a foxhole.

He keeps his hand on my arm, as if he's afraid I'll disappear again if he doesn't hold onto me. "Hen must've known you were coming. She was all in a fluster yesterday, couldn't settle down. The hospital discharged you early, then?"

I nod, then glance over Dad's shoulder into his office. "Are you writing the sermon for Wednesday?" Somehow I can't say what I really want to: *I have so much to tell you.* I know that the moment I try to tell any of it to him, the questions will follow. Questions I can't think about, let alone answer.

"Not yet. Just thinking when I should be writing." He takes off his glasses, folds them, and puts them in his shirt pocket. "I don't know why writing's been harder lately." He smiles, shakes his head. "But that doesn't compare."

My shoulders tighten. If Dad notices, he doesn't acknowledge it.

"I've prayed for today, Richard," he says after a moment. "Prayed for it, and asked God that I would be able to accept it however it came. Or if it didn't come."

I think I've prayed for it, too, although I can't really think of when, or what words I might've used or if I used words at all. It was more of a pull at my chest every time the scream *MEDIC!* reached my ears. So I just nod, our eyes meeting in the dim light.

He adds, "Let's go home." He still hasn't let go of my arm.

It's even chillier with the sun down, but the wool of my dress greens makes me sweat. On the other side of the road, beyond the scattered houses, is a stretch of dark, humming salt marsh. Mike Garley's yard is still covered with old splintered lobster traps and rotting tools, just as it was when I left, and there he is on his porch that seems to be sinking into the marshy ground, giving us a short wave with one hand while the other balances a whiskey glass. The Lees on this side have a new baby, and her two sisters are in the yard with her, wrapped in sweaters, trying to decorate her with grass crowns and necklaces. Everywhere I look there seem to be old, unbroken rhythms. And at the corner of Holland and Queen Street is the yellow glow of my parents' house, effusive with warmth against the indigo woods, the sight of it stirring up feelings I don't understand.

Dad stops at the mailbox, sorting through the letters. "Helen Innes has been back for a while now," he says, glancing at me. "She was at the ironworks in Bath, but Isaiah had a small heart attack last fall and she came home to help him with the hotel. Antonia Hardy's been working on the Mulcahy farm for a couple years now, must be. Who else...Sidney Whitley's still somewhere near Japan or Australia. And Grace Whitley graduated from Boston University in December."

"Oh," I say, "so she's still in Boston, then?"

He gestures for me to go ahead, so I lead the way across the yard. Laurie is at the porch steps, trying to work that nail back in.

"No, she came back and lives with her grandmother again," Dad answers. "She's teaching at the high school."

"I was thinking she might've gotten married," I say, even though I know she didn't. I'm sure he remembers how I used to feel about Grace Whitley without the confirmation of the blush spreading across my face, but even so, I suddenly don't want to talk about her or high school or any of my old friends.

Laurie, muttering defeatedly about rust and decay, trails after us up the porch steps and into the warm lamplit kitchen, where the coals glow in the stove and where my mother hugs me again while I wish she would let go.

M y room is cold when I wake up. I get out of bed and turn the doorknob carefully, easing the door open. I start to feel my way in the dark toward the bathroom to get a drink when I notice a glow of light on the staircase.

He must be downstairs, an insomniac as long as I've been alive. I know he's been waiting for me to talk to him.

I go down and glance around the corner into the kitchen. Dad is sitting at the table, his pocket knife in one hand and a pile of unskinned carrots beside him. He never liked to turn the lights on at night, but now the single bulb over the sink flickers so he can see enough not to cut himself. His chair is pushed just out of the circle of light.

He looks up when the last step creaks under my weight.

"This a new habit of yours," I ask, "peeling carrots in the middle of the night?"

"Well, your mom mentioned wanting to bring a casserole to the Davisons tomorrow—Rebecca had a baby last week. And I thought, as long as I'm up, might as well get a start on peeling these." He shrugs. "But maybe I'm also trying to avoid writing a sermon. Haven't finished tomorrow night's." He digs the side of his knife into the dirt embedded in the carrot. "Actually, it's tonight's sermon, I guess. What time is it?"

"Past one."

"There's always a sticking point, isn't there?" He stops his peeling and looks toward the dark window. "When you talk to God all night and are still no closer to understanding. And I've been doing this for twenty-five years."

I nod as if I do understand. Then I get a paring knife from the drawer by the stove, sit opposite him, and take a carrot from the unskinned pile.

"Seems you're up as often as I am," Dad remarks after a moment.

"You've heard me?"

He smiles in the low light. "This house was so quiet for three years, Richard. Your brother makes his fair share of noise, but then he was at school, and..." He pauses, seeming more intent on whittling away at the carrot than on what he's saying. "And besides, it wasn't like having the two of you here together."

Dad sets aside the carrot, peeled to within an inch of its life, and selects a new one. He says, "We listened for you every night, and now there's finally something to hear. Except it's not what I want to hear."

"It sounds like you're waiting for a baby to cry."

"Sometimes I wish I was."

I glance at him. He's always talking to God, drawing his whole life into one long prayer. Maybe that's why so much more than a table seems to separate us. Trying to steady my hands, I draw the blade down the length of the carrot and flick the peel away with my thumb. I never meant to bring the weight home with me. Never thought I would be here, under this light, looking at the paring blade as though it were a trench knife.

"I think about it, sometimes, what happened over there," he says, unprompted. "Your mother wouldn't watch the newsreels, she couldn't bear it. But I did."

"...why?"

He takes his glasses off, rubs them on his sweater sleeve, replaces them, and squints. "Oh, I've made it worse."

I ask again, "Why did you watch them?"

"The newsreels?" He glances up. "I guess it felt like a betrayal to not know. It seemed like my responsibility."

I find it a little harder to breathe at the thought of him imagining those things. Not until I notice Dad watching me do I realize I'm holding one hand against my rib cage, over my left lung, or what remains of it.

"That star's still in the window," he murmurs, looking up at it. "I suppose I can take it down."

He turns his attention back to skinning the carrot, as if he hasn't just struck a chord of fear in me I wasn't aware existed. For as long as that star hangs in the Dare kitchen window, my parents have a son at war. Take it down and I imagine the last three years will sift through my fists like silt, swirling eddies on a fast current. I've already lost so much of it. I lost the boys and my platoon the moment I was evacuated to the hospital in Liege. But I've tried not to think about it, even as I lay silently awake night after night in dark hospital wards, alone—"lucky to be alive," the nurses told me, because they didn't understand that I'd already lost everything.

"Dad," I say.

He raises an eyebrow and waits as I hesitate.

"I, uh, I...speaking of that—" I tilt my head to indicate the star. "There are things—y'know, things I..."

He doesn't say anything as I stutter my way into unsatisfying nothingness. I run a hand through my hair and try to retrace my thoughts back to coherency, but the words have all evaporated. Where would I even begin? The beginning of my war, the end of it, or the months that followed?

The carrot and paring knife feel suddenly like ballast weights in my hands. I set them on the table and shake my head and say, "Never mind, I think I'm just tired."

Dad doesn't pause in his methodical work. Though he doesn't meet my eyes, I sense he's still watching me. "That's okay. You have some rest to catch up on."

"I'm bored out of my mind with rest," I say before I can stop myself. "...Sorry. I've been flat on my back for a lot of the past few months."

"Is there something you want to tell me?"

"No, not re—well, yes. I don't know. I'm sorry."

"Nothing to be sorry for," he says gently. "It isn't as if I have someplace better to be."

We sit in silence for a long time. Too long. We used to talk for hours, about anything, whatever was on our minds. Then we wrote letters and I learned the art of paring my words, whittling away whatever I didn't know how to explain, which he must've guessed because the war I gave him was a little cleaner, a little more heroic than the truth. Not because he wouldn't understand; somehow I know he would. Or he'd get close. But it's humiliating to be someone's child and then tell him you screamed during a mortar shelling, not your first day in combat or even your second but months in, and it isn't the screaming or the tears that are the humiliating part, it's that you were there at all, and that you know what it sounds like when mortars explode, because you were there and it was a war and you are still his child and war is no place for anyone's child.

"Richard," he says at last.

I look up at him, blinking away my bleariness.

"I'm down here most nights."

A few apricot-colored embers glow in the stove. The shapes imprint themselves in my vision till I see them when I rub my eyes. "I know. Yeah. Thank you."

"You still have time."

"Time for what?"

"You're two, three days home. Not on leave or waiting to jump." Dad sets the knife down. I expect him to continue, but he doesn't. Finally he says again, "You still have time."

But I want to tell you now, I think. *I was in Sicily, Tunisia, Normandy. You know that,* I could tell him, the thought alone making me blush. I was there, I saw those things, sometimes I *did* those things. *I'm sorry,* I could tell him. *I'm sorry I was there. I'm sorry that I know horrible things.*

I stare at the embers. Sicily feels so far away, almost two years ago, the summer of '43 drenched in brown desert and faded scrubgrass light. That boy who first felt mortar fire and saw gunshot wounds on Biazza Ridge wasn't the same one who graduated parachute school and had the gold jump wings pinned on his uniform, and he wasn't the same one evacuated from Belgium four months ago, either. He's sure as hell not the husk of a person who took up a bed in that VA hospital.

If I forget who he was, what he did, I might lose him for good. *So tell him,* I think, eyes flicking to watch Dad without raising my head. *If someone else knows, it can't be lost.*

"It feels like a lot longer than three years," I say, which isn't what I want to say. "Or two and a half. However long it's been."

Dad nods. "Yes. It does."

And that's all. I come up empty. Nothing to say and no will to try to drag the nothingness out of myself.

"I think I'll go back up," I say after a while, and Dad nods and says he hopes I get some sleep. I put the peeled carrots in the icebox for him and climb the stairs slowly.

Back on my bed Hen snuffles in her sleep, curled up in the tangled sheets. I sit on the edge and look at the silhouette of the window glowing in the moonlight and the gauzy curtains filled with the breeze.

I can't tell him yet. But I could tell it to myself. I've lived it already, so maybe if I live it once more, that'll be enough. Maybe then it'll leave me in peace and I'll get on with things.

Here's what matters: My name is Richard Dare, and I was a nineteen-year-old rising junior in college in the summer of 1942 when I enlisted and volunteered for the paratroops, because I was too anxious to let the draft catch up to me and I liked the fifty dollars extra in jump pay every month. I was also lured by the promise that these guys were the best, the elite of the elite. I wanted to be with them and to be one of them. And I was. I spent the whole of my war in the 3rd platoon of Company F, 2nd Battalion, 505th Parachute Infantry Regiment, in the 82nd Airborne Division, dropping into Europe to tell Hitler, *Fuck you*.

Well, the truth is, it was mostly the other guys who jumped and marched with that vitriol fueling them, and that was a good thing because they were the ones carrying M1 carbines and mortars and hand grenades. We were all scared at first, till the fear disintegrated in stages and then we were exhausted and angry and still scared but in a different way. And except for those early worries of stepping on a mine or getting blown to bits, my fear was not the same as theirs. They were scared of fucking up, letting down their buddies, being cowards. I was scared of fucking up and getting one of them killed.

The difference was that their bodies were in my care. What I didn't know at the beginning was that soon would mean their spirits, too, though I wasn't a chaplain. I was a twenty-year-old private, a former theology student who didn't even know how many bones are in the human body, when the Army made me a combat medic. And hell, if that doesn't teach a guy how many bones are in the human body and the myriad number of ways they fracture and how bodies fall apart, nothing will.

I don't want to forget that kid, the young, green medic squinting to see through the smoke on Biazza. He was so fucking scared. I feel sort of bad for him, a side-eyed pity, because I can't make myself believe I was him. Humiliated to have once been him, to have not known anything, to have been so scared.

Humiliated now that I'm no longer him because I know too much.

II.

HUSKY

10 July 1943, Southeastern Sicily, 0115 hours

Total darkness envelops me as I hit the ground. Landing on my left hip, knees bent, I try to right myself to keep the deflated parachute from dragging me through the mud. I slip my trench-knife out from its sheath above my boot, yank the lines of the chute toward me, and sever them, leaving the canvas and lines where they fell. Mediterranean gales whip through the trees and rain plinks on my helmet, blowing into my eyes, which are useless anyway: it's pitch black, darker than the dark behind my eyelids. I whirl around, still kneeling, as rain and wind rattle the countryside, a thousand night sounds rustling on every side.

The pilots must've dropped us all over the coastline. I crouch on my knees in the mud, still feeling that I'm being knocked around in that sardine-can plane. Our platoon leader Lieutenant Walsh was first in the stick, and I was third behind Sergeant Kuhn. There's no telling where I am now, much less where they might've landed, or if they landed. A half dozen practice jumps, both daylight and night, and the weather was never so b—

Voices. A word whispered and a reply. I hold my breath, listening with the challenge word, "George?" on my tongue. The exchange is too hushed to hear what language it is. I tighten my fingers around the grip of my trench knife, the only weapon I have. Then there's a low laugh, and it sounds as if it could be some of the guys in my platoon. I'm about to whisper to them when there's a click and a flame suddenly glows in my eyes, a flame attached to a lighter in the hand of a soldier in an Italian uniform.

Then from out of the darkness, a shout: "George!"

I drop to my stomach on the wet ground and shout, "MARSHALL!" just as the discharge of an M1 rifle bursts into the stillness. I feel the thumps of two bodies, one after another.

I drop my arms and lift my head, breaths coming in short, quick gasps. In the space of a blink three faces appear above me. Or, rather, three pairs of eyes, attached to which must be features that I can't make out because we all blackened our faces with grease for camouflage before the jump.

"Hey pal, you okay? Jesus, but that was a close call." A hand reaches out to grip mine, hauling me to my feet, and then the voice says, "Hold on, you who I think you are?"

"...Pete?" I straighten just as the face breaks into a grin, spooky as the Cheshire Cat's smile floating above Alice in the trees in Wonderland. Like the cat, this grin is full of perfectly straight white teeth because Peter Adler's uncle is a dentist back in Milwaukee.

He laughs softly. "If it ain't the Reverend."

Another voice: "Reverend? You mean we found a chaplain?"

"Don't go getting down on your knees, Simms. But he'd probably listen anyway, wouldn't you, Rev? Got time for a few sinners?"

Before I can answer, the third one steps closer to me and tugs at the armband on my sleeve. "Chaplain, my ass. We bagged a medic."

"Okay," I say, shaking him off, "you didn't bag yourself anyone. What are you, D Company?" I look back at Peter. "Where the fuck are we?"

"That's the question of the night. I ran into these Dog boys back there, they couldn't find their own asses in the dark."

"Hey—"

"Hey nothing. I'm tired of you arguing. You can split if you want." Apparently Peter's figured out how to distill his argument-ending looks into his voice, because the private shuts up. Peter turns his attention back to me. "Rev, how're you doing? You land right on top of them?"

"Almost. I'm fine—yeah, fine. Thank you," I add. "How'd you do that?" I turn in the dark rain, seeing only the shadowy outlines of the bodies on the ground.

"Lucky shots, I guess. Or it's the hunting experience." He grins in that characteristically good-natured, Middle West way of his, an expression I've come to learn over the past year is his truest form. "We have no idea where we're going, Rev," he says, "but I figure we might as well walk."

Parachute gone, I'm lighter than I was when we checked gear in the plane. But my reserve chute weighs me down on the front, and I don't get more than a few feet before I'm pulling it off and throwing it behind me. Peter insists on going ahead of me with one of the privates and the other trails behind, sandwiching me with the protection of their M1s and full clips. The private behind me, the one who thought I was a chaplain, is as jumpy as a rabbit with every rustle and twig-snap on the hillside.

"Simms, I can hear your heartbeat all the way up here," Peter throws over his shoulder. "You should breathe easy now. If we go down, we're in the best hands."

"Sure, but what if *he* goes down?" Simms trots to catch up to me.

"You sure know how to lift our spirits. How about you pay more attention to covering us so he doesn't?"

Without the moon I feel as though we're walking through a dream. Sometimes my outstretched hand scrapes against what feels like the top of a shrub or a hanging branch. All the boys greased the metal on their rifles last night so that the silver couldn't catch the moonlight and light us up like a flare to the enemy, but they needn't have bothered; there's no light to catch on anything. We go as quietly as we can, and though adrenaline ensures no one's guard drops, gradually our collective breathing grows steadier.

I wonder if those two Italians were deserters because we don't encounter any others. Whatever happens, on the ground together is better than getting all our marbles shook up in those planes. Peter and I talk in hushed voices. We don't know if the rest of the boys in our sticks made it, how many of them got out of the planes, how many of the planes stayed in the air.

He and I met on the train to Fort Benning, both having completed basic training but with no idea what awaited us at parachute school. From that first morning, wearing our dress greens and laughing over coffee and crackers and watching the southern countryside pass in a sunlit coach car, we've stuck by each other. A stroke of good fortune landed us not just in the same company but the same platoon. Peter pulls rank as the only sergeant among us, and eventually the two Dog Company boys get too tired to argue with him.

"Real glad it was you we found, Dare," he murmurs.

He's carrying the barrel of his light machine gun on one shoulder, so we can only hope that Branson, his assistant gunner, made it to the ground alive with the gun's tripod. On his other shoulder his M1 hangs by its strap, barrel pointed to the ground.

"No kidding, so am I."

"I mean, hell"—he laughs, short and dry—"you're practically medic *and* chaplain. Simms says he's a Catholic, though."

"I doubt he'd care if I was a witch doctor, if he gets h—"

Though I can't see Peter, I feel his arm reach out, pushing me back by the chest. "Here," he whispers over his shoulder to the privates, because hand signals are no use. Their forms appear beside us. They all have rifles drawn. I hold my breath as if even that will disrupt the tenuous balance of safety, and I slowly move one hand down to my bag.

There's a scrambling that sounds just a few feet from us. Peter raises his rifle—and then lowers it and begins to laugh.

"Fucking rabbit."

Simms swears under his breath, and the other private snorts. I move to stand between them and strain my eyes to see into the darkness, but except for the shadowy lines of bushes and hills that must mean dawn is approaching, I can't see a thing.

"You could see that?" I say to Peter.

"Hunter's eyes. Sharp as a cat's."

"And humble, too."

Rain runs off the rims of our helmets. By the time we all tug our raincoats out of our tightly packed musette bags, our ODs are soaked to the skin. We're all silent. To calm my nerves, I run an inventory in my mind as we walk. In my musette bag on my back I have C rations and a mess kit; my sleeping roll; extra socks; a razor and toothbrush and tiny packets of shaving cream and toothpaste; the New Testament my mother sent me; and a paperback of *Huckleberry Finn,* for which I traded two packs of Old Gold cigarettes. There are two canteens filled with water on my empty cartridge belt. My trench knife is in its scabbard against my calf. I have a shoulder harness from which hang two medical bags, one beneath each arm, and a first-aid kit hanging from my webbing that I thought was so funny when I was given my gear—a personal first-aid kit for a medic, as if I'm not the walking apothecary. But in the steady drizzle I feel grateful that I'm lighter than most of the guys, especially the ones carrying broken-down machine guns or Cochran with the platoon's radio. On the airfield at Kairouan last night, it took three guys to push him into the plane to keep him from ending up like a top-heavy turtle on the tarmac.

I trail after the sound of Peter's footfalls, quiet as a deer through the brush. Night fades and light like dusk outlines the landscape. Except for the rain and the creeping animals, the land is dead silent, eerie, as if the battles have already been fought and we're hunting for the carnage. Even that, we can't find. If not for our run-in with the Italian soldiers, I wouldn't be surprised to hear this is all an elaborate hoax and there's no enemy to fight on this island.

When I joined up, I thought I'd be a soldier like the other volunteers. That isn't at all what I feel like now. The 1st platoon medic, Donny King, was picked because he had two years of medical school at Stanford, and in 2nd platoon, Walt Bruning volunteered for it, I have no idea why. But I was picked at random, as far as I can tell, for 3rd platoon. I've gone over and over it in my head every time there's been a moment to think in the past half year, and I still can't make sense of it. Not once did I give anyone from regimental headquarters a reason to think I'd make a shitty soldier. I don't know what's worse: trying to figure what someone up at division could've seen in my temperament that was unsuited to taking a life, or accepting that the decision—like so much of the Army's chickenshit—was most likely the luck of the draw.

The rising sun reveals a country of green valleys and parched brown slopes, along which are orchards with trees stripped bare of fruit, probably thanks to the kraut occupation. There are long stretches of sandy dirt dotted with scrub and brush, like one of those lawless towns in a western film, and vineyards, whose branches hang empty without a grape in sight. Despite the hours of walking, there's still no road. No trace of an American company, Airborne or otherwise. Substantial cover is sparse and high ground is abundant, which sets us all the more on our guard.

"Looks kind of like California," observes the other private, Garcia. "Not as many wildflowers."

I think of the lupine that grows along the roadsides in Maine and the red trillium in the cemetery behind the church. It's the middle of the night back home, but my dad often goes to the cemetery at night to pray when he can't sleep. I wonder if he's praying now.

With the rain gone, the sky is white over our heads and it isn't long before sweat is running down my back as we tramp along. Every so often we see a figure in the distance, old men in their fields or women holding babies on their hips in the doorways of stone houses, watching us out of suntanned faces. Two little boys pick up sticks from the road and carry them the way Peter and the privates carry their rifles, till a woman runs through the vineyard and calls to them in a scolding tone, and they scuttle back between the rows.

We don't happen upon any towns or see any landmarks that could give us our bearings, just farms and stripped hillsides. Peter and I agree that we should stop and rest and wait for the brilliance of the sun to recede before we keep going. Dusk is better than daylight for marching, and we're trapped among a series of undulating hills that span the horizon like a bunched ribbon. Anyone could be looking down at us.

"You remember those pillboxes they kept harping on in the briefings?" Peter cranes his neck to study our surroundings as we sit on the shady western side of a brown ridge, covered in scrub grass dry as a bone. "No wonder they've built that shit here. Hide at the top, pick off your intruders easy as shooting fish in a barrel." He makes a gun with his thumb and forefinger and mimics popping off a few shots.

"And we're those fish," Simms says as he leans on his entrenching tool stuck in the dirt, "because you know as soon as we find anywhere, we're gonna be climbing up there to clear 'em out."

"Geez, don't volunteer too quickly. Someone'll get the idea you're eager to fight, Private."

Simms wipes his forehead and glances at me. "What about you, Doc? You ready to follow us up with Band-Aids for our scraped knees?"

"I wish you didn't need me at all."

He turns back to his poor excuse for a slit trench. Peter, keeping first watch and rubbing the stock of his carbine with a scrap cut from his parachute, glances over his shoulder at me.

"Someone has to get hit for me to be any use," I add.

"Well, at least you're not the one who has to crawl up a hill as they pound the shit out of us, or whatever the hell it is we're gonna have to do." Garcia shrugs off his musette bag and fishes through it for something to eat. "I'll tell ya, maybe I wouldn't mind playing doctor instead, if it gets real bad up there."

"Hey," Peter says with the sudden sharpness that makes privates listen to him. "You won't be mocking it as an easy gig when Richard is holding your intestines in for you so that your folks back in California don't get a letter that you died a hero on some fucking Sicilian hillside. You show every medic you meet a little more respect or you might find yourself alone when you need one most."

A beat passes before Garcia and Simms say together, "Yes, sarge."

Peter watches the hills and the boys go silent. I'm too wired to sleep, even after all that digging in the hard shale that afforded me a foxhole barely twenty inches deep. When I lean back on my musette bag and close my eyes, I still see the brown hills and the sun bleached across my eyelids. Over and over in my mind I run through a checklist of my supplies, and then through various wound-treating protocols. Everything I learned along with the other battalion medics in the classroom at Benning feels as abstract as ancient philosophy. None of it means a thing until—

Behind me I hear Peter call out the password, and then a voice says, "Marshall, Marshall! Don't shoot."

I sit up and look around. Peter sighs, lowering his rifle, and Simms does the same while Garcia resumes chewing. Three shadows appear on the shallow ridge above us. They all have the 82nd insignia on their left shoulders, with the American flag patch on the right, and one has a white bar on his helmet: a lieutenant. It takes a few moments for me to remember him as one of the recent Officers Candidate School graduates who joined the company when we were camped in Tunisia; Greer, I think his name is. He's a rifle squad leader in 1st platoon. One of the guys with him is also 1st platoon, Stephens, and Tony Rodriguez beside him is one of our 3rd platoon mortarmen. He's got the mortar tripod propped on one shoulder.

"If only that was for a machine gun, Tony," Peter says, nodding to it. "I've got half a Browning here."

"Sorry sarge, I'll keep an eye out for one."

The three of them climb from the ridgeline down to us, into the shade. I listen to Peter and the lieutenant talk in low voices as the four privates cluster together around their musette bags and share rations. Lieutenant Greer has a compass but no map, so they take turns trying to draw one from memory with a stick in the dust. The dry and unforgiving countryside stretching around us doesn't betray a thing.

We rotate throughout the hot day keeping watch. Finally at dusk, as a hazy pink and gray sky sweeps the hills, we move out, the seven of us constituting the size of a rifle squad. If I had a rifle.

"Thank God," Peter remarks to me as we pick our way down the hill. "I'm too Anglo-Saxon for this sunny shit."

"You are a little red."

He snorts. "I'll bet I am. You even know what a sunburn feels like, Rev? You're a lucky Greek bastard."

We walk all night. The moon is out and Greer can see the face of his compass in its light, so we keep on a steady enough northwest course toward, we hope, the Gela beachhead—or "bitchhead," as it's become affectionately known—which was the 82nd's original objective before we were blown so far off course.

I should be watching my step or Tony's back ahead of me, but I can't keep from craning my head back to watch the sky. Sicily's stars are stretched across the blackness like silver pins holding a great curtain from falling and enveloping the countryside. Every winter of my life I've watched the Northern Lights glowing like supernatural lanterns in the blackest of Maine skies, but Maine is covered with trees and I've never seen a sky stretch out as far and wide as this one. Stephens and Simms, both Midwestern boys, seem to think nothing of it and only shrug when I point out the stars. But the sight still thrills me, and for a few seconds whenever I look up, I feel something like peace. I see constellations I've only ever seen in books, like the claws of Scorpius and the Twins—Gemini—as dawn approaches. Funny how it's more dizzying to stare up into the dark expanse, peppered with stars, than it is to stand in the open door of a plane and look down into a bottomless night.

Around dawn, our second night in Sicily over and our second day beginning, a white strand shimmers and crystallizes into focus as we try to keep our heads and shoulders down, crossing a ragged field. *A road.* The whisper runs down our single-file line. Then figures come into view, about a company in size, moving through the ditch alongside the raised road and carrying their weapons.

"Smells like tomatoes," Garcia says.

It smells fouler than tomatoes to me, and in a few steps more I see why. Two bodies lie facedown in the dusty scrub grass, faded bloodstains clumping the dirt under them. More Italian soldiers. Garcia pokes at one with the toe of his boot, and the body flops onto its back. Still fresh, no time for rigor mortis to set in.

"*Buongiorno,* fellas." He crouches, shakes the corpse's hand as if it's an old friend, and relieves the dead man of his gold wristwatch.

"The hell's wrong with you?" Peter mutters, turning away in disgust.

I stare at the stiff face, which is plastered with mud and sweat, his big dark eyes staring up into the white morning sky. Garcia buckles the watch around his own wrist and whistles cheerfully. I try to work up some feeling of remorse or even respectful disgust for my first time really seeing the dead—we'll all go the same way in the end, won't we?—but the bodies look like mannequins or film props, dropped into the landscape so we don't forget we've arrived at the war. And anyway, better them than me.

Rodriguez and Simms loot the bodies for valuables, finding a couple half packets of cigarettes, a gold necklace chain, and a photograph of a woman, which Tony tucks back into the dead fellow's jacket. Peter strips some anti-tank grenades from their belts and passes them out to the boys, though he doesn't seem to take any pleasure in doing it.

"Now leave them in peace," he says to no one in particular, and Garcia stops whistling and rolls his eyes.

Greer lifts his binoculars from the strap around his neck and peers through them toward the road in the distance. "Looks like we've found ourselves some more All-Americans."

As we move closer, I see the 82nd insignia patches, *AA,* on the shoulders of the men hunched to keep their heads from becoming target practice for whatever krauts might be looking down at them. Some more appear to be infantrymen from another division. Greer calls the password. They answer, and we fall in at the back. Peter and the lieutenant move on down the line, and a couple minutes later only Peter returns.

"Greer found part of his platoon," he says to me. "And we've struck gold—that's Krause up there, from 3rd battalion. And Colonel Gavin's supposed to be up ahead, at some hill he wants us to take. They've sent a couple scouts out, but they can't get close enough to see how many Germans there are."

"So even the COs were as lost as we were?" I glance over my shoulder back the way we came. "Are most of these Krause's boys?"

Peter adjusts the barrel of his gun on his shoulder as we walk. "Yeah, it's mostly 3rd battalion 505th, a few other stragglers like us, no one else can find their company. Hey, you got any water?"

"Yeah." I unhook my half-full canteen from my cartridge belt and hand it to him. A headache is beginning to pound behind my eyes, but I can't touch that other full canteen. Someone else will need it more than I do.

Peter tilts the canteen back and swallows, then wipes his mouth on the sleeve of his jacket. "Thanks, Rev. You know, apparently Vandervoort had to come back here and tell Krause to get his ass moving before Gavin and some engineers on that hill got *their* asses blown to bits. Real glad I ain't an officer just about now."

"Sure, but where the hell's our company, or even the battalion?"

"Yeah, I know. Guess we're all fighting with Krause and Gavin till we can find home."

After a couple miles' march past the crimson tomato fields as the sun rises at our backs, we come near a sloping hill on the other side of the clear white highway, the sound of small arms fire growing as we approach. My pulse quickens, and the sweat seems to go cold on my back. The hazy forms of men crawling on their stomachs through the sunburned grass shimmer and solidify. We crouch under cover of the road embankment, and I raise my head enough to see strips of white boxes through the olive trees, perched at the crest of the hill. Those figures crawling against the resistance of the small arms fire must be Gavin and the engineers he's rumored to have found, their objective to destroy those pillboxes.

Officers come down the line, arranging the men into rifle squads, and Peter is charged with setting up the light machine gun on the right flank to cover the advancing engineers. It looks deceptively easy enough: get to the top of the hill and hold it.

"I'll see ya on the other side, Rev," Peter says before rising from the embankment to follow one of the rifle squads. A private holding a machine-gun tripod is on his heels. I realize only after he runs across the highway that this is it, all we've trained for, all we've anticipated through long nights in bunks on a troopship—and while slapping away mosquitoes and puking from malaria at camp in Tunisia, when we were so sick and bored we dreamed of combat just to break the monotony. I don't know why I imagined it as a crescendo, like some Hollywood rendering of what war might be, a heroic rising-up in a moment forever imprinted in my mind. But it isn't that way. Peter crosses the highway and I'm still behind the embankment, and the sound of fire on the hill is distant enough that I have trouble believing in it, even in the reality of this war. It seems so quiet and clean that they can't possibly need me.

Still, can't hurt to be prepared on the chance this isn't just an international game of Cowboys and Indians. The embankment is the perfect natural defilade for what I assume must be the aid station, and I run along its length to the collection of stone huts on the edge of the olive orchard. Some chickens bob about in the dirt before the open door. The tomatoes grow close enough that you could reach out the kitchen window and pick one right off the vine.

It's three structures, actually, one larger and the other two crumbling around it, and I was generous in assuming there might be a kitchen. I picture the apostles themselves loosening their sandal straps and washing their feet before crossing what's left of the threshold. The light dims significantly when I step inside, even though there's only half a roof. A few stretchers crowd the narrow space, some of them occupied. One holds a body covered head to toe with the tattered remains of a parachute. On another is an 82nd boy propped against the stone wall with his leg out before him on the stretcher, ankle bound in bandages with a bit of red showing through. A table quite literally on its last legs is pushed against the wall, and a guy with the 82nd insignia and jump boots counts bandages on it.

"Are you the grave cr—oh," he says, glancing over his shoulder at me and nodding when he sees the red cross brassard on my left upper arm that matches his own. "Company medic?"

"2nd battalion, Company F," I answer. "Are we all there is?"

"Looks like. I'm medical battalion, and Doc Ryder has got one of the infantry boys out rounding up a coupla privates to be runners."

I look past him at the paratrooper with the wrapped ankle. His eyes are closed. "What happened to him?"

"Bad jump." The other medic talks around a cigarette that's all but burned down. "You staying or going?"

"Is the doctor here?"

"Here." A figure appears in the arched doorframe. When he comes into the light, I see he's around forty, with big hands and small glasses over sharp blue eyes. He seems familiar, maybe from camp in Tunisia or back at Benning. "We don't know what to expect or how many Germans are at the top of that hill, so try to conserve your supplies. You need bandages, morphine, anything?"

I tighten my grip on the strap of my bag. "Thank you, I've got enough, sir. I'll just be bringing them to you, anyway."

"Not if you can help it," the doctor answers as the medic tosses me a few rolled bandages. "You let the runners do their job, corporal—"

"Dare, sir."

"And you do yours, Corporal Dare. Just remember your training."

He grips my shoulder for a brief moment, then disappears out of the aid station into the sunlight as a couple of officers come near.

"What training?" I say after him, and the other medic snorts.

I go back out. My brief distraction is gone, nothing between me and the hill except the highway. In the sunlight, the glare off the white pillboxes is too bright to look at. Distant cracks break the stillness farther up the slope. Troopers and infantry advance up through the grass with rifles drawn.

I blink sweat out of my eyes and will my heart to slow. The boys will take the ridge because not taking it is not an option. Because we're the fucking 82nd. All I have to do is follow them. I mean, Jesus Christ, *they* have the tough job.

One more breath, a prayer sent with the exhale, and suddenly the fight doesn't feel like a fairytale. When I step onto the white highway, it snaps into a profound and vivid reality that makes me aware of my rising blood pressure, the hair standing up on my arms, the knot blossoming through my stomach. *Fuck,* I think, squinting at the hillside and the prone forms of the engineers crawling up it. *I don't want to die up there.* But the alternative is cowardice.

I keep myself low and run diagonally along the hillside midway up, to the rear of the pinned-down right flank, where I drop to my hands and knees and take stock of the immediate area. There's Peter and his assistant gunner with their gun set up between two olive trees, firing up the slope to the white pillbox hidden in the grove above us; riflemen on their stomachs, crawling up the hill and ducking their heads as fire intermittently sprays from above; an officer, half-obscured in the ground mist and gunsmoke, hand signalling to the prostrate engineers—it must be Gavin, now taking aim with his rifle, urging them to keep moving.

As the rifle squads provide covering fire for the engineers, the top of the hill doesn't seem so far away, and I wonder again if all this is too easy. Although the crack of machine gun rounds rupture the morning air, I can't help imagining this is just another training exercise, a field drill, and any moment the sergeant will come trudging up the hill with a clipboard in hand to inform us of everything we did wrong.

"Second squad, let's go, boys, give 'em hell!" an officer shouts. "Covering fire!"

A lieutenant fumbling with the rounds on his cartridge belt shouts at me, "Hey, Doc, you follow me. We might need you," and signals for his troopers to stay on him. A dozen pairs of Corcorans and bloused trousers flash across the sandy expanse as soldiers run with their rifles under their arms and their full musette bags bobbing on their backs, making for the trees that line the crest. Bullets from kraut snipers glance through the copse of olive trees and fill the air with shredded leaves and splinters that carpet the sharp grass under our feet.

Then in my peripheral, I see a man fall as quick as a pushed domino, a smoking hole through his helmet.

I stare at him as the lieutenant and his squad disappear in the olive grove.

The world around me slows, the gunshots through the trees fading into an insect hum. Blood rushes into my ears. I don't know how I get to him, legs unsteady, heart pounding, but I crouch beside him and tentatively reach one hand out.

I can't pretend to know war, Richard, my dad wrote in a letter that arrived when we were in Tunisia, *but if I can tell you one thing, it's to listen for the helpless.*

But how do you listen to the dead?

The voice of a medical officer who lectured us at Benning rings in my already-ringing ears: *You're not the grave crew. Your business is to help the living wounded, not move the dead.*

His cheek is warm. A couple of gnats are gathered already in the hole in his helmet, dancing about, waiting to nest in the rotting flesh. Just a kid, just out of high school, barely old enough to shave. His neck is sunburned from traipsing through dry hills under an unrelenting Sicilian sun.

Shit shit shit, holy *fuck,* of course it's all real. It's not fucking Cowboys and Indians and BB guns. Until this moment I never actually imagined what it would mean to touch a dead body. I don't know what the fuck I thought I was training for as a medic, but it wasn't this.

I scramble to my feet and run. Away from the smoking hole, away from the gnats, away from his dead open eyes touching the prickly grass. I leave the body without tagging it for the grave crew. A few yards up the hill I remember and try to turn back but by now the hillside is obscured in smoke and soldiers and there's no going back down and he's gone, trampled because I didn't do the one part of my job that doesn't make me want to retch.

I'll be better, I'll do better, I promise God as I hold one hand on my helmet and crawl on my stomach toward the crest of the ridge, following fragments of boots and jump jackets through the smoke. I hear the soft pop of a mortar gun firing, and then an explosion to my right sends a cloud of white smoke into the sky. There's a haze through the olives where a pillbox used to be. The engineers whoop victoriously.

When I reach the top of the ridge, dead Germans in black uniforms speckle the dusty road that stretches east into the sun. Two white pillboxes are intact, shrouded in the olive grove, and a third was blasted and half-destroyed, though all three appear to be cleared out—of the living, anyway. Gavin directs more paratroopers coming up from the east, and another handful of figures are visible marching below us on the highway. Either someone got the word out that Gavin, 3rd battalion, and all associated waifs and strays needed help, or these boys stumbled on us by luck.

"What've we got down there, half a division?" A captain kneeling on the boot-print-covered road raises his binoculars as he peers down the hill. The exhausted radioman beside him, with that fifty-pound radio on his back, just shakes his head as he sucks wind. A half dozen guys crouch beside them, waiting for orders. Sweat drips through the smeared gun grease melting down their faces.

"Let's go, let's go!" another officer shouts, rifle in one hand as he motions with the other to attack down the hill. Swarming figures shrouded in smoke dart over the grass as the trees ring with shots fired. They're repelled by the stuttering burst of a machine gun trained on the ridge. Men drop to their stomachs with their rifle stocks clutched against them.

The voices of the squad leaders resound through the trees. "Come on, let's *go!*"

"We gotta get down this hill, boys, let's move our asses!"

"Keep—MOVING!"

The sounds beat into my soul, the pounding feet, the hundred rounds per minute, the screaming, till I can't move. I crouch in the grass, hand on the strap of my kit, telling myself to *go* and find someone who needs help and pull my fucking weight and I can't. I want to cover my head with my arms and cry. *This isn't real, it's not real, this can't happen to* me. Bodies move past me. Someone shouts for a medic. "Hey, pal, that means you," I hear a guy yell as he runs past.

"*MEDIC!* Help, I need a medic!"

Two guys right in front of me are cut down by the machine gun the second they raise their heads. A single clear thought snaps into focus in my mind: *If I don't move now, I never will.* I'll get pinned here, either killed or labeled a coward and drummed out of the Airborne, and that's my war over.

Dirt and powder rain on the hillside in black plumes. I crawl on my elbows to the two troopers. One was shot right through the heart; the other got his left jaw blown off. What's left of it touches my hand as I cradle his head to check for a pulse, thick, warm blood coating my palm. The jagged fragments of broken teeth scrape my skin.

I taste bile in my mouth and feel lightheaded and I pull away, turning to be sick in the grass. But I'm not. I stare at my own bloodied hand on the sandy ground and realize that my stomach is holding itself together. Before it has a chance to second-guess itself, I tug my medical tag booklet and a charcoal pencil from my bag and rip out two tags. I hold them on my knee with one hand as I fish for one trooper's dog tags and try to hold my handwriting steady in the thunder upending the world around me.

Just as I pin the tag to the second guy's jacket lapel, I hear a whistle. Without looking for its source I drop to my knees and hold my arms over my head. A spray of white dust and broken rocks blows against me as the roar continues in my deafened ears. The stench of burnt flesh fills the air. At least, that's what I think it is.

"MEDIC!"

There isn't time to even catch my breath. I drag myself forward, not knowing where I'm going through the smoke, following a gurgling cry, somehow audible to me in the chaos of automatic weapons.

An infantry soldier is on his stomach, trying to crawl. Even from this distance I can tell he's delirious. I get to my feet and run in a crouch, and when I reach him I see what I couldn't from a ways off. His progress is so slow because he's dragging himself on one arm. The other is almost completely blown off. I wish it was fully gone, but it's not. Shattered bone fragments and muscles protrude from his left shoulder. I drop to my knees, more to cover myself from the fire than to help him. But he cries out for me. All I can do is stare at the place where his arm is still attached to him by a few tendons. Jesus Christ.

"Please, you gotta help me, I don't know—Jesus—I gotta get to the aid station—"

He whimpers as guys move past us, kicking up dirt and rocks. "Jesus, oh shit, shit," he says, moving his good hand up to touch the other shoulder.

Shock, I think, *he's in shock,* but what paralyzes me is that there's no blood. My inadequate training taught me how to apply a tourniquet, but what the hell am I supposed to do when there's no blood flow to restrict? Gory bits of flesh clinging to his shoulder flap in the breeze.

The kid is crying in pain, repeating "Oh Jesus" every time he sees his arm. I almost run. Away from him and his suffering and his bloodless wound. But there'll only be more to take his place.

It needs to be disinfected—and he's in pain, so morphine—where the fuck's my morphine, it's all slipping out of my fingers—

I tell him it's okay, I'm here, though even to me that sounds laughable, as reassuring as a bucket to contain a hurricane. I still have no idea what to do with that arm. Splint it so the surgeons can try to reattach it? I'm paralyzed again by indecisiveness, staring at it as he sinks deeper into shock. The mortars explode in mushroom clouds across the hillside, filling our noses and ears with powder and dirt. Other boys cry for a medic. The sound is all over me, in me, and if I mess up he's dead and I don't know what to do, I don't know what—

"Jesus, the hell are you doing? Kid's in shock, you *blind,* pal?" Someone shoves my shoulder hard and wedges his way in between me and the guy with the dangling arm. I see the red and white flash of a brassard. "You got plasma?"

Plasma for shock, fuck, I knew that. I fish a plasma bag and tubing from my kit. The other medic pushes up the kid's jacket sleeve and swabs his attached elbow with disinfectant.

"Why isn't it bleeding?" I shout, and then again when he doesn't hear me. *"His arm, where's the blood?"*

The other medic maneuvers the plasma needle into the kid's arm and grunts, "Self-cauterized."

"What?"

"Artillery hits self-cauterize!"

I crouch numbly and watch as he binds the arm in a sling made of parachute canvas. Of course. Shells so white-hot they seal even the stumps of severed limbs.

"You still here?" the medic throws over his shoulder. "Get out of here; see if you can actually make yourself useful to someone!"

I stumble to my feet as the 3rd battalion boys chase German survivors down the opposite slope of the ridge, rifle fire ricocheting on the far side. Dead bodies, theirs and ours, lie entangled on the hillside, already beginning to stink under the Sicilian sun. Cheeks still burning and pulse thrumming from that fuck-up, I pick my way between the bodies, checking for living Americans, hand brushing carotid arteries for pulses as troopers run past me. German artillery pounds the shit out of the ridge, awful screams of metal and gunpowder fracturing tree trunks and hollowing craters in the earth. A shell lands ten feet from me and knocks me to all-fours.

"Help, hey, we need help—medic! Right here!"

In a shell crater in the white road, I make out two forms, but I saw three disappear behind the geyser of dirt. I don't know how I know that the third must've just disintegrated, and when my hand touches something wet and warm I also somehow know that it's a part of the guy who got disintegrated. Though apparently not fully disintegrated, most of him gone, some of him scattered on the blasted white road.

At the top of the slope a trooper is pressing his hand to the bloodied stomach of the infantry soldier on the ground. "I can't—I don't know how to stop it," he gasps, falling back on his heels. His forearms are stained with blood. "I don't know how to stop the bleeding—"

Blood pools on the dusty ground, running in rivulets down the slope till it clumps in the sand. I crouch beside him and push up my sleeves and think of how I almost killed that poor kid with the dangling arm. *They made a mistake, making you a medic,* a quiet voice whispers in me.

Well, even if they did, screw that. What's done is done. I'm here now, and this time I do remember what to do.

"I need to find the artery and clamp it," I say to the trooper, feeling like an outside witness to my own actions. "Look in my bag. There should be metal clamps in there; get me a couple."

I brace one boot on the ground, bite my lip hard, and shove my hand in. My stomach flips over on itself. It feels like raw meat in a butcher's shop. *God, don't let me make it worse,* I think as my submerged hand hunts for a spurting artery. Blood bubbles at the soldier's mouth, and he gags as I shut my eyes. He makes unintelligible noises, legs kicking out, and I shout for the trooper to hold him down.

"Got it, I got—" A mechanical scream slicing through the olives swallows my voice, all but ripping the sky in two. The explosion throws me on my ass and I lose the artery. The barrage doesn't let up so I have to reach back in past this kid's intestines as dirt and rocks shower us.

"We've got you, just stay calm, just hang on." The trooper shouts to be heard over the fire as he pins the kid's shoulders down, "Got the clamp when you're ready, Doc."

Arterial spray stains my jacket. We're out of time and I have no idea what I'm touching, and the guy is thrashing so hard I can't keep my hand steady. I know the possibility of causing him nerve damage, but the alternative is him bleeding out and getting trampled.

Somewhere close, I hear a shouted order that makes my heart nearly drop out of me: "FIX BAYONETS!"

God, please, let me find it.

"Got it. Clamp!"

The other trooper puts the metal clamp in my outstretched hand, and with some maneuvering I guide it into the wound cavity and press it against the spurting artery, sealing it off. The flow stops.

I have no idea how I did that. But none of us have time for me to dwell on it.

"Find me a stretcher-bearer," I say to the trooper as I wipe my bloody hands on my trousers and reach into my kit for sulfa to disinfect the gaping wound.

The soldier isn't crying out now that I'm done rearranging his insides, but I suspect that any relief is fleeting. I grab a syringe and morphine ampoule, break the ampoule's glass neck against a rock, and squeeze the top of the syringe as I draw the liquid up into it. *Talk to him,* I think, so I say, "You keep hanging on." He breathes slow and heavy, his eyes glassy as he stares up at me. "I'm giving you something to help with the pain, and then we're getting you out of here."

He doesn't flinch as I press the hypodermic needle into his rib cage above the wound, guessing as to where it will be most effective. I hear cries for a medic echoing from every direction. As I use a bandage to swab blood off the soldier's abdomen, the sounds of hand-to-hand combat break through the artillery. The screams are so awful that I don't know how to explain that this time, I find myself wanting to run toward them.

"Doc, we'll take him from here," a voice behind me shouts. Instead of stretcher-bearers from the aid station, two troopers have appeared, each holding a rifle with a jump jacket tied between the stocks. One shouts, "Damn medics at the aid station too scared to come out of their hole!"

"Whatever, as long as you get him down there." With one finger still slick with blood, I write *M* on the soldier's forehead, for morphine, so they don't overdose him at the aid station. I'm off before they've even lifted him onto the homemade stretcher.

Most of the dead have been skewered or shot at close range. I find a couple of walking wounded, shrapnel embedded in wrists and bullet fragments in necks. These small wounds suddenly seem like child's play. I finish taping a bandage to one kid's shattered fingers and send him back up the hill with orders to make for the aid station when I hear a buzzing so close it sounds like bees right behind my eyes: 1,200 rounds per minute, none of them discernable from the next. A German machine gun, set up in the trees below us. Out of the corner of my eye, I see a paratrooper fall. Then another. They have got fucking everything zeroed in on us.

I can't reach them going this way, so I trace my steps back. The white sun beats oppressively on the hill through the rising smoke. I pass a radioman shouting into his phone, "The hill to Biscari, Colonel Gavin's group is pinned on the *road to Biscari!*" That's the last thing I hear before the krauts shift the range of their .88 artillery and it hits deafeningly close along the crest.

Across the shale road is an embankment where the rifle squads are taking cover. Down the road to the right, through smoke and olive branches stripped of peace, the hazy outlines of German infantry move to load their big railroad guns. Blood in the grass soaks the knees of my trousers as I duck and listen. Then a mortar lands close and suddenly this whole stretch of the slope is enshrouded in white, a hazy cloud of phosphorus falling like ash on the living and the dead. Finally enough of the smoke clears for me to see soldiers on the slope digging slit trenches.

Then a rumble catches my attention, like an elephant trudging through the olives.

"Fucking *tanks?!*" someone shouts. "Why the fuck didn't we know about the tanks?"

The treads of the Tiger tank grind up the earth as they roll in a death march. It's got an .88 millimeter gun mounted on the front, its barrel wider around than a man's torso, and it rotates as the iron monster trundles toward the American lines. I've never seen anything like it. If our fears could be distilled into one image, this would be it.

"Where are the bazookas? We need heavy weapons on these bastards!" a sergeant shouts. Troopers and soldiers scramble into their shallow slit trenches, which might be slight protection from the phosphorus shells but won't stop a tank from flattening you.

The .88 gun lowers and fires. A shell bursts on a grove of trees behind the trenches, blowing a couple guys out of their holes with a hailstorm of shrapnel.

"Hey, Doc, keep your head down," someone calls, and I glance up to see Lieutenant Greer raising his rifle, trained on the shadowy forms of the kraut infantry in the trees. "I wouldn't put it past these bastards to shoot at you."

Except for shock and dirt-filled ears, the boys in the slit trenches are okay. The artillery and mortars are designed to hit where they'll do the most damage, but the tank gunners appear to be picking off individual men. I see two hit dead-on, blown to bits, limbs scattered in the grass as though hacked off in a gladiator ring.

Some don't get the mercy of dying instantly. I hold the shoulders of a guy who dared to get close enough with his bazooka to try and blow out the soft underbelly of the tank till the gunner found him and shot half his face off. I try to hold him still as his body convulses and I tell him it's okay, he's okay, and then he relaxes for good. I'm holding death in my arms when a half hour ago I ran from it.

Two more Tigers lumber out of the olives, crossing the road at the bottom of the hill. Before I can roll the body of the bazooka man off my lap, I see a figure moving among the bodies. He must be a medic, too—but there's no brassard on his arm, and no red cross on his helmet that would identify him as part of the medical battalion.

He presses his hand to the forehead of a dead rifleman. A glint of silver hanging between his fingers catches the sun. When he glances up, his mouth moving, our eyes lock. The breeze spins the silver in his hand into the shape of a cross. He nods at me, small but unmistakable, then rises and disappears behind the smoke of a phosphorus shell, looking for the next soul to guide to eternity.

A whoop sounds from down the hill, breaking the gruesome symphony. One of the bazooka men must've scored a fatal hit. Fucking crazy, those bazooka guys, getting so close to the tanks they can probably see the gunner's white knuckles.

I follow the marching orders of cries along the slope, bandaging necks and injecting morphine. But when I reach into my bag for the next bandage, my hand finds nothing. There are two ampoules left and some plasma, but I'm clean out of bandages and sulfa. And these Tigers, circling back one at a time to their ammo drops while their companions pick us off, are not through having their fun with us.

The aid station is on the other side of the ridge. All the way up, across the road at the top, down the other side, and back. All while boys cry out for me, dying, convulsing, hearts palpitating in terror as the Tiger guns swivel and decimate everything and everyone in their path.

But more will die if I don't have the supplies to help them, so I run back up the hill, jumping as kraut machine-gun rounds pepper the dirt.

Boys cry out to me as I pass, and I shout, "I'm coming back, I promise, I'll come back!"

My jacket sticks to my sweat-soaked back when I reach the top of the ridge and the road leading to Biscari. The officers have set up a command post. A mortar crew is under the trees, dropping their charges into the gun with shouts of "Fire!" There's a concealed machine gun in a scrub grass nest shooting down the hill into the German line, but it isn't Peter firing, so I hope that doesn't mean the worst.

"They've got two more Tigers!" screams a runner sprinting past me. "Where's Colonel Gavin? Two more Tigers coming up the hill, sir!"

Something touches my shoulder, and I jump and spin around to see indistinct faces behind me in the phosphorus lingering in the stale air. "I'm going to the aid station for supplies. I'll help you as soon as—"

"Rev, slow down, it's me—it's Fish," someone shouts. I'd recognize that voice anywhere, because I spent night after night for months listening to it sing "Don't Sit Under the Apple Tree" off-key from the bunk above mine in Benning. "You okay?"

"Fish?"

"Yeah, it's me, Rev. Shit, you look like you've seen a ghost."

I stare at him, dimly wondering if I'm hallucinating. Maybe he's just a mirage, the product of scrappy hope that my friends could be alive. But the faces of three other Fox Company guys materialize around Fischer, two of them from first platoon and the other, Berkowicz, the best catcher on the battalion baseball team.

"Sorry we're late," Berk yells. "They dropped us on the other side of the friggin' island. We've been fighting alongside the Brits."

An officer at the CP shouts, waving his arm at them to hook up with the rifle squad advancing down through the olives.

"I gotta get to the aid station," I say, all I can muster. The place where thoughts turn to words feels broken in me. Each time a half-breath finds my lungs, the artillery snatches it back.

"We'll see you when it's over," Fischer shouts.

Berkowicz slaps me on the shoulder. "Head down, Rev."

They take off down the far side of the ridge with their rifles drawn, toward the mouths of the Tigers, and I sprint down the other side.

Walking wounded stand and sit outside the aid station, holding soaked handkerchiefs or bandages to wounds on temples, wrists, ankles. Two guys pass carrying an empty stretcher, the canvas stained with blood and bodily fluids. My eyes struggle to adjust to the dusky interior after the bright sunlight as I step over the threshold. The dirt floor is crowded with men lying on their backs and sides, some with wool blankets pulled over their shoulders, others hooked up to bags of plasma or saline. One is completely shrouded from view as the surgeon and medic lean over his abdomen.

"You got any bandages?" I ask them. "I need bandages and morphine."

The medic mutters something I don't understand. I step out of the way as a couple of troopers shuffle into the narrow room and gingerly lower their occupant to the ground. His left ear is gone, the side of his face a mangled mess. He's thrashing and gasping in huge breaths. I help the stretcher-bearers hold him still so the medic can inject something in his shoulder—"Muscle relaxant," he grunts as the kid's shoulders loosen under my hands.

"Take what you need," Doc Ryder says, penlight in one hand casting a weak beam of light into a wound cavity, scalpel in the other.

"You guys aren't getting resupplied."

"You take whatever's there, corporal, and we'll make do."

A thin shaft of sunlight falls through the window onto the table, holding a ragged assortment of what I need, just not enough of it. I take a handful of rolled bandages, some of the little boxes of sulfanilamide wound tablets, three bags of plasma, and as many morphine ampoules as I think they can spare.

Heat waves shimmer in the dead grass as wounded soldiers stumble down the slope. One kid limping along, his arm thrown across his buddy's shoulders, says, "I ain't going back up; they can't make me," repeating it like a broken record stuck in the same perpetual groove as he wipes sweat from his eyes with the back of his hand. The other tries to tell him he doesn't have to go back and their voices fall away, swallowed in the sounds of the barrage from the ridge.

I shut my eyes for a moment. Adrenaline keeps my body rigid, tight as a coiled spring. I don't have time to think about what else awaits on the other side, be it a legion of kraut Tigers or their infantry butchering ours. I'm already done trying to take comfort in the brassard that signifies me as a non-combatant.

I inhale—the stench of sweat and flies and piss and blood-baked grass—and then exhale—the white-hot anger for these boys dying and my own nauseating fear.

Then the cry that simultaneously makes my heart drop out of me and floods me with relief because it holds my only purpose: "*MEDIC!*"

And I run back up.

At the CP, two privates poke their rifles into the backs of a half dozen German prisoners. An officer is interrogating one, a tall, freckled kid who stands with his hands behind his head as if expecting a bullet through his ribs. I hear the private translating say, "He says they're from the Hermann Göring—I didn't get the last bit—" He says something to the prisoner in German. "He said the Hermann Göring Panzer Division."

Paratroopers, just like us.

There's a young, white-faced German on his back on the ground, breathing heavily, drops of sweat trickling past his ears. Judging by the expression of the infantry private guarding him, I'd sweat, too. I kneel beside him and hesitate. Then I take out a bandage and a sulfa pack and begin swabbing the blood and mud from his left shoulder.

"The hell you doin', Doc? Don't waste anything on these bastards," the private says. "We got our own shit to take care of."

White sulfa powder falls over the wound like snow over a bloody river. Without looking up, I say, "Any time you want to switch places with me, private, feel free."

The young German stares at me through feverish gray eyes, at first in fear as if he expects me to drive my trench knife into his stomach, but his body relaxes as I clean the wound. I wipe sweat from my forehead and crouch over him, as much to shield him from any trigger-happy American as to try and see the hole above his heart. I notice a bit of dark metal against torn flesh. A bullet casing.

"It's okay," I tell him as I take the tweezers from my kit. I've never extracted a bullet before and I wouldn't do this if it were one of our boys, but there's no telling if he'll get the attention of a surgeon. If it stays in his shoulder, it could shift down to his heart when they move the POWs out. "You're okay; I'm helping you. You're okay. Shh. I'm just going to take this out, all right?"

The German presses his dirt-streaked hand over his eyes, his breathing ragged and panicked. Muttered ends of words come from his mouth: prayers, almost whispered in my ear as I hunch over him. The foreign words are meaningless to me but for the briefest of moments, I feel a strange sense of comfort.

The privates are herding up the prisoners to move them out, and they won't wait for me. More by memory than sight, I pluck the casing from his shoulder on the first go. Beginner's luck. I have nothing to use for binding his arm, so all I can do is tape bandages over the wound and tell him, "You'll be okay," though I'm not sure he'll make it to evening alive.

While I was working on him, two .75 millimeter field artillery pieces appeared under the trees. Colonel Gavin is talking to their crews as I stop near them to help a couple walking wounded up to the flat part of the ridge. As the guns are wheeled into concealment under the trees, Gavin squints into the distance, where the kraut paratroopers dart like field mice beneath the olives to load their guns. With steel in his voice he says, "We stay on this ridge no matter what."

Our artillery at the CP fires on the tanks, and they must have hit one because a roar spreads along the ridge even faster than the phosphorus. I look up in time from giving the German water from my canteen to see one of the Tigers backing away to nurse its wounds. But no sooner has the cheering faded than an order comes down from the ridge, passing from officers to NCOs who shout it to their squads: "Pull back! PULL BACK TO THE RIDGE!"

Cut off one of the hydra's heads, and two more grow in its place. Isn't that how the story goes?

Three more Tigers are visible through the vineyard at the foot of the western slope, rumbling toward our worn-thin line in the early afternoon sun. Paratroopers with grease and soot-blackened faces scramble and trudge up the slope, and they tilt the last drops of water from their canteens into their mouths, their rifles in the opposite arms.

We stay on this ridge no matter what.

Every one of them looks willing to die up here. As they retreat, I go among the wounded, trying to atone for the fear that pinned me earlier. *I'll follow them.* That's all I let myself think. *I'll follow them into hell if those are their orders.*

12 July, Biazza Ridge, Sicily, 2000 hours

S moky dusk hangs in the sky over Biazza Ridge, a name I heard in
passing from an officer. The Tigers left their trace in the ravaged
landscape and in our wounded. As the last light snuffs out over the de-
filaded olive orchard, some stragglers make it to the aid station, limping
and shaking and sometimes carried on stretchers. Gray blankets cover
bodies head to toe in the dust between the trees. I don't know how many
tanks the boys destroyed, but I know how many of us they took down,
the proof lined up like flat dominoes in a valley we weren't even meant
to fight in.

I move among the bodies with a book of medical tags, checking for
any who weren't tagged properly during the fighting. Another doctor
and three medics from the 82nd's medical battalion arrived in the late
afternoon, and they don't seem to need my help, such as it is. Already
most of the badly wounded have been evacuated—to where, I don't
know. I have no idea if the beachhead has been secured so the wounded
can be loaded onto the landing craft, or if any of the hospital units made
the landing intact. Two men from F Company are dead, Harrison and
Marcotti, and as I write the name of our CO on Marcotti's tag, I wonder
how many more made it to the ground two nights ago.

Night settles over the quiet slopes. I feel like a sleepwalker weaving
through a graveyard. When everyone has been tagged—dog tags removed, eyelids closed, prayers murmured—I climb to the top. I have no
orders and don't know what my duty is here, but I can't shuffle around
by the bodies and the wounded at the aid station, useful only for offering
a light to held-up cigarettes. The memory of the tanks' mechanical treads
grinding up the earth rolls continually through my chest.

The sun was still high when one of the Airborne officers came up the
hill with some forward observers from the 45th division and the Navy,

who fed coordinates into the radio back to their gun crews and Navy destroyers. I've never seen a fireworks show like the one they created when the called-in artillery blasted the area of huts and farm outbuildings, which the Tigers used for cover. Never seen the human spirit so galvanized, either, when a little later half a company of paratroopers marched down the Gela highway and then up the ridge to us. Turns out they were the flag-bearers for a line of Sherman tanks, and boy, if that sight didn't have guys on their feet, whooping and cheering.

An officer at the CP nods to me as I walk through the tattered trees, while his poor radioman looks as though he might pass out on the spot as he relays another message over the phone. Privates patrol the perimeter of the ridge and down the slope, carrying their rifles. To the east, the road to Biscari stretches away free and clear in the moonlight. Wind stirs what's left of the olive branches. The smell of death and gunpowder reeks through the grass, so persistent that I've given up trying to smother it with the scrap of canvas I cut from my parachute.

Crossing my arms against the nighttime chill, I stare through the grove in the direction of the German line, or what's left of it after Gavin led the counterattack before sunset. Smoke still rises from the tree cover and from the spots where the decimated buildings stood a few hours ago. But we took it. *They* took it, I should say. I just followed them and played doctor.

I walk down the far side of the hill, looking for bodies in the blackened grass, but find none. Just soldiers digging foxholes under the trees and cussing out the hard shale as they try to break it with their entrenching tools. The sky that so enamored me last night is almost the reflection of a different world. One where you'd never trip over the body of a friend or hear an after-echo of artillery rupturing the stillness. The landscape tilts surreally, like a film I don't want to see. I know the circumstances that brought me to Biazza, the route I took, but how I arrived *here*—in the midst of rotting limbs and dead boys even younger than me—is too strange a question for my tired mind to unravel.

But leave it to me to start thinking too philosophically, and to Harry Berkowicz to snap me out of it. I hear him before I see him. He must've been one of the scouts sent up the Biscari road, and on their way back he's strong-armed some poor private into listening to another of his bad jokes. "...which is why you never take the subway with a can of tuna in your back pocket. Hey! It's the Rev! How are ya, Rev?" He slaps me on the neck by way of greeting before I can answer. "All right, beat it, Sloane. I got some catching up to do."

He must've filched that subway joke from someone because he's from Fresno, not Manhattan. "You seem in good spirits," I say.

"Well, a fella's gotta keep upright. Can't think about it too much, okay, Rev?"

"Ay-uh."

"I'm serious." He shoulders his rifle by the strap and pulls a cigarette and lighter from his jacket. "I know you. That's why I'm sayin' that. I know you ain't gonna stop thinking about it."

We walk down the hill. Berk slings his arm across my shoulders. He blows smoke into the air and adds, "They don't pay us to eulogize the dead. Not even you, Rev."

"Someone ought to."

"Someone will, but not you. We need you in the land of the living to stitch us up."

I see the red crosses on the arms of the other medics as we approach the aid station and our graveyard. *I had fainted...unless I believe to see the goodness of the Lord in the land of the living,* I think, watching the dim glow emanate from the stone hut's open window.

"What? You fainted up there?"

I glance at him and realize I must've said it aloud. "No, I didn't faint up there. It's a Psalm."

"Oh. Mighta guessed." He flicks his cigarette to the ground and stamps it out.

"For a good Jewish boy, your memory of scripture is abysmal."

"And yet here we both are, in fucking Sicily, and a lot of good the Psalms are doin' us now," Berk says. "Hey, there's McNulty. McNuts! Hey!"

For an hour or so I make myself useful in the aid station, holding a light or unscrewing canteens. Some bandages need redressing. I find that I actually don't mind this part of the work, the steady and methodical tasks. Maybe I even like it. Or maybe it's just nice to be needed.

One of the doctors tells me to take off and get some rest, so I gather up my musette bag and my nearly empty medical kits and step out of the hut. The stars have come out. A Jeep trundles over the uneven ground to pick up the last few wounded. Berk is nowhere in sight, probably dug in on the hill and torturing Charlie McNulty with his jokes. On the far side of the hill, where we first spotted the Tigers earlier, I hear Peter's distinctive laugh from a nearby hole, and Fischer's snort in reply.

"Aw, here's our little Florence Nightingale," Fish coos as I appear.

I drop one of the empty kits on his head and jump into the hole. Exhaustion floods my body, threaded with a morbid joy that it isn't me carried out on a stretcher beneath a parachute shroud. I remember what Berk said—*can't think too much about it*—and force a lighthearted note in my voice as I say, "What's for dinner tonight, boys?"

Peter holds up an opened C ration can of beans in one hand and a hard tack biscuit in the other. "Well, in the left hand here we have an entree of freshly harvested kidney beans marinated in a brown gravy, just lovely, and in the right we have one of those French pastries—"

"A croissant," puts in Fish through a yawn.

"Yes, a croissant, flaky as you like and just out of the oven." Peter looks between his two options as though weighing their sins on a divine scale. "Or maybe I'll be creative and have beans on toast, like the Brits."

"Separate or together, it makes no odds how they'll fuck up your stomach," I say.

"Mhm," Peter agrees, dumping a liberal helping of the beans onto his biscuit and holding it out like a flute of champagne on New Year's Eve. "Bottoms up."

Fish flicks the flint on his lighter and then holds it out to me. The tip of my Lucky Strike glows dull against the dark sky. We all sit with our knees to our chests in the shallow hole.

"As soon as it's light"— Peter stuffs the C rations back in his musette bag—"we see what we can do about finding Lieutenant Walsh and the rest of Fox Company. And now," he adds, freeing himself of all encumbrances except his rifle as he climbs out of the hole, "I'm going to see how the boys are getting on."

Fish blows out smoke. "Keep your head down, sarge."

I take advantage of the extra room to stretch out, such as it is, my head on my bag. Over us the sky covers the hill and the valley and the highway like a blanket.

"Can you believe we came from up there?" Fish murmurs.

I twist my neck to glance at him, then look up at the night, and we're quiet for a minute.

"Still don't know what kinda screwed up idea this was, jumping out of planes," he says at last, and then we both laugh, though there's no humor in it. The hillside still reeks with death's perfume.

The ground is hard and cool but it might as well be a mattress stuffed with feathers, the way my body settles into it. There's something to be said for the proximity of foxholes to graves. All it would take is another Tiger rolling up from the valley and to bury us alive in a flood of dirt, or artillery blasting one of the olive trees so that it falls over the hole, and we'd be—well, not six feet under, these holes aren't that deep what with the shale, but under enough to do the trick. I watch the arc of the stars like a dead man sans coffin.

"You think we'll find them tomorrow?" Fish's voice beside me is almost contemplative. "I feel sorta homeless, out here with these guys we don't know."

"At least we found each other, and Pete and Berk."

Fish taps another cigarette against his dirty fingernail but doesn't light it. "You know, I never saw a body before today. A dead one, I mean. Except for at my grandmother's funeral when I was a kid, but she was laid out all real nice, you know. Sunday best and her pearls and all that."

"Heart attack?"

"I dunno. My old man"—he draws the sleeve of his jump jacket over his hand and coughs against it as the wind blows the scent of the dead to us—"my old man, he said she just went in her sleep, peaceful as anything."

He drops the cigarette back in its pack and tucks the pack in his pocket. The silver undersides of the leaves on the olive trees flutter in the breeze, and mosquitoes hum over the blood in the cooling grass. I watch the sky through the frame of the branches, listening in case someone needs me.

We're alive, I think drowsily, eyelids falling shut.

For now. But for now is enough.

III.

SPRING

April 1945

I n the bright light of the late afternoon sun, I sit on the porch steps with a colander of shelled snow peas by my right knee and a matching pile of pods by my left. Hen snuffles about with her nose to the porch, sometimes stealing an empty pea pod and slinking away with it as though she expects to be scolded. We weeded the garden earlier and I cleaned out the shed, and then Mom didn't know what to do with me. She finally gave me the peas so she can make soup tonight, leaving me on the porch to shell in silence. "Really, Richard, it's okay if you take a break," she said, eyebrows drawn together as she wiped her hands on her apron, but I told her I didn't want a break and would rather catch up on whatever chores they've been putting off.

I have trouble enough with the long, dark stretches of night, when the boundary between my memories and the present blurs. Maybe I'll weed the garden a second time at midnight just to give my hands something to do. Spring is coming. That's something. I always put an unfair amount of faith in summer to heal any and everything, to restore what winter killed. And Grace Whitley will be home at the end of the week from a visit to her great-aunt's. I try not to dwell much on daydreams of what seeing her will feel like. It doesn't seem fair to heap expectations on our reunion when there's every chance the last three years changed her as much as they did me.

Still, I find it hard to keep from thinking about her.

As the sun is setting, I leave the peas draining in the colander by the sink and walk with Mom and Laurie to church. Gray dusk falls like ashes beyond the windows as Dad prays under the white vaulted ceiling. I shift, cross my legs, uncross them. Tell myself to stop and not annoy Mom, sitting so still beside me. It feels as if I never left—and at the same time, I hardly recognize this place. Of course, spend long enough in a church and you've got to try talking to God at some point. I don't think I'm ready to do that yet. I'd just like to sit here, and if he sits with me, then maybe we'll talk. But I won't hold my breath on that chance.

When the sermon is done, the last hymn sung, and the neighbors clustered together—many of them hemming me in and welcoming me home and congratulating me (for what?)—I spot two familiar heads, one dark and one light, going out the side doors. My heart jumps at that blonde hair.

I say thank you and shake hands and slip away down the side aisle along the windows to the big doors. On the sidewalk, both girls turn around and I realize that the blonde isn't Grace Whitley; it's Helen Innes. Of course it's Helen. I should've noticed, taller and paler than Grace.

Antonia Hardy, smile as big as I remember it, runs up the steps and hugs me. "Richard Dare, you scoundrel, you didn't tell us you were home!"

"Hi to you too, Toni. I got here Monday."

"How are you? Laurie told us all about what happened in...France?"

"Belgium. I'm okay."

She steps back to let Helen hug me too, and Helen says, "It's a long time coming."

We grew up together, spent endless summer days frog hunting in the marshes and playing baseball at the Whitley farm. Toni and I were each other's first kiss at thirteen, both laughing so hard during we swore it would never happen again, and it never did. For a few minutes, listening to her catch me up on town gossip and laughing with them, those days seem close, our childhood selves not so far away. But when we turn to walk home beneath a cold, deep-blue night sky, that reassurance snaps away like a candle flame extinguished.

"You see Mattie much?" I ask as we begin walking north.

Helen snorts. "Only every day. He hobbles into the hotel and orders coffee just so he can lean on the counter for an hour to talk to me. Except he also passes the time of day with every girl who goes past on the sidewalk."

"Of course he does."

"You and Mattie are home," she says after a moment. "Sidney's still somewhere in the Pacific, as far as we know. And Sam and Joe..."

We only lost two childhood friends. *Only.* Joe Carson dropped out of high school to enlist when he was 17, lying about his age on the enlistment papers, and he was already in the Pacific when America declared war on Japan. He was a supply officer in the Navy, and he was killed over there before I even enlisted. When he died, all I knew of the war was that it was being fought in places I'd never heard of. And Sam Norberg, my oldest friend for as long as I can remember, was killed on some Pacific atoll called Saipan last year. Grace wrote me about it and didn't say much, because what is there to say that would mean enough?

Helen says, "Well, at least we have you back."

"Any word from Sidney?"

Toni draws her arms around herself. "Last Grace heard from him a few weeks back, he was still stationed in the Philippines."

We break off from Toni at York Road, where she turns east to go home, and Helen and I walk a little further together. At the intersection of Queen and Holland, my house glowing white in the rising moonlight across the empty road, Helen shifts from one foot to the other. "Grace missed you a lot, you know," she says. "Goodnight, Richard." She buttons the top of her coat and waves and hurries, ashy blonde head down, along Queen Street.

I wake to the scent of spring filling my bedroom. Standing in the upstairs hallway, the breeze at my back, I close my eyes and listen to my heart beating, the slight rattle of my lungs even in the clear air. Before, on a morning like this, I'd have been up before dawn to run, timing my six-mile route through sleeping streets. That old impulse still burns in the rest of my body. I try to swallow it back, pretend it doesn't matter even though it does. But it can't happen.

In the kitchen Dad turns the page of the newspaper as a forgotten piece of toast half-spread with jam grows cold on his plate. I go out barefoot on the porch and announce that the temperature gauge says fifty-nine degrees.

"Almost warm enough to jump in the river." Dad holds open the sports section with one hand while his other hand drops below the table with a crust of toast, which disappears into Hen's mouth. I bite my lip to keep from laughing. Who was so adamant we'd never feed her from the table, not even scraps?

I sit down opposite him. "What're you doing today?"

"Oh, I'll probably wander over to Jim's store, see if I can't find a replacement for the knob that fell off Laurie's door. You know he's never going to get around to doing it himself," he adds, with a good-natured roll of his eyes. "Then I'll keep hammering away at that end table in the shed, unless Dolores Hardwin finds me and corners me into her pitch for new hymnals we don't have the budget for. Of course, I know where you'll be today."

I look up. "You do?"

"I saw Hannah in town yesterday," he says. He doesn't lower the paper, but I catch his eyes on me. "She told me she'd be picking Grace up at the station, late."

"Well, maybe Hen and I thought we'd wander down to the farm."

"Mm. I'm sure you will."

I reach for the paper and pull out the crossword before he moves past it. "Leave me the classifieds, too, if you don't mind."

He lays the paper on the table and finally notices his cold toast. Hen, at his feet, lets out a small whine. "Any leads?"

"Not yet." I draw a seashell spiral beside the crossword grid, digging the pen deep into the paper till it punctures. "Every returning GI in Maine is after the same jobs I am, and some of them have bachelor's degrees."

Dad scrapes a thin layer of butter over the toast. "You must be thinking about going back to school, if I know you."

"...yeah. I guess. I don't know." My eyes fall on 17 down, *Nick and Nora Charles's pooch,* and I write A-S-T-A in the boxes. "I guess I don't know if I want to go back to Brown."

"No one would force you to."

"I know."

Dad went to Brown, too, twenty-something years before me, and I don't want to tell him that my time there feels as meaningless and insignificant as a dream compared to what came after. There's no point in going back now.

He drums his fingers in a pattern over the letters to the editor. After a few moments' quiet, he scoots out his chair and says, "Right now, it's a beautiful day and there's a girl who doesn't even know you're home. Go on, go see her."

G race and I wrote occasional letters to each other these past few years. There were times when the thought of her was the only thing that picked up my dead spirit and kept me going. That isn't to say she owes me anything or even that I still feel the same as I did in high school. Only that when the ground is mud and shit and you're sick and the nights are bitter cold, you become hungry for something good and warm in a way you can't describe. And Grace was what my mind held onto.

But so much has changed, and the last Grace of whom I have a memory outside her letters is from three years ago. She isn't static like the photograph of us I carried with me throughout the war. We grew up, and maybe I've grown out of love. I don't know if I have, but I know I probably made up another version of her that she's never even met. I didn't mean to. It was just inevitable.

Warm light falls on the road as Hen and I walk together along Queen Street. She stops at every corner to sniff at the sewer drains and lampposts. When she starts to trot off toward Salt Pond, where we always used to go on Saturday mornings to watch the birds and wade in the water, I whistle her back and tell her, "We'll go later, maybe with Grace. Come on now."

The road to the Whitleys' that breaks off of the curve in Queen Street is dirt, bordered by a low cedar fence over which the honeysuckle and trumpet vine will entangle come June. Hen runs along the fence with her nose going. She bounds out across the wide pasture, empty now but for dead grass, that fluffy tail waving in the sunlight.

I walk slowly, watching the wind move through the stubbly fields. A bank of trees to the west breaks the light, tall oaks brushing the pale blue sky and willows sweeping through the dust of the lane. We used to sit under their canopy to do our homework and argue and throw grass at each other. I missed it all so much that it hurts to look at it, the oaks, the glowing clouds, the bare apple orchard waiting for fruit. Seeing the dirt road that stretches to the pond where the cows—before they cost too much for Mrs. Whitley to keep—would sit in the summer to cool off, stirs up melancholy in me. So does the white farmhouse nestled in the folds of the valley. I left it all so quickly, with so much finality. Maybe because I never expected to come back.

For three days I've been holding on so tightly to Helen's comment that Grace missed me that I'm afraid I'll bruise the idea of it. Hen trots beside me as we walk along the lane between the pastures, before the valley dips. "It's just Grace, isn't it?" I say to her, trying to quiet the quick tempo of my heart. "What am I afraid of? You've seen her more recently, do you think she missed—"

"Richard?"

I turn and see someone behind us on the road. The sun is so bright that she's only a silhouette moving down the hill as I squint. Then Grace comes into focus, a strawberry-blonde-haired figure in mint shorts and a white blouse, the awkward elbows and knees of adolescence gone but the light step still there. All the words I agonized over are gone at the sight of her.

She sets a couple of empty egg crates on the road and shields her eyes from the sun with one hand, and then her face breaks into a big grin, as illuminating as if it drew all the sunlight out of the sky and into her.

I half-expect the dead honeysuckle vines to blossom as she passes them, hands in the pockets of her shorts.

Stopping a few feet from me, she says, "It's really you," with such a softness that for a moment I wonder if her days of teasing at my expense are behind us. Then she adds, "At first I thought 'No, it can't be—he'd never be such an ass as to not tell us he was coming home,'" and the edge of her mouth lifts in the impish grin that drives me wild.

"Sorry I didn't give you enough time to batten down the hatches and set off the warning b—"

Grace cuts me off by crossing the space between us and throwing her arms around my neck, laughing and saying things I don't really hear because her skin is so soft and her hair tickles my cheek and she smells like rosewater and fresh linens. Not a memory or a black-and-white photo or ink on stationery—her, flesh and blood and color, fitting perfectly in my arms.

She steps back and tilts her head as the light falls in her eyes. "Where's the hurricane? I don't believe it's really you."

"The Army must've drilled some of the nerves out of me," I say, aware that I'm grinning like a fool and I can't stop.

"But not the paranoia?"

"Of course not. If anything, you have to be *more* paranoid in the Army."

"Look at you." She flicks my shoulder and gives me a disapproving look. "You're skinny as a stringbean. Do they not feed the boys in these VA hospitals?"

"We have to give my mom a few more days, and I promise she'll fatten me up. You should come over tonight and help us eat all the baklava she keeps making," I add.

"I'd love that." Grace smiles as the breeze blows her hair back. "Richard, I'm so glad to see you. I really am. How long have you been home, you sneak? You just let me waste away at Aunt Meg's for the week!"

"I wanted to actually show up, not just write it."

"Did you get into any trouble? Wheelchair races in the hospital hallways?"

Making my voice light, I answer, "No wheelchair races, but I did flirt with as many nurses as possible."

"And I bet a hundred bucks you talked some poor nurse to death about Calvinism. And probably the Red Sox. Or maybe Calvinism *and* baseball. If anyone could draw theological parallels there, it's you." She crouches to receive a twig Hen proudly offers her. "Wait, I know—you tried to teach the nurses some Greek and had them calling their mothers goats."

"I don't know why you'd think I would ever ramble about anything," I say dryly, feigning an innocent expression. "Or spread Greek lies."

Grace snorts. "Uh-uh, you don't get to pretend you didn't tell me in ninth grade that *spanakopita* is Greek for *hello,* and that you didn't happily let me say that to Mrs. Marsden every morning for two weeks in Latin class till she thought I had a brain aneurysm. And there I was thinking I was a linguist, impressing the language teacher."

"Well, I can't be held responsible for you not fact-checking me in a Greek-English dictionary. Intellectual curiosity, Grace." Before she can protest, I add, "So you graduated in December? A semester early?"

She waves her hand like it was nothing. She studied French and Latin classics in college, a linguist after all despite the ninth grade *spanakopita* incident. "It wasn't as though I had much of a social life to keep me busy, just the girls at the Red Cross sewing bandages together every Friday night."

I think of the bloody gauze all but disintegrating at my touch as I helped move wounded soldiers in an aid station in Belgium and wonder, as I follow her across the lane to the egg crates she dropped, if any of those bandages ever passed through Grace's hands, too.

"I took eggs to the Lewises and the MacKinleys," she says over her shoulder. "The hens are laying well. Thank goodness we don't have to rely on ration books for them."

"Oh, that reminds me." I take the dime and nickel from my pocket. "From my mom. She requested a half dozen but a dozen if you can spare them, and she'll pay you the difference tomorrow."

"What's this now, a party at the Dares'?"

"Let me take those," I say, reaching for the empty egg crates, and Grace lets me pick up one but insists on carrying the other. "And yes, it's always a party at the Dares'. You know her open-door policy at dinnertime."

She turns around, walking backwards. The sun, rising higher in the sky, catches the back of her head and glints her hair reddish. "It's not *the Dares* without you there, no matter how many neighbors show up for dinner. It's been a different life without you. All of you."

We walk along the dusty road together as she tells me about life in Boston and on the farm. Finally we stop under the shade of our old willow tree. We sit knee to knee, just brushing, cross-legged in the grass under the sweeping arms of the tree as Hen rolls around on her back. The bright morning is subdued beneath the leaves, flickering sunlight moving in and out between the breeze-stirred branches. Grace turns her face up to the patches of blue sky peeking through. Her hands are busy picking pieces of brown grass, which she then scatters onto my legs, as though it were a ritual offering.

"Should I ask you the usual questions?" She rips a clover into neat shreds. "Like if you have any good stories, or what you're going to do now, or if you really tore up London like the stories say about paratroopers...?"

"I did go to London a couple times, but I promise I had no part to play in raising hell in Piccadilly Circus. Whatever you heard, that was all the 101st Airborne. We 82nd boys were better behaved."

"Oh, of course."

I lean back on my arms and watch the changing light. "And I don't know. Your guess is as good as mine for what comes next. But what about you? I thought you had all of Boston in your grasp and a teaching job anywhere you wanted. What made you decide to come back to Caspar?"

She shrugs. "It seemed like time to come home, what with Sidney still being gone, and I just didn't want Gran here all by herself. And it happened that Mrs. Marsden only just retired last year and the high school was hiring for new French and Latin teachers, so"—she shrugs her shoulders—"I took that as providence. With me, they only needed to hire one person. And I had to make sure you made it home all right."

"Toni said it's been a little while since you've heard from Sidney."

Grace nods, seeming about to say something, then doesn't. I wish I knew how to be more of a comfort, but all I know is that when I couldn't write home, it wasn't because I was too busy having a good time. Her older brother is a navigator in the Army Air Force, and I'm sure she knows even better than I do the casualty rates for airmen.

We sit for a while in the grass. There's something bittersweet about knowing that we could wake up to snow tomorrow, that just for this suspended moment the spring world is ours. Then Grace's shoulders lift, and she looks at me and smiles again. How she's always been able to do that so easily, move from fear or sadness into her lighthearted self, I've never known. "Have you had breakfast yet? We've got *plenty* of fresh eggs."

I can almost hear the self-satisfied whistles of my 3rd platoon buddies if they were able to see this. *What're you waiting for, Rev? Get that girl!* they'd cajole, and Berk would buy another round of drinks.

They'd ask, *Status of the Grace dilemma?*

And I'd have to answer, *Situation Normal All Fucked Up.*

I was thirteen when Grace and Sidney came here from the North Shore of Massachusetts, where they were raised by their maternal grandmother and assorted relatives after their parents died. I don't know as much as I'd like about their lives before they came to Caspar, mostly because Sidney has always been silent on the topic and Grace, who usually chats away about anything from French literature to styles of drinking glasses, still clams up whenever conversation tends toward personal history. Even as children, the rest of us understood it must be an era of painful memories that still stings when touched, so we tried not to.

What I do know is that their other grandmother, Hannah Whitley, who's lived in Caspar all her life and whom I've known all of mine, used to be a much quieter woman. Then her grandchildren came to her, only after what seemed like a bitter struggle against her late daughter-in-law's family. The Whitley farm was always a lonely place, especially in winter when the wind stripped the oaks to skeletons and the windswept valley lay shrouded in ice and snow. None of us ever liked going there on errands, to pick up fresh eggs or to bring bread to Mrs. Whitley, because we were uncomfortable with her steadfast solitude, which I now know was grief.

That all changed overnight in the fall of 1935. Excitement ran in an electric current among us at school the day before they came. Our little gang—at that time me, Antonia, Helen, Sam, Joe, and Mattie Faucheux—rode our bikes along Queen Street after school that day and stopped at the head of the road that sloped into the valley, hoping to see something or someone. We rode back and forth all afternoon and into the evening until our curfews called us home for supper, having seen nothing. This prompted an anticipatory feeling in us all that night like Christmas Eve. I could hardly sleep and kept getting up to look out my bedroom window at the empty street.

Their appearance in the schoolyard the following morning was my first encounter with love, that kind of quick, head-over-heels adolescent infatuation that makes you swear you'll kill yourself if the other person so much as glances back. Grace was the most beautiful girl I'd ever seen, and I was mortified that I couldn't look away from her and that I blushed every time she turned in my direction. The first time she called my name, I wanted to dig a hole beneath the swingset and die there.

But I wasn't the only boy who thought she was cute—who'd do anything to see that smile light her up—and worst of all, she was popular, genuinely well-liked because she was good-natured and could make anyone laugh. It became immediately and painfully obvious to me that I wasn't distinctive in her line of suitors, a line that was getting long. I wanted to make an impression on her, so I promised myself I wouldn't be one of those puppy-eyed boys asking Grace about school dances or going to the pictures or the pharmacy after school for sodas. Maybe if I was different than them all, she'd notice me.

What I didn't expect, in maneuvering myself out of the line of potential beaux and finding other ways to claim Grace's attention, was that when we were together I often forgot about love and my own very dramatic heartache. Sidney and I became close, too, "thick as thieves" as my dad said, and in a month or two I was no longer thinking of ways to win Grace over. Not to say that I wasn't still in love, but only that my heart—and hormones, I guess—began to settle down.

I'd stop at the farm in the mornings to help them feed the chickens and goats, and then we'd all walk to school in every kind of weather, cutting through the pastures instead of taking the roads. But our favorite time was summer, when there was no school, only swimming and baseball, and the world was so wide and green that it felt endless, as if winter was tamed for good. I know that's a romantic perspective, but being around Grace makes me say things that I'd not be caught dead saying in a chow line.

IV.

DESERT

I f it's not the dysentery, it's the fucking Atabrine tablets.

"Just swallow it, Bill. One pill that tastes like shit beats malaria." I cross my arms up on my oil drum perch by the mess tent. There are two chow lines, and Lieutenant Walsh is stationed at the end of the other. Turns out we have a lot of jokers in F Company who tuck their Atabrine under their tongues and pray for malaria to get them a few nights in the hospital.

"You sure about that, Doc?" the private says sullenly through what sounds like marbles in his mouth.

I turn my head to look pointedly at the sign beside my oil drum. Back in the spring, during our first week in the desert, Charlie McNulty found what appeared to be an animal skull of some kind with all the flesh long gone. It now sits gaping atop a plank, scrawled with the macabre warning, "He forgot to take his Atabrine!"

The private refuses to acknowledge GI Yorick, pouting at me instead. "It makes me see things. Real fucked up things, you know, that ain't really there."

"A hundred-and-four-degree fever would also make you see real fucked up things that aren't really there." I slide off the oil drum and stare at him till he grumbles and reluctantly swallows. Then I make him open his mouth and stick out his tongue. The state of his teeth leave something to be desired, but at least there's no place for a tablet to hide. He carries his mess kit with its sour-smelling beans out of the line while pulling a face of disgust—at the pill or the beans, I can't tell.

They keep coming, mess kits in one hand and tablets in the other. I know it tastes like shit as much as they know it. But the evacuation hospitals here are already so overcrowded with malaria and dysentery cases that they've begun discharging sick men after twenty-four hours and sending them back to their units, even if they're too dizzy and feverish to walk. It was the same back on Sicily, and it'll be the same wherever they drop us next. Forget the krauts and the Italians. These diseases are our worst enemy, and half the American invasion force is welcoming the enemy in right through the main gate.

"Evening, Doc," Harry Berkowicz greets me, turning from telling some stupid joke about kangaroos to the privates behind him. He plucks his tablet from his mess kit, holds it up so it catches the harsh desert sun that glows right in our eyes, and pops it in his mouth. "Just pretend it's a shot, boys. Ooh, she burns as she goes down."

"That's what I said to your wife last night," McNulty pipes up from a few spots back.

"You know what, McNuts? Fuck you," calls Berk good-naturedly. He coughs hard. "Son of a bitch, that aftertaste."

Jim Garrett mutters, "Don't talk about shots."

"That'd be just what all our poor intestines need right now." I wave Berk along. "All right, beat it. Yes, I'm *very* proud of you."

He goes off whistling. Sergeant Autry relieves me from Atabrine duty just in time, because my patience is wearing threadbare for this kind of chickenshit. I fill my canteen from one of the fifty-gallon Lister bags in the mess tent. Skinny Santorini, eating on the ground in a half-moon with a handful of other 2nd and 3rd platoon boys, calls after me, "Don't worry, Rev, we'll save ya some!"

"Chicken parmesan, I think Joe said it was."

"The Rev loves Italian food, don't he?"

I call to Santorini without looking back, "Skinny, tell them to fuck off for me, would you?"

Skinny's the only other Greek guy in 3rd platoon, a waiter in his parents' restaurant in Chicago since he was old enough to balance a tray. He balances mortars now as the leader of 3rd's mortar squad. He didn't believe me back in basic when I told him I was also Greek, and it took reciting my mother's moussaka and shakshuka recipes to him before he was convinced. "Anyone can learn Greek." He sniffed as he looked down at me from his top bunk, a porn magazine flipped open in front of him, and I was offended he didn't think my accent sounded authentic. "What'd your ma cook on New Year's?"

The white-hot sun hangs heavy beyond the strip of the Atlas Mountains to the west as I walk through camp. During the 115-degree days we sweat so much that we probably lose a couple pounds of body weight each, then at night when the temperature plunges below sixty and the wind howls, the sweat freezes under our wool blankets. There's no good time of day or night to wash with the half canteen of water we're each issued, because we'll either be sweating again minutes later or shivering as we strip in the cold darkness. No wonder it seems like half the division, Fox Company included, has malaria. We can't regulate anyone's body temperature.

I take a deep breath through my nose—the hornets take open mouths as an invitation, we had a couple close calls during the tablet checks—and take a swallow of the water. Nectar of the gods. Smells like warm cat piss, tastes worse.

A few of the cots are occupied in the 3rd platoon barracks, just tents with useless mosquito netting hanging over the openings. Anyone laid real low by dysentery or malaria or the local treat, sandfly fever, is moved to the medical battalion tents, and those bad enough are sent to the field hospital five miles from our camp. But most of them are sent back if they're not actively dying, so you can have fever visions of your dead grandma or a kraut hurling a grenade at you, and you better fucking get it together on your own because being sick is a disgrace to the United States Military. At least that's the attitude of some of our superiors, not just General Patton at Seventh Army. They all talk a lot of bullshit until they're the ones doubled over with stomach cramps and body-shaking chills.

"Hey, Fish." I kneel next to a cot in the back corner of the tent I live in. There are a few other 3rd platoon boys in here, most of them in the third stage of malaria—exhaustion. "How you doing, buddy?"

Fischer mumbles something unintelligible. He was at the hospital for less than a day before they kicked him out because there are others "more in need" than him. Others more in need, my ass. He has a fever of 103. Last night he was trembling so hard before the ambulance came for him that he probably bruised himself. I could wring his neck in frustration for his obvious lie last week before we left Sicily that he was taking his tablets.

He's past the cold stage. Judging by the way he's kicked the three blankets down past his waist as he lies bare-chested on the thin mattress, this is the heat stage.

The evening is hot and dry, though maybe the nightly temperature plunge will cool him off. Malaria keeps coming back for a lot of the boys who've already had it once, but this is Fish's first time. If he makes it through tonight, his fever could be down by the morning. But making it through tonight is no easy order.

"Can you drink anything?"

Fish opens his eyes, which are glossed-over with fever. I breathe out with relief when I see he recognizes me. Supporting the back of his head with one hand, I hold the canteen, but then he shakes his head weakly and turns his face away.

I lower the canteen and instead pour a few drops onto a washcloth, then ball it up and hold it to his mouth. He lets me this time, though I can't tell if he actually swallows any.

"Good job," I tell him as some of the water falls down his chin. I wipe it away with the corner of the blanket. "You'll be past this soon. We'll be out of this hell hole soon, too."

I mean, a guy can hope, right?

"Well, it's Friday night. They're showing a Rita Hayworth film when it gets dark. *You'll Never Get Rich,* I think. You like that one?" I screw the lid on the canteen and hook it back on my belt. "Of course you do. You'd watch Rita watching paint dry." He had three pin-ups of her over his bunk at Benning. "I think my favorite of hers has to be—"

Still lying on his back, Fish makes a choking sound. With one arm I quickly pull him up to his elbows, turning his head to the side. My other hand reaches for an empty ammo case near the cot I saw when I came in. Just in time. He retches into it. I don't know how; he hasn't eaten in three days.

"It's okay," I murmur, my arm around his shoulders. "There you go. That's fine. You're getting better, Fish, this is just part of it."

I come back to sit with him for a while after I dump the vomit-desecrated ammo case into the sand outside the tent. His sleep is fitful and restless till finally, as the moon is rising, his breathing seems to settle and I feel a little of the rigid tension go out of his arm. When I'm sure he's okay and sleeping deeply, I leave the barracks in search of Rita Hayworth.

The film is halfway through by the time I squeeze on the end of the bench beside Tommy Morgan, who's staring fixated, his cigarette forgotten in his mouth, at Rita on the side of the mess tent as she spins around in Fred Astaire's arms. My usual suspects, Berk and Peter and Skinny, are sitting a few guys down. Skinny leans across to tell me that Peter and Donny Macklery from 1st platoon are engaged in a spirited debate of Rita versus Veronica Lake, and I don't need to hear them to know that Peter is advocating for Veronica. Peter would walk off the edge of a cliff for Veronica, if she asked.

"Hey, Rev. Rev!"

I glance away from Rita's sheer skirt fanning out around her as they glide through the dance. Peter is gesturing to me.

"Rev, help us settle this." He waves his hand at a guy behind us complaining that he can't hear. "All right, pal, they're *dancing,* there's nothing to hear. Fuck's sake. Rev, you rather one night with Rita"—Peter inclines his head to the screen—"or Veronica?"

"Barbara Stanwyck."

"Barbara Stanwyck's not an opt—"

"She is if this is my night we're talking about. If Barbara Stanwyck teased me just once, I'd die happy." I tap the end of Morgan's cigarette. "You're about to be eating ashes."

Skinny pipes up, "Yeah, but if the Rev had one night with *any* girl, you know he'd choke. Sit on the bed all night and bore her to death talking."

"Bet even the Rev couldn't ruin it with *Barbara,* though."

"How am I supposed to be the pinnacle of chastity to you all if you—"

Berk throws his head back laughing, which earns us more shushing. "Wait, wait, you're admitting it? The chastity?"

"I didn't admit anything because I don't kiss and tell." I flick on my lighter for Morgan, who came back to his senses long enough to stamp out the first cigarette and is starting on a new one.

"It's Rita for me," Skinny remarks. "That smile of hers, goddamn. It *does* things to me, y'know?"

Berk makes a face and takes a drag on his cigarette as he says, "Jesus Christ, no more, *please.*"

Thank God for Rita and Veronica and Barbara and every other symbol of the normalcy for which we're so hungry. When you feel like shit as much and as often as we do, you gather up whatever scraps are dropped and hope they're enough to buy a few moments of peace in between trips to the latrine.

After one such trip toward the end of the film, I trudge back to barracks to check on Fish and maybe write a letter home. I'm so used now to feeling like I have a perpetual stomach flu—we all are—that being in pain is more a frustration than anything else. Not to say that anything's gotten better, at least not consistently, but there's a certain numbing effect. Felt like I was going to die the first morning I couldn't get off my cot, way back in the spring when we first made camp in Kairouan before the Sicily jump. You learn to live with things, I guess, even cramps and piss-tasting water. And there's no quicker bond than the one between a bunch of guys with dysentery sharing quarters.

I check on a few of the guys in 3rd platoon's first tent who are bound to their beds, emptying vomit basins and helping a few of them clean up, the details of which are best left forgotten to history. But rinsing my hands outside the tent with lukewarm water from my canteen, I wonder if maybe I don't feel so much animosity now toward the red cross tied around the upper left arm of my field jacket.

27 August 1943, North Africa

To:

Elizabeth Dare

19 Holland Rd.

Caspar ME 04462

Dear Μαμά,

I'd send you a postcard and say I wish you were here, but there isn't much of a tourist industry where we are, and you wouldn't want to be here anyway. Hope all is okay at home. Did Laurie go back to school? I need his new address. I think he wrote something about living in a new house off-campus.

Have you picked any tomatoes yet? It's very hot here, I'm working on my tan. My Irish friends are suffering. It's all the annoyance of going to the beach and getting sticky with sand without getting to jump in the ocean.

How are Nana and Pop? He better not be trying to use the table saw again. Maybe you could siphon some of his energy and package it up for me. I sure could use it out here. Also, could you call Nana after you get this letter and read it to her? I know she's probably upset I haven't written them more. Tell her I'm trying. They keep us pretty busy, but I guess that keeps me from getting too homesick.

Has anyone interesting been over for supper? Write me any neighbor stories if you remember them. All the guys like hearing those. It's nice to read all the letters from home out loud. We especially liked your retelling of Marvin Bridges explaining to Dad how he brews his own moonshine, while drunk on that moonshine at the minister's table—some things in Caspar really don't change.

I've written it a hundred times now but please try not to worry too much about me. I'm okay, feeling fine, they feed us enough (even though it doesn't always taste like food, ha). And here we even have beds to sleep in, so all in

all I'm better than I have been. I know you'll still worry, but I'm taking
care of myself, I promise.

Tell Nana and Pop I love them, and Dad, too.
All my love,
Richard

28 August, 0500 hours

Milky white moonlight washes the dust-packed roads of the camp
as the stars fade. The mountains glow in the gray stillness, ethereal as dawn comes over the desert. In an hour reveille will sound and
the lines for the latrines will snake around the tents, and the grumbling
of guys washing in the cold will harmonize with the buzzing sandflies.
Hornets will gather in the mess tents and try to drown themselves in
the beanpots on the camp stoves. On the thermometers hanging in the
mosquito netting by the tent flaps, the mercury will slog higher till it
reaches its peak at noon, a toasty 110, give or take a few degrees. I like to
get out of camp in the mornings ahead of all that.

I pull the laces tight on my jump boots and hop down the tent steps.
The camp is quiet except for a couple guys coming and going to the
latrine and the three privates peeling potatoes behind the mess tent, this
week's unlucky bastards on KP duty. Swatting a mosquito out of my
eyes, I set off running. I woke up this morning for the first time in two
weeks without stomach cramps and I feel sixteen again, brimming with
restless energy.

The first time I ran in Corcoran boots in Georgia, I and every other
guy limped back to barracks after a three-mile training run, barely able

to stand on our new blisters. Some of them would've been in pain no matter what because they weren't runners, but I was three months out from the end of my sophomore track season at Brown and my feet were desperate for some cleats to navigate the rocky, twisting paths on our runs through the Appalachian hills. I felt as though cinder blocks had been strapped to me. But after enough times out, the callouses hardened and the boots didn't pinch so much till I barely noticed them anymore. It mattered more to me that I could still run.

As I run I think of older days and cross-country practices, also in the shadow of mountains. Running in the foothills at home was like steeplechase, jumping over streams if they were narrow enough or going right through so the cold water splashed the sweat on our shins. The woods were deep and the trees shut out the sunlight, but then we'd come to a clearing or a plateau in the hill and see the whole valley below us, with the white dots of houses and the little white crosses on the church steeples. Most of my friends ran cross-country and track, too, though I haven't yet been able to convince any of the guys in 3rd platoon to run with me. Berk just laughed the time I asked, so I never asked again. Peter promised to come "one of these days," but that day hasn't arrived. Santorini maintains that running is dangerous for a Greek's health after the incident at Marathon two thousand years ago and does only the bare minimum that Airborne training requires of him. And Fischer cannot be roused before dawn even if the tent were on fire, and besides, he's still laid up with malaria—the only valid excuse of the whole rotten lot of them.

Out of camp, the tents behind me, the air loses its sour tang. The desert stretches in unbroken vastness all around. I run along the road that leads to the hospital, trying to enjoy the cool air without inhaling a sandfly. My heart rate climbs and I swat away mosquitoes that take hits at my chest, and I feel a way I haven't felt in a long time. I tell myself it isn't how a soldier should feel, not with talk of us moving out again next week. But that doesn't dampen it. So I run faster, feet beating on the dusty brown road and feeling stronger than I have in months. I could run till I hit the end of the world.

A figure on the road up ahead wavers in the haze. I slow as I approach him. By his height and blond crew cut I can tell it's Lieutenant Walsh, 3rd platoon's CO. He's also in running shorts and has stopped to lace his boot.

"Sir," I say and drop to a walk.

Walsh straightens and says, "Morning, Dare."

I salute, and he raises his hand to his temple and drops it quickly. I've seen him from a distance out here some mornings, running, but I never wanted to bother him. He's the quiet sort, and I think he must run before dawn as much for the exercise as to watch the sunrise alone.

"These things are hell to run in, aren't they?" he remarks, scuffing the toe of his boot in the sand.

"Sure are, sir."

He jerks his head at the road stretching away. "Run with me a ways, Dare."

"Yes sir."

He keeps a steady pace at a jog, so I force myself to go slowly and keep in step with him. He's probably five or six years my senior, transferred from the 3rd battalion into F Company just before Sicily. We were anxious and a little jumpy going into combat for the first time with a guy none of us knew, but our old CO had been a stuffed shirt from West Point trying to work his way up the military ladder through nepotism, and at that point we would've preferred Mickey Mouse leading us into battle. Walsh turned out to be a competent leader, cool under pressure, as trusting of us as we grew to be of him. But I still don't know who he really is because he keeps himself at even more of a distance from the men than most officers do.

"Where are you from, Dare?" Walsh asks between short breaths. Then he adds, "You don't really get to know a fellow using his last name. Do you go by Richard, or...?"

"Yes sir, that's fine." I rub sweat and dust out of my eye. "I'm from Maine, sir."

He waves one hand to dispense with the "sirs," at least while we're out here alone, I assume. "That so? All I know of Maine is the lobster boats."

I huff out a laugh. "Sure, on the coast. I'm from up north, in the mountains. Where are you from, si—sorry."

For a minute the only sounds are our feet in rhythm, the wind blowing disparate notes through the desert, and the labor of our breathing. "I come from a little town in Indiana. Not much more than a crossroads for trains going to Chicago."

"Cubs or White Sox?"

"Cleveland Indians," he answers, and I catch his smile in my periphery. "And Maine, that'd make you what, a Yankees fan?"

I bristle. "If you weren't my CO, sir..."

He laughs.

As we run, dawn breaks over the hills, light that begins at the bottom of the sky and spreads up like mist in a gradient of color. My dog tags beat a pattern into the sweat on my chest. Walsh slows and then stops, staring out at the blush of the horizon. "You know, all of us in Fox owe a lot to you and Donny King and Walt Bruning. Wouldn't get far without our medics. How're you holding up?"

"I'm doing fine, sir," I say, and bite my tongue not in time. "Tired of the Atabrine checks."

"It is silly, guys tough as nails scared of a little aftertaste." He laughs and then looks at me. "But you like the 3rd platoon, the men there? The noncoms, Evans, Adler, Hayward...?"

"They're good men, sir. Sergeant Adler was my first friend in the company, actually."

He nods, hands on his hips. His face has been sunburned and tanned and sunburned again. For a moment he seems about to say something more about Fox but can't find the words, so he settles on, "You must've been a runner before the war."

"High school and college." When he raises a curious eyebrow, I add, a little reluctantly, "I was on the track and cross-country teams at Brown."

"Brown, that right?" Walsh whistles. "Bet they've given you hell for that."

"No more than Jimmy Whitlock and his economics degree from Fordham."

In a few more minutes the sun will be bright as it climbs over the mountain peaks. Walsh nods in the direction of camp. "Morning reports await and I'm just slowing you down now, Brown. I'll see you around."

"See you around, sir."

After a few seconds, his jog slows and he turns around, running in place. "Richard," he calls back. "That nickname you have—I've heard it among the guys, *Rev*—where'd it come from?"

"I made the mistake of telling them I studied theology."

"You mean to say you could've been a minister instead of getting caught up in all this?" Walsh tilts his head, pink light clinging to the sky behind him. "Medic and chaplain all in one—listen, when I get hit, you're the one I want."

He continues on toward camp, and I keep running past dry desert scrub blowing in the wind. The border between opaque sky and baked orange land is blurred, and the hills at my right arm are draped across the landscape like a sheet flung out and not yet flattened over a mattress. Any farther and even I risk a sunburn, so I turn back, the sand sticky on my arms and shins.

The green-peaked tents of the barracks come into view. A figure appears on the road out of camp, and at first I think it's Walsh again, but then the form solidifies and the hair is dark. I stop and watch him. It's Peter, who's politely put off all my invitations to come running. I start to grin because finally I won. Then I have a frightening thought.

As he approaches, I call, "Is it Fish?"

"What?" Peter slows. The front of his white t-shirt that says "U.S. Paratroops" across the chest is already damp.

"Fish, is he...?"

"Geez, no. He's fine. Sleeping like a baby when I left him."

I let out my breath. "Then what are you doing?"

"Well." Peter looks down at his boots. "I'm running, what does it look like?"

"C'mon, you don't run. Not unless you're ordered to."

"I just thought you might be lonely out here. But it looks like I caught you at the end," he adds, a hopeful note in his voice.

I smack his shoulder and steer him away from camp. "I'm not letting you off that easy."

Peter tugs off his shirt, slings it around his neck like a rich woman's mink, and begins to sing an old Airborne song through short huffs for breath. *We pull upon the risers, we fall upon the grass...*"

"*We never land upon our feet, we always hit our ass,*" I take up, and then jog out ahead of him, turning and running backward as I watch him. "All right, sarge, let's go, pick it up!"

"I'll...kill you. How do you...still have so much energy?"

"Can't kill me when you're dragging that far back."

He speeds up and snaps the t-shirt in my direction. I jump out of the way, crowing and taunting him to try and catch me as the sun climbs to warm our backs.

H arsh light glares in through the open mess tent an hour later. To make up for the overcooked potatoes and stale biscuits, Skinny Santorini's describing the roasted lamb and mint sauce and *loukanika* and *pastitsio* that his mother made on Pascha. "But seein' as your folk are Protestants and all," he says, pointing at me with his fork, "I don't suppose you make such a big deal for Pascha."

"What do I have to do to be Greek enough for you, shower in olive oil and walk on my hands all the way to Athens?" I lean across the table and steal his last piece of leathery bacon. He tries to stab my hand but misses. "My γιαγιά makes lamb on Easter, too."

"My grandma would paddle us out of the kitchen with a broom and throw pieces of bread to us through the window, like scraps for ducks," Peter remarks.

Berk tears a piece of biscuit and starts to say something about latkes when Charlie McNulty crashes in, nearly pushing me off the end of the bench. "Watch it, you crazy mick," Skinny mutters, lifting his mess kit to keep potatoes from falling in the dirt.

"Hey, Berk." Taking no notice, McNuts leans across the table and all but presses an opened envelope into Berk's face. "Tell it to me straight, would ya? If you thought your gal was takin' up with some 4F bastard, what would ya do?"

"Fuck's sake, Nuts, let a fella eat a spell, won't ya?" Berk leans out of the way as McNuts jabbers on. Then we hear the cough of a Jeep on the main avenue through camp, followed by the shout of everyone's two favorite words: "MAIL CALL!"

We all scramble up, and I almost trip untangling my legs from beneath the bench. A cloud of dust hangs like a halo around the officer sorting letters and calling out names in F Company: "Carter, M—Coleman, T—Dalton, S..."

"Berk, c'mon, listen," McNuts says, bouncing in Berk's face, annoying as a sandfly. He must've flagged down the Jeep the moment it drove into camp and badgered the mail officer. "If your gal—"

"Would you shove off, McNuts, I'm tryin'a open this." Berk ducks away as the mail officer calls "Dare, R," and hands me a V-mail envelope.

"I'll take anything for Private Fischer, too," I tell the officer. "Fischer, Jack." He flips past a few envelopes, then hands me another.

"From Grace?" Peter appears beside me, unfolding his customary two letters, one from his mother and one from his girl, Chrissy, a welder at a munitions plant in Milwaukee.

I rip the seal. On the "from " line is scribbled *Laurence Dare,* and the address of his fraternity house at the University of Maine in Orono. "No, from my brother, actually."

"Hey, has he asked out the redhead yet?" Skinny holds the edge of his letter up to his nose, presumably to smell Eva's apple perfume.

Laurie's flirtations with a cute ginger named Faye, a history student, have been the source of much entertainment for us—especially his graphic description last week. A game of catch on the quad went pear-shaped when cute Faye clocked him in the nose with a baseball. "There was blood everywhere," Laurie wrote, and all the boys liked that.

"Let's see." I straddle the bench at the table where our half-eaten mess kits still lie, picked over now by hornets. "Aw, look at that, he says he took her out to the pic—"

"It's a girl," someone says, and I glance over to see 2nd platoon's Lieutenant Carter still standing in the dusty road as the Jeep trundles off through camp. He looks up from the letter as if in a daze, and then comes over to the mess tent, which is the enlisted men's mess but he doesn't seem to notice or care as he sits on the end of a bench. "My wife—she had the baby, it's a girl..."

"All right, lieutenant, well done!" someone calls out, and someone else wolf-whistles and we all gather around him to see the photograph.

"She looks like you," Garrett remarks, though to me she just looks like a baby. Carter's wife named her Iris, which was his idea, and if there's anything that could make a bunch of combat-weary paratroopers feel a tickle in the throat, it's that hint of a smile around Iris's little mouth and her balled-up fist, as if she's making to slug a guy.

"Can't wait to be through with this fucking war," says Berk, leaning his elbows on the table and reading his wife's letter for the third time, "so I can get back to Fresno and me and Emily can have some Irises of our own. Makin' babies, not war, I'm tellin' ya."

McNulty has folded and refolded his letter so many times that it's gray and wrinkled. "Would ya listen, Berk? If your wife—"

"McNuts, I gotta be honest, if I'da thought Em would go around with some 4F while I was gone, I wouldn't have married her."

"You didn't know there was gonna be a war when you married her."

"War or no war, you gotta find a girl you can trust. And if yours don't wanna wait for you, let her and the 4F have each other."

McNuts does not seem placated by this advice. He chews at his dirty fingernails, apparently convinced that there's no other girl in all of Queens he could ever love.

"C'mon, Rev, what'd your brother say about the redhead?" Skinny wonders.

"Sounds like they're going steady. At least, they went out every night the week he wrote this."

By his expression, I can tell McNuts thinks 4F guys like Laurie have got it made, but to his credit he doesn't say so aloud. He runs a hand uncertainly through his greasy red hair and asks Berk how he knew Emily was the one. As the only married man in 3rd platoon—and one of the only married enlisted men in Fox Company—the boys all look up to Berk with reverence and respect, and torture him with their love problems. He seems a little offended that I've never come to him for advice. As often as he can, he likes to remind me just how much he knows about women.

"You know what, though?" he says now, tapping out a smoke from the packet. "It's our anniversary in four days—two years married. Seems a hell of a shame we've spent most of it apart."

"What're you giving her? Perfume? Earrings? Pop down to Woolworths on the corner and pick out a dress?" Peter winces as he takes a drink of rancid water from his canteen.

"Something even better—a letter none of you guys will ever get to see."

"My condolences to the censor office," I say, and we're having a good laugh about the poor clerks who are forced to trawl through all the smutty letters when Skinny says, "Yo, if it ain't the walking dead!"

I glance up. Fischer has wandered into the tent, looking like a skeleton in a white t-shirt with his hands shoved in his trouser pockets. His face has lost its Sicilian tan and his cheekbones stick out, but he's on his feet, and three days ago that was a sight I wasn't sure we'd ever see again.

"Morning, fellas," he says as I slide down on the bench to make room for him. I hand him his letter, which lifts his shoulders a little.

"You want something to eat?" Berk swats a hornet away from the remains of his breakfast. "God, I hate these little fuckers."

Fish shakes his head weakly and crosses his arms on the table. "Thanks, I'm not too hungry just yet."

"Not sure it's a good idea for you to be up, anyway," I say. Feeling like my mother, I touch the back of my hand to his forehead. Besides the usual sweat from the North African sun, he isn't abnormally warm. The fever must've broken early this morning. "But at least now you're not 103 and still rising."

"I know, but a fella gets real bored lying there. My back needs a break from that cot. Say, Rev, you think you could lend me a book? I liked that last one, Gatsby."

"Sure thing, Fish, you and Pete are my favorite library patrons. Unlike some people"—and here I level my V-mail envelope at Skinny—"who borrow books without returning the last one and never pay their fines."

Skinny blows out smoke and scoffs. "Whaddya lookin' at me for?"

"I know you gave my copy of *Lord Jim* to someone in Dog Company, and I'm never gonna see it again." I hold my hand out. "And I'm in a collecting mood. What've you got?"

"Let's see—" Skinny, company magpie, fishes in his jacket pockets. Books are valuable currency, so I know he must've made a good trade for poor old *Lord Jim*. But it was missing a couple pages in the front and also the back cover, and that's why I don't try my luck making a demand on one of the several Italian wristwatches he nicked off dead soldiers in Sicily. "I got some chocolate here—oh, it's melted...a piece of chewing gum, unwrapped, I promise, half a carton of smokes..."

"I'll take the smokes," I say, and he grumbles as I catch the carton of Camels. Less than half full, and most of them will end up back in his mouth anyway, the way he's always bumming them off the rest of us.

Peter asks Fish how he's feeling, and I read Laurie's letter again. The table is quiet for a minute or two till McNuts bursts out, "But how do you *know* if you love a girl?!" Berk yells at him to lay off and Skinny shoves him and the peace of the morning evaporates.

V.
VICTORY

F lashes of green and yellow light glimmer past in the long mirror behind the bar at the Green Moth, as the feet tapping across the dance floor set the drinks on our table to trembling. I watch the brandy sloshing its level, thinking I might need at least two more before I get up to dance again. There are less male dancing partners now than there used to be, and Mattie Faucheux and I have both already danced two full sets tonight with the girls and with other girls we didn't come with but know. Everyone in Caspar knows everyone, and we all end up here in the restaurant inside Helen's father's hotel on Saturday nights because this is our only semblance of nightlife. At least Caspar's girls seem happy to have dancing partners again who aren't their younger brothers or their 4F neighbors or even one another. If they notice how much more work Mattie and I have to do to keep up with them, they're too polite to say so.

"You know, back in our day," Mattie begins as we watch the girls from our table off the dance floor.

I throw him a look. "Back in *our day*? What, four years ago?"

He takes a swallow of his drink, which is his third while I'm still working on my first, and says, "Try telling me those four years haven't been their own lifetime. But back then, we could lindy with the best of them, couldn't we?"

"I wouldn't say the best of them, but we did try."

"Ay-uh, we did." Mattie tilts his drink back again while also tilting back on his chair.

We watch the girls dance with some high school boys to Tommy Dorsey's "Swingin' on Nothing." Well, Helen and Antonia found partners. Grace and Mary Heath are victims of the men shortage and are dancing with each other, and when Mary spins Grace out as they all dance the Charleston, I catch a half second of Grace's open-mouthed grin. On the next spin, she calls, "Hello, Richard, dance the"—gone again, and I wait; a few seconds later—"next dance with me?" Then she's off and Mary's dark curls are closer to me, glinting in the smoky light. It takes until Grace comes back around for me to tell her, "Mary's a much better partner than me—"

"You've had enough of a break!" she calls through the blur of movement. "Besides, you've already danced twice with Toni—and I haven't had you at all yet."

She and Mary seem to be having the time of their lives. I don't know how they have the stamina to both dance and laugh so hard, but it makes me laugh watching them. Just as funny is Toni's obvious displeasure with the freckled sixteen-year-old whose idea of dressing up is his varsity letter jacket, and who seemed to forget how to dance the moment she took his hand. Mattie lifts his glass in reply to her look of appeal.

"I should've worn my uniform," he remarks, setting his glass down and immediately picking up mine.

"Hey—"

He finishes it off before I can protest further. "Relax, Dick, you know you would've been nursing that all night. But imagine how many girls we could get if we'd worn our uniforms."

"If your sparkling personality can't get you a girl while dressed as a civilian, then what makes you think your uniform would be more successful?"

Mattie takes out a pack of cigarettes and lights one up, and I don't have the energy to ask him not to smoke. "Please. I owe Toni a drink because I lost a bet that you'd have got down on one knee to Grace within one week of getting home." He breathes out a cloud of smoke in the dim light. "Maybe try your uniform, and the veil will be lifted from her eyes."

"Grace isn't the kind of girl that cares about uniforms. And besides, we're not kids anymore, so you can take your bets about puppy-love and shove them you know where."

"The women in London didn't do a double-take when you passed them in your dress greens? Huh," he says, blowing out more smoke. "Guess I'm just better-looking than you."

"Or women in London prefer guys who're white as ghosts and have a million freckles," I add, "which must be true, considering that their country is still reproducing."

"You wanna get out there with the girls? Go on, get. Oh, they're starting a new one—go on, Dick, don't let your sweetheart down."

I reach for his cigarette and snuff it in the ashtray next to our empty glasses. "If you call Grace my *sweetheart* when she's in earshot, I'll free you from this mortal coil."

"Oh, thank God." Mattie tilts his chair back again as he signals to the waiter for another round. "That better be a promise. Hey, Grace—"

"Okay!" I stand up, pushing back my chair and shrugging off my jacket. "I'm going, you don't need to announce it to the whole room."

"Aw, you're blushing. Look at that!"

I almost scoop up a handful of peanuts from the glass dish to throw in his face, but someone catches my wrist and pulls me onto the dance floor. It's Grace, smiling at me. When the opening bars of Artie Shaw's "Traffic Jam" resonate through the club, I know I'll be dead before the end. But I see Grace's eyes crinkled at the corners with laughter, and I think that death by lindy hop might be worth it.

Maybe her touch is magic, because I make it through the whole dance and am only a little out of breath by the end, hardly more than she is. I don't know if the glow between us is a spark or sweat or the drinks. Maybe all three. It seems to shimmer like gold in the haze as she tugs my hand and pulls me back toward her. The band picks up a slower tune, and instead of returning to our friends at the table, we keep dancing.

"What do you suppose they're talking about?" Grace says as she tilts her head toward our table. "No, don't look! Cripes, Richard, you're anything but subtle."

"Why do I have to be subtle?"

"Because now Mattie is waving at us, and I knew that would happen. Toni did say something about winning a bet, but I don't know what she was talking about..."

I clear my throat, almost coughing in my hurry to redirect Grace. I'd like to talk to her about feelings that may or may not exist, but not here in the crowded hotel on a dance floor with other couples twirling past and our own personal peanut gallery watching from the wings. "Probably just some stupid stunt of Mattie's, like that time he tried to ride your grandma's cow bareback. Anyway. Have you, um—are you reading any good books?"

Grace cocks an eyebrow at this abrupt turn of conversation, but she eases into it as naturally as from a Charleston to a waltz. "I'm almost done with *Cannery Row,* you know, that new Steinbeck—you'd like it. It's very atmospheric, all colors and sounds and smells and not much of a plot. Sort of the thing you just fall into and get swept along with. Sometimes it's nice to get swept along when you read."

"Yes, I guess so," I say distractedly, taken in by the rose petal scent on her neck and the feel of her back beneath the fitted bodice of her green silk dress. "Oh, speaking of books, I have one for you, that French poet you love...Boudin?"

"Boudin was a painter. Are you thinking of Baudelaire?"

"Baudelaire, that's it. I found it in an old shop in Scotland, and I hope it's worth it because I inhaled a pound of dust pulling it off the shelf."

"Your poor lungs. And that's sweet, but you didn't have to bring me back a book."

"I wanted to. And I actually read it cover to cover, too, on the side with the English translations; that's how boring it could get over there." Wait, no, that's not what I meant to say. "Not that I think Baudelaire is boring—I really don't—only that I'd never read much poetry before that because I hated it in school. It was always so dry how our teachers taught it, and especially French...Grace, any time you'd like to stop me, feel free."

She was grinning through that whole spectacle, happy to let me dig myself an even deeper grave. "And give up the chance to see you blush? Never. Tell the truth—did you actually like it?"

I only read it for you, I almost say, but catch myself just in time and say instead, "I think I did."

We fall silent, listening to the clink of the piano keys, instinct taking over my movements in the dance. The last time I danced was in England, last summer, after Normandy but before Holland when we still thought the war might be over by Christmas. The locals gave it their all to take our minds off what we'd just come back from, but I'll never forget the weight of death that hung on my shoulders. Even with the dancing, many of those evenings were melancholy. They were in fear of losing their

country, had watched the newsreels of London in flames, and had given
their sons in sacrifice. We had lost our friends, and between campaigns
with time to think during marches and close-order drills, I noticed that
my own naïve faith—a belief that the world could still come out okay
in the end—had taken a direct hit somewhere in the Italian hills or the
French hedgerows.

"What're you thinking about?" Grace is watching me with that per-
ceptive gaze of hers that feels almost indecent in public.

"English country dances, actually. But I'd rather be here," I add
quickly, which is true.

"You know Mattie claims he had three girlfriends in England?" She
arches her arm to twirl and her skirt spins out, joining a dozen others
around us. "But if I know you, asking you that question would make
you blush the color of a plucked chicken."

"I'm willing to bet there were three girls he jilted, probably more, who
all owe him a slap, if that's how he defines *girlfriend*. And excuse me, a
plucked chicken? Is that what I look like to you?"

"No, no, not at all!" Grace laughs, shaking her head. "Red as a rose, is
that better? You'd blush red as a rose if anyone asked you about English
girls. No, you look very handsome—very snappy outfit, too." She tugs
on the cuff of my shirt, which I rolled up to dispel some of the heat of
dancing.

I look over her head to the slow-moving, silver-and-gold reflections
mixing like wet paint in the bar mirror. For a little while time seems to
pass us by. I guess the band plays at the same tempo, and that old Cab
Calloway song "Sunset" doesn't suddenly have two new stanzas, and it
isn't as if everyone else has left the hotel. But even though we're far from
alone, Grace is framed in my vision and all else falls away: the smoke, the
feet rocking the wood floor, the lingering scent of whiskey and vodka, the
raucous laughter in the corner booths. I only hear the steady thrum of

the bass player's strings, an undercurrent girding Grace and me to these same few steps in rhythmic motion.

If the mood of those English dances was tempered by a sense of "we only have tonight," then this evening is the mirror image, an open and eerie road stretching endlessly ahead of us. In the military, our lives were never our own, and there was some freedom in that constraint—freedom enough to try to dance our cares away, despite that it never worked. But now there are no orders from division, no jumps or objectives, no screams to follow to the wounded. Just us and whatever lives we're brave enough to try for.

"...Richard? Are you listening?"

I snap back. Grace's eyes are on mine, and I realize she must have been saying my name before I heard.

"Sorry, say again?"

"I asked if you want to take a break after this one."

"Oh—yes, let's."

As the last notes of "Sunset" fade out, we head back to our table, which has accumulated a concerning number of empty glasses. When Grace leans over to say something to Helen, Mattie catches my eye and makes the shape of a heart with his hands and then breaks it apart. If he didn't have a prosthetic leg, I'd kick him under the table.

We drift out of the hotel around midnight. Mattie, probably thanks to his iron liver, is not as drunk as I expected him to be. We wave goodbye to the girls as Antonia, who drew the short straw of alcohol-deprived chauffeur tonight, climbs in behind the wheel of Grace's red 1939 Chevy, a convertible that may be the most frequent reason for me breaking the tenth commandment. The lights in the hotel still burn yellow for late-night revelers, the only place awake on deserted Linden Avenue, under the oaks with their tenuous new buds.

Mattie slides into the passenger side of the truck, but I watch until the Chevy's taillights disappear into the darkness under a sky dotted with silver stars.

There's a suctioning sound behind me. Mattie, working the window crank, calls out, "Whenever you're done composing your poetry about pretty girls and starry nights, Dick. I'm in no hurry."

"As if you have anywhere to be."

"Listen, if you don't get me home I'll fall asleep right here, and I don't think you want me sleeping in your truck all night. Ferry me to my bed, if you will," he adds, slurring the last words, so maybe he really is three sheets to the wind.

When we were kids, no one else got under my skin like Mattie did. One moment we would be pounding the shit out of each other in the dirt, hurling expletives like spit watermelon seeds, then minutes later we were best friends again after the others separated us. As furious as he made me, he could also make me laugh till I cried, and most times I'd forget whatever heinous thing he'd said or done to upset me. None of my other friends treated me with the needle-sharp honesty that has always been Mattie's curse and gift.

But tonight the short drive passes in uncharacteristic quiet for him. I know we've crossed into Caspar's French-Canadian neighborhood when the steetlamps grow sparser and the road more rutted. The potholes in the rest of the town are annoying, but here they're egregious. Petit-Canada has no one to advocate for it on the town council, and the potholes are the least of its communal concerns. Before I met Mattie in fifth grade, when his family came here from Quebec looking for mill work, I had only passed by these streets on my bike and never gone down any of them. White American families here try to pretend that their lower-class Franco neighbors don't exist, and the latter are so insular and wary of everyone outside this neighborhood that the town might as well be two separate countries.

It wasn't till halfway through high school that I finally saw Mattie's house for the first time, and I've still never been inside. There are no lights on when I pull up, and he waves a hand at my offer of help. "I may have a fake leg," he says tiredly as he opens the truck door, "but it is still a leg, last I checked." He shuts the door, then leans on the open window. "Night, Dick."

"Goodnight, *Matthieu.*"

"Who's that? I don't know him." He gives me a half-hearted salute, crosses the crabgrass yard to the dark, gray little house, and disappears in the shadows.

I continue on home. Caspar asleep feels like the northernmost outpost of the world. I think about the glow when I danced with Grace; was it really just the brandy? I didn't imagine her touch on my arm, holding me a little tighter than she needed to. But it's easy to be swept up in the thrill of dancing and believe the illusion that our lives don't have these gaping wounds at the center.

Dad's hunched shoulders are framed under the kitchen bulb when I pull into the driveway. On the porch I try to open the screen door gently in case he's fallen asleep at the table. His notes are spread in front of him, but his chin is propped on one hand and he's looking at the blackness through the front window, as if expecting the Lord to set a burning bush down on Holland.

"Were you waiting up for me?"

He turns, apparently so lost in his thoughts or prayer that he didn't hear me come in. "No, no, I was writing. Lost track of time. How was the dancing?"

"Exhausting." I slump in the kitchen chair across from him. The stinging in my ribs has finally hit, a delayed reaction to lindy hop.

"Did you dance with Grace?"

I look up at him. His gray eyes are tired but not without some good humor. "I did. And I don't think I stepped on her toes at all." My elbow brushes his scattered papers. "You must've finished Sunday's sermon."

"No, these are just notes." He leans back in his chair, runs his hands over his face. "I thought I had it, and then it just disappeared. I think this will be one of those 'wee hours of Sunday morning' sermons."

"Maybe God just wants you to go to sleep and agonize a little less," I offer.

"Tell you what." He stands, glasses in hand, leaving the papers. "I promise to try if you do, too."

At the stairs, he flicks the light switch and the bulb dims into a bare glow in the kitchen. Then he turns and glances at me in the moonlight, and says, "I know I don't need to wait up for you anymore, but old habits are hard to break. It was a long war."

M y mind unspools every moment of the interview I just left as I drive home, offering me a front-row seat to an agonizing reel of my own embarrassment in Technicolor. In the reception area of the *Bangor Daily News* office while I waited for the editor, my heart began beating harder than it ever has before a job interview. It was only a copyediting position, but it was still the best chance I've had so far. A few minutes later, the editor's tapping pen was a drumbeat, his eyes unwavering. Why did I suddenly develop a stutter while talking to him? I couldn't *not* hear the pen tapping, couldn't look away from it even when I felt him watching me. It seemed to grow in decibels until I could barely hear his voice, or even my own as it stammered out inadequate answers. The clock on the wall began to match the pen's rhythm, and so did the blinds on the open windows banging against their frames in the wind, and even through the wall I could hear the receptionist in the front chewing bubblegum. The typewriter keys in the newsroom behind us were staccato bursts punctuating my rising blood pressure.

In the moment I was vaguely irritated with myself for ruining the editor's first impression of me, but for no good reason I was even angrier at them, the editor and the blinds and the receptionist and the typewriters and their cocktail of sounds that clawed through my eardrums and made me fucking livid. I held my hands together as tight as I could in my lap to keep from reaching out and snapping the pen in two. The reel becomes a silent film at that point in my memory, because I have no recollection of what he asked me or what I said. I think he did say, "Thank you for your time, Mr. Dare. We'll be in touch." But they will not be in touch because I am positive I convinced him I don't even know the basic rules of grammar.

The first bars of that Glenn Gray song I hate, "My Heart Tells Me," come over the truck's radio. I hit the knob to turn it off more forcefully than needed. Up ahead of me the train whistles, and the red-and-white striped arms cross over the tracks as I come to a stop. It's the coal train passing through on its way to Presque Isle. Maybe I should ditch the truck here at the railway crossing and swing up onto one of the empty cars like a vagabond. There can't be a single job in Maine—aside from shoveling coal or plowing or working in a mill—for which I haven't applied. Every town is flooded with more boys returning each day. I wonder how many of them lose their shit at the sound of bubblegum popping.

When I pass the train station, there are a handful of people on the platform in front of the ticket office, more than I've ever seen there. Before I get to town I sense something isn't quite right, but can't say what or why. I glance in the rearview mirror. No cops behind me. No one at all, just an empty, deeply cracked road guarded by dense pines. The air is warm and the sun blinding, even through my sunglasses.

At Main Street I pull up to the stoplight between the post office and the hardware store, and glance out to see the sidewalk in front of the hardware store crowded with people. At three o'clock on a Tuesday? I still feel stuck back in the newspaper office, so the pieces haven't quite fit together when there's a tap on the truck window. Some high school kids are bouncing around between the curb and the street. When I crank the window down, Lydia Norberg—Sam's little sister—sticks her face in and crows, "Richard, Richard, turn on the radio!"

Around me traffic has stopped, and folks are getting out of their cars and joining the cluster of adults on the sidewalk, huddled around the open door of the hardware store.

The Glenn Gray song is long-gone. When the radio picks up the signal again, it catches a man's voice mid-sentence: "...fly over all Europe. For this victory, we join in offering our thanks to the Providence which has guided and sustained us through the dark days of adversity..."

Were it not for the context, I wouldn't have recognized President Truman's voice. I turn the volume up, and folks who can't hear at the store begin gathering around the truck. For a minute the whole street is silent, engines turned off, and even kids hold their breath as we listen.

"Let us not forget, my fellow Americans, the sorrow and the heartache which today abide in the homes of so many of our neighbors," the president says gravely, "neighbors whose most priceless possession has been rendered as a sacrifice to redeem our liberty."

I take off my sunglasses and put them on the dashboard. Lydia's face, framed by her friends', rests on the open window. "We must work to finish the war. Our victory is but half-won," Truman is saying. I think of Sidney, still flying over Pacific atolls that I can't even imagine. Whispers of "is it over?—Germany surrendered?" move through the clusters. The voices are hushed, afraid of trampling over the president's speech that the homefront has waited four years to hear.

Truman's voice is interrupted by a crackling on my radio, the signals crossing, and the dissonant chords of a jazz song drown him out. I turn the dial by a hair's breadth, and it picks back up. "…will our fighting job be done. We must work to bind up the wounds of a suffering world—to build an abiding peace, a peace rooted in justice…"

I feel eyes on me and glance up. Grace leans on the open door of her fire-engine-red Chevy at the curb, listening to the president on her radio speak in unison with mine. She watches me as though no one else on the street exists, and her expression says, *Can you make any sense of this?*

An Augusta announcer's voice follows Truman's. I press the knob, though the street is still abuzz with the broadcast. Grace crosses and puts her hand on the open window. "Drop me back here when it settles down?"

The open street suddenly seems very small, and I don't want to hear everyone's relief and worries and questions. I nod and get out and go around to the other side to open the passenger door for her. She climbs in, settling her leather satchel by her feet and smoothing the pleats of her wide-legged trousers.

"Should've stayed late at school, after all," she remarks as I navigate through the clusters of people and parked cars in the middle of the lane. I haven't seen Caspar this alive since that Sunday afternoon when people poured from their homes calling out the news that the Japs bombed Pearl Harbor.

"War's over. Go home," I mutter at the people taking their sweet time vacating the street. "Well, one of them."

We must work to bind up the wounds of a suffering world. On Water Street, women and old people congregate on porches with children clinging to their legs or cross between yards, calling to one another, "Did you hear the president?"

At the stop sign intersecting Water and Queen streets, I sit for too long, looking across at Holland and our house on the corner. I imagine my parents sitting in the kitchen together at night, when Laurie was at school, listening to the radio on the windowsill and wondering if it would be them or their neighbors receiving a Western Union telegram that week. Or waiting last fall for an announcement from Roosevelt that he never gave: "The war will be over by Christmas." I'm sure that was spread just as much here as it was among us over there.

"It seems so sudden." Grace glances at me. "I know it isn't, but it seems that way."

"All these years, and it's over with one radio announcement."

"But are we sure it's over?"

No other cars are in sight as we idle at the stop. I cut my eyes to her. "Isn't it?"

"I don't know. We should be celebrating, shouldn't we?" She laughs—well, not really a laugh. "What a pair of sad sacks we are."

I drive past the church to where the road ends at the marshes. We watch two herons swoop low over the wetlands that stretch out from the foothills of Mt. Katahdin. Above them the sky has darkened, and the air feels heavy like rain. I stare at the farthest point of the sky and hope for lightning to cleave it in two. The furious thunderstorms that form over the mountains and roll down onto Caspar used to frighten me, but now I wish for some deafening thunder, just to have a place to hide. Even from Grace.

Some of the guys in Fox Company will get to go home, but just as many will be shipped out to Japan to jump on Tokyo. How much longer do we have to hold our breath, till the moment we can begin binding ourselves up without fear that another wave of wounded will come in?

These are not flesh wounds, stabilized by sulfa powder and a half dozen quick stitches. How do you bind up the suffering when the wound is still gushing and there isn't enough light to find the veins to clamp and the most you can do is hold his head and tell him it will be okay, when you know it won't be?

"Richard," Grace says. She's turned in the seat, watching me with worry in her eyes. "I can tell you're already thinking about it. Obsessing about it."

"Obsessing about what?"

"That there are still boys fighting the war and you're not."

I look down at my hands in my lap, at the winter scars etched across the knuckles, some from the elements and some from my own clumsiness that pissed me off at the time. And now I'm pissed off that the same clumsiness got me knocked out of this thing, wasting myself when they need me. Grace knows she's right, so I don't try to pretend she isn't.

"It isn't fair to them," I say. "That some of mine will have to keep fighting because they don't have enough points to go home."

"Points?"

"We all got points for jumps we completed, any medals we won, any wounds. Some guys never got wounded, so it doesn't matter if they've been with the company since '42. If they don't have enough points, they're not getting back." I shrug. "Not that there are many of the original guys left in the company at this point, anyway."

"Oh."

"We had this stupid game"—I smile and shake my head thinking of it—"all of us taking bets who'd get a nice clean wound that week, not enough to kill you or get you shipped home but just to get a few days in the hospital with the pretty nurses and hot food, you know. It was morbid, but it made us laugh. A lot of stupid things made us laugh."

Grace smiles too and says, "Guess you had to laugh or you'd go crazy."

"Yeah," I say after a moment, "that's true."

We sit for a long time watching the slate-gray clouds tumble across the sky. She said it. What a pair of sad sacks, sitting alone as the town rejoices.

In time the wounds will turn phantom, though I know that doesn't mean the pain will end. Where's our promised new heaven and new earth—hasn't this earth been beaten and burned and decimated beyond recognition? Did God look away when the Nazi high command gassed His chosen people in cattle cars? Will the black boys who fought in segregated units for a country that hates them ever partake of Truman's peace and justice?

How much longer will we wait for the old order of things to pass away?

"I spent so long cleaning other people's wounds." I shake my head, press my fingers to my eyes. "Sorry, I don't even know what I mean by that. It's just—I don't know how to make sense of anything anymore, much less…"

"Much less bind up the suffering of the whole world?"

And how do we begin to bind ourselves back up, Mr. President, when we've lost limbs and lungs and our very minds?

She touches the cameo necklace around her neck and says, "No one's asking us to take care of the whole world. Only to start with each other."

I stare out my window without answering. After a moment I'm aware of something hovering above my shoulder blades, as if drawing static from the fabric of my jacket. Instead of touching my shoulder, Grace draws her hand away. I pretend I didn't notice.

There were men I had to leave as they were dying because I knew they wouldn't make it but their buddy nearby would. They died alone, in snow and mud and choking on their own blood and vomit, crying for their mothers. A gold star and some dog tags and diaries are all that immortalizes them. How do I atone for that? How would anyone ever begin to draw a stitch through the wounds of those families?

Grace turns the volume down, voices in the background discussing the surrender in Reims. Then a broadcast comes from Augusta reporting on the president's announcement and proclaiming that today, May 8, is being celebrated around the world as V-E Day: an Allied Victory in Europe.

VI.

CHIESA

J im Garrett from 3rd platoon is dead, and I can't even go out to drag his body back. Every time someone so much as twitches, the belfry sniper tries to blow off a head from his position in the church on the corner opposite. He has the best vantage point in the town, first zeroed in on us across the street, now swinging north to pick off 2nd platoon. Like any sniper, though, he won't last long.

The street is littered with broken bricks and chunks of plaster. There was a fountain in the center of the square till a hit from a German .75 millimeter gun knocked out its base and flooded the cobbles. Mortars have torn through the palm trees lining the median, and bits of their trunks are scattered in the wet street.

The command post across the square from the church is little more than a shed filled with straw and the stench of animal waste. At the far end, a couple of officers are huddled around maps spread on work tables, taking turns barking orders over the radio. Another one scopes the upper windows through binoculars. None of them seem to notice me.

Leaning in the doorframe, I chew on a ragged fingernail and watch Lieutenant Walsh with 3rd platoon a hundred yards away. They're sheltering behind a low stone wall, a dozen guys on their stomachs. I squint at the shuttered upper windows of the buildings lining the street. 3rd has to secure each of them.

A black plume of powder mushrooms into the air from half a mile away in the village. Out of our sight line, 2nd platoon has got a hell of a fight on its hands, and even from here I can hear someone screaming for a medic. It takes all my will to stay put. Donny and Walt will take care of their own platoons.

The village resonates with gunshots as Walsh and Dennis, one of the demolitions NCOs, try to decide what to do with the church. It's a cultural landmark and we're under orders to preserve such places to the best of our abilities, which more than likely means someone else will die before we're justified in calling the British artillery down on it. I stare at Garrett's back, covered in dirt and plaster dust. Although I can't hear Walsh from this distance, I know what he's saying to Dennis: "Save us a lot of pain if we could blast the damn thing."

I watch as he signals the NCOs. Peter will take 1st squad along the left flank to clear out those buildings—and if they're lucky, get a bead on that sniper. Walsh will take half of Evans' 2nd squad into the church, while Evans takes the other half to root out the surrounding buildings. He orders Haley and Reynolds to provide a base of suppressive fire. Then he signals Cochran, his radioman, to stay on him. Peter's squad is the first to go. They crawl on their stomachs below the stone wall, their rifles under their arms, and disappear into an alley.

Something rustles behind me. It's either the replacement officer who caught a stray bullet in the shoulder on our approach into Arnone, or it's an upset goat stamping on its straw. That's what happens when an occupied stable becomes your aid station. I move back from the opening and go over to check on him. The officer, not the goat, though the goat stops chewing to eye me with a skeptical expression, from one disgruntled European to one displaced American.

This lieutenant, whose name I can't remember, is our only casualty of the day so far. I crouch beside him and look at his shoulder without touching it. The blood hasn't spread, and the sling I rigged up seems to be holding. Once the boys secure the town and we can bring up the surgeons from the rear, someone will get the bullet fragments out of his shoulder. All I have to do is make sure he doesn't bleed out before that.

I've got him on a stretcher at the back, farthest from any more strays that might pepper the square, and out of the goat's way. He's not asleep but not fully conscious, either, pain evident in his face when he shifts a little. Finding a syrette in my kit, I say, "Sir, I know it hurts, but I need you to try to lie still for me. I'm going to give you some more morphine, sound good?"

Walsh must give the order because Haley begins firing. Emptying the syrette into the lieutenant's shoulder, I try to hold my attention fully on him, even as I'm listening to the firefight outside.

I move the bandage a little to check his bleeding, and then a scream cuts clear through the gunfire: "MEDIC!"

His odds are good. I smooth the bandage back into place, pull the wool blanket up around him, and take off. Haley and Reynolds, the nose of their machine gun propped on the sandbags, quit firing when they see me and point at the white stucco church. Another cry—"MEDIC!"—emanates from it.

I run in a crouch across the wide stretch of empty street, right past Garrett's body and the watery bloodstains. Either the sniper is dead, or he's following the rules of war because I'm not shot at. The sounds of close-quarters fighting come from the nearby storefronts—shouting, falling plaster, M1s discharging.

A shaft of gray light falls through a hole in the ceiling above me when I enter the church.

"Lieutenant?" I shout. "Berk?"

There are two chapels on either side of the chancel, and a carved oak door in the transept that I assume must hide the belfry stairs. For a few breaths, the inside of the church is eerily silent. No shots echo off the barreled vaults. I feel the peaceful eyes of the Virgin and the Saints on me from the wood-paneled triptychs hanging behind the chancel.

There's no answer. I have to make a choice. Just as I head for the belfry stairs, an explosion shakes the foundations of the church and throws me on my ass, the force of it pushing me backward ten feet across the stone floor.

...

Up. Get up.

...

Go—you need to find the others—get up—

Plaster dust fills my lungs as I climb to my knees, coughing, a whine like a pulled fire alarm ringing in my ears. As the smoke clears, the hole in the dome of the church—over the center chapel—becomes visible.

"Lieutenant?!" I shout, gripping the edge of a pew. My voice sounds tinny, as if transmitted over a radio. "Lieutenant! Berk!"

Why the hell would the Germans shell the church, burying their own guys alive? I stumble to the belfry steps and call out for someone, anyone, a sign of life, but if there's an answer I can't hear it. I reach into my bag and wrap my fingers around a syrette. Picking my way through the heaps of rubble that fell from the ceiling, I shout for the lieutenant again.

Then there's another shell, and I throw myself down on the cleaved stones, heart pounding as if to drop out of me. My mouth opens in a scream, swallowed by the whipcrack of the shelling.

Bits of the ceiling fall on my back and I taste blood, dripping into my mouth from my nose. It's on the third shell that a thought comes to me.

Fuck.

Walsh would've told Cochran to get hold of the artillery crew and make sure they're holding fire on our coordinates. But I haven't seen Cochran.

A white haze envelops the sanctuary. I crawl through the rubble as sweat and tears burn my eyes. They must all be dead already. They have to be.

Shit shit shit shit shit shit.

I get unsteadily to my feet and run, almost tripping down the center aisle, screaming for Cochran, for the radio, anything, *anyone.* Wind blows back the door of the church, which hangs by one hinge. A whistle slices through the white sky. I duck behind a crumbling half wall and cover my head with my hands.

O Lord, my Lord, the strength of my salvation—

The shell's tremor reverberates through me as it hits the shops beside the church.

—you have covered my head in the day of battle...

Stumbling and dizzy like I knocked back too much Italian wine, I shout for help, and then I blink and see Cochran: slumped against the blasted wall of the church, two holes in his chest. I ran right past him when I came in.

His eyes stare straight ahead and his pulse is long gone, but the radio is still on his back, so I drop to my knees and grab the receiver.

"*This is Company F 3rd platoon,*" I scream. "We're in the church—3rd platoon is in the church, CEASE FIRE—"

I can't hear a thing in reply. Someone from the British artillery crew is talking, but the words are disjointed, reaching my ears only half-formed. Then I make out one word, "coordinates," and I shout, "I don't know the fucking coordinates. It's the church in the village, the *church*—I'm an F Co medic, my guys are still in the church—"

Something hits my shoulder, and I whirl around. A private has appeared out of the smoky gloom from the church, his face streaked with white dust and blood. He's heaving in great gasps of air, and though his mouth moves no sound comes out. Then he's pulling at my jacket.

"Doc," he shouts, and at that moment it all rushes back in: the machine-gun fire, the burst of a grenade in a storefront window nearby, the artillery man on the radio whose voice falls away when I drop the receiver.

Walsh's blond head is outlined in the light streaming in through the holes in the façade. He's knelt over a body on the ground before the chancel, at the very place someone would stand to receive communion. Blood pools beneath his knees and runs in channels between the gaps in the stone floor. The lieutenant shifts, his hand gripping another, bright scarlet staining both men's hands as if they made a blood pact. It's Berk, trembling so hard he's nearly convulsing, shallow breaths turning to gasps of pain.

"We got the sniper," the private pants, "but then those shells started coming..."

He and the other private talk over one another while Walsh tells Berk to hang on. Precious seconds are lost as they hover around him, seeming to forget I'm here—"it's okay, Harry, we're gonna get you out of here"—so I shove the shoulder of the private closest to me and snap, *"Move!"*

Chastised, they all scoot back. I put my hand on Berk's forehead, startled not at the sweat on his brow but the coldness of his skin—like touching a corpse. Talking to him with quiet reassurance, I reach into my bag for wound dressings and disinfectant, eyes tracking his body and landing on the dark bloodstains spreading across his right thigh.

Bandages will be no use. His trouser leg is soaked through with blood from his groin to his knee. Embedded in his upper thigh is a chunk of twisted steel, razor-sharp at the edges and still smoking. Bits of exposed muscle brush my fingertips. Artillery wounds often self-cauterize, but not when the shrapnel severs the femoral artery. He's in shock, his skin bone-white and freezing even in the humid air. We might already be out of time.

"Hold him, hold him," I say to Walsh as Berk thrashes his legs out, his body jerking involuntarily in reaction to the pain. "Hold him down! Keep him still!"

Walsh orders one of the privates to find us a Jeep as I use my scissors to cut Berk's trousers away. I throw all my weight into my shoulders to bear down on the artery over the wound, where I can feel a pulse throbbing through his leg. Theoretically he has a couple of minutes before he dies from blood loss, but two months in combat has taught me that you can shove your textbook theories up General Patton's ass for all the good they are in the field.

"Put your jacket over him; keep him warm," I tell Walsh. "And get a tourniquet from my bag."

My hands slide off his blood-slicked skin as he writhes in pain. I shout again for them to hold him still. One of the privates pins his other leg as the wound spurts arterial spray in my eyes. I set my jaw, up to my elbows in Berk's blood, feeling the pulsing arteries tap out death warnings like Morse code through my shaking muscles.

We have to get that tourniquet on or I'll be carrying my friend's dead body out of this church, so I give up with the pressure—not that my finger in the dyke is doing any good—and ball up a handful of dressings instead. I maneuver them into the wound cavity, where the scarlet arterial blood saturates them into uselessness. Another and another, till I've stuffed the wound three times and there's no room left for anything but a prayer.

"I'll need your help getting it under his leg"—I duck my forehead to wipe blood and sweat on the arm of my jacket—"when I tell you, lift his right side."

"And the shrapnel?" Walsh asks.

"Leaving it in for the surgeons." It's likely already caused enough nerve damage, and I won't risk the chance that the way it's embedded in there is the only thing keeping him alive. "Okay, lieutenant, tourni—"

There's a sudden stutter of machine-gun fire and Walsh shouts, "HEADS DOWN!" Both of us cover Berk's body with our own.

Before I'm even aware of what's happening, the private is on his feet with his rifle. In my peripheral vision I see him crouched behind a pew as dark figures, rendered featureless by the sun at their backs, spill through the opening in the side of the church. At first I'm not sure they realize we're in here, but then a head jerks around at the sound of Berk's blood-soaked gasps, amplified in the cavernous sanctuary.

There's the spring and release of a cartridge. A body hits the floor. It must be one of theirs because the firing continues. Some set of balls on that replacement. There's a shout from the other end of the church and the exchange of fire grows more intense, but I don't have time to watch.

"Stay with us, Harry, you're almost there," I lie as Walsh puts the tourniquet in my hand.

The lieutenant kneels with his arms under Berk's. "Ready?"

"Go."

I relieve the pressure and as Walsh lifts Berk, cries of pain escaping through his gritted teeth, I slide the tourniquet under his thigh. My hands are slippery with blood, and I can't get a good grip on the buckle. Even if I could, these Army-issued tourniquets don't come with a windlass. There's no way to get it tight enough with just my hands.

I lean over Berk, pulling the strap as tight as it can go, but I know it's not enough. "This isn't going to work."

His face is damp with sweat, lips turning blue. We don't have time to sit here hoping for the best. Shock or blood loss or both will take him if I don't figure out what the fuck to improvise.

"Lieutenant—"

Someone pops off three shots with an M1 and then the church, except for Berk's shallow heaves for air, is silent. It startles me more than the first shot did. A familiar voice calls out orders and then two figures loom over us, blocking out the dusty sunlight gloom.

"Doc!"

Caught in one last desperate attempt to yank the tourniquet tight and cut off his pulse, I grunt, "I'm a little busy—"

"Let us help you," Peter's voice says.

He and McNulty crouch on Berk's other side, dropping their rifles on the bloodied stone. With quick hands that are steadier than my heartbeat, I unbuckle the useless tourniquet and put pressure again above the shrapnel and stuffed wound dressings.

"Oh shit," McNuts breathes out, then quickly adds, "yeah, Doc, whaddya need?"

Berk's pulse in his carotid is sluggish beneath my touch, his eyelids drifting shut even as Walsh tries to keep him awake. This is it. One chance to give Emily Berkowicz a reunion with her husband instead of a corpse.

"McNuts, get one of the blood plasma bags from my kit, and my scissors and tape. Sarge—" I crane my neck back to see the altar, which is covered with a white cloth. On top of it, a collection of silver candlesticks and a crucifix stand untouched as if Providence guards them from falling plaster. "Cut off some of that cloth, enough to tie around his thigh—make it three or four inches wide. And Lieutenant, I'm gonna need your trench knife. Berk, you're gonna be okay, but I need you to stay awake. Can you do that for me? For Emily?"

His eyes flick toward me, feverish, uncomprehending. I press as hard as I can, setting my jaw and glancing upward at the vaults, as if expecting to find reassurance there. Anything to keep from looking at his left arm, draped over his chest, and his wedding ring glinting in the cobalt-tinted sunlight through the stained-glass windows.

Walsh holds his trench knife ready as Peter returns with the desecrated altar cloth.

"Lift him up again."

With Peter holding him, I bind the cloth a few times around Berk's thigh, then pull it up into an X and tie a half-knot. I stick Walsh's sheathed trench knife over top and finish the knot. Bracing one boot on the stone, I pull the tourniquet with the knife as torsion, tighter and tighter around Berk's thigh till I can't feel an arterial pulse.

"Let him down gently. Pete, hold his head. McNuts, alcohol pad, and get the plasma ready."

Peter cradles Berk's head in his lap, hand in his hair. McNuts puts the pad in my hand, and Walsh holds the plasma bag while I push up the sleeve of Berk's field jacket and swab the crook of his elbow. His chest heaves. Plasma won't be enough to save his life—he'll need a blood transfusion at the field hospital—but it should boost his system long enough to pull him out of shock and hold him till then. I crouch over him and slide the hypodermic needle in—and miss. No vein.

I draw it out and try again. Another miss, and now my hand is trembling. I drop to my stomach as bullets whistle outside in the street, staring at the blue vein that crawls the length of Berk's inner arm.

"You're gonna be just fine, Harry. You got the best damn medic in the whole 82nd takin' care of you," Peter says.

Deep breath. We're out of chances and time. I can't let my fear be the nail in his coffin.

Head of the needle poised between my fingertips, I try a different vein, and it slides in. Holding it there, heart momentarily buoyed though it's far too early for relief, I tell Walsh to tape the needle just below my fingers, and then the plasma bag is secured.

Berk's eyes have fallen shut, but the tourniquet has cut off the blood flow from his leg. Holding my thumb beneath his jaw, I feel his pulse gradually steadying. It seems pointless to deny him a hard-fought rest.

"Harry, I can't give you any morphine," I tell him quietly as I swab away the excess blood around the wound. "It's a respiratory dep—it'll fuck with your breathing. Can you hang on through the pain?"

Though he doesn't open his eyes, he swallows and nods, head slipping to the side till his dirty cheek rests in Peter's hand. Sweat and smoke cling to the air. The fire in the street has dissipated, the lone voices and calls of paratroopers drifting in through the open side of the church. McNuts and the other private are knelt behind the pews with their rifles on their knees while Peter and Walsh speak in hushed voices, still sitting with Berk and me in the aisle.

The private sent to find some transportation reappears and says, "Lieutenant, there're no Jeeps; the road to the aid station is mined. All the doctors say they can't risk it. Captain Robinson's holding the wounded at the CP, sir."

Walsh pinches the bridge of his nose. "Okay. Thanks, private."

The sacrilegious tourniquet on Berk's leg has held, white cloth soaked through now to crimson, like a passion narrative played backwards. *Ironic,* I think with a sort of exhausted hilarity, *because he's a Jew.* Jokes aside, he can't wait hours at the CP while the damn doctors huddle at the aid station, afraid to come treat their patients. Sure, the road is mined, and bears shit in the woods.

Swallowing my frustration, I scribble out his medical tag and pin it to his jacket, then scoot back as two stretcher-bearers come down the center aisle. I hold the plasma bag and tubing as they transfer Berk onto the stretcher. "He has shrapnel in his right thigh. Be careful."

I grab my helmet and walk beside the stretcher with the plasma in hand. Berk closes his eyes, the rise and fall of his chest less frantic than three minutes ago. He winces in pain as they maneuver down the steps, though he doesn't seem fully conscious. I press my hand to his forehead. It's still cool and damp with sweat, but his pallor is dissipating.

The aid station filled up while I was gone. Wounded lie in the straw and on blankets and jackets, some trading smokes or laughing weakly, others unconscious. Donny King, 1st platoon medic, sits beside one guy lying on his stomach, stuffing the shrapnel wounds in the guy's back. Maps and equipment are strewn on the workbenches, and runners come and go from the street with messages relayed for the officers. Fox Company's CO, Captain Robinson, is on the phone with the aid station, or so I guess from his body language and the rising of his voice as he paces in tight circles, nearly yanking the phone's cord out of the radio block.

"Hammond, goddamnit, if you don't get yourself to the CP—I've got a dozen wounded here, at least three critical—"

He listens a moment, then argues louder, countering the surgeon on the other end. "Bill, I haven't *got* any fucking transportation. I can't get them to you! You get yourself forward or I will march the goddamn mined road myself and kick your ass up here to the front..."

I give him a wide berth as he and the surgeon have their tête-à-tête. "Donny," I say as the runners lower Berk to the ground beside the guy with the back wounds, "I've got a couple out there still to tag. Keep an eye on him for me? He needs to be in the first wave. That tourniquet can't stay on his leg for long. Needs a transfusion, too."

"Sure thing," the other medic answers around an unlit cigarette. "What's the story?"

"Shrapnel in his femoral artery, right thigh."

"No shit?" Donny cranes his neck back to look at Berk, whose chest rises and falls weakly. "And he's still alive?"

"Grace of God."

He tapes a bandage across his patient's lower back. "I'll take care of him."

"'Preciate it." I bend down by the stretcher and give Berk's bloody hand a squeeze. "Hang tough, buddy." My stomach twists suddenly with the thought that we may never see him again.

I put my helmet on and return to the street. Lieutenant Walsh is standing on the porch of the church, staring at Cochran slumped against the broken wall.

"You might as well take his ammo, sergeant," he says to Peter.

At Peter's order, McNuts strips Cochran's cartridge belt. He also unhooks the personal first-aid kit hanging in Cochran's webbing and says, "Doc," tossing it to me. I turn the canvas packet with "FIRST AID" printed on its front over in my hands. Unopened. Cochran never had so much as a stubbed toe.

Walsh kneels beside his stretched-out legs. I drop Cochran's aid kit in my bag and watch the lieutenant. He takes off his helmet, runs a hand through his sweaty hair, bites down on his thumbnail. Then he glances at Garrett's body in the street, and the resolute tightness in his shoulders falls away.

"Sir," I say.

He glances up.

"I can tag them, sir."

Walsh looks back at Cochran. "Yeah. All right." He reaches for his radioman's dog tags, snaps one off, and drops it in his jacket pocket, then stands. "Tanner, Edwards," he calls to two privates, "move Corporal Garrett's body out of the street, boys."

"Yessir."

"Don't want anyone..." Walsh stops, bites down on his lip. Flies crawl across the caked blood and exposed muscle in Garrett's cheek, half-smashed on the cobbles. "Don't want anyone driving over him. His family deserves an intact body to bury, at least."

"He was the best point guard on the 505th basketball team," Peter remarks.

As the lieutenant watches the privates, I notice he's gripping the strap of his M1 so tight his knuckles are white. But for the grace of God go us, or something like that. He squints at the bright white façade of the church and says, "I don't know how we weren't all hit in there. Never heard such a shellacking in my life."

Peter flicks the flint on his lighter. "Artillery's got a hell of a lot to answer for."

"No, it was my fault. Poor communication." He turns to Evans, who appears with half of 2nd squad. "Sergeant, your men okay?"

"All fine, sir, sounded like you took the worst of it. What's this I hear about it bein' friendly fire?"

Their voices fade as I finish Cochran's tag and pin it to his jacket. I think of the day I met him in Georgia, his big grin all out of proportion to the fat mosquitoes and the Army noodles in the mess tent.

Touching his eyes shut, I say a prayer for him, as I have for each one. A few months ago I would've laughed at the idea of praying over the dead, but I speak the language of the dying now as I didn't then, one foot perpetually balanced between life and death and the twilight of in between. And I can't imagine reaching past their organs to find an artery, or holding them still as they scream from the nerve damage, and not tell those things back to God, desperate with a hope bordering on pain that he binds up the wounds I can't.

I do the same for Garrett, a double portion of grace because the Catholic chaplain will pray over him, too. His aid kit was dropped in the street. I go out to fetch it, and as I crouch I feel eyes on me. Thinking it's Lieutenant Walsh, I stash the kit with my supplies and say, "Sir, if it's all right with you I'll go hook up with 2nd platoon, see if Bruning needs h—"

I glance up and the words die in my throat.

A little girl stands alone in the street. She stares at me and I stare at her, and then I look over my shoulder, but no one else is around—no one who could claim her, anyway, just other 3rd platoon boys checking down alleyways.

"Ciao," I say softly.

She doesn't say anything, just scrapes one bare foot over top the other. Damp strands of black hair cling to her cheeks, and her big dark eyes watch me in unblinking intensity.

Without a word, she scuttles over to me and wraps her arms around my neck. For a moment I stay completely still, unsure what to do. But she can't stay here in the street where a stray bullet from either side might find her, so I stand with her in my arms and hoist her on my hip. She must be about five or six years old and is light as a feather.

"What's your na—uh—*come ti—*" Shit. Should've paid more attention during the rainy afternoon foreign language classes at Benning. *"Come ti...ti chiami?"*

No answer again. Even if I knew how to ask where she lives, I doubt she'd make a sound. She presses her face to my shoulder. Her heart beats quick and frightened against mine, but she doesn't appear to be hurt.

I go back to the church with her in my arms. Peter frowns, shouldering his rifle by the strap as he comes down the steps. I hold a finger to my mouth. She's spooked enough as it is.

"I'll go hook up with 2nd platoon, sir, after I find her mother," I whisper to Walsh.

He nods and tilts his head to the side, watching the little barnacle clinging to me. Then he reaches into his jacket pocket and takes out half a bar of our C ration chocolate in its crumpled silver wrapper. Stepping around me, he says, *"Ciao"* in a gentle voice. A few seconds pass, and then I feel her arm reach out to take the chocolate.

"Keep your head down, Rev," Peter says, patting my other shoulder and smiling at the girl before following his squad across the square.

I stand in the shadow of the church gables and look around. There are no civilians in the street. Even though I'm sweating in the heat, her cheek is cold against my neck. She shivers in her thin little cotton dress.

"It's okay," I whisper. When I treat wounded men I can't always tell how much they understand, but they panic less under steady hands and a comforting voice. "It's okay. You're scared, I know. Listen, I'll tell you something. I'm scared, too. Can you believe that? I'm scared all the time. My name's Richard, by the way—*mi chiamo* Richard."

I glance at her hand clutching the chocolate. "You ever had chocolate? Here."

It's not easy to unwrap one-handed, but finally I break off a sliver of it and hold it out to her. She takes it and nibbles as I walk across the square, my hand on the back of her head, moving gently through her tangled hair.

"I want to take you home, but I don't know where you live. You can't have wandered very far with no one noticing." Going north past the church feels right, assuming I'm not wrong in thinking that's the direction from which she came. "You've probably given your mother the scare of her life, but that's okay, she'll just be hap—"

Some troopers across the street knock a door in with the butts of their rifles and she jumps, almost dropping the chocolate. Her body is tense with fear. If I wasn't holding her tight, she'd jump right from my arms.

"Shh, shh, shh. It's okay. I know them. They're friends of mine, they won't hurt you. We won't hurt you, I promise. It's okay. Shh."

Hoping that she'll make some sort of sound or signal when I stumble on the right place, I go slowly past the storefronts and narrow houses, picking my way carefully over the rubble. She burrows her cheek into the crook of my neck as her frightened little breaths grow steadier.

"Gianna!"

I turn, and the girl raises her head. A young woman runs across the street from a shop that says "Il Panetteria" in the window.

"Gianna!" she calls again, and Gianna says "mamma" in a very small voice.

The woman looks as though she might weep and laugh at the same time when I put her daughter in her arms. "She was by the church—um—*ch-chiesa*, I found her there."

"Grazie, grazie, grazie," the mother is saying, her hand in Gianna's hair as the little girl clings to her, and I tell her it's fine and *prego, prego* and she kisses me on both cheeks. She notices the chocolate and says something with the lilt of a question.

"It's chocolate, um, candy—sweets," I say, and then she takes up the *grazies* profusely once more and kisses me again.

I glance back as I turn down the street the way we came. Gianna watches me from her mother's shoulder, her eyes as wide and curious as a fawn's and the chocolate safe in her hand.

I rub my eye with the back of my dirty hand, realizing that the poor thing still came to me when my face and neck were streaked with blood.

Whatever sent her running into the street scared her more than I did. My legs feel suddenly unsteady, the stretch of crumbled street and gutted façades and little clusters of paratroopers tramping through the hazy air all looking unreal, spiraling away from me though I'm standing still. Under the shade of a tattered red and white awning, I sit heavily on the remains of a limestone wall and hunch forward till my forehead touches my knees. My breath leaves me in shallow exhales. Berk would've died without me. He could've just as easily died regardless of my actions or even because of them, so the fact he didn't seems to have everything and yet nothing to do with me.

Gianna made it home safe, but for each child like her there'll be a hundred who don't. It's wrong. It's just all so wrong. I turned twenty-one in June. I should be in my senior year at Brown, running along the river in the early mornings, not playing this stupid game of war where children are caught in the crossfires. For a horrible moment of self-pity, I wonder bitterly what heinous sin I must've committed to be punished like this.

"Richard?"

I lift my head as the shadow of a tall figure approaches. Peter appears out of the harsh sunlight, hand on the ammo pouch on his belt. He plants one boot on the remains of the wall and watches me, cutting off my asinine line of thought.

"You okay?"

"Yeah." I rub my eyes again, probably creating a breeding ground for infections. "Yeah. Sorry. Needed a moment."

Peter extends his hand and I take it, letting him pull me to my feet. "You find that little girl's family?"

"Yeah, she's safe."

We walk back through the village together, past the church and the hole in it, through which the altar and crucifix are visible. Peter lights a cigarette, then passes it to me. He doesn't try to reassure me or lift my spirits, and for that I'm grateful.

"You think Berk'll make it?" I say finally as we cross the cobbles still stained with Jim Garrett's blood.

"I think he's a tough SOB who'll fight harder than a cockroach." Peter kicks a rock through the rubble with the toe of his boot and shrugs. "Wouldn't surprise me if he pops back up one of these days like a bad rash."

"Hope so. Hey, what happened—krauts must've scattered, huh?"

Peter nods. "Brits pounded 'em with the artillery; they retreated back across the river. Some of the footbridges must still be intact."

We stop outside the CP. An ambulance idles in the street, engine running—one of the surgeons must've braved the mines. Shadowy figures move about inside the barn, gathering wounded to be loaded. I hear an engineer tell Captain Robinson he's pretty sure they disabled all the booby traps on the road to the aid station, less than reassuring, but for the critically wounded, that risk has to be taken before they die of shock in this stable.

"I should go help," I say to Peter, hooking my thumb toward the aid station. "I'll see you tonight?"

"Yeah. See you tonight. Hang tough, Rev," he adds, gripping my shoulder momentarily before going off to catch up with his squad.

I touch the warm hood of the ambulance and take a deep breath as sounds of pain come from the barn. I don't want to go in; I don't want to wade back to the festering wounds, to watch friends suffer. The thought alone makes me sick to my stomach, not because of the gory nature of my task but because I don't know how much more of this pain I can witness before it breaks me for good.

But that doesn't matter in the end. I gather myself, silently repeating the words that have carried me this far: *Whatever it takes, whatever you ask of me.* I go in, unscrewing the lid of my canteen in case anyone needs water. My eyes adjust from the bright sunlight to the shadows and the men inhabiting them.

VII.

TRILLIUM

June 1945

L ow voices on the porch murmur about a cold front moving
east from Aroostook County. Scrubbing the supper dishes at the
kitchen sink, with the porch window open to the conversation and
the cool night, I see Jim Harrison—foreman at the lumber mill in
Millinocket and one of the church deacons—come through the gate and
join the men on the porch. From night to night there's no telling who'll
come into our yard, and it fascinates me how this slow practice appears
to have changed very little, if at all, with the country still at war.

They're talking mostly of weather patterns and the missionary fund
at church. Dad's voice carries through the window every couple minutes
with a gravitas that quiets everything else. After so long away, the slow
voices of old Maine men sounded strange to me at first. Before I enlisted,
I never thought much about my voice, till my friends from places like
Chicago and California teased me for the *r*'s dropped into *uh*'s and
one-syllable words stretching out and *h*'s where there is no *h*—"ovuh
they-uh" and "cahn't." The first day of parachute school when I said to
Berkowicz that the mess tent was "down they-uh apiece," he asked how
far that meant and I couldn't answer. I told him it was just what I said:

"down there apiece." He about laughed himself into a coughing fit the first time I called a lobster a "bug" without thinking twice.

But I hear the difference now. These old Mainers talk slowly and deliberately, without pretense. "Ay-uh," I hear through the window screen, the calling card of a native. *Ay-uh.* In Fox Company I learned to bite my tongue to keep from answering every question with that old affirmative, and also how to tell someone my name with all the r's in the right places instead of "Rich-ahd Da-ah." I tried to talk as though I could be from anywhere in America, undefined and indistinctive. I don't know how well it worked. Since coming home it hasn't taken long to slip into the country dialect.

Dusk is coming on when Laurie and I finish the dishes and head out to the porch. He goes into the yard with Hen and throws her tennis ball while I sit on the steps and listen to the hum of voices drifting into the night. If only I could sit there beside Dad and talk to him, and maybe then some of the constricting pressure on my heart would ease. *You'll feel better once you find work,* Mom said yesterday, when I must not have done as good a job as I thought at masking my restlessness. *If, if, if,* I keep thinking. If only there was a way to tell him. If only I was braver.

I drape my arms over my knees and watch Hen tear after the ball. The conversation seems to be about the church budget. Tipping my head against the post, I let my eyes fall shut, knowing I should go to bed. But it doesn't matter when I go up because I'll barely sleep anyway, and when I do, the nightmares will be the same. White everywhere. White snow forest, white linen sheets, whites of eyes, white walls, white knuckles.

"I'll tell you this," a drawling voice remarks. They're on the front porch, around the curve of the house, where I can't see them or them me. "I'm more 'n a little worried about what folks been calling the readjustment."

I open my eyes and glance in their direction.

"What readjustment?" Dad's voice says.

More deliberation. A puff on a pipe. Then the same voice answers, "You know as well as anyone, John. You're livin' it. All these boys comin' home in droves, boys who got good at just what we don't want 'em to be good at to be civilians."

"I reckon three years ago you'd have been more disturbed if we'd gotten into this war, Jed, and none of our young men rose to it," Dad answers.

Someone else says, "Give 'em jobs. Best way to keep 'em off the streets and away from my daughters."

"It might keep them busy, but that sounds to me like a cheap treatment." Dad again. "Seems to me we should be trying to help them, whatever they need."

"They've got cocky," Jed rambles on. "Think they have a right to anything and everything, and turn up their noses at good work."

"Who's done that?"

Jed laughs. "Your own son done it, John. Looked at me with that holy look o' his like he's too good for farming now he's been off around Europe."

I hear Dad sigh. A beat passes, and then, "I'd thank you to let me attend to my own family, Jed. You worry about your children, and I'll worry about mine."

"As you say, Pastor."

I wait motionlessly, listening to the quiet from the other side of the porch. After a minute the talk moves on, and they say nothing more about it. For a long time I sit staring at the porch railing and the murky green leaves poking through the slats, indistinct in the dusk. A numbness comes on slowly that fills me to my fingertips. We talked so much about home. About girls and siblings and soda counters and backyards and high school football fields and lakes and kitchens. And here I am in the middle of it all at last, sitting right at the heart of the patterns of my old life, and the people who used to know me think I'll get violent with nothing but empty time on my hands. Maybe the fucked-up injustice of it would make me angry if there wasn't a hard, bitter kernel of truth in it. Just another boy who got good at just what they don't want him to be good at in civilian life.

Finally I stand. Some of the neighbor kids have stopped to pet Hen and talk to Laurie at the gate. He didn't hear. I go into the house, careful to shut the screen door without a sound, and slowly climb the stairs. I wonder if that conversation should've upset me, but in my room, as I tug my shirt off over my head with a jingle of my dog tags, all I feel is a resigned dread of the long night ahead.

"**D**ad! Wait up."

Loosening my tie and shaking it off with the jacket I wore to my interview today, I catch the screen door behind me at the last second so it doesn't slam. I let Hen through the gate and join Dad on the sidewalk. "You walking to church? Can I walk with you?"

"Be glad of the company."

Hen trots between us, happy to be in the center. The setting sun cuts through the clouds and lights the tips of the grass on fire. Along the road the trees have come out in full brilliance, jade and emerald leaves standing out starkly against the white, clapboard houses. The air is fragrant with a coming rain.

"How did the interview go?" Dad asks.

"Well, he stared at me blankly while I was talking, and that threw me off, and I probably rambled. Didn't want it anyway; it smelled like a latrine in there."

Dad smiles, and we walk in silence. Linens on wash lines in the Harrisons' yard snap back in the breeze, for a moment catching the slanted light as it glows in our eyes. The white squares stay imprinted on my vision after I look back at the road. It occurs to me, not for the first time but maybe the first time in a while, that there's so much about Dad that I don't know. I wonder if most fathers tell their children more than he has. His favorite story from before Laurie and I were born was meeting my mom, but he's always backed out of the light when he's a solitary player and there's no one else on the stage to fall back on.

I glance at him, the familiarity of his set brow and searching eyes welling up the affection in me. Those sharp gray eyes still frighten me sometimes, as if they mean to seek out everything in my soul.

We come to the churchyard. At the steps, I say, "Could I ask you something before you go in?"

"Of course." He turns and sits on the bottom stone step, wrapping his arms around his knee as he looks up at me.

At the same moment a glimmer of scarlet at my feet catches my eye: the trillium originally planted on the graves of Nicholas Lewis and Laurence Kalikredes. The latter was my uncle, and Laurie's namesake. I stare at the letters of his name etched into the granite and try to imagine what he looked like, not as in the posed photographs I've seen but just in everyday life. It's been twenty-seven years since he was killed at the second battle of the Somme, but I know not a day goes by that my mom and my grandparents don't grieve for him. He and Lewis were Caspar's only combat casualties in the Great War, and back in 1919 the church ladies had wanted to plant poppies for them—but poppies won't grow in Maine; it's too cold. So they settled for red trillium, which has long since grown past the boundaries of the graves and the two headstones to speckle the whole front of the churchyard's little cemetery like our own Flanders Field.

"What is it, Richard?" Dad, watching me, tilts his head invitingly.

I look at him, the trillium still dancing before my eyes like the white linen, thinking of an uncle I never met who never got the chance to come home like I have. And despite only having a handful of stories through which to imagine him, I feel as though I'm letting him down, playing at civilian life in fits and starts. What would he do in my place? Would the memories of the French trenches follow him, or would he try to put all that behind him?

"When you couldn't fight," I say at last, sitting on the step beside Dad as Hen lies at my feet, "in 1917—were you upset?"

A curved spine kept him out of the Great War. "I was twenty-one when America took up arms. You can imagine I felt pretty much how your brother felt when he was denied. To borrow a phrase from your generation," he adds, turning his head to me with a wry smile, "yes, I was pissed off about it."

Laurie tried to enlist the Monday morning after Pearl Harbor, going with his friends to the recruitment office in Bangor, where a doctor told him that his genetic scoliosis rendered him physically unfit for military service. His friends returned with their signed enlistment papers, pledging themselves to the various branches; Laurie, with a black 4F stamp on his Selective Service slip. We'd both just arrived home that weekend for Christmas break, me from Providence, him from Orono, and he ripped into me in an uncharacteristic fit of rage because I made the egregious mistake of having doubts about enlistment. In eighteen years of backyard wrestling and bruised ribs and black eyes, all laughed off minutes later, we'd never fought like that before, every flung word in the kitchen that night as sharp as barbed wire. "You're so selfish!" he shouted, eyes full of white-hot passion. "You've got nothing stopping you. Just admit you're scared!"

So I did. I told him maybe he had no second thoughts about throwing himself into the jaws of the war machine, but I remembered that our own uncle had died in that machine, one that had annihilated a whole generation of boys. "Not wanting to sign my own death certificate doesn't make me selfish," I argued. "Waiting a little to see how things play out makes me *smart.*"

Of course we know what happened in the end, which is that I got fed up waiting for the draft to catch me, and by that point my friends were all going and the peer pressure sunk in and I didn't want to be left behind, just as Laurie predicted would happen.

"Maybe if I had gone," Dad says, "I would've been more resistant to you going. Not that I could've stopped you. I've long since given up trying to reason with all the Greek hard-headedness in this family." He raps his knuckles against the side of my head, and I smile and duck out of the way.

We sit on the steps and watch the sun dip below the mountains. The storm clouds rolling in cast the eastern sky in a dramatic light.

After a long silence, he says, "There must've been parts of it that weren't as horrible."

"Some."

"But you don't want to talk about those, either?"

"Well. Even the good memories are...tainted."

He picks at a brittle bit of leather on his watch strap. "I don't say this to put myself front and center, but it's a new experience for me, a strange one, to have a son who knows more than I do."

"That isn't true."

"Of course it is. You know it is. You're still just a little too scared of me to say it. And how desperate I've been for it to come untrue—for that burden to not be on you, or if there was some way I could take some of it..."

"Dad—"

"You shouldn't have to carry this."

"I'm not bitter." I glance at him, but he doesn't look convinced. "I'm not bitter that it's me and not you or Laurie. I can't go down that road of shoulds and shouldn'ts. I'll never get back. It's only what happened, not what should or shouldn't have happened."

A new expression passes over his face, respect, maybe. Before I can think better of it, I say, "But there is something else I wanted to talk to you about."

Dad nods, the lines of worry in his face easing. "Sure."

"I was wondering—I—" My eyes stray to the trillium, petals turning back in the wind. How do you say to the man who raised you to love the Lord that you feel nauseous every time you enter the sanctuary? That though you screamed promises to God in the midst of artillery barrages, prayer now feels as much a confrontation, as much a reason to duck and cover as those whistling mortars?

He's watching me expectantly but kindly. It's all I want to just pour this all out, like Christian losing his burden at the cross in *Pilgrim's Progress*. But my heart falters even before the words do. Has he always looked at me with so much love? I never paid enough attention. It's a love so inexorably bound up with the faith he built and encouraged that the thought of losing it terrifies me.

I feel sick at the thought of that light going out of his eyes because of me.

"Actually...it's nothing." I shove my hands in my pockets, shoulders bent to the wind. "Never mind."

"It's only me here. No one else is listening."

"I'm fine, Dad, I promise," I say, holding his gaze. "It's just a lot to get used to, being home."

"I understand, but if you try to suppress it—"

"I'm not suppressing anything."

He gives me a look, as if to remind me what a bad liar I am. "If you're not suppressing anything, why haven't you said a word to me about what you did for three years, beyond what I could read in any newspaper?"

"Then read the papers." I shrug. "I'm sure what they reported was accurate. Robert Capa or Ernest Hemingway can tell you whatever you'd like to know."

"Ernest Hemingway is not my son," he says. "You are. I could do without the trussed-up anecdotes of war correspondents. They'll never be able to tell me what you can."

I don't say anything, wishing he would sweep the light away.

"Richard," Dad adds after a minute. "I've told you before how I worked with some veterans after the Great War, haven't I?"

"Ay-uh." I've been dreading this moment. "You were a chaplain in one of the VA hospitals in Massachusetts."

"A chaplain's assistant because I was still in seminary, but yes. More or less." Rolling back his shoulders and staring out at the marsh, he goes on, "I know that doesn't mean I understand—"

"No."

It comes out harsher than I meant it, and when I wait too long to pedal it back, I can tell it stung. Instead of apologizing, I tighten my arms rigidly around my legs and wait for him to make whatever point he intended. Like everything else in his life pre-Caspar, that young version of him is so shrouded in mystery that I don't know what relevance it has to me. He ministered to sick and dying men in hospital wards, the victims of trench warfare with their blown-off mouths and gassed-up lungs. My lungs aren't *that* bad. I'm certainly not one of his dying charges. And I'm not crazy. I'm not one of the so-called psychoneurotic cases.

Dad finally says, "It's not my place to draw a comparison. I'm sorry."

He watches me still, then puts his hand on my knee for a brief moment before standing. There was a time when that expression could have prompted me to admit to anything, even if I didn't do it. It troubles me now that I can stand opposite it and yet still feel the secrets repressing deeper in my chest.

"I'm sure it's something," Dad says, "or you wouldn't have brought it up. But you think about it, and remember that my door is always open."

I nod, but he adds, "*Always*, Richard. You know that. Here, or at home."

"I know."

He doesn't believe me. But then he nods, too. Right as the last of the light sinks behind Mt. Katahdin, he turns and goes up the steps into the church. My eyes move to the steeple, which is filmy in the dusk. The white cross stands guard like a lighthouse for Caspar.

W hen I first met Jack Fischer at parachute school in Georgia, he told me he was from New Hampshire and he could tell I came from New England, too. He asked whereabouts. I said Maine, north of Augusta, and he looked confused and said, "There's Maine north of Augusta?"

I doubt that my grandparents, whose six years in Boston did little to wash the old country off their feet, even knew the name *Augusta* when the New England Presbytery sent them north to a place colder than they dreamed existed. While half the families in Caspar trace their lineage back to the town's founding in 1851, neither the Kalikredes nor the Dares can claim that. We're just sojourners, Dad says, blown in off the logging roads or the railroad tracks to a town where no one really ever intends to stay but somehow they do.

He was a twenty-four-year-old seminary graduate, a "from-away" just like the Kalikredes, when he swung off the train into this mill town in 1920. Pop, my maternal grandfather, built the house on Holland Road with his own hands, in between bettering his English and reading theology books and holding babies and writing sermons for the same congregation that still gathers twice a week in the church's pews. My grandparents' home was a beacon in a dark country, especially in winter when darkness seeps into the daylight. He welcomed Dad into it, and sometimes I imagine them as much younger men, sitting in front of the kitchen stove at night talking about Chesterton or Augustine or the Early Church.

I assume that Dad was sent here after graduating from seminary because the heads of the presbytery in Massachusetts must've known that there was no better man than Dimitrios Kalikredes to shepherd this literal orphan and teach him how to minister a church. But how Dad got from Portland, where he was born, to college at Brown and then to seminary in Massachusetts, is a story Laurie and I have never been told. Even Pop, who loves a good raucous tale to accompany his pipe in the evening, has never let slip so much as a hint about who Dad was before he was the lonely figure climbing off the train at the Caspar station, with no money and barely his name to hold onto. And I know he knows.

He does take pleasure, though, every holiday, in reminding the family that "John was all set to get this irritating assignment in Maine out of the way, so he could get back to Boston and become someone," but then Dad was welcomed to the minister's table and met the minister's oldest daughter and maybe Maine suddenly didn't feel so cold and desolate. That's what I think, anyway. She says no one ever called her "Lizzie" before she met Dad. I can see her smiling at him and him trying to reconcile the plan he'd had for his life with this incongruous, black-haired figure in a landscape she wasn't built for. And I mean both that she was born in a sun-bleached and white-cliffed country four thousand miles away where it never snows and ice is only a myth, but also that she was—is—a wild spark of electricity in a place more packed with stoics than any ancient Greek philosopher's *stoa*.

The same year I was born, 1922, the old minister at the Presbyterian church in Boothbay Harbor died suddenly, and after so long away from a coastline, I think my grandparents were desperate to live by the ocean again. They left the Caspar congregation that was so wary of them in the beginning, with many tears, I've been told. Growing up I could never pass anyone on the street without hearing "How are the Reverend and Mrs. Kalikredes? I certainly do miss them, tell them I say hello!" They're still healthy as oxen, which Nana attributes to the clove of garlic she eats every night before bed, except on Saturday nights, because she doesn't want to smell of garlic at church. The church here became my dad's, and because he was a Kalikredes, in a sense, they welcomed him into the fold.

So the tradition of ministry trickles down to me from both branches of my family tree, going back generations—my great-grandfather was an Orthodox priest in Corinth. The choice of giving one's life back in service to God was always my foregone conclusion. It was a map showing the path for me to follow, and I had plenty of encouragement to follow it. Pop had none of that, yet he still defied his family's old faith when he converted and then ensured his estrangement and his wife's and children's by immigrating half a world away because he had faith that God told him to. Still, he would say now, just as Dad would, that he's only a sojourner, straining his eyes through the snow and rain to catch a glimpse of his true country.

Hen waits at the gate as I look back at the road, into the gray night with porch lights flickering on, trying to see the way that Pop and Dad do. To see past the tired clapboard houses and scrub grass and rusted cars and understand that it's only a passing shadow, this life. But it's a shadow

I still have to live in. And you don't tell a man whose house is swept into the eye of a hurricane that the sky will soon clear. By that time, the floodwaters have already washed out the foundation and swept away the roof like a raft. And he's left staring at the flotsam, realizing he doesn't even have the materials to rebuild.

The screen door bangs open. Laurie comes out on the porch with a trash bag in hand. "I don't know if you've seen a ghost, or if you *are* the ghost," he calls. "Mom wants to know if you're ever coming in."

It feels like the moment of sobriety that occasionally punctuates the mood after too many drinks. I open the gate and Hen trots through, bounding up the porch steps to follow Laurie inside.

B y the time the sun rises, I've given up on sleep. A soft mist hangs in the trees. When I say hello to the chickadee poking his sharp little beak at my window screen, he cocks his head with a jerk, as though a puppeteer controls him by strings. He hops with odd, stilted movements and then disappears with a rush of his wings, off to find breakfast. Just in time, too, because a second after he's gone, a rock hits the side of the house to the right of the window. I turn my face away as another rock bounces off the screen. Then a shower of pebbles rains around the window.

"Richard?" someone calls from the yard.

Hen's head lifts from the puddle of her curled up at the foot of my bed. I hold my finger up to her, and the whine in her chest turns to a disappointed rumble as she settles back down. I climb out of bed, reaching for the white t-shirt on the bureau as I look out.

"Richard!"

It's Grace, wearing tennis shoes, rolled-up jeans, and an incongruous green raincoat, even though the sun is glowing in the valley. Her Chevy is pulled up cock-eyed at the curb, as if she couldn't even wait to reach the driveway. She's bouncing from one foot to the other, and she has another handful of rocks in her fist and looks ready to hurl it till she sees me.

"Okay, Romeo, what are you doing throwing rocks at me on a Saturday morning at"—I glance at the clock on my nightstand—"it's barely seven."

"Oh," she says, seeming not to have noticed that the daylight is so fresh. "Sorry. I couldn't wait any longer. I tried to eat breakfast..." She shakes her head as if to dislodge the night's cobwebs. "I can't sit still, Richard, and I needed someone to talk to, and now you're here again and I can talk to you."

I hesitate with the t-shirt over my head. "What's wrong? Is your grandmother all right?"

"Yes, yes, she's fine—listen, my neck is getting stiff, maybe you could—"

"Yeah, of course, sorry. I'll be right down."

Hen follows me out into the hall and halfway down the stairs before I realize I'm still in my pajama pants. I run back to my room and change them out for a pair of jeans so quickly that it takes three tries to get the button through. As long as I'm here, I reach for the crenelated bottle of Dunhill cologne on top of my bureau, almost dropping it, and maybe I steal another half a minute to slip into the bathroom and brush my teeth just long enough to smell vaguely of spearmint. I need to shave and I have the Greek side of my genetics to thank for the unkempt mess of my hair, but I don't have time to put any of that to rights. Grace Whitley started the morning throwing rocks at my window like the signal between forbidden lovers. Whatever that means, it doesn't leave an opening for a razor.

She's sitting on the top porch step with her arms wrapped around her legs, staring at the dew-tipped grass. The raincoat has been discarded beside her, leaving her in just a thin gray sweater with fraying sleeves. As I close the screen door, I notice her left foot bobbing up and down and an envelope dangling from between her fingers.

"Is it Sidney?" I ask before stopping to wonder if I should. "Is that a telegram...?"

Grace climbs to her feet. She doesn't look like she's been crying.

"It is from Sidney, a letter." She bends the envelope back, studying it, with her and her grandmother's names scrawled across the front in spidery handwriting.

"Oh. Good. That's a relief."

"Mmm. It must've come in the mail yesterday and dropped under the table, and I only noticed it this morning. Couldn't sleep."

"I thought you'd be thrilled to hear from him. He's okay, isn't he?"

She glances up, and I see what I couldn't from a floor above her: she's biting back anger. Twice she tries to say something and falters before getting hold of it. "I—he's—yes. He's okay. But he won't be once I get my hands on him," she adds, setting her jaw. That bobbing foot wasn't anxiety; it was simmering.

I must've left her to simmer too long, because instead of trying to explain Grace just holds the envelope out to me. I shake the letter out. A folded snapshot falls into my hand. It's of Sidney in his Army Air Force dress blues, his arm around the waist of a young dark-haired woman with a pretty smile. The exposure is high and there are palm trees rising behind them, water glittering behind the woman's shoulder.

"Well, that's nice," I say, looking from the photo back to Grace and not really understanding what upset her. "So Sidney found a cute Australian girl to go with—"

"To go with *forever,*" Grace interrupts.

"What?"

"He married her!" She points to the crisp, white-edged photo. "Richard, he *married* her."

M attie bolts up so quick he bangs his forehead on the fender of the cream Plymouth Coupe he was stretched out beneath. "He *what?*"

"He married this Australian girl." I toss him a potato chip. "Sometime in May. Guess that's why Grace didn't hear from him for a little while."

"She pretty? The wife?"

"Looked like, from the photo."

"Shit, I'd have been a little too busy to write my sister, too."

I snort. "Well, the honeymoon's over now. He told Grace he'd be back in the Philippines by the time the letter'd get posted."

"So what's the story?" Mattie says. "He knock her up?"

"I don't know. Maybe they just fell in love. People do that, you know."

"No shit, Sidney getting married on a whim without tellin' anyone...I never would've guessed."

"Me neither."

"And she—what was her name?"

"L-e-n-a. I'm not sure if that's Lee-nuh or Lay-nuh."

Mattie disappears again beneath the Plymouth and says, "So this Lee-nuh Lay-nuh, she's just staying in Brisbane, waiting for him to come back?"

"I guess so."

"Wonder if that means we'll never see him again."

I eat the last chip, ball up the bag, and toss it into the trash a few feet away. "Sidney'll come back. I can't imagine him leaving Grace and his grandma here alone to fend for themselves. Not that they can't—but he wouldn't do that."

"Would you come back to Maine if you had a reason to stay in Australia?"

"Dunno, I've never been to Australia."

"Ay-uh," Mattie answers, a disembodied voice, "that's the point."

Late afternoon sunlight falls through the dusty windowpanes of the garage. There's a Ford stripped of its wheels up on the blocks, and a green pickup in the other bay with "Pepper's Dairy" emblazoned in butter-yellow script on the driver's door. Harlan Wagner also owns the car lot at the edge of town and a good chunk of the Caspar residential real estate. He painted the "Wagner & Sons" in an aesthetically pleasing arc over the front of the garage to give the place a familial sense, but Wagner has about as many sons as he does truthful bones in his body.

"So what's Grace make of it all?" Mattie wonders. "She planning to give Sid a little dust-up or what?"

"She'll probably box his ears on principle, but she's torn between being mad at him and excited about having a sister. Now," I add, slinging my arm across the top rung of the stepladder I'm sitting on, "if they tried to stay in Australia, or even California, then yes, ten bucks says she'd book a ticket just to knee him in the Whitley family jewels."

"Here's what I think." Mattie sounds as though he's speaking around a screwdriver in his mouth. A lug nut rolls across the concrete, and I stick my foot out and kick it back to him. "I think maybe Sid's got it right. If a Caspar girl was wanting to marry me, I'd have known by now, don't you think? I can't believe I got out of this town only to come back. I had the whole world—"

"And any girl you wanted, right?"

"All I'm saying is that if you didn't know how to use the uniform to your advantage, Dick, that doesn't mean the rest of us wasted it."

I eye my watch. "I thought you said to pick you up at five to meet the girls at the pictures. We'll miss the shorts."

"Oh, Dick, don't you know I need at least an hour to freshen up…"

When he slides out again from beneath the Plymouth, he could use an hour to freshen up, grease streaked across his cheeks like camouflage for a night jump. He puts his tools away and clocks out. As he fetches his clothes from a metal locker at the back of the garage, I say, "Listen, some ground rules for tonight."

"I don't need ground rules."

"Yes, you do. No mentioning Sidney and Lee—Lay—whatever—to Grace unless she brings it up first. It's still a sore point. Don't make innuendos about it, either, or vague jokes about servicemen and foreign girls—"

Mattie began trying to interrupt about three words into that so I plowed through until finally his voice rises above mine as he backs toward the employees' washroom, clothes in a bundle under his arm. "You underestimate what a gentleman I can be when I want to."

"The trouble is you never want to."

He closes the washroom door and continues talking. I hear the water running as he calls, "Did I tell you about Annemarie in London?"

"I really don't want to know how many times you scored in London, with Annemarie or anyone else."

"She had this one gown, blue silk, and the neck plunged down…"

"Was she a working girl?"

"Why does every girl who emphasizes nature's endowments have to be a working girl?"

I check the time again. The girls will be through with their first round of popcorn. "She doesn't, but it's just like you to have gotten fooled. More than once."

"I think I'd have remembered paying Annemarie for those nights in Piccadilly."

"That's the whole deal about Piccadilly," I say. "No American fellow ever remembers what happens there, not when he's plastered."

"And I guess you were too well-behaved to ever go there yourself?"

"As a matter of fact, yes."

I let him talk to the empty air of the garage, and go out to my truck parked in the dusty yard out front, waiting in the driver's seat. I roll the window down to let in the early summer air while I listen to Mattie's distant voice remonstrate about the wicked good fun of Piccadilly girls.

VIII.

REPRIEVE

3 March 1944, Quorn, England, 0630 hours

A gray-throated heron dips over the canal, wings skimming the glassy surface. I slow to a walk and watch as he alights in the reeds on the opposite bank. Mist clings to my arms, a perpetual damp film that might as well be Quorn's calling card. Crouching to catch my breath, I watch thousands of tiny drops disturb the mirror-like water, their light patter synchronizing with the bird calls in the thickets on the green hills. The countryside is still in the fringes of winter and it's too early for most flowers, but even the grass smells sweet and the marsh stink seems washed in the rain. If it wasn't a Friday with scheduled training, I could sit here for hours listening to the raindrops and the rustles of wildlife in the tall grasses.

Flecks of dew and sweat and damp grass stick to my ankles, the marks of a good run—six miles through the dales and the rain in some of the most beautiful, verdant countryside I've ever seen. I love England, a love that might be all the stronger for having come from Italy and Tunisia, places I'd not soon scramble for postcards of. This feels the most like home. The locals love us (poor taste on their part), the food is always hot if not always good, and we're encamped on the Farnham Estate, a farm abundant in creeks and crab apples and blackthorn trees. A farmer told us the blackthorn berries are crushed to make gin, which was of great interest to the boys. Best of all, there's no dysentery, malaria, or hornets, and no wounds to clean, just ankles twisted on drunken larks and once in a while a black eye from boys feeling too frisky in the pub with the local girls.

The heron stalks through the shallow water with deliberate movements. He pokes his beak in and claims a wriggling fish the same shade as the silver sky, then swallows it in one go. I watch his hunt, admiring his patience as he lopes through the water so gracefully I can't help thinking he must be enjoying himself and this solitary morning. He arches his long neck back and looks out at the canal, where a few unoccupied punts and wood-paneled barges bob at their moorings along the bank. Then his eye lands on me, blinking once.

"Do you like being alone?" I murmur as he drops his beak to the water once more.

As if in answer, he blinks again and tilts his head.

I'm just straightening up, stretching tired muscles, when a quiet voice behind me says, "Careful, don't disturb him! This is perfect, if he doesn't move..."

It's Fish, moving through the grass with a hunter's soft tread, in his field jacket with sketchbook and colorbox beneath his arm. He stops beside me and watches the heron in fascination, a smile playing at the corners of his mouth. "Look how his legs bend backwards, like the opposite of our knees. But how to differentiate him from the water? He blends in so well."

"You were born in the wrong era, Fish," I say. "Should've been an Impressionist, painting rivers with Monet and Renoir."

He sets his supplies in the grass and sits. "You're telling me."

"How do you do the surface of the water?"

"Some gray and white, but it's all about the colors reflecting. And the light, mostly." He props his sketchbook on his bent knees and begins to sketch the heron's form with a charcoal pencil.

I check my watch. Still an hour till reveille. "Mind if I watch? I'll go if it's too distracting."

"No, stay. You were here first anyway." He thumps the ground beside him. "I'll draw the heron, and you philosophize about him. He's probably a metaphor for something or other."

"A gatekeeper to a magical world beneath the river," I say as I sit, and Fish grins, but he's already engrossed in his drawing. The heron lifts one spindly leg after the other, wading soundlessly through the water as weak sunlight tries to break through the mist over the countryside.

4 *March 1944*

My head is swimming as I leave camp. I have no idea how I ended last night's outing to the Blacksmith Arms'. All that's left is vague, glittery impressions of pretty English girls who smelled like lavender and their laughing mouths outlined in red lipstick, and the laughter itself, as unexpectedly welcome to us GIs as it seemed to be to the girls. As though any such happiness has been too long suppressed here, and in chancing upon it now they no longer recognize it.

A stone wall thick with moss borders the estate. As I pass it, buttoning the cuffs of my jacket, I suddenly remember stumbling along the sidewalk in the predawn hours this morning, my arm around Skinny's waist, and him collapsing on the wall and announcing he would sleep there. He was much drunker than I was, and last I saw was still sleeping it off in his bunk.

Rain falls lightly in my eyes as I walk the half mile from the estate at Northage Close to the post office in the village, carrying two letters, one to my parents and one to Laurie. A Jeep passes and I salute to Captain Robinson in the passenger seat as the driver weaves slowly through an in-street basketball game, ball dropped when the guys see the lieutenant and hold their hands to their temples. I turn off Leicester Road onto Meeting Street and see the post office, white brick next to the butcher's shop, with the canal winding behind it. I've been to it a few times since we got to England in February, and each time picked up my mail from an old white-haired man whose vocabulary consisted of grunts from deep in his chest. That's why it's a surprise when I open the door to see a young woman with her back to me, sorting mail into the many niches along the back wall.

There are two old ladies ahead of me, apprising one another and the postal girl of the village gossip. I hear *GIs* sprinkled in a few times and feel some glances at my back as I pretend to be interested in the stamps on the carousel. Really I'm raising my eyes every so often to watch the girl as she laughs at their stories. She has a wide smile and high cheekbones and looks so familiar. Maybe I've passed her in the village.

I take the letters from inside my jacket as the ladies scuttle past me and out to the street. "Good morning, Mrs. Herring, Miss Cardin," the girl says as they leave. She turns to me and starts to say something when the telegraph machine behind her sounds its alarm, and she holds up one finger. "One moment, please, sir."

She goes back into the office behind the counter, though only a narrow doorframe without a door separates it from the front and the customers. While she takes down the message, holding an earpiece to a black metal headphones set up to her ear, I turn and look out at Meeting Street. A public garden bordered by a green wrought-iron fence is tucked onto the corner. All the trees are still bare and the rosebushes are only thorny sticks, and it all looks exceptionally dreary in the drizzle. Inside the post office, though, the dampness and chill has retreated, and for the first time I wonder if spring might be coming early to the north of England.

The Morse code blips on the telegraph machine stop and I look back as the girl sets the headphones down, standing with a sheet of notepad paper in her hand. She has a lot of dark hair pulled back from her face with a silk scarf. Her eyes are dark, too, and friendly, although I wonder if it's tiring to see all these GIs, a constant reminder that her country is still at war.

"Thank goodness," she remarks, coming back to the counter. "It's only for Mr. Breedlove down at Grange—well, down at one of the farms. You probably wouldn't know it. Just from his daughter about when her train comes in tomorrow. Every time I hear the telegraph I pray it's not another of *those* messages, you know—the ones that'll make even a tough old farmer weep. So much life and death passes through a post office. Have you noticed that?"

I set my letters on the counter. "No, I haven't. You must know everyone here. Makes those messages even harder."

"Oh, it does, especially so when it's a lad I was in school with. Folks in Quorn are kin to each other, like as not—except for some who really are kin and will go to blows over a few quid borrowed." She picks up the letters and smiles at me brightly, as if I'm another of those school lads.

"Sounds an awful lot like an Army camp. Just sending those out and picking up, if there's anything for me. Corporal Dare, 505th."

"Ah, *you're* Corporal Dare?" She shakes her head and goes over to one of the niches at the far left of the wall before I can wonder why my name precedes me. In a playful voice, she says as she raises an envelope to catch the light, "This one's from Elizabeth Dare—your wife? Or a sister?"

"My mother," I answer with a laugh as I take the letters. "She'd appreciate the sister compliment, though."

"You're one of the lucky ones. There's always a letter for you. Some of the American boys have stopped coming in, and it breaks my heart, never having anything for them. It makes me so sad to think there's no one waiting for them at home."

I put the letters inside my jacket and say, "Well, I think your neighbors—or kin—are making us feel as at home as possible, what with Army cots for beds." She makes a sympathetic face, and I add, "No, we're used to it. When you come from sleeping in a hole in the mud, a cot in a town like this feels like the Ritz. I just wish it didn't take a war for me to get out and see the world."

"I'm not sure Quorn is the best place to come if you're trying to thaw out or see the world," she remarks.

"I saw enough of it last year. And this feels more like where I come from than London, say."

"You're not one of those infamous paratroopers, just dying for the chance to tear up the city and leave your mark?"

"I'll say not. My friends would tell you I'm not nearly that much fun."

The bell over the door rings and an older man comes in, glasses speckled from the rain. "Be with you in a moment, Mr. Merriweather," the clerk says to him, but I say, "Oh, no, don't let me keep you from your work."

"A soldier and a gentleman, there's something you don't see every day." She goes to help Mr. Merriweather, who has two brown paper packages tied with red string waiting for him. After he leaves, tipping his hat to the girl and giving me a polite nod, she taps her fingers on the counter and watches me.

"Would I be correct in guessing that you never stay this long to chat when our postman, old Jack, is behind the counter?"

"Guilty," I answer, feeling myself blush, and she laughs. She still looks so familiar, and it isn't until she adjusts the scarf holding her hair back that it suddenly clicks. I lean forward on the counter. "You were at the dance last night, weren't you? At the Blacksmith Arms'?"

"I only just remembered myself," she says, the arch of one eyebrow quirked up. "We danced, but I don't think we had much of a conversation. Too loud and crowded."

"Did I behave myself? You can tell me the truth."

"Oh, you were scandalous, you American cad!" she answers mockingly. "No, you needn't worry. You were sweet. And I had a wonderful time."

"Listen, if I made any promises to see you again, I'll need you to remind me of when and where, because I have no idea what happened after they played that Irish drinking song."

She smiles. "You didn't make any such promises."

"Can I make one now?"

"Without any drinks in you first?"

"I think I'm braver without it. And so you don't think of me as just that stupid GI who had to drink before he could dance with you—I'm Richard."

"Jenny," she says, holding her hand across the counter, which I take and shake awkwardly in a way that makes us laugh even more. "And why not, Corporal Richard Dare of the 505th? You're cute—you can promise you'll take me out dancing again tonight."

"Eight o'clock, the Arms'?"

"I'd love that."

G old from the gas streetlamp glitters in the puddles as we leave the Arms'. It must be after midnight. I didn't look at my watch all night, and I hardly touched my drink, either, noticing when I did pick it up that it had gone warm and watery.

Jenny and I ducked out before we could get swept up in the drunken exodus of my brothers-in-arms. The pub was full to bursting with 82nd boys tonight, all out on the prowl, and Jenny could name every girl who left on the arm of a paratrooper, just as she's doing now. She danced a couple dances with Peter and one with McNuts, and probably would've danced with Fish too if he hadn't let himself be happily pulled from the pub by a cute blonde an hour ago. God knows where he'll wake up.

We walk along dark, quiet Meeting Street, past the closed post office and the public garden and the butcher's sign swinging in the wind. Jenny's high heels click on the pavement, and she draws her blue wool coat closer to herself.

"I'm only just down here," she says as we cross the bridge spanning the canal.

"Have you always lived here?"

"Mhm. Just my dad and me now, though my little brother and sister are up at school in Scotland. Have been since the Blitz. Dad thinks it's safer for them, and he's right." She kicks a pebble ahead of her. "I've an aunt in Edinburgh, so I go up to see Alex and Marnie once in a while and I stay with her. Edinburgh's a lovely city; you should see it if you haven't yet. Actually," she adds, turning to me, and the sky is clear so I can see her face in the moonlight, "You *would* love it—Athens of the North, they call it. What better place for a Scottish Greek, and a scholar, no less?"

"Don't talk about Greece. I was so close to seeing the homeland, and instead I had to wade through Italy."

Jenny laughs and hops over a wide puddle. Without thinking, I reach for her hand so she doesn't slip on those heels. She takes it and holds on for a moment before letting go. "When there's not a war on, most folks dream of a Roman holiday."

"Rome, maybe, but definitely not Naples."

A car bobs past us toward the village, yellow headlights illuminating the wet street.

"It's just an odd time to be alive, isn't it?" Jenny murmurs. "Who knows how long it'll last."

"Not that the rest of it is much to write home about, but I wouldn't mind if this part lasted a little while longer."

She glances at me. "I wouldn't, either."

We walk slowly down the lane past the sleeping stucco and plaster houses, dark blue and mint and white-washed, attached to one another with their doors opening right onto the street.

"This is where I get off," Jenny says, stopping on the sidewalk before a two-story brick home with a garden out front and a stone wall as a barrier from the street. There's a vine climbing up the front that looks as though it'll bloom in the summer. Most interesting is the building behind the house, or in front of it, I suppose, if you're coming from the proper direction. A stone cross is visible in the moonlight.

"Your father—"

"Is a vicar, yes." She looks over her shoulder at the stone church. "Sorry I forgot to mention it, out of habit, most likely. Most boys turn tail when they learn it's the vicar's daughter they're trying to seduce."

"Actually, I know what it's like, growing up under a watchful eye." I nod to the church. "My father's a Presbyterian minister."

"Is he? Are you only saying that to woo me?"

I'm sure even I could come up with something more romantic than the sexual dampener of mentioning my minister father, were that my intention. "If you don't believe me, I can recite the Heidelberg Catechism for you. 'What is your only comfort in life and death? That I am not my own'—"

She puts her hand against my mouth with a clear laugh that's more likely to wake her father than my Heidelberg is. "All right, I believe you."

Before I can lose the nerve, I touch her cheek as her hand drops from my face. A raindrop has fallen on her eyelashes and mascara is smudged across her cheekbone.

"Richard," she whispers, and her hand moves to touch my wrist. "Listen, before we...before anything else...no promises. No plans. We don't know what will happen to either of us."

"I know."

"I want to dance and laugh and have fun. That's all."

"That's okay. I can't even make any promises now, anyway," I say, "and I don't know how long I'll be here. They don't really tell us anything..." My voice trails away and even though I think I see a light flicker on in the window, I hold her cheek and kiss her.

Jenny's hand relaxes and she leans into me, returning it, sending my heart racing. As my hand moves down her waist, she moves back just enough for the light to pass between our faces again.

She whispers, "No promises?" and I agree, no promises, though I would've said whatever she wanted just to get the chance to kiss her again.

I walk slowly past the canal along the road that leads back to the Blacksmith Arms', drunker now than when I left it. After touching Jenny's face that felt as smooth as silk—after kissing her, my mouth still full of the taste of her lip gloss—the thought of going back to barracks and being surrounded by men is about as appealing as sitting at the bottom of a damp Italian foxhole. I wonder if it would seem too eager of me to show up at her father's church tomorrow morning, but I don't know if I can wait till next weekend to see her again. I've been so little in the company of women since leaving home that being with her is more intoxicating to me than the beer dimming my friends' senses right now.

Quorn at night reminds me an awful lot of Caspar, not so much in appearance but in the smallness of a place encompassing much more than its narrow houses and bridges suggest. I think of my younger self, so restless to leave backwater Maine and see the world. If I had it to do over again, I'd be in no hurry. Pay attention, I'd tell myself. To the way the sun set over the white cross on the church steeple and the glances of affection between my parents. To the warmth of my friends beside me as we huddle after climbing out of the cold river, the crack of a baseball bat, the slice of hockey skates across the frozen pond. The way blackberries taste in the early summer, the rhythm of my grandparents' voices, the thump of Laurie's heartbeat beside mine in bed on winter nights when we were really little.

As I approach the Arms', the door opens and a uniform appears under the streetlamp. When he turns I notice it's Jacob O'Connor, the new replacement runner for 3rd platoon's headquarters squad.

I don't know him but in passing, which is my fault, not his. Like most veterans, I suppose I have some trouble welcoming replacements. Every time I look at a guy like O'Connor, I see Jim Garrett's gray face pressed to the bloody street in Arnone, or Billy Marcotti with a bullet hole right through the center of his helmet on the slope of Biazza Ridge. I know it must be hell being a replacement. Their war begins with our loss. But I saw more replacements wounded and killed in Italy than I did any of the guys I'd come up with, so loss begets loss begets more loss. They have an alarming rate of attrition—I don't know if it's that they had less training than we did, or if they want to impress us older guys—but whatever it is always leaves a bitter taste in my mouth. It would be easier not to know their names, not to laugh with them or hear their letters from home read aloud so that I know the names of their sisters and girlfriends.

Of course, in theory it would be easier never to get close at all, replacement or veteran. But you don't survive by keeping apart.

"O'Connor," I call, and he glances back. He pauses outside the Arms' and waits for me to catch up.

When I do, he looks unsure of himself, skinny kid in a uniform tailored too big for him. He shifts from one foot to the other and nods at me as he takes out a cigarette, then offers one to me, which I pass up.

O'Connor fishes in his pockets but comes up empty, so I take out my lighter and hold it up for him. "Thanks," he says, lowering the lit cigarette and blowing out smoke. He seems uncertain how to interact with me. Come to think of it, he's probably only ever seen me in the company of guys like Peter or Skinny, all us "old-timers" from whom many of the replacements shy away. Even they're probably a bit easier to understand than I am, because after long enough—if you make it as a replacement and don't get yourself blown up—you start to fall in with the other guys till the line blurs between original and newcomer.

But I'm not his sergeant or just one of the guys. I've noticed that some replacements are particularly wary of me, as if an aura of death follows me. They'd rather not talk to me, just in case it jinxes them so they'll need a medic. Or maybe it's only that they're not quite sure where I fit in among the squads of riflemen and mortarmen and machine-gunners.

"Are you heading back?" I ask him.

"Yeah, it's gettin' too rowdy in there for me."

He seems to forget the cigarette between his fingers as we walk toward the Estate. For a few moments the only sound on the quiet street is the wind stirring the beech trees, till he gets up the nerve to say, "I know the other guys call you Rev—Sergeant Adler explained it—but I didn't want to just assume that—"

"As far as I'm concerned, you can call me anything that gets my attention." I shrug. *"Rev, Doc, Richard,* just *Dare* if you want. I'm not picky."

"Is that story true, then? That you were in...I already forgot the word for it. The college where you go to be a minister."

"Seminary. And no, that's been exaggerated. First thing you oughta know about that bunch—they'll spin any story you give them way out of proportion. Even if you don't give it to them. These guys are blood-hounds."

Out of the corner of my eye I see him smile. I go on, "I was an undergrad when I joined up, two years away at least from seminary. But imagining I was two steps from the pulpit gives *Rev* a better ring to it, I guess."

"Cripes, I hope they don't give everyone a nickname that style. I'd be...*postal clerk* or *tobacco farmer.* Those don't really roll off the tongue."

"No shame in the ambition to be a postal clerk. About your third night on the line, sorting mail will start to sound real good."

O'Connor grins. He reminds me of a wide-eyed child, a little gullible, not always in on the joke but laughing anyway. "I saw you earlier, with that English girl. She's real pretty."

"Well, there you go. She's a postal clerk. You want any career advice—"

"You went to college, though." O'Connor raises the cigarette again and looks at me. "That's your advantage when it comes to gettin' a job after all this is over. I barely left home before I joined the Airborne."

"Where're you from?"

"North Carolina. I'd never been farther'n Raleigh before."

I glance at him. "Is that why you joined the Airborne? You must not've been far from Fort Bragg."

"All you northerners think the South is just the same as your little states crowded together, but y'all don't know how big North Carolina is."

"No," I agree after a moment, "I guess I don't."

"That bein' said, no, I wasn't far from Fort Bragg. But that's not why I wanted to be a paratrooper."

"Why did you want to?"

"Hell if I remember anymore," he answers, and I snort in agreement.

I watch our reflections pass in a puddle at the base of the canal bridge as it slopes up. "It must be kind of intimidating, being a replacement. Guys like Branson, Vandenburg, Rodriguez…takes a lot to keep up with them. Hell," I add, "I've been there when they've been puking their guts out, and I'm still scared of them sometimes."

"Well, I guess. I didn't even know if I'd make it through parachute school, but I was pretty determined. Get through or die trying."

"So was I." Drizzling mist falls on our heads as we pass quiet stone houses with blackout curtains in their windows. "I was so terrified of getting drummed out and sent to the infantry, I never went home even when we had leave in the States. Just my luck a late train would mean the difference between you guys and some nervous draftee who gets me blown to bits."

"That really happened? Guys who were late, they'd kick 'em out of the Airborne?"

"I saw it a couple times. It ensures discipline, I'll say that. It only had to happen once in Fox to scare the shit outta us all. No one was ever late again."

We walk through the drizzle in silence. Near the Estate, three black American GIs cross the street when they see O'Connor and me coming. One of them is a lieutenant, yet he defers to me.

I haven't witnessed it myself, but I've heard the stories from guys who've been there when fights break out in the pubs, instigated by 82nd boys who are drunk, full of themselves and full of shit. As if we aren't all foreigners in this village. Some of the white boys assume they arrived on foreign shores with a God-given right to the women and the resources, and pity the fool that gets in their way. These black soldiers still go to battle on their behalf, for a country that'll still treat them like dogs the moment they arrive home.

What the 82nd would look like if not for military segregation, I've often wondered. I bet these guys could do a hell of a lot of damage as "devils in baggy pants," as the Germans call American paratroopers, if they were given the chance.

The lieutenant glances at me as we pass. I touch my forehead in salute, and he does the same.

"I bet his family's been in America at least a hundred years longer than mine," I say to O'Connor as we turn down the wooded lane. "Probably longer."

"Mine too." O'Connor shrugs. "But we blend right in."

My mind turns back to Jenny. I can almost feel the phantom of her hand on my shoulder as we danced. I'll go to church tomorrow and if it's too eager, she can send me on my way. But I don't figure I have anything to lose.

"This is me," O'Connor says, jerking his thumb at the first of the 3rd platoon barracks, a green tent on a platform under the dripping limbs of the ash trees. "Hey, I got a deck of cards in there, you wanna play a little something?"

"I don't know," I answer, realizing how tired I am and suddenly longing to crawl into bed and fall unconscious. "I want to get an early start tomorrow, fit in a run before church."

"Church? Where?"

"Jenny's father's, but it's Protestant, and you're—"

"As Irish Catholic as the day is long," O'Connor finishes. The flood-light at the tent door glows on his face. For the first time I notice how startlingly lonely he looks. He bites at his fingernails, then seems to realize what he's doing and drops his hand. "Listen, you sure you don't want to...? We found some coffee yesterday. I could fix it up."

His voice falters. Under the light's glare he looks like a lost child, begging for reassurance. I lean on the railing of the steps up to the tent and say, "How old are you, O'Connor?"

"Nineteen back in January."

"You got friends in the platoon?"

He shrugs. "Yeah, but y'know, they're all replacements too, and it's...well, we sorta feed off each other's nerves, if you know what I mean. Y'all've already fought. You know how it's gonna be."

"No one can ever know before it happens, even if he has two stars on his jump wings."

"Are you scared?"

I glance at him, then crane my neck to see the stars, thinking of the nights I've dropped down from the door of a plane. There's only one reason I made it through both Sicily and Italy without losing my mind. When I look back at O'Connor, alone and afraid and only nineteen under the light keeping away the darkness, I think how I'd have felt if I hadn't met Peter on the train to Georgia.

"We're all scared," I say, "but you'll learn how to control it, how to use it to your advantage. You stick with us, and you'll be well looked after." I sling my arm across O'Connor's skinny shoulder. "Fix up that coffee, okay? Hope you like blackjack."

" **A** re you blind, pal? That foul was so far out it's probably in Scotland!" Berk throws off his catcher's mask and stalks up to the 1st battalion corporal acting as umpire, who backs up a couple paces.

"It went over the chair. That was in!" the corporal says, pointing at the wooden bar chair someone must've stolen from a pub. "Maybe if you weren't using furniture for a foul pole—"

Berk's one of those short guys who'll kick anyone's ass with or without provocation. Wind him up and set him off, like turning the key of a tin soldier, and he looks in the mood to go twelve rounds with this kid. He caught up to us in Belfast in the winter, full of stories about how the surgeons wove his leg arteries back together, including details he couldn't possibly know unless he'd been awake and on his elbows on the operating table.

"You ever seen a baseball game?" he shouts as I shake my head and trot back to what passes for centerfield. "See, there's this thing called a *foul*—"

"Jesus Christ, c'mon, is this baseball or politics?" Skinny shouts from 1st base.

We put down metal trash can lids for bases out behind the 2nd battalion barracks. It's already been the site of three bloody noses in less than a week, one from a misjudged pitch, two from another disagreement about a foul ball that came to blows. I eye the argument and prepare to run to the barracks for my aid kit. Put a bunch of twenty-something guys on a baseball diamond, and most of them abandon all sense of human decency, even forgetting that we've got an audience. A cluster of officers and enlisted men has formed under the trees in the rare English sunlight. Lieutenant Walsh watches in apparent amusement, his arms crossed and eyes hidden behind dark sunglasses.

Peter pushes Berk back with a hand to his chest. I can't hear what he says, but this isn't the first time he's had to hold Berk back from throwing punches. With a scowl to the corporal that makes me think I'd watch my back in the latrine if I was him, Berk grabs his mask and goes back behind home plate. The contested hit is safe, and now we've got the first and second bases loaded, the runners bouncing from one foot to the other as they watch Peter.

"Any day now, Romano. This sun won't last," Peter calls from the pitcher's mound, raising his mitt to catch a new ball Berk throws to him. The score's 2-2, bottom of the fourth and last inning; we cut the game in half to squeeze it in before the dinner bell rings. We still need three outs to win this. Able Company's best batter Joe Romano comes up, swings his bat, and squints in the sunlight. Bright reflections glint off jingling dog tags. Out in centerfield, I wipe the sweat from my eyes with the edge of my t-shirt and push back the brim of my baseball cap emblazoned "AA." O'Connor kicks the dirt around third base, blowing out a shiny pink bubble with his gum. Fish out in left field smacks his mitt and leans forward with his hands on his knees.

"Beat their asses, Joey!" calls one of his buddies, warming up his swing beneath the willow tree. All the Able boys begin chanting and heckling us, bunch of jerks who think they're the best in the regiment because their company comes first alphabetically.

I cup my ungloved hand by my mouth and shout, "Crush 'em, Pete!" The others on the field follow suit till it sounds like Fenway on game day out here.

Romano, Staten Island born and bred, grins and spits on the ground like he thinks he's up to bat for that New York team. Peter adjusts his silver sunglasses, nods at Berk behind the plate, winds up, and pitches a hell of a fastball. Romano swings and the bat cracks, a grounder to center. I take off running. Most of the time the scores in these games don't really matter to me, but beyond our team rivalries, I think Joe Romano is a little bitch and I'd like to knock him down a peg. Also, I'm sick of him bragging about his sexual conquests in the chow line, so as my friends shout my name I decide this ball isn't getting away, come hell or high water.

Turns out it's the latter. My chest hits the creek first when I dive for the ball, cold water soaking my arms and t-shirt, but I scoop it up. Romano's instantly out, but we've still got two runners who both take off. I scramble to my feet in the creek and hurl the ball to O'Connor at third base, who jumps up to catch it and comes down on the trash can lid—one runner out—and then he chucks it underhand fast as a whip to Berk at home plate, the second runner out with a couple inches to spare. The umpire jerks his thumb back and calls, "Out!"

"You boys see that?!" Berk shouts, jumping up so quick it's a miracle he doesn't undo all the surgeons' hard work. The Able boys groan and kick the grass as I run across the field in squelching wet Corcorans. I grab a laughing O'Connor around the waist, spinning him around like my prom date. Fish sprints across from left field, shouting "Fox, Fox, Fox!" and Peter runs off the pitcher's mound to thump me and O'Connor's backs. The field resounds with laughter and whistles. Berk spins the hat backward on my head and slaps my chest. McNuts hooks his thumb at Romano and the two runners and drawls "Youuu're *out.*"

Skinny smacks his glove and says to O'Connor, "Fricking beautiful! Where'd you learn to jump like that, Toothpick?"

Our laughter can probably be heard halfway across the county. One of the Able boys calls, "Geez, y'all are celebrating like you won the World Series."

"We're romanticizing the hell outta this, Thompson, 'cause if we don't, who will?" Peter shrugs and grins. "Lighten up a little."

"Yeah, swell, you can have your laughs. We'll get you back next weekend."

As some of the officers walk across the field, Lieutenant Greer calls, "That'll teach 'em not to mess with foxes, eh?"

Walsh touches the brim of his own baseball cap to us and smiles.

"Nice to put a Yankee in his place," he mutters as they pass, giving me a wink.

We're all talking over one another, pointing at the field to rehash plays, when the regimental photographer appears.

"This is swell, all this," he says, gesturing to us. "If you fellows can hold still, I'll take your photo. Be nice for the company scrapbook."

Peter herds all nine of us into a cluster, though holding still is another matter. I'm sure the photo will come out blurry. I loop one arm around O'Connor's neck and the other around McNulty's. We smile for the camera, and there's some shoving and smacking till the photographer tells us to knock it off.

In this moment, sweaty and laughing in the sunlight, we're all together, and nothing can ever take that away.

IX.

SKELETON

"Deep breath for me, Richard, as you're able."

I arch my back as Dr. Linstead presses the cold metal bell of the stethoscope along my spine, his other hand on my shoulder. He asks me to breathe in again, and I try. Then to exhale, and I try that too, but not very impressively. He moves the stethoscope to the right side of my back to my good lung.

"You just speak up if I'm hurting you," Dr. Linstead says. "Or tap the table."

"I'm okay."

He asks me about physical activity. I take another breath for him and close my eyes, trying not to think about baseball and cleats and cross-country races on windy fall days.

"Are you sleeping enough?" Linstead loops the stethoscope around his neck and guides my shoulder with his hand so I sit up straighter. He presses against my ribs and chest in that way doctors have that's hard enough to be uncomfortable but not enough for you to say so.

"Probably not," I answer after hesitating, when I know he can't see my face.

"How many hours a night, do you think?"

"Three...four." That's too generous.

"And the shrapnel wounds in your back—it was all removed, as far as you know, in England?"

"That's right."

"Hm. You do have quite a few good scars back there." As he listens to my lungs, he says almost as an afterthought, "Your collarbone seems to have healed nicely, and you said it doesn't give you any pain?"

I nod.

"Good."

His hand presses a spot on the left side of my back, not far from my spine. It makes me inhale sharply, and I clamp both hands on the table edge to steady myself. He takes his hand away and waits while I try to catch my breath.

As I blink stars out of my eyes, Dr. Linstead moves around me and says in a kind voice, as though speaking to a wounded animal, "All right now, Richard, you can get dressed."

He goes out of the room that doubles as his office and the exam room and shuts the white door with a click. I watch the door and the afternoon light that shines in rectangles across it. A chill crawls up my spine, needling at my lungs. Reluctantly, wishing I could delay him from coming back in and diagnosing me with something much more serious than obstinacy, I get dressed.

After a gentle knock, the door creaks open and Dr. Linstead pokes his head through. "All set, son?"

I nod as he comes in and pulls a chair from his desk around to me. He sits himself down in it, folds one leg across the other, and rests the clipboard with my chart on top of his knee. Removing his glasses, he looks up at me—still sitting on the exam table, legs dangling down—and softens the blow with a precursory smile. He has the same smile as his daughter, who was my high school English teacher.

He slips his glasses onto his nose and refers to my chart. "First, your sleeping and eating habits. I could've said just by looking at you that you aren't doing enough of either. 5'11" and 130 pounds soaking wet."

"I know. I'm trying. I don't really have much of an appetite."

"I understand that, but you need to get stronger," he says, peering at me over the glasses, rather pointedly. "You could stand to gain a few pounds, son."

"Yes sir, I'll try. I will."

"But," Linstead adds, "getting stronger will only get you so far. Sooner or later, and I'd place my bets on sooner, what's left of that left lung is going to collapse again. It's called a pneumothorax. Think of it like a burned-out house, only the skeleton structure still standing, but barely. It's significantly weakened."

"I know what it is."

When he tilts his head curiously, I add, "Pneumothorax, I mean. It happened in the field hospital."

"Then I'm sure you don't want it to happen again."

He scoots the chair back on its wheels and retrieves the stack of x-rays from his desk, then gets up and goes over to the illuminator, a white panel mounted on the wall opposite me. After lining up the films side by side, he flicks it on. Blue light glows through my x-rayed ribs. He points a bony finger to the top of my chest. I broke five ribs, two on the right and three on the left. Now they appear whole and healed while protecting the real trouble that still lives in my chest.

Linstead circles the area with his finger. "You can see here the damage to your left lung." I don't, because it all just looks like a white cloud behind the thin stripes of ribs, but I'll take his word for it. "Damaged lungs are a tricky thing. When one lung can't function at full capacity, you'd expect the healthy one to make up the deficit, wouldn't you?"

"I guess so."

"But what actually happens is that the weaker lung drags its brother down with it, as though spreading poison. With a damaged lung taking up so much unused space in your chest, the other one isn't able to compensate.

"What's interesting, though," he goes on, switching off the humming illuminator and returning to his desk chair, "is that sometimes, people with all or part of a lung removed are physically healthier with just the one—after the poison, so to speak, is extracted."

Phantom tingling spreads through my ribs. The corners of my mind darken. A white forest, running with rivers of blood. Not just mine.

"It can't stay there forever. The damaged lower lobe will need to come out—a lobectomy." Linstead watches me with concern, which forces me to look out the window between his shelves crowded with glass bottles and tablet tins. "You're at a high risk for lung infections, including pneumonia, and your immune system is weakened because of it, too. And if there's one thing that Maine winters are generous with besides snow, it's sickness."

My mind leaves the snowy forest and travels instead to the moment I struggled out of a medicated fog in the English hospital, staring uncomprehendingly up at the harsh white lights and the shadows moving above me, oxygen mask strapped over my mouth like a gag. I couldn't feel much of what they were doing, just some dulled pain, but I heard it. Even yesterday, the sound of Laurie putting the silverware into the kitchen drawer made my throat dry.

"Would you like to speak to your folks about it before we decide anything?" Linstead scribbles something on a note. "This is the address for the veterans hospital in Augusta. Your treatment there would be covered."

He holds the note out to me, and I look at it but can't move to take it.

"I...I don't know if I can do that," I say finally.

He doesn't say anything, and I look anywhere but at him, convinced I'll die of humiliation if I have to explain myself. And why? Humiliated from the pain earlier, or the memory of the surgeon in England cutting shrapnel out of my chest, or the confusion of all this, or that I can't stand to be confronted with my own necessities because that means being noticed, dissected. It means that all my worst fears are given a grounding in the world instead of just in the racket of my own head, but most of all it means that I can't back away into the darkness and be forgotten—

Linstead scoots forward and sets the note on the exam table by my leg. "You have to, son. Perhaps I understated the severity—if you don't have that damaged lobe removed, I do think you'll face the consequences this winter, and it's possible you could lose the whole lung. The complications I mentioned are not just a passing cold that can be shaken off."

If only to satisfy him, I take the note and tuck it into my back pocket without looking at it.

He settles his clipboard on his knee and writes something. Without looking up, he says, "What about your chronic pain level, on a daily basis? 1-10, one being nearly unnoticeable."

"Around three, I guess."

"You notice the discomfort, but it doesn't keep you from your life?"

I nod.

"Worse at night?"

I nod again.

Linstead writes something else, then looks up at me. "If you'd like, we can think about some painkillers to help you manage the pain until you can have the lobec—"

"No." I surprise myself, and him, with the decisiveness of that answer. Clearing my throat, I add, "I don't think I need that. The painkiller, I mean. It isn't so bad."

"Okay," he says simply. "You let me know if you change your mind. I could give you something to help you sleep."

"I don't think so."

He doesn't press anything on me, but in the following silence I can tell there's much more he wants to say. But I don't want any painkillers or sleeping pills. I don't need anything that would "help." For fuck's sake, I shouldn't even be alive, so what right do I have to anything that would ease the pain?

"You will tell me if anything gets worse, won't you?" Linstead is watching me, and I force myself to meet his eyes. "It's all right if you don't want to talk to your parents—you're an adult—but just remember that I'm here to help you."

He worked in a veterans hospital here in Maine after the Great War. That's probably why he and Dad became such close friends so quickly after Dad arrived in Caspar—I doubt anyone else understood the things they'd seen and heard in those wards. I immediately regret putting my stubbornness on display for him, when I know all he wants is not to lose another patient to the aftereffects of war.

"Of course," I answer, knowing I won't say a word.

O ne of Dr. Linstead's favorite stories to tell, and one I've heard a hundred times throughout my life, is of the night I was born—a heavy, stormy, end-of-June night, with bone-jarring claps of thunder and rain that blew sideways. My mom will nod and say that she can still taste the rain scented with the crushed flowers from her garden. She'll pick up the story threads then and always enjoys reliving the first year of sleepless nights in memory, to guilt me, I assume. "What a set of lungs you had," she'll say, which has for a long time been a favorite family irony considering that after that first year of non-stop screaming, I didn't speak till I was about four. It was Dr. Linstead who first performed hearing tests on me, and who gave us a referral for a hearing specialist in Bangor.

The hearing specialist—I still remember his wood-paneled office, the scratch of the chair upholstery on my legs as I fidgeted and he talked to my parents—confirmed there was nothing wrong with my ears. He officially diagnosed me with "obstinacy." Those were his exact words, and they've been embedded in Dare family lore ever since, mostly because my parents were irritated to have spent money on a specialist doctor who told them what they'd known from that first stormy night. Growing up, whenever I put up a fight about something, Mom or Dad or Laurie would say, laughing, "Looks like someone's come down with a case of obstinacy," which of course would only harden my resolve that I was not going to do the thing in question, whatever it was—recite a verse in Sunday School, or attend the Cub Scout club that Dad signed me up for, or sleep in the attic room above my grandparents' garage in Boothbay because I was convinced it was haunted.

Or willingly submit myself to the dismantling of the burned-out skeleton house in my chest. I leave the practice, trying to come up with ways to put off the inevitable, just as Grace comes out of the pharmacy next door. She waves to me; otherwise I might not have noticed her. She comes over to me, squinting in the sunlight.

"What are you up to? Isn't it a beautiful afternoon? It's so warm that I walked to school this morning. I was picking up Gran's arthritis prescription and some more aspirin. I've been getting headaches from all my exam grading..."

She looks up at Linstead's practice, and an edge of worry creeps into her voice even while she tells me about the rhododendron tree blooming in their kitchen yard. At last she can't keep it in any longer and says, "Everything okay? How're the lungs?"

"Oh, everything's fine—relatively."

"Good." Grace pulls the straps of her leather satchel tight. Her red cardigan is tied by the sleeves around her waist, and the scarf wrapped in her hair doesn't do much to keep the loose waves from blowing out in the wind. "I almost forgot; I need to stop at the post office—I have a letter for Lena." She holds up the envelope, addressed to *Lena Whitley*. "How many stamps do you think it takes to send something to Australia?"

"You wrote to her? So does that mean you're not gonna kill Sidney?"

"Oh, I am," she says lightly. "But that's between him and me, and Lena has nothing to do with it. It's that he thought he could get married without telling me first."

"Well, I hope she turns out to be everything you want in a sister. And I hope we all actually get to meet her."

"I'll dig Sidney up and kill him a second time if he thinks he can stay in Australia." She taps the edge of the envelope with her fingernail. "But he's always been picky, you know? So that makes me think Lena must really be something. He wouldn't marry just anyone on a whim."

We pass the general store where old men sit on the porch, playing checkers in between half-grunted conversations. We used to spend half our summer lawn-mowing and babysitting money on the ice cream and popsicles in the freezer by the door. The other half went to baseball cards, which we bought in packs from the cardboard display box by the till. At the top of the potholed street—why bother repaving every year, reasons the town council, if the ice is only going to crack it all again in three months?—the marquee of the Caspar Cinema glints in the sun. *Mildred Pierce* and *The Picture of Dorian Gray* stand out in those block letters.

"Have you seen that yet?" I say to Grace when she comes out of the post office. I nod at the marquee. "Dorian Gray."

"No, but I loved that book. I think it was you who lent me a copy."

We leave town behind and approach the footbridge that spans the creek. Grace makes us stop in the middle, select a couple of skinny twigs, and drop them in the slow trickling current below for a game of "Pooh Sticks," which entertains us even more now than it did when we were kids. We turn to the other side of the narrow bridge, leaning over the stone wall, and watch as they come out side by side, hers just ahead.

"How is it I've never won this game against you?"

She straightens triumphantly. "Come back to the house. We have half a blueberry pie that needs to be eaten, and I don't want to eat alone."

"Well...Dr. Linstead did say that I need to be fattened up."

"And he used those words?"

"Something to that effect. It made me feel like a sacrificial calf."

Grace kicks a spray of pebbles ahead of us with the toe of her shoe and says, "Then that must make me the witch from Hansel and Gretel, tempting you home with candy and blueberry pie."

"You're not going to stick me in your oven, are you?"

"Of course not. The oven's filthy from the blueberries that exploded out of the pie."

We sit on the stoop outside the kitchen door long after the pie is gone, a colander of leftover blueberries and half a bottle of elderberry wine between us. We talk and laugh and the sun is warm on our backs, sinking into evening, though I barely notice the time till Grace points to the sunset. She tells me about her letter to Lena, and I don't pay attention very well because she looks so beautiful in the fading light.

"Oh," she says, straightening up, her arms wrapped around her knees. She turns from the sunset and squints at me. "Tomorrow is June 6—I wasn't sure if I should say anything, but, well—I wanted to tell you I remembered. That's all. Is that okay?" She tucks her hands beneath her knees. "Sometimes I don't know how to be when it comes to...all that. I'm sorry."

"No, it's okay," I say. "It's nice of you to remember, Gracie."

Our eyes meet as I reach for the wine bottle.

"I wish I could understand," she says. "Sometimes you seem so alone, Richard, and I don't want you to be."

We sit in silence for a minute, washed in a sunset as beautiful as the one over the English airfield a year ago tonight. Finally I say, "On the plane that night...we lost someone, one of the guys in my company, and I..." My throat goes dry despite the wine, and I wish I hadn't said anything. "Well, I know I'll dream about it tonight."

"Was it your fault he died?"

I look up at her. "Not necessarily—"

"But you're still blaming yourself."

I don't answer, staring instead at the white-flowered weeds poking through the dirt at the bottom of the steps. A little black shadow appears among the apple trees, Grace's cat Baxter, stalking the field mice. He harbors suspicions of me for reasons I can't understand, but when he sees us, he slinks across the lane and pushes his face against Grace's legs.

Scratching between his ears, she says, "Would it be wrong of me to assume that being a medic—well, that it wasn't only saving lives—that it was about comforting people, too?" She knocks her knee against mine, our old signal to say, *All okay?* "I didn't have to be there to know that's what you did because that's who you are. And it probably made all the difference, more than you'll ever know."

Before I can think how to react to that, the screen door behind us opens and Grace's grandmother pokes her head out. She must not've known I was here because when she sees me, she says, "Oh! Sorry, you two." When she starts to close the door, Grace tells her it's okay.

"Well, the chicken's ready, Grace. Richard, will you stay for dinner?" Mrs. Whitley smiles kindly but with a definite hint that she, too, thinks that I need to be fattened up. I say yes because I want to put off the inevitability of going home and facing tonight's spate of nightmares. As I follow them into the kitchen, I look over my shoulder at the rose and lavender blushing in the western sky, imagining C-47 engines roaring through the clouds.

X.

OVERLORD

6 June 1944, over the English Channel, 0045 hours

The interior of the C-47 is oppressive with the smell of sweat and fear. Someone is praying the rosary. Vandenburg beside me pulls the buckles on his webbing tight. Three boys on this plane are replacements, and I don't know what's worse: not knowing what to expect or, like the rest of us, knowing too much.

Lieutenant Walsh crouches at the open door, watching the darkness over the Channel. I'm second in the stick after him, and sitting opposite the opening I can see some of the other planes flanking us. The drone of hundreds of engines fills the night sky as three Airborne divisions—the 101st, the British 6th, and us in the 82nd—fly in V formations toward the Normandy coastline.

I scoot forward to see the water below us. The shadowy forms of the Allied fleet skim through the darkness, Navy destroyers and landing craft as far as I can see and beyond to break the Atlantic Wall. Something in me feels drawn to that cold water and the men in the holds of those LCIs as they clutch their rifle stocks and pray. I think of my friends in other planes, Peter and Fish in the second stick and Berk and McNuts in the third, counting down the minutes till they see the green light go on. We each feel it, all that lingers unspoken in this plane, of being a part of something far greater than we could ever have imagined.

Maybe it's that communal understanding that reassures me whatever happens, we'll take our battalion's first objective, the town of Ste.-Mèr e-Église, and the Allies will take Normandy as our foothold into Hitler's Fortress Europa. And we won't fail because the weight of the free world is on our shoulders. I still remember the steel in Colonel Gavin's voice at the top of Biazza: "We stay on this ridge no matter what."

So we take Normandy no matter what. And I know too well what those words mean.

O'Connor watches me from across the aisle. Our faces are smeared with blackening, but his eyes glow gray in his skinny face as he bites his top lip. I tug at the straps of my musette bag and smile at him. His mouth presses into a hard line, a grim smile in return. Skinny sneezes. Rodriguez's unlit cigarette dangles from his mouth. Fingers drum on legs, and rosary beads tap against one another.

As we geared up last night on the tarmac of the Cottesmore Airfield, light fell on us from the most beautiful sunset I've ever seen in England, a deep orange sky fading into rose as if to tell us, *Goodbye. Good luck. Give 'em hell.*

Did I remember everything? Do I have enough morphine? Will we even get out of the plane? The same anxiety that accompanies every jump, only this one seems to carry so much more weight than both Sicily and Italy did.

But as long as we get out, I have full confidence in every man wedged around me and in every plane flanking us. Maybe I wouldn't say that if I didn't have two stars to my jump wings already, but I know these men better than I will ever know anyone else, and I know they all feel the same.

Whatever it takes, I pray. *Whatever You ask of me.*

I touch my dog tags, warm on my chest beneath my jump jacket. *No matter what.*

"Hey," Vandenburg says beside me. "Rev?"

"Yeah?"

He has to shout to be heard over the engines and the rattling aircraft. "Seems like you got a wire to the Big Fella. Think you could say a prayer for me, too?"

I start to answer him that I already have when flak erupts in the sky around us. Boys dozing off because of the airsickness pills I passed out at the airfield jolt awake, the whites of their eyes glowing in the dark interior. We must be passing over the Channel Islands and a battery of antiaircraft guns.

"Hold on, boys!" Walsh shouts. He hangs onto the anchor cable running under the fuselage, stumbling and then catching himself as another artillery shell screams past. He sits beside O'Connor. "Not far now."

More shots ring out, but our pilot holds steady. Then the night is quiet again except for the plane's engines.

"Are we close to Normandy, sir?" someone calls.

"Very close."

If those were Guernsey and Jersey, then the Cotentin Peninsula must be rushing out to meet us. Just as I wonder how the pilots keep from flying into the other planes, we pass into a cloud bank and my view out the door goes opaque.

I think about my parents, my grandparents, Laurie. Grace. I think about a gold star pinned in the front window. I ask God that if this is it, then please let it be quick.

No one speaks. Our heartbeats are strung together as we all make promises to the Big Fella, whatever that looks like for each man.

"...and I will walk before the Lord in the land of the living."

The clouds fall away. A line of white surf breaks on Normandy's shores under the bright moonlight. For a moment the night is crystalline, glistening in the blackness.

Then the plane jerks to the left, and the guys opposite almost pitch over onto the rest of us. We all try to stand, but antiaircraft fire screams through the sky, and we're knocking against the sides of the C-47 like pebbles in a can as other planes dip and dart to avoid the flak. Ack-ack lights up all around. You'd think the top of the sky is made of paper, the way the shells rip across it. Guys are knocked to their knees in the aisle. I feel someone hanging onto my harness straps.

The crew chief crouching by the cockpit door shouts something to Walsh as red and blue tracers slice like searchlights into our cross-section of sky. Just below us both engines of another C-47 go up in orange flames, and the plane drops altitude as if a giant hand has yanked it back to Earth. The white-capped coastline disappears, flashes of light and antiaircraft fire lighting the trees and fields. Shells explode over the French countryside as tracers go up like bottle rockets on the Fourth of July. We have to be close to our drop zone now. It takes all of my willpower to hang onto the anchor cable and plant my feet and not hurl myself out the door.

Someone shouts, "What the fuck are we doing, lieutenant? Let's jump!" I wouldn't mind getting the hell outta dodge, either—anything is better than being a trapped passenger—but the light still isn't on, and the pilot has climbed to avoid all the flak. We must be at 1,200 feet or more, and we gotta go down through all of that shit. Out the sliver of door I see thousands of deployed canopies, attached to paratroopers falling right down through the hellfire.

Walsh pulls his head in just as a sapphire-blue tracer zings up and peppers the side of the plane. Guys are shouting behind me and crowding up against one another; no one wants to get caught last in the back. Other planes drop out of sight. I watch one do a nosedive into a field, its cabin engulfed in flames.

The lieutenant shouts something to the crew chief about missing our drop zone, but we're going so fast that drop zone or not I don't see how we can jump at this speed and altitude. Then the red warning light by the door blinks on and casts bloody light across Walsh's cheeks. I can't hear a word he says even though my face is inches from his, but his gestures are enough: *HOOK UP!*

I hook my static line to the anchor cable and feel the cable pull taut as everyone else does the same, guys stumbling to keep their balance and holding onto one another. *Let's go, Jesus Christ, come on—*

I see the shape of the words Walsh shouts as the plane knocks us from side to side: "EQUIPMENT CHECK!"

Vandenburg behind me yanks on the straps of my shoulder harness, where my medical kits hang. Walsh screams to sound off for equipment check. From the back of the plane come the desperate confirmations: "Twelve okay!—Eleven okay!—Ten okay!"

Vandenburg smacks my shoulder and I shout, "TWO OKAY!"

As the words leave my mouth, the jump light flashes to green.

We feel a weight drop from beneath the plane, Walsh hitting the button to unload our supplies and weapons that have as much chance of making it to the ground as we do. He's at the door about to jump when we fly into tracers. Then the crew chief gets too close and takes a bullet right in the head, and we watch his body hit the floor of the plane.

"Holy *SHIT, let's go!*" Santorini's distinctive voice screams from a few men back.

For a second I think it's only the force of the firing that's knocked Walsh back. "DARE, GO, GO!" he screams, gesturing to the door.

"Sir—"

"Damn it, get out! GO!"

There's a strange note in his voice, like orders given through a gurgling choke. Then light from a shell illuminates the interior and the blood bubbling at his throat.

"Shit." I unhook my line and push Vandenburg past me. "Go, get out!"

"Dare—" Walsh chokes out my name even as I'm telling him to stop, to be quiet, to hang on. I hook my arms under his shoulders and drag him back from the door. The plane takes flak and staggers, losing altitude rapidly. We fly through more ack-ack, which lights up the stick in intermittent flashes. I hear the prop blast flinging off bags and equipment as the rest of the stick begins to jump, each trooper pushing at the back of the man in front of him and screaming to be let out.

"Rev!" Santorini shouts, and I scream at him to jump, just fucking jump, and he's gone.

I hold my hands to Walsh's throat. His warm blood soaks my wrists and the sleeves of my jump jacket. "Okay, sir, just hang on," I tell him, his pulse labored beneath my fingers. "Sir, you have to stay with me. We're gonna get you back to England. You're gonna be okay."

He kicks his legs out, reaching for my hands. The bandage I'm using to try to stanch the blood flow is sodden and I drop it and reach for my kit, but I can't get to it what with the other gear weighing me down. Then I hear someone shout, "Doc, let me, I'll get it! DOC!"

O'Connor hovers over us, unhooked from the cable—still here in the plane while the kraut artillery tries to blow us out of the fucking sky.

"The fuck are you doing?! Get out, you need to jump! O'Connor, *go!*"

"I can help you, Doc! Let me help you!"

He stumbles as the plane pitches downward. Gravity pushes me against Walsh, who's in agony, clutching at my hands clutching him. In the darkness I can't see the wounds or how many there are or if there might be more besides his neck. I feel a tug at my shoulder harness, and then O'Connor sticks a rolled bandage in my hand.

The fabric is soaked instantly. Walsh can only get out half-words now, in unimaginable pain each time the pilot dives to take evasive action.

"Hang on, sir, it's okay it's okay it's okay! I've got you!"

He mumbles something that might be "don't waste that bandage," knowing him. But I'm already dousing the wounds I can feel with sulfa powder. O'Connor gives me another bandage, and I lift Walsh's heavy shoulders toward me so his head falls on my shoulder. I wrap the bandage around his neck, stuffing another into the wound.

"Will you go?" I shout over my shoulder at O'Connor. "You need to jump!"

"I'll jump when you jump, Doc."

With the crew chief dead, I have no way to communicate with the pilots, no way of knowing if we're over our drop zone or long past it. But I don't need the pilots to tell me that if we don't get out soon, we're not jumping into Normandy at all.

Walsh grips my hand and tries to say something. I see blood running down the sides of his mouth. He gathers up enough breath to stutter out, "D-Dare—you n-need to jump—that's an order."

"Sir, I can't leave you here—"

O'Connor shakes my shoulder. "Doc, we gotta go!"

"Richard," Walsh says, and I meet his eyes, seeing the tiny reflections of a fiery sky in his irises. "They need you d-down...down there more than I do."

I try to answer him, but my throat has suddenly closed up.

"DOC!" O'Connor is shouting. "Doc, come on!"

"You get out of this p-plane, trooper. That's an order." Walsh's grip on my hand weakens. "Or do y-you want me to c-court-martial you?"

I hook my arms under Walsh's again and drag him to the center aisle, sitting him on the floor between the seats, where I hope he won't get tossed around. The green jump light glows in my peripheral as Walsh gasps for air that won't come.

Crouching beside him, my hand on the bandage sticky against his throat and the rims of our helmets scraping, I close my eyes, a prayer caught in my mouth that I can't get out, *for thou has delivered my soul from death mine eyes from tears my feet from falling,* flak drumming our wing as Walsh's face twists in pain. *The sorrows of death compassed me...*

There isn't time to say anything else. He clutches the bandages at his throat as a kraut bullet bleeds him out. I hook back up to the cable and stumble after O'Connor and jump into the shaking night.

The force of the prop blast jerks my head back and then yanks off my leg bag. Tracers cut past me so close I think I must be dead. But we jumped so low and so fast that that's my only thought before my left hip meets a soaked field and I hear O'Connor a few feet away whispering, "Flash?" into the damp darkness.

I answer, "Thunder, it's me, thunder," taking a deep breath as I try to sever my chute's cords, the trench knife bloody and slick in my grip. At least there's no wind tonight.

"Where the hell are we?"

"Not where we're supposed to be, that's for sure." I push the lines and canvas of the parachute away, feeling sick. The dewy grass is a cold relief to my bloodied hands. Tipping my helmet back, I look up into the sky, watching C-47s try to evade the antiaircraft guns. O'Connor flinches at the discharge of an .88 gun not far away. When its shell flashes through the darkness, we see paratroopers falling under full canopies, pulling on the risers to keep from getting skewered in the treetops.

We got out. I imagine the ground crews at Cottesmore unloading a single body from our stick. *Poor bastard,* I hear an English voice saying. *Never even had a chance.*

I'm sorry, sir.

There isn't time to dwell on it. We're on the ground in Normandy, together.

"What've you got?" I whisper to O'Connor. "Prop blast took my leg bag."

There's just enough moonlight to see him nod. "Mine too, but I've still got my rifle."

"Then let's walk."

6 June 1944, Ste.-Mère-Église, Normandy, France, 0730 hours

I don't know why I imagined the sun wouldn't rise. In my mind, the night of nights heralding the day of days drew out perpetually. Passing green-shuttered stone farmhouses and lush pastures, I'm surprised at the dawn lighting the tops of the hedgerows. Somehow it disappoints me what a beautiful place Normandy is. A couple of cows the color of cream in coffee stare over their barbed-wire at O'Connor and me as we march past with the other 2nd battalion guys we've come across since the jump. The countryside is eerily quiet, and though we've been wandering through hedgerows and along dirt tracks for hours, we haven't seen any evidence of the enemy.

"You know," O'Connor says, inhaling as we pass honeysuckle tangled around a gatepost, "the farms and all, it kinda reminds me of home."

Church bells ring in Ste.-Mère-Église as we approach. The road turns to cobbles, and members of our bunch break off to greet buddies and hook up with their companies. Scraps of cloud drift through the beryl sky over pale brick rowhouses. I stare up at the gabled attic windows that would make perfect kraut machine-gun nests, and probably did. By the look of things, 3rd battalion completed its objective of capturing the town. Still, knowing how snipers sometimes lie in wait for hours, I keep my head low.

O'Connor wipes sweat from his eyes and says, "Guess we missed the fight."

"Yeah." I squint in the bright sunlight glaring off the stucco façades. "Come on, let's see if we can find any…"

Two stretcher-bearers pass us on the narrow road, a body between them covered with parachute canvas. O'Connor's head swivels as he watches them head toward the church.

"…any familiar faces," I finish, smacking O'Connor on the shoulder. "Hey. Jacob. Let's go, okay?"

I almost add that because he's the platoon's runner, we ought to find Lieutenant Walsh. Then I catch myself. The wet field washed all the blood off my hands, but I still feel its warmth as though it seeped through my skin. The phantom touch of Walsh's throat, quivering as I tried to hold it together, and the plane tumbling through the antiaircraft fire and the sky flashing with tracers so that every couple of seconds the interior lit up with blinding light and I saw his whole chest drenched in crimson—

"Rev, hey, Rev!"

I blink, realizing I was walking without even seeing the street in front of me. Santorini appears. Behind him a handful of F Company boys crouch and lounge in the thin shade of a corner building, its white shutters brilliant in the sun. O'Connor crosses the street to say hello to McNuts. Tired laughter moves through the boys gathered. Smokes and C rations exchange hands, and bits of improbable stories float in the warm air—*ran into a fella who told me he'd seen another guy who said* he'd *seen...*

Santorini grips my hand. "Glad you fellas made it down."

"You too, Skinny."

"We ain't much yet"—he jerks his head toward the other Fox boys, and I see Vandenburg and Haley bartering kraut souvenirs—"but more keep tricklin' in." Skinny runs a hand through his black hair and glances off down the street, dotted with paratroopers and Jeeps. Somewhere close by a fire is still burning. "I, uh...I probably don't need to ask about Lieutenant Walsh."

"No, he didn't jump." I take my helmet off, wipe my forehead with the back of my hand. "I guess that's obvious."

Skinny squints and watches me for a few moments, then shakes his head. "Fucking shame. That makes Greer our platoon leader. Oh," he adds as he taps out two smokes, giving one to me and fishing for his lighter, "that's the aid station, just up there. Doc Ryder's all set up. Promised him I'd send him any medics I found."

"Guess that means me." My nerves feel all twisted up inside me. "You see any of the fighting?"

"Tail end. Tony and me popped a few shots off with the mortar, but it was all 3rd battalion clearing this place out." Skinny breathes out smoke. "Hey, Rev?"

"Yeah."

"You know there wasn't anything you coulda done, right? You know it ain't your fault?"

I lower the cigarette. "Skin, that doesn't change that he's still dead. Absolving myself won't bring him back."

"Absolving yourself?" Skinny repeats. "Jesus Christ, Rev, this is a war we're in. If we all try to *absolve* ourselves, we'll never get to Berlin."

An officer nearby calls for him, and Skinny sets his helmet on his head and touches the brim to me. "Gotta go set up some mortars. Hang tough."

I exchange greetings with the boys, give McNuts a smack on the helmet for good measure—"Who let you into France?"—and then head for the aid station, a freestanding brick structure set back from the street, maybe a hotel or a school before. A gray brick wall with chunks blown out of it surrounds a courtyard, and tattered, flowering bushes hang over the wall. Walking wounded sit in the grass. Some others are on stretchers. I see bloody heads, crushed legs, arms pressed to chests in makeshift slings. I'm just thinking that wherever McNuts is, Berkowicz is never far behind, when I see that familiar stance: leaning up against the open doorway, all swagger and full of himself even when he's standing still, his right hip jutted out as if bragging that he lived to tell the tale of his busted femoral artery.

"Hey, Berk, why should you never carry a can of tuna in your back pocket on the subway?" I call.

He turns and grins. Sweat has washed most of the camo grease off his face, and the knees of his trousers are soaked through with mud.

"Morning, Harry," I say, knocking his shoulder and trying to force the lightheartedness with which he's so often lifted my spirits. "Good to see you."

"You too, Rev. What a night, huh?" Berk smacks my shoulder and gives me a reassuring nod. His expression is sober as he adds quietly, "Skinny told us about Lieutenant Walsh. I'm real sorry."

Hollins, company 1st sergeant, pushes out of the door past us and says, "Berkowicz—hey, Dare, nice of you to join us—Berk, with me, they want Fox to hold the line by the cemetery."

"On it, sarge. Rev—I'll catch you up later?" Berk follows Hollins, then turns back when they reach the road. "Oh, Rev. Fish is inside. He's okay, but I think you should talk to him."

From what I gather of snippets of conversation between officers inside, our 2nd battalion is holding this northern end as well as the eastern approach of Ste.-Mère-Église, with 3rd battalion in the south and west. I look into some of the rooms, mostly offices where company CPs have been set up and officers consult with one another over maps. Troopers mill through the main vestibule, some helping to bring in wounded. I poke my head into an oak-paneled dining room, its walls adorned in neoclassical, Greco-Roman hunt scenes of mossy green hills and golden-leafed trees. The glass doors at the back are open to let in air and light as Doc Ryder, our battalion surgeon, bends over someone on the long table. A medic is on the other side, holding a plasma bag and tubing in place for a guy I can't see.

Across the hall is a drawing room, where a gilt-framed mirror on the mantelpiece shows the reflection of a half dozen or so walking wounded. A musty smell of sweat and festering wounds hangs in the air. Fischer is sitting on a deep windowsill, looking like a forlorn cat who's found the last patch of sunlight. His head is down, dark hair falling over a cloth pressed to his right eye.

"Fish," I say, and when he doesn't answer, I scoot around a stretcher and a guy with a bloodied knee. "Hey, Fish."

He looks up, blue eye unfocused for a moment. Then he blinks and notices me. He takes a deep breath but doesn't speak, just looks at me and then back down at his lap. His rifle is propped on the wall beside him and he's still wearing his musette bag on his back.

"Berk said you'd be in here." I lean on the wall and tilt my head to try to see what he's covering. "How're you doing? What happened there?"

Fish turns his face to me and takes away the cloth. Blood is smeared along his temple. A laceration has cut through his eyebrow, narrowly missing his eyelid. "Piece of flak. I was fighting with 3rd battalion here."

"Did you pull it out yourself?" I reach out to touch his temple, and he starts to flinch away before I hold up my hand. "I'll be careful, I promise."

He lets me touch the area around the cut as he says, "No, Doc Ryder did, but then some worse wounded came in and he got busy I guess."

"It's pretty deep. Let me stitch it up for you." I take an alcohol swab and suturing kit from my bag. "I haven't seen anyone else from the second stick yet, just you."

"White and Avery are around here somewhere. So is Lieutenant Greer."

"Yeah, I need to talk to him."

Fish picks at a loose thread in his jacket sleeve. His shoulders are slumped but tensed, and although it's not my finest hour, either, he seems uncharacteristically miserable. Last time I saw him this dispirited was when he was puking his guts out from malaria in Tunisia.

"This'll sting a little, just hang tight," I tell him, but he barely reacts when I wipe his cut with the alcohol swab. His eyelid is swollen and bruised blue and gray, like he took a nasty left hook to the face. When it's clean, I wipe it with some analgesic to numb the area and then thread the needle. "Okay, the best way to do this is if you're lying down."

He twists the bloodied white cloth in his hands, wrapping it around his fingers and letting it go again. I wonder if he sees a parachute canopy in the fabric. The room is busy behind me, wounded limping in and stretcher-bearers pushing their way out. Every time footsteps creak over the threshold, Fish tries to see past me, as though waiting for a ghost to walk in.

"Fish?" I say.

His cheeks are white, though whether that's from pain or anxiety, I can't tell.

"Jack."

Finally he glances up at me.

"I need you to lie down so I can get a better angle at this, okay?"

"I, uh...yeah. Yeah, sorry, Rev." He sits up from the windowsill and follows me to the green brocade couch, where blood and dirt have soiled the gold embroidery thread on the cushions. Fish lies down with one leg bent at the knee and plants his other boot on the burgundy rug.

Crouched behind his head, I use my tissue forceps to open the wound enough to see where to insert the needle. There doesn't appear to be any shrapnel still caught in his skin, but this is a pretty good gash.

"You're going to look like Frankenstein's monster when I'm finished with you," I joke. "Hold these, would you?"

Fish gives a half-hearted snort as he takes the scissors for me. I brace my elbow on the edge of the couch, clamp the sterilized and threaded needle with the holder, and push the needle through his skin. Sunlight falls across his forehead, bright in my eyes.

I hold my breath and tug the needle gently. It feels calming to do something so precise and methodical, and I fall into the rhythm of stitching, wrapping, tying off, cutting the excess. For a couple minutes it eases the knot in my chest, suppressing the anger I've felt all night since the floor of the plane.

"You're gonna have a nice little scar right through your eyebrow, Fish," I tell him as I lean over his forehead, "and girls always like that sort of thing."

He doesn't answer, so I work in silence. As I'm tying off the last of five stitches, he rubs his other eye with the heel of his hand and says, "I don't know if he got out, Rev. I don't know how many of them got out."

"Who?" I snip the thread.

"Peter." Fish's eyes flick up, trying to see me. "I don't know if he jumped, or if any of them at the back made it out..."

"It's early yet, half the company's still missing. We all missed the DZ."

Fish sighs as I shake the contents of a sulfa packet over the stitches. "No, I—I was at the back of our stick, you know? And Pete was s'posed to jump second, after Greer. Only we switched places, me and him. We switched 'cause that new replacement in our squad, Akins, he was all worked up and panicking so Pete went back there to try to calm him down and told me to go to the front, and then suddenly the light went green and I jumped."

I sit back on my heels, cutting a bandage in half to tape to his temple, and say, "Then I don't see how you did anything wrong, Fish."

He lets me fix the bandage, which won't even be visible under his helmet. Then he sits up, gingerly touches the bandage, and looks around as if noticing the room and the other wounded troopers for the first time. We stand together, and I reach out to hold him steady.

"We jumped from real high. I thought I was gonna get torn up with all those tracers," he says. "But I had enough time to see the plane. I saw it going down, it just lit up all these hedgerows. Greer and I got out, and White and Avery, but I don't—"

He glances away, his voice catching.

"If I hadn't switched places with him, Rev, y'know?" Fish runs a hand through his hair. "Maybe it would've been me."

"Fish, we're not going there. We're not thinking about that." Just because only four of them from the second stick are accounted for doesn't mean that Peter and the others are all dead. "Are you sure it was your plane you saw go down? It was such a shitshow up there, there's no way of knowing, not yet. Chances are it wasn't a Fox plane at all."

Yesterday afternoon—a lifetime ago—we outfitted one another on the tarmac in the shade of the wings of the C-47s, buckling clasps and tightening packs and hooking pouches to our webbing. "Hey, Rev," Peter said when I passed his squad on my way to my plane assignment. He gave a tug on a private's shoulder harness. "I'll see you over there?"

"See you there, Pete," I said.

I can't step into the tidal currents of grief. They need me whole. What we know for sure is that Walsh is dead and Greer is our new platoon leader, and with those uncompromising facts we keep going, because it's D-Day and there's no other choice.

But that doesn't help Fish, convinced he let Peter step into a breach that could've claimed him instead if not for a replacement's nerves. And I know there's no way to reassure him.

Except, maybe, to keep him busy, so when another battalion doctor and medic arrive to help and Doc Ryder sends me out to scrounge for supplies in town, I take Fish with me. He carries his rifle as we walk down the narrow street filled with cigarette smoke and American voices. On a street corner under signs for Montebourg and Carentan pointing back the way we came, a couple of French civilian men talk to a huddle of 82nd officers. Thick emerald ivy clings to the sides of stone houses, and the window boxes spill over with roses like coral seashells. We pass a storefront painted the color of robin's eggs, "Poissonnerie" in yellow letters over a door hanging off its hinges and swinging over a splintered threshold. Hell of a beautiful place to fight a war.

"Rev?" Fish says.

"Ay-uh."

"...you really think girls like scars?"

I glance at him and grin. "Sure they do."

He tilts his helmet back and touches his eyelid. He'll probably have a monster headache in the next couple hours, but at least the flak didn't hit an inch lower. With a short laugh, he says, "Maybe they'll give me another Purple Heart for my collection."

We come to an intersection, a café with windows blown out to our left. Beyond it, up a sloped street covered in broken tree limbs and piles of bricks and shrapnel, is the dark stone church presiding gothically over Ste.-Mère-Église. Glass glitters on the pavement in the town square that smells of powder and burning wood, and some of the row buildings are missing roofs and chimneys. Troopers sit with legs dangling on the stone wall around the church or crouch under the blossoming apple trees. I slow to stare at two of the trees: one unbothered and swaying in the early summer wind as it drops white petals to the grass, the other beside it split right through the trunk and scorched black.

"See if you can beg some personal aid kits," I tell Fish, "on Captain Ryder's orders. Anything you can find will help, but morphine especially."

For a few minutes we weave between the clusters of troopers, pocketing whatever they're willing to spare, though some part with their morphine syrettes suspiciously. The white-faced clock on the church bell-tower ticks to 0830. I'm tucking a packet of wound tablets into my bag when some figures gathered under the trees in the square catch my eye. They're staring up into the branches. An officer rubs a hand over his eyes and then points and says something I'm too far away to hear.

"Hey, Fish," I call, jerking my head toward them. "What're they looking at?"

"You haven't seen?" A 3rd battalion kid with a mouthful of crackers glances over his shoulder at us. "They might be friends of yours."

"Yeah, word is they're Fox Company," his buddy adds, giving us a sympathetic look.

The color drains from Fish's face, and my heart drops.

There are tree limbs and shell craters in the dirt around the church. Tangled in the fractured trees, caught by their lines like macabre marionettes, are six lifeless bodies that died only a few feet above the ground.

They hang stiff in the branches, faces gray, knotted beyond hope by torn parachutes and equipment straps. Fish and I stare at them.

"Oh my god," he murmurs.

Colonel Vandervoort, F Company's first CO back in '42, stands by the church with the Protestant regimental chaplain Lieutenant Forrest, talking and eyeing the laden trees. I walk around one of the suspended bodies, hoping to see who it is, but the leaves obscure his face.

Every few seconds a burst of gunfire sounds from the cemetery behind the church, the front line for defending the town. 1st platoon's machine-gun nest is angled between the headstones. The gunners are crouched behind it watching the line. One of them glances at the trees, his expression unnerved.

"You don't think—" Fish starts. "I mean, can you see…can you tell who they are?"

"I don't know. I can't tell." Any of these bodies could be Peter. Any of them could be from the missing second stick, but whoever they are, they jumped into every paratrooper's nightmare. Hanged from a tree, an Airborne grave, and shot by the enemy before they could even try to untangle themselves.

I walk around another tree and see a blue-lipped face hanging above me. A rifleman, Jimmy Halloran. He and Mickey Russo reigned the craps tables back in Quorn.

Vandervoort, leaning on a pair of crutches and favoring his ankle, says something to the chaplain, grips his shoulder, and then hobbles off with another officer. Forrest calls over a couple of privates and 1st platoon's Lieutenant Winger from the cemetery, and they walk over to us.

"Fischer, Dare," Forrest says quietly, nodding.

"Sir," we answer.

He tucks his hands under his arms and looks up at the bodies. "The colonel—well, we need to get these men down. You can't hold the line when your buddies are done up like this."

"Sir—" I glance at Fish, and he nods—"we want to help."

Nothing could prepare me for the way their bodies feel. Maybe I've been working on the living so much that I half-expected them to be warm. But rigor mortis has set in, and as Fish and I hold Halloran's legs while Winger cuts the lines with his trench knife, the cold of the body frightens me.

I turn my face away so Fish can't see the tears in my eyes. A year in combat and it's taken getting here, to the blossoming churchyard of Ste.-Mère-Église, for me to run out of words to put to this war.

All we can do is get them down and wait for the grave crew to come for the bodies. I can't even reassure them, right at the end, that it will be okay. That they'll make it home. They were slaughtered without a fighting chance.

Lieutenant Forrest collects their dog tags. We lay the bodies in the dust of the churchyard, where petals have been crushed under trampling feet, and cover them with their parachutes. And then there's only one left, and when Lieutenant Winger and the two privates lay him down, Fish and I let out our collective breath.

Not Peter. Not anyone from the second stick—they're all from headquarters and 1st platoon, missing their drop zone by a few yards. I look at their covered bodies and repeat each name silently to myself. Danny Taylor, Walter Weston, Jimmy Halloran, and Michael Cotter, all enlisted men barely out of high school. Nicholas Hughes and Eugene Hill were officers. Two of the good ones.

Lieutenant Forrest kneels beside Taylor's head, clutching a leather-bound New Testament as he murmurs, "'I will not leave you comfortless; I will come to you.'" From the Gospel of John, at the Lord's table before he went to the cross.

Bursts of machine-gun fire at the cemetery line cut into his voice. The early summer day is cold on my neck as I watch. He moves to Walter, praying scripture aloud and then closing his eyes to pray silently.

I see Walsh's face in theirs. Like Walsh, each died alone.

"'Then shall be brought to pass the saying that is written,'" Lieutenant Forrest prays, "'death is swallowed up in victory. O death, where is thy sting? O grave, where is thy victory?'"

Fish glances at me, but I can't meet his eyes. I fight the urge to grab Forrest by the jacket and shout, *This—this is the sting! This is the victory!* And then I feel a revulsion at myself, that I've said and believed those things, too, that I assumed a grave or a parachute shroud held no stretch of ground won in some cosmic battle. Try telling these men's families this isn't a victory for death.

Last night when the roar of the C-47 engines and the artillery drowned out my voice so I felt the shape of the Psalm more than I heard it—who did I say that prayer for, to comfort Thomas Walsh or myself?

This fucking war.

I kneel beside Forrest, hearing my dad's voice in my mind as the chaplain prays, and I take out my tag booklet to begin labelling the bodies.

XI.

SUMMER

June 1945

The heady scent of night phlox floats through the air as we slip and hop down the steep incline of the river bluffs. I hold onto Mattie's elbow to balance him, though he says he'd crawl if he had to. Sapphire water glistens through the rustling trees. It'll be bone-cold, the way we like it.

I told Laurie we'd make it just fine, so he went on ahead with Helen, Toni, Hen, and our picnic baskets, but Grace has hung back. The short white dress over her swimsuit ruffles out in the wind, and she claps a hand on the kerchief in her hair to keep it from blowing off. She walks ahead of Mattie and me, pointing out familiar pine trees and rocks, all the places we used to climb to look out over the river. Silk spider webs shimmer between branches and a swallowtail butterfly flaps past, the color of the tangerines the Moroccan vendors sold in the souks we passed through on our way to Tunisia. Grace reaches her hand out and with a gentle flutter the butterfly lands on her finger, so still for a moment that its dusty, veined wings are lit by the sun, the edges burnt black and freckled with white like a doe's coat. She glances back at us with a grin.

The butterfly lifts off and disappears into the woods. She watches it go, hair sweeping her collarbone as she turns her head. I wish I could save this moment as a postcard to look back at in the winter: Grace on the path framed by the pine forest, squinting in the sunlight, with the river filling the horizon beyond her. Watching her, I'm not sure if it's love or just summer.

She reaches for a handful of strawberries clustered in the foliage alongside the path. Slipping the kerchief off her hair, she gathers the berries in the green fabric and ties it off like a cartoon hobo's bundle. "You boys want some?"

"You may feed me one when I make it to the bottom alive," Mattie answers.

Before I can say anything, Grace comes over to me and drops a couple of berries into my hand.

"They taste best in June," she says, flicking a leafy green top away.

We pick our way along the path as it snakes through the rocks and the berry thickets. Below us the river currents thread over one another and gather in little pools among the granite ledges. Even the ducks shaking their tail feathers in the shallows look happy that Maine is warm again. Grace glances over her shoulder at me, an expression of concern for Mattie and I in her eyes, and nods to the water and the old trestle bridge. *Go on*, I mouth, and she smiles and disappears around the curve in the path.

Mattie and I take our time. Getting back up will be a trick, but none of us would ever dream of leaving him out. Times change and folks grow up and some lose their legs or a lung and you adjust, but you don't let go. At last we reach the bridge spanning the shallow part of the river. Scrubby honeysuckle bushes dot the sandbars, where the others are already wading. Grace and Helen pair up against Laurie and Antonia, two fair heads against two dark ones, and the pool becomes a maelstrom of white waves. Hen bounces between them, taking no one's side.

I hold onto Mattie as he lowers himself carefully to sit on the bridge. He can't get the prosthetic wet, and making it to the water without it would be impossible. He bends his real leg at the knee, leans back on his hands, and stretches the prosthetic out in front of him. I sit beside him and dangle my legs over the edge of the bridge, staring down into the slow current as it spills clear across the rocks. It's odd to be here and not watch Mattie beat everyone else down to the water, lying in wait with wet mud or a worm to stick down one of the girls' swimsuits.

I nod at his prosthetic. "Is it a pain in the ass at night when you have to go to the bathroom?"

"Yeah, you have no idea." He snorts, then reaches behind him for his Red Sox cap as we watch the others in the river. Toni waves at us, and we wave back. For the first time in the more than ten years I've known him, Mattie looks wistful.

Grace walks up the path on her toes to avoid the sandspurs. On the bridge, wrapping her arms about her middle and looking cold as wet hair clings to her forehead and neck, she says earnestly, "Cutest one-legged boy in all of northern Maine, Mattie."

He grins up at her. "Can't imagine I have much competition."

"You're in a league of your own." She disappears into the trees and reappears wading into the water, across from the other three, making for the flowering thickets that grow sprawling on the sandbar in the middle of the little pool. The blackberries won't be in season till late July, but blush honeysuckle and star-petaled goldthread grow there, too.

I push up the sleeves of my flannel shirt and brace my hands on the crossbeam that spans the trestle, leaning forward to watch for minnows in the water, although I'm really flicking my eyes up to Grace every so often.

"I'm not as good at saying things as you are," Mattie remarks after a minute. I feel his eyes on me, and I tear my attention away from Grace on the sandbar and look at him.

"Unless it's flirting with Helen?"

"Sure, unless it's Helen. But it means a lot that you haven't just ignored it. And I know I can't do everything now that I used to, and you guys know that, but you..."

He trails off. After a few moments, he adds, "You're the only one who knows how it was, I guess. How it is."

"What happened doesn't make you any less of yourself, not to us. And whatever we do, you can bet we're dragging you with us, even if we have to carry your sorry ass."

"Aren't you getting in?"

"You're sure you don't mind?"

"I'm touched by your thoughtfulness, but I'm a lot warmer up here in the sun than you'll be."

I stand and say, "I guess I'll go down."

"You still have to get undressed."

"Geez, Mattie, stop flirting with me."

"C'mon, Dick." He tilts his head at me condescendingly. "They're all going to see eventually anyway. Could anything be worse than half a leg?"

When I toss my shirt on the rest of my clothes on the bridge, Mattie whistles and I almost pick it up to put back on so I don't feel so much like an exhibition. I leave him on the bridge—a reckless choice considering he's up there alone with our lunch baskets—and walk to the path in the trees. It curves steeply through blankets of pine needles and levels out at the smooth stones along the water's edge. Helen laughs as I step into the water and wince at the temperature. Little eddies from the current swirl about my ankles and flow on under the bridge. Laurie's making a lazy effort to poke at fish with a stick, and Grace and Toni are lying on their backs on the sandbar.

"Richard," Grace says I wade in, "will you please tell Toni she's crazy?"

"Toni, you're crazy," I say to Antonia, on general principle, and she grins languidly up at me, too content on the sandy verge between blackberry bushes and water to put up a fight. "What for?"

"She thinks Bogart is more of a sex symbol than James Stewart," Helen answers. "Sorry, Grace, I have to side with her on this one."

Grace sits up and drops a handful of sand onto Toni's stomach. "You're both ridiculous. Bogart's always so, 'Look at me in my trench coat holding this big cigar, and we'll always have Paris, darling,' et cetera et cetera and he's only sexy because he's so mysterious. James Stewart has a personality. Charm. Don't those count for anything?"

"He's also got ears the size of my father's Buick. And so what if I want a mysterious personality?" Toni adds without much fervor. "I like the stoic, cryptic types. They're always ready to sweep you off on an adventure."

"I don't know if I want to go on an adventure." Grace leans back on her hands and squints. "I just want a nice, quiet life."

"Married to James Stewart?" I say. I try to imagine what he would say to woo her, but all I can think about is Toni's observation of his ears.

She smiles. "If he'll have me. But if not, I'm sure I can arrange something else."

"Oh, I'm sure you can," Laurie remarks, cryptically enough to make Bogart proud.

I watch the glow that seeps through the water as the light moves across it. All the science in the world about tides and currents could never sufficiently explain to me why water moves as it does, running together and then apart and then together again seamlessly, like a zipper up the back of an evening gown. I look from the water to Grace as the others talk and laugh. She picks more goldthread, crossing her legs in front of herself and threading the ends together. We ran together and then apart, further apart than I ever imagined we would. And despite all the obstacles in their way, the disparate streams always come back together, the river returning over and over to itself, two currents continually flowing in and out of one another. Like hands held, let go of, held again.

Mattie waves to us and calls out that he's going to eat all the food and if we want any, we'd better come. Up on the bridge, we spread it all out. The hot sun dries the water off our skin as we pick through bread and cheese and jars of blueberry preserves, and Grace's Scottish shortbread, which is saltier than it used to be thanks to sugar rationing. Helen brought leftover chicken and half a sweet potato pie from the hotel. We divide it carefully six ways. Mattie contributes some cheap wine, glinting cherry-red as we pour it from the green glass bottle into paper cups.

Once most of the food is gone, the sun beats odd patterns through my closed eyelids as I lie on my back. I lose track of the conversation, a low background hum moving in rhythm with the river below us.

Someone kicks my leg, and I open one eye. Laurie pokes me again with his foot. "You forgot to tell them, didn't you?"

"Tell them what?"

He snorts and says, "I'll tell them, then, if you're too busy daydreaming." Turning back to the others, he announces, "*This one* got a job at Linstead's practice, and he doesn't think it matters."

I sit up as the others pepper me with questions: "When did this happen?" and "When do you start?" and "So the war really did make a doctor out of you, huh?"—that last one from Mattie, as if the only qualification for becoming a doctor is asking the local physician if it's okay with him.

"I was there last week to pick up a prescription for my mom," I say, "and you remember Mrs. Carr, that old widow who's been his secretary forever?"

"Oh, she retired," Toni comments, popping a grape into her mouth. "My aunt plays bridge with her."

"You're a secretary?" Mattie sits right up, mouth open and eyes dancing with piqued interest.

I throw a grape at his head. It hits him satisfyingly on the ear and falls between the slats to the river. "It was this or working Don Harrels' soda counter. Anyway, I noticed she wasn't there and Linstead and I got to talking, and he's running himself ragged trying to do everything. He pays more than Harrels, and it won't be as sticky. I start on Monday."

"Given the right patient, I should think a doctor's office is far stickier than a soda counter," says Mattie, who can't seem to decide which of his quips to get out first.

"I won't be assisting with surgery, you idiot. I'm filing his patients' records and answering the phone and running errands."

"You have an incredible talent for making everything as boring as possible." He sniffs and then tries to take the last bit of Toni's pie when he thinks she isn't looking, but she smacks his hand away like she would a fly.

Grace pushes her sunglasses up onto her head and smiles at me. "I think you'll make a wonderful secretary."

"Actually," Mattie adds, crunching on a saltine, "I've got myself a new gig, too. Helen's trying me on for size."

I look from him to her. "Helen's paying you to be her call boy? How sweet."

"Wait, is that—would you consider that, Helen?"

"Thanks, Richard, giving him ideas. C'mon," Helen says to Mattie with an incline of her head, "tell the truth, fool."

"It's just that, isn't it? I'm Helen's new musical fool." Mattie grins at her, and she rolls her eyes. "Two nights a week, playing at the hotel. 'Trial basis,' Mr. Helen's Dad says, if I behave myself."

"It was between him and Eleanor Hartman," Helen says in a pained voice, as though she feels an explanation is necessary.

Laurie snorts. "Our church pianist? Can you imagine, the liquor flowing and the couples lindyhopping and then 'Come Thou Fount of Every Blessing' starts."

Grace uncorks the wine and refills the cups, then holds hers in the air. "Speaking of drinks. To Toni's birthday this past Wednesday, and Richard's tomorrow—and to his new job *and* Mattie's, well done, you two—a toast." She tries to clink her cup with mine, but paper is a poor substitute for a wineglass, and the sides of our cups just crumple in depressingly.

There's something else we haven't toasted yet. Grace knocks her knee into mine, smiling as the sun brushes her shoulders, so I say, "To Sidney and Lena, too, and to the hope they'll join us soon enough—congratulations on the new sibling, Miss Whitley, it's a girl."

She laughs and everyone toasts Sidney and Lena, shame they aren't here to see it. As the sun falls below the hills, lighting the river downstream in moving watercolors, we all go quiet for a while, lost in memories or worries. Grace is watching the water tumble over itself into the rock hollows, and I watch her, glancing away now and then to follow the swallows across the filmy sky. If we were alone here...

"Isn't it odd we all came back here?" Toni wonders into the stillness. "Caspar, of all places, when we had every chance to escape. Some of us more than others," she adds, glancing at Mattie and then me.

Helen hums in agreement and says, "I didn't really think we'd all still be single now. Except Laurie, of course. Is that a sign of something for the rest of us?"

"It's a sign that you stubbornly refuse to let me take you out," Mattie remarks, at which Helen rolls her eyes again.

Laurie says, "Faye wouldn't mind setting you up with some of her Bangor friends, I bet, if anyone needs a break from the Caspar pickings."

"'Pickings' makes us sound like the last of the runt piglets to be auctioned off at the county fair," Grace laughs, wrapping her arms around her legs as she turns back from watching the river to face the others.

"Well, you can't be too picky in Caspar. We don't all have a handsome Navy boyfriend proposing to us." Toni says it with her usual good-natured humor, but as soon as she does, she presses her mouth together. The strangest expression passes over her face. If I hadn't happened to be facing them, I would've missed the even odder moment between her and Grace. Toni looks as guilty as she used to when she'd let slip the ending of a film the rest of us hadn't seen yet; she never was good at keeping secrets. Helen bites her lip and looks at Grace with a concern that seems to frustrate Grace.

"What's this?" Mattie leans forward, lowering the wine bottle that he'd been about to tilt up to his mouth. "Who has the handsome Navy boyfriend?"

"No one," says Grace, her shoulders drawing together.

"He has to be *someone*—"

Mattie doesn't mean anything by it, he never does, and I've never known Grace not to laugh and then dish it back to him when he needles her. But she cuts him off with an irritation completely unlike her: "He's no one. He doesn't matter. He was a stupid boy in Boston who thought he wanted to marry me, and I didn't want to marry him and that's that. He's gone."

"Grace, I'm sorry, I shouldn't have..." Toni's voice trails away. Then she adds, with more conviction, "That wasn't my story to bring up. I'm sorry."

"It's okay, Toni," Grace says, the irritation gone from her voice. "He was just a boy who got ahead of himself, falling over his own feet to propose when he hardly knew me."

I had dates in college, Jenny in England. But I never got anywhere near a proposal with any of them, and for some reason I never imagined that Grace could, either. *Just a boy who got ahead of himself.*

After a minute, Helen clears her throat and says, "I ought to be getting home…"

"Right, me too—goats to feed." Grace stands and dusts pie crumbs off her swimsuit. "That was a lovely afternoon. Let's go again soon."

Toni looks as if she'd like to crawl beneath the bridge trestle and hang there till we all leave, but she hauls herself to her feet and helps me gather the remnants of the picnic.

"I'll get that. You go on ahead with Mattie," says Grace, holding out her hand for the basket. Happy for the escape route, Toni gives it to her and she and Helen start up the path with Mattie between them.

Laurie glances at me, one eyebrow raised when Grace is bent to gather up the paper cups and can't see us. *I don't know,* I mouth, which seems like the answer to any question he could ask me. He must feel himself a third wheel because he wordlessly pats my shoulder and follows the girls and Mattie off the bridge into the gray-lit trees.

I crumple the aluminium foil and stick it in the basket beside the pie dish. We crouch at the same time to pick up the utensils. Grace glances at me, barely raising her head, and tries to smile, but it falls away.

"Sorry about that," she says. In the trees around us, the frogs are beginning their opening act of the evening.

"What for? Toni not being able to keep a secret?"

Her damp hair falls in front of her eyes as she deposits a handful of utensils in the picnic basket. "I guess I didn't want you to think any less of me."

"How could I ever do that?" I pause in stacking the plates, jarred at the very idea.

"I don't know." Grace shakes her head and rests her elbows on her knees, head turned to look out at the silvering of the water. A trio of swallows swoop through the dusk with a soft rush of wings. "It just seems so trivial, compared to—"

She doesn't finish, but I hear the end of that sentence anyway. I bite my tongue. One of these days I won't bite it in time to keep from snapping at someone that the lives they led here while some of us were overseas were every bit as worthy in their joys and pains as any suffering we experienced.

"What happened to not much of a social life," I say instead, forcing the corners of my mouth into a light smile, "and only the girls at the Red Cross rolling bandages on Friday nights?"

Grace looks up at me at last, and a hint of a smile plays at her mouth, too. "That was true. Especially after I said no to a marriage proposal."

"Well, and a good thing." I stand, stiff knees cracking, and hold my hand to her. "You have to hold out for Jimmy, after all."

She laughs a little, which I consider victory enough. Then she takes my hand, and I pull her to her feet. I take the picnic basket and we walk up the path wordlessly. If she wants to tell me about it, she will.

When we reach Helen's car at the head of the logging road, I say that Laurie and Hen and I will walk home instead. We watch as the girls and Mattie drive off, and then Laurie says, "Good talk?"

"Sort of." I shrug, casting a glance at him. "She'll tell me more when she's ready. Maybe."

We emerge from the woods and walk up the dirt road through the farmland. A few Caspar lights are coming on in the distance. Laurie is quiet for a while until we cross from the river road to Queen Street, when he says into the twilight, "So she didn't tell you anything?"

"Not really—not about him, at least. You didn't know anything about it?"

"Handsome Navy boyfriend in Boston is news to me."

"I guess it shouldn't matter to me."

He shrugs. "I don't know. Only you can decide that. But," he adds, "does this mean maybe you'll finally do something about her? Was ten years long enough for the feelings to percolate?"

"I don't know what to think about those feelings anymore."

Laurie looks at me, but doesn't say anything. Finally I add, "I was in love with her when I was nineteen. That's puppy love, you know? Even without what came after."

"So you're not in love with her?"

"I don't know, Laurie. Even if I am, it's not fair to her."

"How so?"

"Well, if I were her, I'd probably rather stay single than settle for me."

Brow furrowed, Laurie says, "If that's you fishing for some reassurance—"

"It's not."

We walk in silence, my words lingering in the dusk between us, till I say, "Maybe..."

"What?"

"Maybe she should've said yes to him."

Laurie gives me a reproving look as he tugs on the white towel draped over his shoulders. "Richard, you have no idea who the hell this guy is. You're going to cast your girl to him?"

"She's not my girl, and that's not it. If it wasn't him, then there would've been someone else. And some Navy officer with old money Boston parents is a far better marriage than...damaged goods."

"Don't call yourself that—"

"What would you call it?"

"Shit, I don't know, but there's nothing wrong with you. I mean, it's not like the shell blew off your balls and you can't marry her because you can never satisfy her or father her children, à la *The Sun Also Rises* or whatever."

"Do we have to talk about this?"

"I know you hate it because you're a Puritan like Dad, but I'm just reminding you that you have nothing to worry about there. Unless there's something you didn't tell us…? No, okay. I mean, your lungs aren't much better when it comes to wedding night concerns—"

"God, Laurie."

"Okay! I'm done."

We walk along as the light trickles below the mountains. The white clapboard houses of Queen Street look like delapidated ghosts set back from the road. We say hello to Walter Perrin, the town flaneur sitting on his porch with his pipe in mouth. He nods and lifts his hand as we pass.

"Oh, boys," Mom calls from her vegetable patch under the kitchen window as we come up the sidewalk, "come see this slug I found. He's huge. I know it's him who's been eating my lettuce. Laurie, go get the table salt—"

"Don't salt him!" I drop my towel and the picnic basket in the grass and go to the slug's rescue. He is huge, and I think about how funny it would be just to fling him into the air toward the woods, or drop him into Laurie's hair, but I dutifully deposit him on a rock behind the toolshed instead. At least it'll take him a few days to make his way back to the lettuce.

"I forgot what it's like having you around, *yiannaki.*" Mom strips off her gardening gloves as I come back. "No pest can ever be killed; it must be rehomed."

"God created the slugs, too."

Laurie, ironically, swats a mosquito dead on his arm right then, but I have no wish to rehome mosquitoes. "But wouldn't you say that most pests exist now in their post-fall state?" he wonders. "What would a slug have been in Eden?"

"Probably still eating Eve's lettuce, and she had no way to get rid of it," says Mom decisively. "Are you hungry? There's moussaka from Thursday in the freezer."

B lue-tinged candle flames flicker in the wind, stretching toward the porch screens and snapping back. I strike another match and light the last wick. In the center of the table is a bunch of lavender from Mom's garden, which she tied with twine and dropped in a little cut-glass vase. The wind settles into a breeze that lifts the flower heads in the garden and blows gently through the screens, and the candle flames stand up straight and glowing, as if to stand attention for the longest days of the year.

Laurie comes out to the porch from the kitchen with two bottles of wine in his hands, raising them aloft as if he expects us to drink one apiece.

"Since when could we afford more than one?" I say, shaking the match out. "Or even one."

"We can't. These are from Dave, you know, one of the editors at the paper? His in-laws left it with them"—he sets the bottles down—"and they don't drink white, so I brought it home. He says to tell you happy birthday, by the way."

"Thanks, Dave. Does Mom need help?"

"She just swatted Dad and me out of the kitchen with a dish towel, so I think we're safer out here." He smooths out the cloth napkins and folds them, and then lays out the silverware on them, making the porch table look like it's laid out for a cocktail party, even though it's just us tonight.

We sit and after a minute, Laurie says, "I haven't asked you yet about going back to school. Should I?"

I reach for one of the wine bottles and the corkscrew next to it and say, "I don't think it's that easy."

"You should take advantage of the GI bill."

I look up as I work on the corkscrew. "You think so?"

"Yeah, the GI bill, you know, you can get free—"

"I know what it is."

"You don't want to let the government pay your tuition, after what you did for them?"

The bottleneck is damp with condensation and my hand, slippery against it, feels unsteady. Not willing to risk stabbing myself in the thigh with the corkscrew, I put it and the bottle back on the table, where water droplets melt into the linen tablecloth. "Don't say that, Laur. Or think of it that way. I didn't do anything for them. The government doesn't owe me free tuition."

"Ah, the natural Dare modesty," he says, tilting his chair back on two legs. "Now just admit that you deserve something. So you got fifty extra dollars a month for being a paratrooper? Can you really put a price on what you—"

"You are." I shrug. "Free tuition is an exchange, too."

Laurie takes up the corkscrew and works on the bottle. "I know you too well. You'll never be happy with a job here in Caspar, working at a doctor's office." He taps his temple. "Too much of an intellectual, even though you won't admit it."

A few minutes later I hold Laurie's hand in my right and Mom's in my left as Dad says grace. When our eyes are closed and our heads are bowed, he clears his throat, and after a few moments he thanks the Lord for a beautiful day and asks a blessing over the food. He pauses, and I shift slightly, preparing to get comfortable for the long haul. The warm pita bread is right under my nose. I hunch forward slightly as my stomach growls loud enough to be heard in New Hampshire, and I can feel Laurie trying not to laugh.

"And I thank you for Lizzie," he continues as the cricket song grows louder past the screens. "And for our boys. Tonight, especially, for bringing Richard home to us."

"Quickest one ever, Dad," says Laurie a few seconds later, after the three of us, startled, follow Dad's 'Amen' with our own. "Clocking in under thirty seconds."

"Well, God knows everything we don't say. Besides, the dinner's getting cold." He passes the roasted potatoes to Mom. If I'd not been paying attention, I would've missed the half-second glance he gives me, that hint of a smile, because only on June 29th does he shorten his prayers to accommodate my discomfort at being the center of attention.

We sit for an hour after the spanakopita and tzatziki are gone. My seat faces the yard, and in the clovered grass and webs of leaves and the knotted trunk of the apple tree, everywhere light can gather, it's as though a million candles have been lit. I refill the wine glasses as the wicks burn down. The screen door with the broken latch bangs against its frame in the wind. There's laughter, and I smile, leaning back in my chair and stretching my neck to see the fading daylight beyond the porch beams. Even so, it feels like part of me has separated from the rest of my body and is sitting here with them, while I watch from the stairs inside, hearing the faint note of untruth in my laugh.

The last time I had a birthday at home I was someone else completely. Still had the baby fat in my cheeks. And at that time I still harbored a belief in absolutes that didn't come and go with the tides, a naïve assumption in the goodness of the world that I don't see now in the blue light as dusk falls. Only what lies beneath it, pulsing like a wound.

There's nothing very much different about the Dares now than in 1942. For that matter, unless you go looking for the gaps in families, Caspar appears to have hung in stasis throughout the war, too. To come home and find everything different and unfamiliar, that was what my friends and I were afraid of, though we rarely voiced that fear. But maybe I shouldn't have been afraid that life here would move on without me while I was gone, because it seems irrevocably clear now that what I should have feared was coming home to walk alone on a road none of my family have ever known. To be among them but to never really be with them.

"Richard?"

I snap back.

"You keep doing that," Mom says gently. "Getting lost somewhere up there."

Dad's voice is measuredly lighthearted as he asks, "What're you thinking about?"

"Oh, I don't know," I say, fiddling with the crumpled ends of my napkin. I search for something innocuous to offer. "Just thinking about how things here haven't changed—"

A shot sounds from the road, a bang as distinct as a rifle shot, and next thing I know I'm on my feet staring out the screen at the dusk, listening for the screams that are sure to follow. Someone says my name distantly as bright light pops in and out of my vision. The bang fills my ears, all the air flees my lungs; my chest and hands are suddenly clammy as my throat closes up.

That sound, again and again and again, the quick release and fire hurtling on a path to kill and maim. I feel their blood, the stumps and shattered bone fragments of blown-off limbs, the warm, slippery, ruptured organs. They need me. But everything goes black and I don't know where I am, the rush of my hyperventilation consuming even the repetitive shot ricocheting through my mind.

...

Richard. It's okay. You're at home. You're with us.

I lift my head. Watery shapes hover before me.

Richard.

I press the heel of my hand to my eye. My cheeks are wet.

Then the voice rises to the surface. "Richard, it's okay," it says, and I sense more than see Dad crouched beside me. He talks to me quietly as my breathing trips over itself. The porch begins to tip alarmingly sideways and I plant one hand on the wooden slats, trying to force breath into my lungs, panic rising when none comes.

I feel something on my back, and I jerk away and hear my disembodied voice saying, "Don't touch me—"

"I'm sorry. Can you hear me?"

"Yes..."

"It was only a car backfiring. It's okay—there's nothing out there."

It's not real, I tell myself, but my body hasn't caught up. Gradually his face comes into focus, gray eyes watching me with worry.

I hunch forward till my head is between my knees. The salty taste of tears fills my mouth. I feel them watching me. My discomfort grows into revulsion till I wish I could break out of this body, throw a match on it, and watch the flames light up Caspar. I wish I could become unknown. They all saw every humiliating moment.

One small breath leads to another. Dad says, "All right, there you go. Feel a little better?"

The dizziness fades, but anger flows in like a tide to take its place. Mom and Laurie are standing behind him, their expressions a cocktail of concern, pity, and shame, as if they could be more embarrassed to have witnessed this than I am at causing it.

Dad reaches out a hand to help me up from the floor of the porch and I push him away, shaking my head but not finding any words.

He backs away. A silence falls on the porch. I press my face to my hands and hope if I try hard enough, I can disappear, or at least make the last five minutes come untrue.

Finally I plant one hand on the floor and push myself up on shaky knees. Mom and Laurie ask at the same time if I'm okay.

"I'm fine."

The porch air is so warm, and their faces are all so close to mine. I go back to the table and sit, propping my elbows on the cloth. The only thing worse than what just happened would be to flee inside and let my absence fill this seat. If I do that, it's all they'll remember.

But it's also clear that the night has been spoiled. Laurie stacks the dirty dishes and slips into the kitchen. Mom and Dad both sit again, apparently thinking that I won't notice the silent communication, the telling glances passing between them. The silence lasts a long time. In the woods the frog song has grown so loud that it could probably drown out a backfiring car now. Finally Mom reaches out, puts her hand over mine, and says quietly, as if a neighbor might be listening at the fence, "I know that it must be hard to talk about some things, but your dad has worked with men who fought, who went through the same things you did…"

She says more that I don't hear because I'm giving her until the count of ten to get her hand off mine. I stare at the dull pearl of her engagement ring, simmering at their compulsive need to be so gentle with me.

I pull my hand away, skin still tingling at the touch. Neither of them acknowledge it. I realize it's gone quiet and that she's waiting for me to answer. They both look so desperate for me to give in, maybe even assuming that I'll be grateful if I do—"of course you were right, this is better," all that bullshit that would apply to some single, tangible sin weighing on my conscience. If it were so easy, we wouldn't be sitting here pretending I'm not as spooky as a rabbit.

"Thanks, but I'm not like Dad's Great War veterans, okay? That was...well, I don't know, but I'm not crazy."

"I didn't say you were," Mom begins, "but..."

They glance at one another, a look perhaps meant to be subtle but that is glaringly obvious to me. Their faces hold the exact same expression, lines of worry drawn in the same places. Maybe that's just what happens when you've been married long enough, but there's something odd in it.

"What?" I say, looking between them. "What was that?"

When Dad hesitates in answering, I scoot my chair back and stand. "If you want to use those poor guys as a cautionary tale for me, then...go ahead, I guess. But I don't need to talk about things, okay? There's nothing to talk about. I just want to get on with it. It's not like I've lost my mind like they did. And I don't need a chaplain the same way they did. I'm not dying."

Before either of them has a chance to answer, I go in, letting the screen door flap shut behind me.

XII.

FOXHOLES

19 June 1944, Le Bois de Limors, Normandy, 2145 hours

"Berk, if I was still in England, the last thing on my mind would be drinking."

"So you're telling me," Berkowicz leans forward, dipping a spoon from his mess kit into the .50 cal ammo box he's using as a coffee pot, "that you couldn't go for a nice stiff finger or three of Scotch?"

"What I'm telling you is if we were on leave in London, I'd be asleep in the hotel bathtub." I set my elbows on my knees as I crouch at the lip of his foxhole. "So where's your other half?"

"Nuts? He said he had social calls to make." He tastes the coffee off the spoon and grimaces. "Think if I try hard enough, I can imagine this is Scotch?"

"Maybe if your sandfly fever comes back and you start hallucinating."

"It ain't as though I have the freshest ingredients to begin with. I'm sorry the Army doesn't issue me coffee beans straight from Greece—"

"Christ, it smells like feet over here." McNulty appears in a low silhouette against the yellow French twilight. "Gentlemen. Guess who just scored two packs of Lucky Strikes off the mortar boys?"

Berk scrambles up. "You're shittin' me."

"Did you steal them?" I say as McNuts lights one up and passes it to me.

"Traded 'em. You know in those film noirs, there's always some guy in a trenchcoat and he opens it up and there's a hundred fucking things in there, watches and cigars and a hot cup of coffee and shit? That's Skinny. The guy in the trenchcoat."

"Film noir? I think the hot cup of coffee was Harpo Marx."

"He's pretentious about coffee, too," Berk says to McNuts, as though they've been comparing notes about me. He holds out the ammo case, sloshing it around. "Want some?"

McNuts gags in reply.

"I'm not pretentious. All I said was that I'd literally rather drink this mud. Because I have standards," I add.

"Fuck your standards. You want the sheets turned down, too, and a rose on the pillow?"

I flick the glowing cigarette butt at him. "If it wouldn't put you out." Then I realize what he said when McNuts interrupted him. "Wait, you think coffee beans come from *Greece?*"

"Sure, they're exotic, ain't they?" Berk leans back against the dirt wall of their hole as McNuts jumps down. It isn't the commissary that Santorini's foxhole is, but it's cozy. They've even got a green tarpaulin stretched across the muddy ground. "What'd you trade for the smokes, Nuts?"

"My extra pair of socks."

"You traded your *socks?*" I reach down to smack his helmet, and he yelps. "The hell is wrong with you? Charlie, you're going to give yourself trench foot, and guess whose problem *that* turns into?"

"Yours," the two of them drone in unison like scolded children.

"Yeah, mine. We can't afford to lose you to the aid station or worse."

"Oh, I ain't going to no aid station. You wanna see them?" McNuts tugs out his laces and slides off his boot.

"And you were the one bitching that it smells like feet down here. I wonder why," Berk mutters.

McNuts slides off one of his socks, damp with a couple of holes, and with a grunt he props up his leg and wiggles his toes at me. "Look at these toes and tell me you see a spot of trench foot, Rev."

"They look fine now, but what happens when you can't change your socks? If your feet stay wet, those toes'll start going black."

"Bet you all your morphine I can cut myself a deal before it gets to that."

"Well, fine," I give in, losing steam for the argument as this doesn't seem like a hill to die on. "What's sharing socks between guys who share latrines?" I tap my collarbone. "But I want you to dry those out first chance you get. Boots off, socks around your neck. If it rains, you put the boots right back on. Any wetter than they are now, and you won't be able to."

McNuts sighs, but he drapes the socks around his dirty neck like a bacteria-laden Christmas garland. "You know you nag, don't ya?"

"All right, wise-ass, consider it a wedding present. The only thing I hate more than Berk's coffee is trench foot."

"Harry Berkowicz's all-purpose war ailment cure: coffee that burns right through your small intestine," Berk says. *"L'chaim,* or—what is it your family says, Rev?"

"Yamas."

"Yamas, ladies," he announces, and downs it like a shot.

The night is eerily quiet, only whispers here and there from nearby foxholes. I make out the forms of two officers walking under the trees a few yards off. We took a hard hit in casualties the last three days to take the town of Saint-Sauveur-le-Vicomte, and the line is spread thin. Word down from division headquarters is that we're getting replacements as soon as we get back to England, but a shit ton of good that does us right now, camped out in the mud under impenetrable hedgerows in the Bois de Limors forest in Normandy.

"You know who I miss?" McNuts stretches his legs out as much as he can in a tight hole. "Lettie back in Quorn."

Berk grimaces at his second sip of coffee. "I thought her name was Lottie."

"Was it? Huh. Maybe so."

"You two doing okay?" I glance between them, their faces hard to make out in the falling dusk. "Besides the imminent trench foot."

"Yeah, we're okay—you okay, Nuts?" Berk says, and McNuts shrugs. "Don't fret yourself over us, Rev. We hold up pretty good."

"It'll probably go in one ear and out the other if I tell you to be careful."

"What's that?" McNuts says, cupping a hand to his ear innocently, and I kick him with the toe of my boot.

"Sleep tight, you two," I say. "I've gotta go check the boys on the line."

"Sweet dreams, Rev," Berk calls, and McNuts flaps one of the socks around his neck at me.

I walk with my hands in my jacket pockets, collar open to the warm night air. We got showers four or five days ago back in Picauville when they took us off the line for a day. By our standards, a shower four days ago means you're fresh as a daisy. Last night I shaved in the side mirror of a supply truck parked on the western road out of Saint-Sauveur after we'd set up our roadblocks there. Maybe tomorrow we'll find a creek to bathe in. You make do and thank God we all have numbed senses of smell.

Under the trees the light is a soft gray, disarmingly peaceful even though there's a German battery not half a mile away. I go among foxholes and check on the 3rd platoon boys, crouching at the edges to shoot the shit with them. That's the only way we've stayed sane. Some minds are stronger than others, and there's no telling what one guy will withstand when same event breaks another. Last night Lieutenant Winger sent a rifleman, Ray Allison, off the line to battalion HQ to be a runner for the XO, because Ray was shredding his fingernails down to the cuticles and about shit himself at every rustle in the trees. No one held it against him.

I don't stay long at any one foxhole, always on the move, like a hummingbird searching for nectar. In Sicily, we all learned how many interminable hours of waiting frame five minutes of action—action that, if God is on our side, ends without casualties. The best possible outcome is that no one needs me. I only treat wounded men in brief snatches, but the moments are so heightened in pain that they feel like a thousand years. Then the boys wait days at a time marching and digging holes without a trace of the Germans, forced to listen to me nag them about trench foot and gonorrhea and *I swear to God, McNuts, if you shack up with another French whore and come down with a venereal disease—*

Anyway, there's so little I can do to relieve their boredom and their nerves and their exhaustion, when it's my charge to take care of them. So I make my rounds with these small things, talking to them and trying to making them laugh to take their minds off home and pain and their girls, anything to remind a guy he's not alone. It'd feel like a dereliction of duty if I didn't.

Farm boys, city kids, guys like me from small towns no one's ever heard of, all our lives as wildly different as strangers from distant planets—it's still the most confounding experience I've ever known, being bound together tighter than brothers. An army of citizen soldiers.

"Dare," someone whispers behind me, and I turn.

Lieutenant Greer is coming through the trees, holding the strap of his rifle hanging from his shoulder. The guys all respected Lieutenant

Walsh but I know they thought of him as a tight-ass, not the kind of man you could just have a beer with, not that officers and enlisted should fraternize like that anyway. But Greer has been a favorite among us all since he was transferred to the 2nd battalion in North Africa. He's tall and lanky and mostly elbows, and if you watch him from behind you can see how pigeon-toed he is; the arches of his jump boots must be collapsed. Before Officers Candidate School at the University of Washington, he was a farm boy, picking cherries in his parents' orchard every summer. He laughs easily but he also takes good care of us, always asking how we're doing, making sure that our minds are holding up. I've met and answered "yes sir" to enough officers to know how many of them aren't competent even of remembering their boys' names, but Greer is the kind of leader you always hope to have.

Of course, the relief of him as our platoon leader is tempered by the fact that he wouldn't be if Walsh hadn't died on D-Day, but my agonizing over the past doesn't do the guys any good.

"Evening, sir," I say.

"Pretty, isn't it?" Greer chews gum as he looks up at the sky.

"Nice to see a sky without smoke in it."

"How are you on supplies? Captain Robinson just got off the phone with division, told me we aren't getting resupplied anytime soon. So whatever you've got and can scrounge is it."

"I thought that might be the case. I've gotten good at rationing."

"I wish you didn't have to make those choices." He shakes his head. "I've just come from Branson and O'Connor at the line."

"I'm on my way there now, sir."

"Good—they'll be happier to see you. Richard, listen," Greer adds, pausing in his gum-chewing, looking first down at the soft mud beneath our boots and then back at me. "I try to talk to them as much as I can, keep up their spirits. But I have a feeling they tell you more than they do me, the line between officers and enlisted…or maybe it's just that you're their medic, and they love you."

I feel myself blush at that, though I'm dirty and sweaty enough that it probably doesn't show.

"So if you—well, I hope you'll tell me if you think any of them needs a break. I can always send someone up to HQ to be a runner for a day or two."

The respect I already had for him grows stronger. I nod. "Yes sir, I will."

"All right." He grips my shoulder and gives me a brief smile. "Oh, and have you seen Sergeant Dennis? He wasn't in his hole."

"He was back at Rodriguez and Santorini's hole a few minutes ago, sir."

We part ways, and I keep low as I approach the line where Scott Branson and Jacob O'Connor are keeping an eye on that German battery across the hedge-rowed cow pasture. I move quiet over the bed of pine needles under the trees and whisper the password as soon as I see the dim outline of the two helmets in the slit trench. O'Connor lets out his breath and lowers his M1.

"Boys," I say, dropping to my stomach and crawling to the edge of their gun emplacement.

Branson, a dry-humored Ohioan who never minces words, checks the cartridges in their machine gun propped at the lip of the trench, camouflaged in the brush. Mountain ash and silver birch trees shelter us like watchful saints. "Anything happening, Rev?"

"That's what I was gonna ask you."

"Eh, it's quiet. And you know what that means." Branson squints into the night as the sky deepens to cobalt. "I don't like it quiet."

Propped on my elbows, at the height of their shoulders as they sit watching the fields, I glance between them. A breeze blows back O'Connor's dirty blond hair as he takes off his helmet for a moment. He was promoted from runner in the headquarters squad of our platoon to assistant machine-gunner in Peter's squad, after Nolan died on D-Day. In the thirteen days since we jumped into Normandy, the runt of the litter has endured a baptism by fire.

"Y'all remember that Cary Grant movie with the leopard?" He glances over his shoulder at me. "You know the one. He's a professor studyin' dinosaurs, and Katharine Hepburn's there, too? And the little dog, you know."

"*Bringing Up Baby,*" I say.

"That's the one."

Branson slowly swivels the barrel of the gun to the right, watching the hedgerows across the flooded field, then he sits back. "I thought it was a tiger."

"It was a leopard, wasn't it?"

I shrug.

"What about it, Toothpick?" Branson asks.

"I just thought of it. I don't know why."

I press the back of my hand to my mouth to keep from laughing out loud at O'Connor's impression of Grant and Hepburn running around the garden calling "George!," as George the terrier trotted just out of reach with a thousands-of-years-old dinosaur bone in his teeth.

"Spell me a minute, would you, Rev? Been holding this pee in for an hour." Branson hoists himself out of the slit trench, his jump boots squelching in the mud, and disappears into the trees.

O'Connor moves over to man the gun, and I drop into the hole beside him. As we watch the line, slate-gray clouds fill the sky and a drizzle starts to fall.

"Shit," he says.

The rain plinks on our helmets steadily. O'Connor sniffs and wipes at his nose.

"How're things, O'Connor?" I zip up the collar of my jacket, crossing my arms as the wind bites at us.

His eyes flick toward me. "Whaddya mean?"

"Just wanted to check how you're holding up."

"Oh." He nods. "I'm okay."

His hand moves along the full ammo clip, eyes straining to see through the rain. I'm not sure if it was brave or foolhardy of him when he stayed with me and Walsh in that plane on D-Day, but I wonder if there was even a choice in his mind. Although I certainly don't keep score—imagine if I did, a medic tallying up favors owed—I can't help feeling that I owe him something. He was willing to go down in flames with me.

"Hey, Rev," O'Connor says softly.

"What is it?"

"What's college like? Do you want to go back when this is all over?"

I tuck my hands under my arms and think. "I don't know. I've made better friends in the Army than I ever did there."

"My father doesn't think much of college. He never went, and his dad sailed from Ireland when he was sixteen. Neither of 'em ever had any use for it."

"What about you?"

"Well, I send my jump pay home every month, you know?"

"Yeah, me too."

"And I got a letter from my mother when we were in Picauville," O'Connor continues. "She said she's been puttin' it away, in a college fund just for me. Dad doesn't know. Makes me feel sort of rotten, but it might be the only way."

"It's your money," I say, tilting my head toward the darkness and the German line. "God knows you've earned it and can do what you want with it."

"I guess so. He doesn't see it that way."

"Where do you want to go?"

"University of North Carolina," he says decisively, so he must think about it a lot. "I don't know why, just always had it in my mind. Don't even know what I'd do there. But I like the thought of writing for a newspaper."

"Maybe you'll be a correspondent in the next war."

He glances at me and laughs, the sound of it muffled in the rain. "You know, maybe."

But let's hope it never comes to that, I add to myself.

Branson slips back through the trees. I climb out of the slit trench, whisper goodnight to them, and cut back through the trees the way I came to continue my rounds. I have my own foxhole, but I've spent an hour or two in it, tops. It gets lonely without a buddy.

I pass 2nd platoon's foxholes, two or three men in each, some covered with tarpaulins against the rain, others huddled against the wet earth as disgruntled as half-drowned cats. Back in 3rd's territory, I say goodnight to Lieutenant Greer and Sergeants Dennis and Evans, taking cover under the arms of an oak tree to look at a map. At one tarp-covered hole that looks much the same as every other, I kneel and lift the flap. "Anyone home?"

"Careful, you'll wake the baby. I just got him down," Peter's voice whispers mockingly.

I drop into their hole as Fischer, wrapped in a damp wool blanket, kicks at Peter without bothering to open his eyes. "Shut the fuck up," he mutters.

"Sarge, this baby swears like a fucking sailor." I take my helmet off and set it on my knees. "Is he always so fussy?"

"Yes, actually. Keeps me up half the night..."

Fish's indignant head emerges from beneath his blanket. "*I* keep *you* up?"

"See what I mean," Peter says.

"You got any coffee? Berk made some, but you know what that means."

Peter laughs. "Not to worry, Rev, we'll fix you up."

He hands me his tin cup. At least the contents smell and taste vaguely like coffee. And it's hot. Fish tucks his arm under his head for a pillow and says, "You see anything interesting out there?"

"Just Tony showing off that kraut holster he picked up yesterday, and Berry and Morgan arguing about Babe Ruth's home run record. Oh, and O'Connor does a real good Cary Grant impression."

"He does Sinatra, too. All he's gotta do is hide behind a leaf," Fish says, and I snort.

"You spending the night?" Peter stretches one leg out and pops a cracker from a C ration packet into his mouth.

I set the tin cup on top of his mess kit. "If you'll have me, and if you don't charge an arm and a leg for room service like Hotel Berkowicz."

"On the contrary, we offer a full continental breakfast," says Peter, tossing me a cracker. "When in Europe."

I lift the edge of Fish's blanket and lean against him for warmth. Judging by his breathing, he's nearly asleep already.

Peter lies down with his knees bent, too tall for all foxholes, and puts his head on his musette bag. "There were three guys in my stick on D-Day who fell asleep over the Channel," he says reflectively. "I didn't understand that at all."

"Did you hear about General Taylor?" I prop myself on one elbow. Fish mutters something, grumpy that I tugged his blanket off him. "I heard Cole and Winger talking about how he didn't even have his jump wings when he jumped into Normandy. You're the fucking general of the 101st Airborne and you aren't even qualified to make combat jumps?"

Peter snorts. "That's the 101st for you. Screaming Eagles, yeah, I'll bet he was screaming on the way down."

"That's not the worst of it, though. Apparently he brought a pillow on the plane, took off his whole harness and chute, and stretched out in the aisle. He slept the whole way to Normandy."

"You're shitting me," Peter says, and we try to keep our laughter down, for Fish's sake and to keep noise discipline. "There's no way."

"He did!"

"So did his pilot find a special, secret way to France where no one was shooting flak at them?"

"Nah, I think it's just Taylor. He could sleep like a baby right under one of those kraut railroad guns. Kinda like Fish."

Peter shakes his head. "Christ. What if they'd gotten hit and had to jump—"

"And no parachute."

"It's all chickenshit, all their showboating about strict discipline. We'd be out of the Airborne if we so much as thought about doing that. Not that we're dumb enough to even consider it."

We listen to the rain drumming on the tarp. I close my eyes and feel my bones settle against the soft ground. Besides Fish and Greer and a couple others who got out early, the rest of the second stick missed the drop zone on D-Day by miles because their C-47 flew through such heavy flak. But the plane Fish saw go down wasn't Fox Company at all, and you never saw a happier reunion than when Peter and 1st squad trickled into Ste.-Mère-Église that evening at sunset. This company is carried on the shoulders of good NCOs, but Peter might be the most beloved, as evidenced by the cluster of guys gathering round him in the street outside the aid station. I'll never forget the color returning to Fish's cheeks when he realized who it was. After the tragedy of our boys hanged in the trees outside the church, it renewed our collective spirit to have our ghosts back from the almost-dead.

I turn onto my shoulder and try to quiet my mind, exhausted but wired. The Germans know we're here and I can't imagine they'd try anything after they got their asses beat in Saint-Sauveur, but that's a gamble I'm too smart to bet on. All you ever know out here is that you know nothing. Though I can't see him, I know Peter's sleeping with his rifle tucked in his arm. Well, he's quiet, anyway; who's to say he sleeps at all? Mine and Fish's shared body heat makes the blanket too toasty so I slip it off, feeling stray raindrops through the tarp cracks fall on the back of my neck.

"Rev," Peter whispers.

"Yeah?"

I hear him sit up. Then the glow from a lighter illuminates the hole, Peter's hand cupped around the quivering blue flame. But he doesn't light a cigarette, just sits with the flame warming the palm of his hand, its short arc of light casting long shadows on his face and the earthen wall of the hole. The light is safe beneath the tarp, though I'm beginning to doubt that any Germans will venture across the flooded fields and into this muck tonight. Still, uncovered light is a beacon for artillery.

Peter drapes his arms over his knees, and the flame makes shadow puppets on the tarp stretched out on the ground. "Got a letter from Chrissy the other day," he says. "She says the lake's still too cold to swim, but the magnolia trees are blooming."

"Oh. Those must be pretty."

"Growing up we spent all our time in that lake in the summer, till our skin was all wrinkled like prunes. We'd get waterlogged and go over to the five-and-dime for popsicles, jump back in the water when we got too sticky."

"My friends and I were the same with our river."

"Some nights I don't even remember coming home. We'd just stay out under the stars." He laughs and adds, "Seemed like such an adventure back then. If only we could just run back to our beds in our nice dry houses now."

I look up at him, his face just beyond the range of light. "You been bit by the nostalgia bug?"

Peter moves the lighter to glow between us. He smiles. "I know you weren't asleep. Thought you might want to talk about home."

I don't know if that's such a good idea, feeding each other's memories of everything we've lost. It doesn't change anything. But the alternative is being alone, even though there are three of us in this foxhole, and not being alone is the very reason I don't sleep in my own hole. Besides, I doubt I'll sleep tonight. The hours seem long till dawn. So I sit up and say, "Tell me more about that lake."

XIII.

MEMORIAM

July 1945

T he trees cast long shadows, touching the tips of the white flowers in the grass. Hen trots down the porch steps, takes to the privacy of a bush by the shed to conduct business, and then after a short silence bounds out again, a filthy tennis ball in her mouth. She drops it and picks it back up three times before making it to the porch, then stands at the foot of the steps and looks up at me, biting down on the ball as if it'll squeak if she presses hard enough.

We leave a trail of crushed weed-flowers in our wake, me out of breath, her a little golden lion happily ducking past my reach. I can't keep up with her so I sit in the clovers instead, calling to her to bring me the ball. Her tail flicks uncertainly to one side as she watches me.

"Come here," I say, thumping the grass as if I have something here more delicious than a disgusting old ball. "Come on, bring it to me. You have to bring it if you want me to play."

If Hen was human, she'd raise a skeptical eyebrow. I crouch forward on my hands and knees, feeling the evening dew from the grass on my jeans. "Hen, you let Laurie have it yesterday. Did Laurie bring you home in a snowstorm wrapped in his coat?"

Her attention is caught by a dragonfly, and her jaw slackens. I lunge for the ball, then toss it straight up in the air as she whines. "What if I accidentally threw it on the roof?"

We're having a full conversation about fair play and sportsmanship when I hear someone say, "I came here for my daily portion of nonsense, and you didn't disappoint."

Grace leans on the gate, the setting sun at her back. Hen barks joyfully, abandons the ball, and runs to the fence, stretching up on her hind legs so Grace can scratch her ears.

"I aim to delight." I start to get up, but she motions me back down and unlatches the gate. Hen follows her through the yard, nearly under her feet.

Grace sits in the grass beside me and puts a book between us. "I wanted to return this cookbook to your mom. I forgot to bring it to church last night and I thought she might be missing it."

By the cover, which I don't recognize, my mom isn't missing it, and it could hardly be an urgent enough excuse to walk all the way here from the farm this late in the day. I turn my finger through the pages past charcoal illustrations of blueberry pies and rice puddings, waiting for her to say something. What happened at the river isn't mine to bring up.

"I had to use extract for the lemon bars, because where are you going to get a fresh lemon in Caspar?" Grace shifts as she unbuckles the straps of her sandals and tosses them in the grass. She looks at the grass stains on my jeans and then tugs the sleeve of my white t-shirt. "By the looks of it, Hen was winning."

"Of course she was winning. She plays dirty."

When she smiles at me, it catches me so off guard in its affection that my heart jumps and my mouth goes dry. I think I forget to smile back. I hear Santorini's voice, two years ago on a dusty desert night as he stared slack-jawed at Rita Hayworth projected on the canvas of the mess tent: "*That smile of hers, goddamn. It does things to me, y'know?*"

"Are you mad at me, that I didn't tell you?" Grace says.

It takes me a moment to remember how to form words as she watches me. "Mad at you?" I shake my head and let the cookbook fall closed. "I'm not mad at you, Grace, why would I—"

"It's only that we used to tell each other everything. And I don't know—well—I guess we grew up."

It was one thing, seven or eight years ago, to ask each other about prom dates, but it's something very different to exchange notes on love now. Especially because I'm wondering if I can ever be neutral when it comes to Grace. If I really loved her I'd want her to be happy no matter what, and if she'd said yes to that Navy fellow in Boston because he made her happy, then my conscience would tell me to be content with that. But I know I wouldn't be. I'm too selfish for that. Even though I have no right to it, and no reason for it, a twinge of jealousy goes through me.

"I know you want to ask about him." Grace makes a go-ahead gesture. "Get it out."

I rest my elbows on my knees, knowing that it's no use pretending I'm not curious, not with her. I start with the first thing I can't compete with. "Was he rich?"

"Of course you would ask that and not 'What's his name?' Or 'Where did you meet him?'" Grace rolls her eyes. "If it tells you anything, his parents had a townhouse in Beacon Hill."

"You told me when you were a freshman that you'd *never* go on a date with a rich Boston boy, and Beacon Hill is the epitome of—"

"Oh, I'm sorry that freshman Grace had plenty of boys to choose from, but the Grace of last year was a victim of the man shortage that plagued us here on the homefront."

"So did his parents buy his way out of the draft?"

"Richard, you have to know that not every person whose parents own a townhouse in Beacon Hill bought his way out of fighting."

"But this one did."

"He graduated from Northeastern with an officer's commission," Grace says with a long-suffering sigh. "He was an engineer. And no, he didn't go overseas. For all I know he's still at the Shipyard."

"Was he really heartbroken?"

"I don't know. I saw him once after, and he wouldn't tell me a thing, even though he's the one who asked me to have coffee."

"Then you made the right call. Any guy who'd embarrass you like that is an idiot."

"I embarrassed him first." She pulls a white-topped dandelion from the grass and picks off its fluffy seeds one by one. "Can you imagine proposing to a girl in a nice restaurant and her saying no? Honest to God, I had no idea he was going to do it. I never knew he was that serious."

"He proposed in a restaurant?" Tacky, proposing in public. "I would've run out of there, too."

"Are you only condemning public displays of affection because it's what Andrew did?"

Andrew. There's a name we can never give to our future child. "No, only because you don't like that sort of thing."

Grace laughs. "He was better than the boys who drank too much punch at prom and thought they were Bogart, trying to woo me with thoughts of Paris when all they wanted to do was feel up my skirt and make out in the locker room."

"Pity the fools. If they'd been paying attention, they would've channeled James Stewart to woo you."

She grins and blows the remaining dandelion seeds at my face.

"I'm sorry I didn't tell you about any of it," she says after a moment. "I don't know why I didn't."

"You don't need to be sorry. It's your story, to tell when you want."

We sit in the grass in the fleeting handful of moments after sunset and before night. Strands of stray hair cling to her neck. Briefly my mind flits back to Jenny, who'd make me wait in the kitchen of the rectory if she wasn't done with her makeup.

Hal Stuart's Model T trundles up Holland and turns left on Queen Street, leaving a little plume of exhaust lingering over the rutted asphalt. On the other side of the street, a herd of kids kick a soccer ball around the Demarests' front yard. Their laughter fills the dusk with a hopeful note. For all the ways we've grown up, the way she looks at me hasn't changed, that perceptiveness that sees so much of me, all that I want seen and understood and all the parts of which I'm ashamed. I'm sure she's noticed what I don't want her to notice, the anxiety that I'm not very good at hiding, but she graciously hasn't mentioned it.

"Do you mind if I ask you something, too?" I say, and Grace nods. "Why did you say no to Andrew? Besides that he put you on the spot, in public."

"I felt like we wanted different lives." She leans back on her elbows and starts to say something when a honeybee lands on the knot of her gingham shirt, above her shorts. "Oh! Hello. Isn't it late for a bee to be out?"

"As if bees have a set bedtime."

Grace laughs as it crawls up her buttons. "Of course they do. Nighttime is for fireflies—you never see a bee out with the fireflies."

"How would you know? A bee's ass doesn't glow in the dark. You wouldn't know it was there."

"A bee's ass," Grace repeats, grinning.

The bee hesitates on her stomach, then lifts its thin gossamer wings in the breeze and alights on the back of my hand in the grass. Grace pretends to pout. "I've been stood up."

The bee settles on my wrist, like a small passenger boarding a bus and waiting for the doors to close and the journey to begin. Its translucent wings would be invisible if not for the intricate pattern of bronze veins. From so close, I can see tiny individual hairs on its body, powdery pollen clinging to them.

"So you wanted different lives?" I say, tearing my attention away from the bee, who's joined together his two fat front legs as if folding them in prayer.

"He wasn't the sort of person I could imagine spending my whole life with. He was nice, but...just the thought of marrying him made me feel stifled. And that isn't what marriage should be."

"No, probably not."

"It may be for some people, and maybe they want that comfortable security he could've given me," she continues, "but that's never what I wanted."

"You said at the river that all you want is a nice, quiet life."

Grace scratches Hen behind the ears as Hen, lying on her tummy in the grass, licks dirt off the tennis ball. "That's still true, but a nice, quiet life with a person who doesn't put me to sleep faster than the six o'clock news."

The bee lifts his wings again and sets sail for fairer skies, his legs dangling beneath him. Grace watches him go as I watch her and wonder what sort of person she does imagine spending her whole life with. I'm so focused on that thought that I jump when someone calls out, "Hi, Miss Whitley!"

"Oh, hello, Katherine," Grace calls back, twisting around to see a group of girls, all about fourteen or fifteen, standing outside our gate with bubblegum popping in their mouths. They must've come from the river, because they have damp hair and towels slung over their shoulders.

Grace adds with a glance to me, "Katherine and Marjorie and Rebecca were all in my freshman Latin class in the spring."

I realize that the Katherine is Katy Greene and the Rebecca is Becky Langford. When they were in grade school together, they would make mudpies at Salt Pond after heavy rains, and would pelt us high schoolers with them when we came down the wooded path to fish for trout. I assumed they would remember me, too, or at least know that my dad is the one who preaches to them every Sunday morning, but then Becky calls as though she's just caught us making out under the willow tree, "Is that your boyfriend, Miss Whitley?" and they all dissolve into laughter, calling out, "Aw, you two are so cute." Before Grace can stutter out a reply, they run down the sidewalk into the night, laughing about love and boys as their towels slap their legs.

"The imaginations of high school girls," Grace says as she turns back to me, smiling, not even a blush on her cheeks.

Just as she turns her head to look at me, there's a crash from the house across the street—someone dropping a ladder or something on the ground—and I jump, sweat instantly prickling my back, heart climbing to my throat. Grace glances toward the source of the sound, then looks back at me, though I see her only out of the corner of my eye, unable to tear my attention away from the street.

"Richard?" Grace leans toward me and I feel her hand touch mine. "Everything okay?"

I look at her finally. Her expression is soft and patient and curious, no hint of secondhand embarrassment in it. "Sorry," I glance over my shoulder again, "I...that just...it startled me."

"I know. It wasn't anything, though." She says it so gently and matter-of-factly that I believe her. It wasn't anything. Still, we sit in uncomfortable silence for a minute or two.

Grace says finally, "Maybe I better be getting home."

This is just what I've been so afraid of her seeing. It's what I couldn't explain to Laurie, walking back from the river: If she's smart, she won't settle for me. What if the next time I think I'm caught in the middle of a shelling, she's caught there, too, where the shrapnel can hit her? Not the shrapnel that lives now only in my memories, but the very real kind that I'm afraid I could create without even knowing what I'm doing?

I nod. "Right, of course. I'll give you a ride."

When I drive her home, she asks me to let her off at the top of their lane. I watch her go until she becomes just a golden-haired speck, with her hands in her pockets and her head down.

Instead of going straight home after, I turn right onto Holland under the gloaming sky. The church's white frame stands starkly against the thin line of dark trees behind it. Most nights Dad comes here after dinner, when no one else is around. I park at the curb and go up the steps to the side door. Inside it only takes my eyes a second to adjust because the sanctuary is also dusky. At the first pew on the left, facing the altar, my dad's strong frame is bent forward. For a few moments I stand in the doorway and watch him, trying to pray, too, but finding only an emptiness where devotion used to be.

"Richard," he says, shoulders straightening. He looks back at me.

I go down the center aisle past whitewashed pews. Our stained-glass cross in the window glimmers with the votive reflections. "I didn't mean to bother you—"

"You're never bothering me." He nods for me to sit beside him. I do, and we stare together up at the stained-glass. "I love how the church looks at this hour," he remarks. "Well, at every hour. They all tinge prayer differently."

In the last two weeks, we haven't said a word of what happened on my birthday. He hasn't asked, and I pretend I don't notice Mom's concerned glances at me when she thinks I'm not paying attention.

Dad crosses his feet and seems to have no trouble simply staring at the pulpit and the communion table, draped with a white cloth and empty silver plates. "Is it about Grace?" he says, without taking his eyes from the communion plates or the cross or wherever.

"How could you tell?"

"Wait till you have children. You'll be surprised at how good you get at reading their anxiety from a mile off. Especially yours."

"I wouldn't hold my breath about the children."

"Well, the breath-holding might prove difficult anyway," Dad remarks.

I snort and then say, "If it's okay for me to ask—"

"Yes?"

"Did you—when you first met Mom, did you know? That you wanted to marry her?"

He leans back, his arm along the top of the pew. "I think I did. It doesn't serve anyone well to believe in love at first sight, or soulmates, if you want to know what I really think. But some part of me knew that there wasn't going to be another woman after her. That she was the end of my line, and that's just how I wanted it."

"End of the line," I echo. "Yeah."

"What did Grace say?"

"She said no to a proposal in Boston. I think that's why she came back to Caspar. And I guess it should encourage me, that she said no to the other guy."

Dad nods. "Do you love her?"

No one has ever put the question that simply. I look at him. He's waiting patiently, tracing a knot of wood in the pew.

"Yes," I answer, and I know that it can't be taken back. Nor would I want to. But it doesn't feel like a relief to have said it.

"And you can't tell her?"

"I…" Pressing the back of my hand to my eyes, I add, "It happened again. With her, just now."

"Ah, I see."

"I just don't want to hurt her."

"No, of course not."

After a few moments' silence, I go on, "Besides that, I'm afraid of the finality. If we talk about it and she doesn't love me, that's not just the possibility of love gone; it's her friendship, too. And I could live without the first, if I have to, but not the second."

"Only you can decide if the risk of loss outweighs the never knowing," he says. "With every kind of love in this world, we run the risk of being turned away. Of showing up with our whole hearts to a locked door." He tilts his head to me and smiles as he adds, "Did I ever tell you how your mother almost got away?"

"She did?"

He looks back at the stained-glass as he says, "I was young and stupid back then, making a mess out of courtship. She was ready to get married and I wasn't—or I didn't think I was—and I still hadn't learned how to balance the duties of the church and community with love and family. In the end, I let down the person I cared about most in this town. She decided to go to Boston to live with her aunt for a while, and I nearly made myself sick with grief, I suppose, in the days before she left."

"I can't imagine that."

"It's no mystery to me where you got the overthinking from." He laughs. "On the morning she was set to leave, I ran from the church to the train station and got there with a minute to spare. You can piece together the rest, but she never got on that train to Boston."

"I didn't know any of this."

"I think sometimes about how things could have gone differently, if I hadn't run after her," Dad says, his voice oddly reminiscent of its cadence when he's working through a difficult passage in scripture. "How I might not've stayed in Caspar or built a community with these people. Or how I might never have married. How you and your brother wouldn't be here."

The two votives he lit flicker under the blue glass of the cross. I glance at Dad, his profile set against the muted sanctuary. His black hair is graying at the edges, but his jaw is still set with that firm Scottish resolution, his shoulders tensed and strong, his eyes somehow always seeming to move upwards.

He says, "Richard, I don't think there's a part of you that really believes that girl doesn't love you, whether or not she knows it yet."

"But what if that isn't enough?" The fear rises to the top of my voice. "What if there are things the war changed that I can't even see yet?"

"I'm sure there are," he answers. "But you can live the rest of your life afraid of those changes, or you can let her in and trust that she's smart enough to make the choice for herself."

Then he stands and touches my shoulder for only a moment and says, "Let's go home." As I follow him down the center aisle of the sanctuary, I look back at the stained-glass. Gray clouds are gathering in the night behind it.

T he streetlights on Water Street glimmer in my rearview mirror as I make the left on Boucher. Potholes big enough to swim in are filled with last night's murky rainwater, and there are no lights and no sidewalks. Low houses with dark windows are set back from the road, some depressingly overgrown with crawlers and hedges that block out the moon's glow. My headlights cut across patches of dirty white siding. Feeling conspicuous, I flick them off as I pass two men standing at the edge of a driveway, glowing cigarettes in their mouths as their eyes track me.

As neighborhoods go, I don't mean to give the impression that the rest of Caspar is immaculate compared to here. There's barely a family in town who didn't suffer during the Depression, and it shows. But Petit Canada is distinctive because of who lives here and the very clear boundaries these residents draw between themselves and the rest of Caspar. They have their own Catholic church, which also has its own school, and there were always kids my age I'd see at the drugstore or the river I didn't know at all because they'd never set foot in the public schools. And, of course, while there are plenty of poor American families in other parts of town, every narrow street in this neighborhood is impoverished. Most Franco men and many of the women work at the mills north of town, labor jobs all they can get thanks to poor English and inadequate education.

They keep themselves to themselves. There are easier places to shake off the label "immigrant" than a rural town whose greatest pride is its generations. Never mind that those generations only go back about a hundred and twenty years, at the most generous estimate. "At least we're Americans," I've heard women at church remind one another, once a year when they feel charitable toward their Canadian neighbors and set up winter coat drives for the children in the church basement.

I pull up to the curb in front of Mattie's family's house. There are no lights in their windows, either. But the grass has been cut, and there are some bunches of forget-me-nots around the mailbox. The house is small, another indistinct white cottage that the Delfinches probably own if they don't own the whole neighborhood already.

In the old days, I'd flash the headlights to alert Mattie I was here for him. Now, I sit in the truck and watch the house through the passenger side window.

Mattie's family doesn't own a telephone, so I left a message for him with Wagner at the garage. It's the one-year anniversary of our friend Sam's death, and I thought the two of us should honor it together. Then Helen rang this evening and told me that Mattie called her five times last night, each call sounding more drunk. He must not've gone home at all. The last one trailed off in what she described as raving. She expected him at the restaurant tonight to play, but he never came.

"I should've been paying closer attention," she said anxiously on the phone. "You know, before it reached a point where I don't know if he's okay or if he's safe..."

I told her that she can't blame herself for anything, that Mattie is an adult and not her responsibility, but I feel the same as she does. That without someone watching out for him, he'll destroy himself.

Nothing happens, so I get out of the truck and try to decide if I should knock on their front door when it opens and Mattie's mother comes out holding a cigarette and lighter. She stands on the sagging wooden porch and lights up, watching me without expression. She can't be any older than my mom, but her face is so weather-beaten and weary that she somehow seems even older than my grandmother. Her hair is the same brown as Mattie's, her cheeks dotted in the same freckles.

I go around the truck to stand on the curb.

"Mrs. Faucheux?" I say. The yard between us seems a long distance.

"Adrienne's not here." She flicks a spark away. *"Es-tu son petit ami?"*

"Sorry?"

Mrs. Faucheux gestures vaguely to all of me. *"Es-tu le petit ami d'Adrienne?"*

"Oh, sorry. I, uh, no—I'm not her boyfriend—*Je ne suis pas son petit ami*." I step onto the grass, but her look keeps me from coming any closer. "I'm Richard. I'm a friend of Mattie's. Is he here? I was—"

The screen door slaps open behind her and before I can say anything to him, a torrent of Quebecois flies like shrapnel between Mattie and his mother. I step back onto the road. Mattie looks like he hasn't slept in a week. He takes the pack of cigarettes from his mother as she argues with him, shakes a few out, then turns as he lights the cigarette and sees me, because I couldn't make up my mind whether I should leave. I half-turn back to the truck, then look at him, knowing that I've transgressed one of the unspoken rules of our friendship by coming here.

"Richard, wait."

Mrs. Faucheux's cigarette butt glows like a firefly in the darkness. She watches Mattie as he crosses the yard. She looks tired, too, but a different tired than her son. Perpetual. I realize that, if some things had gone even slightly differently for my family, this could be my own mother or grandmother, carrying the beaten-down kind of tired that gets into your bones from always working and never belonging.

She disappears into the dark house as Mattie reaches the curb.

"I'm sorry, Mattie, I shouldn't have—"

"Why? It's okay. Sorry she didn't recognize you. Been a few years, I guess." He takes the cigarette from his mouth and holds it out to me.

"You know I don't smoke anymore."

He shakes his head. "Sorry, don't know what I was thinking." He hesitates, blowing out smoke that the wind carries away from me. Then he says around the cigarette, "Didn't know you were stopping by."

"I left a message with Wagner."

"That son of a bitch never tells me things like that."

This isn't the mood I had pictured for tonight, and I don't know what to say about Sam, so instead I tell him, "Helen expected you at the restaurant tonight."

"So she sent you over here to check on me?"

That comment annoys me more than the offered cigarette. "I guess I shouldn't have bothered. You look busy, so..." I trail off, not bothering to finish, then go back to the driver's side of the truck.

The passenger door opens at the same moment, and Mattie climbs in before I do. He drops the glowing cigarette on the curb, reaches his foot out to crush it, then pulls himself back in and shuts the door, as if we've made plans to go somewhere together. Trying to redirect him from his set course is as fruitful as Sisyphus rolling his boulder, so I just get in and look at him and ask, "Where are we going?"

"Oh, let's just drive around." He taps the cigarette pack nervously, clearly wanting to take another out and light it.

"How many of those are you smoking a day?"

His eyes cut to me with a look that tells me to drop it. "Not all of us are blessed enough to have our habits kicked for us."

"Why haven't I thought of it like that?" I say, wrestling the gearshift into first and flicking the headlights on as I pull away from the curb. "Listen, Mattie, I know you don't ever want to take my advice—"

"If I took your advice, I'd never leave the house and I'd read five books before breakfast."

"Don't see what's wrong with that. But I just don't want you to have made it all the way home for nothing."

This is met by a quiet that depresses me more than anything he's said. In my peripheral I see that Mattie is slouched in a way I didn't know was physically possible for him anymore, right knee bent with his foot on the seat, head against the window, prosthetic left leg stretched out straight in front of him. The headlights of a passing car light up his profile as we drive past dimly glowing houses that grow farther and farther apart.

"You made it through the Hurtgen Forest. I wasn't far from there in Belgium. I know what it was like." I try to keep my voice light as I add, "If I were you, I wouldn't waste that."

"That's not true."

I glance at him. "What's not true?"

"You made it through the ETO, too." His voice is downcast. "And yet look at you—turn left."

Why I do turn left without thinking about it is a mystery. When he doesn't continue, I say, "What about me?"

"I don't know. Never mind."

"Yes, you do. You always know. You've never been neutral about anything in your life."

Mattie straightens up. "You're afraid. That's what I think. You could get out of this town; you were always one of the ones who could just snap your fingers and come up with a new life for yourself. Never seemed to occur to you it's not that way for everyone."

"I don't know what you're talking about. And anyway, Mattie, I'm not the one calling Helen drunk five times a night, and then standing her up when you've agreed to play for her."

"No, go straight here," he interrupts, pointing.

"That leads out of—"

"Out of town, yeah."

I bite my lip, vaguely feeling as though I'm being kidnapped driving my own truck, but I go straight through the stop sign at the deserted intersection. It's quiet, the blue night and dark pines looming over the pock-marked road, till Mattie says, "You need to loosen up a little. You're wound tighter than a two-dollar watch."

"Okay?"

"Always have been." He flicks my shoulder. "D'you expect Grace to take care of a neurotic husband?"

"Do you think Helen finds it romantic when you ask her why she hasn't fallen in love with you yet?"

He's probably rolling his eyes. If only Sam were here to tell us to knock it off. We both know the narrow seat between us is occupied by ghosts, but I'm not brave enough to acknowledge it.

"I forget where it happened," he says after a minute. "Makes me a shitty friend."

I slow as my headlights sweep a deer and her white-speckled baby in the middle of the road. They stare at the truck with huge desolate eyes, till Mattie leans over and tries to sound the horn at them, and I smack him away and snap, "Cut it out." The deer skitter into the woods.

After a moment, I answer, "Some place called Saipan."

"Wish that name meant something to me." He lets out a huff of breath, as if he meant to laugh but couldn't gather it, and adds, "Guess it does now."

We drive in silence for a couple of minutes till Mattie says, "Here," around his unlit cigarette. He taps his window, and I turn left onto a road I've been down only to get somewhere else. I pull into a dirt lot with a couple of derelict gas pumps. Beyond them is a low, gray building with windows set too high to see in or out of. There's no sign, and a couple of old junker cars that don't look as if they run are parked at crooked angles in the weedy grass.

"Where are we?"

"I need a drink, and we're all out of the good stuff at home. That's where." Mattie opens his door, climbs stiffly out, and limps across the lot past the pumps. A few old guys in rusted metal chairs sit behind the pumps, watching the street with beer bottles in their hands. Their faces look like a hundred miles of bad road.

After some deliberation, I get out and run after Mattie. He might not get home if I just leave him here. The old guys are muttering to each other in what sounds like broken French, too local of a dialect for me to understand. I take a wider path around them than necessary and they go silent. Four pairs of eyes track me. It's the same superstition with which Mattie's neighbors, even his mother, regard any outsider.

Mattie stands in front of a metal door on a concrete stoop. When I catch up to him, the stares of the old Franco men burning holes into my back, he opens it and lets me go in first. Dim lights glow over a bar, but the corners of the room are drenched in shadow. Smoke wafts through the air. The surfaces I can see look as if they haven't been scrubbed since the Great War, if ever. Otherwise it's startlingly nondescript, nothing specific about it so that if I got knifed here and then had to describe the place to a detective, I'm not sure I could.

My eyes take a minute to adjust from the darkness outside to the light. Then I feel the gazes. There are a couple of middle-aged men at the end of the bar, probably mill workers, and I notice a few others at two tables pushed up to the concrete walls. I have a sense of others watching me that I can't see, burrowed deep into the recessed corners, men who think me as much a foreigner here as the Americans think these men are in Caspar.

With his non-prosthetic foot Mattie pushes a barstool out, nodding at me. He says something in French to a figure behind the bar. The guy comes into the light as Mattie orders for us, I don't know what. *Had to have been a lumberyard worker before this,* I think, watching the guy's back, broad as two barrels.

I'm still holding my keys in one hand and am considering backing slowly out the door and then making a run for it. Unintelligible conversation has picked up at a table a few feet away, but there's no light over it to illuminate the faces of the talkers. No one's staring at Mattie, only me, so he must be a regular here or else there's just something un-American about him and something too American about me.

Something cold and wet touches the back of my hand. The black-bearded bartender has slid a glass across the counter to me, filled with an amber-colored liquor.

Mattie raises his. Cigarette smoke drifts past it in the light. "To Sammy," he announces and downs it like a shot. Who knows how drunk he already was when I came to his house, but I know the difference between sober Mattie and wasted Mattie, and we're much closer to the latter.

"Don't do that to him," I say, leaning my elbows on the bar and angling toward Mattie as if doing so will dispel the suspicion from the other patrons. "If we really want to toast to Sam, we shouldn't do it in...well, in here."

"You mean the Francos aren't good enough for you?" Mattie crunches a piece of ice from his glass.

"I didn't say that."

"Sorry, Dick, that my dives aren't up to your white standards, even though I've assimilated into every fucking part of American culture. Even lost my accent for it."

"White standards?" I repeat, unsure what he means by that or how the conversation suddenly took this turn. Also, since when does he use words like assimilate? Apparently drunk Mattie turns into sober Sidney. "I don't know what you're talking about, but I just mean that this place isn't really Sam's kind of—"

Mattie pushes my untouched glass closer to me and says something that sounds like *gosses*. "Yes, it's exactly what you mean. Sam's dead. I want to remember him. I knew you wouldn't do anything about it."

"You don't want to remember him; you just want an excuse to drink. And if 'by do anything about it,' you mean get drunk on his behalf, then no, I won't. Can we get out of here?"

He pulls out a cigarette and lights up and shakes his head. "Not till you loosen up. Try a sip of that."

"I'm not drinking anything. I have to drive us both home."

"*Câlisse.* Do you know how difficult you are? Trying to be friends with you is like bargaining with God himself. Smite me down with your righteous holy judgment. I'm ready."

"Mattie, come on," I whisper. "I just think we're both smarter than to get wasted 'in memory' of Sam in a place that'll give us tetanus."

Mattie signals to the bartender. They talk in French for a minute, and at one point the bartender looks at me with an inscrutable expression. Then he reaches down behind the bar and comes back with a beer, popping the cap on a bottle-opener beside him. He puts the beer on the rough bar in front of Mattie.

"Well, since you seem to be such good friends with these guys, maybe one of them can give you a ride home." I stand, keys in my closed fist.

"Relax and quit giving them a reason to look at you suspiciously."

I sit on the stool again. "Why are you doing this? Drinking won't bring Sam or Joe back or Sidney home. It's only going to make you more miserable."

"Do you mind keeping the fuck out of it?" he says sharply. "Thanks for the ride. Now you can fuck off. I'll find my own way."

Now I can't leave without him. I watch as he finishes the first beer and starts on another. I don't think this is what Helen had in mind when she asked me to check on him.

"You can go on home to your perfect family." Mattie raises an eyebrow at me. "The American dream, the Dares, aren't you? What gives you the fucking nerve to think that everyone else has to be just as good as you?"

I set my chin on my hand and wait for him to get it all out. It won't matter what I say; he'll still find a way to dredge up old resentments. Even after all this time, he still thinks of himself as an outsider among us. I wonder if he knows who he is without that distinction. Wonder how much bitterness it holds.

"Well?" He knocks my leg with his. "What else have you got to say on behalf of white Caspar about the Francos? *Dirty illiterate immigrants, you better not slip up and say a French word in school, boy...*"

"I don't know why you keep saying 'white.' I've got a foot in both worlds, just like you." My grandfather likes to say that the only good immigrant is a Northern European immigrant, and then he laughs that huge laugh of his and thanks God for his brown skin.

Mattie snorts derisively. "But this town loves you. You might not be white the way they're white, but they don't notice anymore. That's the advantage of birth, I guess."

"Why'd you start coming to public school? I thought the Catholic church had its own school."

His words are starting to slur as he says, "That's what I mean. It's all about advantages. You think my dad wanted my sisters or me to repeat his life?"

"You mean he wanted you to learn English."

"Remember that son of a bitch Mr. Steiner's class in fifth grade? Where we met, yeah, of course you do. I was the only Franco in there. He used to make me come to the front so he could whip my hands with that old leather belt if I said something in French on accident."

"I remember."

Mattie snuffs his cigarette out in the ashtray. The acrid smoke all around us is burning my eyes and each minute it gets a little harder to breathe, but I'm trying to tough it out for his sake.

"It doesn't matter now, anyway," he says, as though he doesn't care, yet I know he does. "Learned English and graduated from an American high school even though everyone thought I wouldn't, went to war, left my leg somewhere in Europe, came home to work at the same garage I have since I was fifteen and for less money than I made in the Rangers.

What's the fucking point of it all, anyway? That's why I'm drinking for Sam. Because what the fuck else do I have to drink for?"

"The chance at a better life?" I pick up my drink and clink it against the brown glass of his beer bottle. "*Yamas,* as we say in my white American household."

He watches me suspiciously, which forces me to actually swallow the sip I took. After swallowing it takes me about twenty seconds to come back down, the back of my throat burning. I don't know what's in that, and I hope to never experience it again. But Mattie has shed the bitter expression and grins at me as he lowers his empty bottle.

"You're okay sometimes."

"For what it's worth, I think you're right," I say. Thank God I actually ate dinner tonight. Can't imagine drinking that on an empty stomach. "None of this is worth drinking for. Nothing worth having is."

"Uh-huh. No sermons until you finish that and earn the right to preach."

"Then I rest my case. It's not worth it."

Mattie looks pleased at his small victory, and before I can stop him he's taken my drink and downed it. Just watching him makes my stomach twist. "I can't believe that was all it took to silence you. We should go out drinking more often."

"No, we really shouldn't." I look at the clock over the bar. 9:57. Long past my self-imposed curfew, the time of night when I lose all ability to function in the presence of other people.

"I always just wanted to be good enough to be friends with you and Sam and Sidney," Mattie says, apropos of nothing. He's staring into the dark corner of the room as though he can see them there. "And now Sam's gone, Joe too, and Sidney might never…"

He doesn't finish that thought, and I don't answer. It would be easier to tell him that he never needed to try so hard with us, if he wasn't so drunk that he won't remember any of this tomorrow. But I know too well how the fear of never being good enough is paralyzing, and if I don't drown those fears in drink like he does, it's only because I'm exactly what he always says I am: self-righteous, disdainful, holier-than-thou, whatever you want to call it. Judging him for whatever he does only because it's what I don't do.

"So let's give him a proper goodbye, him and Joe both," I say finally, looking up at Mattie. "Let's do it right, the way they'd have wanted. Let's not drink them out of our minds."

I pay the bill and when we go outside, Mattie's arm slung over my shoulder, the night is pitch black with no moon or starlight. I turn my face away from the smoke on his breath. The men's eyes follow us in the dark. After I get Mattie into the truck, I go to the other side and let out the breath I've been holding, turning my face into my elbow to cough out the smoke filling my lungs. The clean night air rushes back in and leaves me lightheaded for a minute.

Darkness engulfs us as I drive, dispelled only by the headlights. I never realized how eerie Maine can be until I left it and came back to it. Mattie taps his fingers on the door, as if to let me know he's awake.

"You're sure you want me to take you home?" I say as I turn onto his street in Petit Canada. "If you need to stay at my house—"

"And let the Reverend smell the whiskey and smoke on me? Thanks, but I'd just as soon not."

"He's not like that, you know." I pull up to the curb. Hand on the gearshift, I add, "It's me who's a judgmental ass, not him."

Raindrops tap the windshield as Mattie's eyes glow in my direction. "Nah. You're not so bad. I give you shit." He starts to turn away, his hand on the door handle, and then looks back at me. "Can we switch places for just a minute?"

"Well—" I glance from him to the steering wheel. "I'm not letting you drive, if that's what you—"

"I don't mean literally," he says. "I meant, can I tell you what I think about something, and maybe because you're not me, it won't fall on deaf ears?"

"...oh. Okay, I guess."

"Tell Grace." Mattie's face is unexpectedly and impossibly sober, not only as though he never had a drop to drink tonight but stripped of all its characteristic mockery. "She's been waiting."

"She told you that?"

Mattie raises his eyebrows. "She didn't have to. Do you really think she came back to Caspar because she had no other options? A girl like her won't wait forever."

He opens the door and holds his hand up when I start to get out, too. "I'm fine. I can make it." Standing on the curb, hand on the open door, he adds, "What I'd give for what you two have, you've no idea. Go get her, Richard."

XIV.
ANGEL

28 July 1945

Rain skitters down the lattice windowpanes in Grace's kitchen, gathering in deep pools outside in the lane. The mint-colored clock over the pantry door ticks to five. Wilting wildflowers lean out of a glass jar on the drain board by the sink, and a sleeve of crackers, half-eaten and forgotten, lies beside them. The coffee pot drips on the counter while I shuffle a deck of playing cards at the table. I deal the cards around, to Mattie on my left and Antonia across from me and Grace and Helen on my right, who've teamed up because bridge is technically a four-person game. Mattie, who never trusts me to deal, fans out his hand of cards and counts them to make sure he has thirteen.

Thunder rumbles over us and the scent of coffee fills the kitchen as we play, more half-heartedly than we ever have before. The sky was bright and clear when I left the house this morning to pick up Mattie and meet the others at Chimney Lake, but clouds gathered while we were there and drenched us soon enough. Our clothes are draped across a laundry rack in front of the woodstove to dry. While Mattie and I stripped halfway to our skivvies in the kitchen, the girls disappeared upstairs to change and then Grace reappeared, her wet hair wrapped in a peach-colored towel, with some old shirts of Sidney's for us. They smell like mothballs but it beats being wet, so I just pushed the sleeves up to my elbows and told myself that Sidney would give any of us the shirt off his back if it came to that.

"Pass," Toni says at her turn. With her cards splayed in her hands, she looks over her shoulder out the window into the half-flooded lane. Rain and wind blow in sheets through the leaf-heavy apple trees and against the house siding. "It's fitting, though, don't you think? Sam loved a good storm."

Mattie tilts his chair back and says, "I always thought he'd get struck by lightning, actually. Crazy sonuvabitch."

Sam has no ashes. His family never got the closure of burying a body, unlike Joe Carson's family, who buried him in our church cemetery three years ago after he was killed by friendly fire in the Philippines. He was with a Navy supply unit, for God's sake, not even combat. No one had even thought yet to worry about him. But seeing as Sam didn't get a burial and Joe already did, our pilgrimage to the lake was only symbolic. A time for all of us to remember them in a place untouched by war. Except it isn't. All of Caspar, every stream and tree and bit of lakeshore here that they loved—all are stained now with their absence.

"Have you heard from Sidney or Lena?" I say to Grace as she starts to push her chair back to get the coffee. "No, stay, I'll get it." My motive is selfish, though, because I don't want them to notice my hands shaking as I hold my cards or the incessant bobbing of my foot. It could all come to nothing if Grace and I don't get a moment alone after the others leave. What if Toni and Helen decide to spend the night, or Mrs. Whitley comes home early from her visit to Aunt Meg in Bangor? Then it's back home for me, to let these anxieties ferment until the next time I work up enough courage to tell Grace that I—

"Oh, thank you," Grace says as I get up for the coffee. "No, I suppose the last letter was about a month ago." She tries to keep her voice light as she sets a card on the pile. The mood is already somber, and if anyone is astute at reading emotions, it's her. Sidney not writing for a month is uncharacteristic, and I know Grace doesn't want to bring us down more, not after it seemed to finally hit us collectively this afternoon that Sam and Joe are never coming home.

"Richard, can I play your turn?—wonderful, you've got a nice hand." I hear Toni set down a card for me as I pour the coffee into mismatched mugs, then Mattie passes, and Toni wins the round for her and me.

It takes two trips to bring the mugs to the table and a third to get the sugar bowl, because I know Grace won't drink coffee unless there's more sugar than coffee in the cup. She lets Helen play the next round, seeming troubled. She has such a well-crafted, thought-out façade that I have to pay close attention without appearing to pay close attention to see past it.

"I'm sure you'll get three letters from him tomorrow, and they were just lost in the mail for a bit. That's all," Helen says, brushing her shoulder against Grace's.

"Yes, I'm sure that's it." But Grace's smile doesn't reach her eyes.

She gets up to switch on the radio balancing on the sill over the sink, and that Cab Calloway song we danced to in the spring at the hotel fills the warm kitchen. After three sleepless nights of wrestling in my mind, I realized that if even Mattie was clear-eyed enough to see what I need to do, then there's no sense putting it off. All day I've been swallowing down my fear. Mattie's right that a girl like Grace won't wait forever. But what if I make a mess of it—what if the ten years of waiting turn out to be flat and useless to me now and I can't say what I really mean? I know I have to because Grace and I have a chance that so many others will never have, but it's that very pressure that tears me up inside and what if there are some things that mean too much in essence to ever be distilled into words—

"Toni, play my cards," I say, scooting my chair back.

A couple minutes later I wash my hands under the bathroom tap and look up into the mirror reflecting the dark green wallpaper behind me. I brush back through my hair with my wet hand, but it doesn't do anything to tame the beginnings of a tangled mess thanks to the rain. I wonder if there's a bit of floss around, just in case, and I open the medicine cabinet. Inside is a tin of St. Joseph's aspirin, a glass bottle filled with a light pink liquid—"eau de toilettte rosewater," the label says—jars of salves and creams, Pond's digestive tablets...aha.

Dropping the used string in the wastebasket, I check my teeth—all clear—and take a piece of spearmint gum from the pack I grabbed while I was running out of the house this morning.

I open the bathroom door and almost step on Baxter the cat, a silky black puddle on the green hallway rug. He jumps to his feet, arches his back, and shows me his impressive teeth. I show him mine back. We watch one another, he, I think, just a bit too judgmentally for my comfort.

"What? As if you don't have your own fun wooing all the nice little house cats in town, you lady-killer," I say to him, crouching and holding out my hand. After a moment of deliberation, he steps closer and brushes his tiny nose to my palm. It might be the first reconciliatory moment in our long history of me trying to bond with him and him regarding me suspiciously, as if he thinks I'm out to ruin the women of his household, whom he protects with only the most marginal effort. I add, "We can exchange notes later, Baxter. Right now I have a bridge game to rush through."

I straighten, roll up the sleeves of Sidney's shirt again because they keep slipping, and go back toward the kitchen as Baxter disappears upstairs on silent paws. But in the living room, where we always used to push the furniture aside on New Year's Eve to dance, I notice movement out the wide front window that looks out on the lane.

An idling engine hums outside. I go to the window. Through rivulets of rainwater down the panes, I see a black Model T parked in the drive and a boy walking across the yard with shoulders hunched to the rain.

An angel of death in a black Western Union raincoat.

"Grace!" I call, even as I wish I could blink the sight of the black car and the courier away. "Grace, can you come here?"

"Hm?" A few seconds later she appears in the hallway, her bridge cards still in her hand. The glare of the foyer light over her head glows on her damp golden hair. Her feet are bare on the stone floor, and wearing a pair of rolled-up jeans, she looks ready for an afternoon of fishing or picnicking—or card-playing—not for whatever is typed on that telegram. She tilts her head and says, "What are you—"

The courier knocks on the door.

Grace looks from the door, then to me. She makes no movement to open it. "Richard?"

The other three appear behind her. The courier knocks again, and I go from the living room window to the foyer and open the door.

When the courier, poor kid, holds the letter out and says, "For Mrs. Hannah Whitley," Grace makes a sound from her throat that's not quite a cry and not quite a word, either. I look back over my shoulder. Both hands are pressed to her mouth. In the rainy shadows shrouding the foyer, her green eyes are shimmering with immediate tears. Taking the letter feels like a betrayal to her, as if I'm the one signing Sidney's death certificate.

"No, no, no," Grace breathes out through her hands. Toni and Helen have their hands on her shoulders.

"Thank you," I say in a low voice to the courier as he puts the telegram in my hand, and I drop a quarter in his.

He nods, lips tight together, and then disappears into the rain. We hear the Ford's engine sputter to life in the driveway and then it bumps away through the mud.

I shut the door with a click and turn back to Grace. With one hand still over her mouth, she takes the telegram. She stares at it silently for nearly a minute. If I didn't know her better, I might call the expression in her eyes uncomprehending. But I do know her, and know that she understands it all too well, better than I do.

She breaks the seal on the telegram but doesn't open it.

"Grace, I think we need to read that," I say quietly.

She shakes her head, her "no" barely audible. She wraps her hand so tight around the telegram that it creases. "No, Richard, don't. Please don't."

But she doesn't resist when I take the telegram and unfold it. Stark black capital letters dance across the page, and I have to blink a few times to focus.

The secretary of war wishes me to express his deep regret that your grandson Lieutenant Sidney C Whitley has been reported—

Unable to trust my own sight, I read back over it three times before I understand it.

—missing in action since 25 July over Borneo if further details or other information are received you will be promptly notified.

And then signed with the name of a general I've never heard of.

Grace lowers her hands, and I feel her staring at me pleadingly.

"Missing," I say, finally meeting her eyes. "He's missing. Since three days ago."

"He's not dead?"

I have no idea what to say to her. She's seen the newsreels herself that depict Japan as a squint-eyed torturer, no conscience in its brutality. How much of the propaganda is true, I couldn't say. But I do know that Japan never signed the Geneva Convention and isn't bound to the rules of war the way Germany was, never mind how often Germany itself broke those rules. What the Japanese Empire does to prisoners of war is unconscionable, *if* Sidney survived what sounds like the crash of his plane, *if* the Japs haven't already killed him, *if* dysentery or starvation or whatever other South Pacific malady doesn't do him in first.

Given those odds, who's to say that a killed-in-action telegram wouldn't have been less heartbreaking in the long run for Grace and her grandmother. For Sidney, too.

And Lena, God. Lena.

I put the telegram back in Grace's hand. "I don't know. I'm sorry, Grace, I don't know."

"But missing?" Grace looks at me, then at Mattie, who's standing in the doorway biting into his fingernail. "That means he could still be out there, doesn't it? It doesn't say killed." She frantically smooths out the paper edges she creased. "It doesn't say killed; it says *missing*. He could be—he could be a prisoner, or stranded?"

Mattie and I look at each other. There's no way Sidney could still be alive, even if he survived an emergency water landing, unless he was picked up by Japs.

"Richard, tell me that he could be alive."

"He could be," Mattie concedes before I can say anything. He means it honestly, and I wish I could agree, but I falter at the possibility of giving Grace false odds. Even if Sidney is alive at this moment, that doesn't mean he's coming home.

Grace takes a deep breath. She's hyperventilating, in shock, pressing the back of one hand to her eyes as she tries to keep from crying. Anyone else would do the same, though I sense there must be another thread running through this grief, one not yet fully illuminated and which the rest of us can't understand. There's a history she's kept buried for so many years.

"It's drafty here. Let's go in the kitchen and get warm," I say. She lets me take her hand, and in her other she clings to the telegram as if dropping it would mean letting go of her brother. Helen gathers her dropped playing cards from the slate floor.

In the kitchen, Grace stands before the stove, staring glassy-eyed at the telegram. At first I think she might drop it in, but she doesn't even seem aware that it's still in her hand. Toni gathers Grace's hair off her neck and whispers something to her, and Helen loops her arm through Grace's. I stare at the cold coffee in the mugs as Mattie shuffles the cards and drops them back in the box.

"It's never going to be over, is it?" he says to me. "Even after it's ended."

Helen looks over her shoulder at us and gestures with her chin to the doorway. As Grace sits down ghost-like at the table, we cluster under the arch.

"The three of us should go home." Helen's voice is quiet, but I doubt Grace even hears us. "If it's too much of a crowd, she'll just get overwhelmed. You stay, Richard," she adds.

"Me? You're sure? Shouldn't you and Toni—"

"It's not Helen and me she wants right now," Toni answers. "You saw her a few minutes ago. She was only looking for you."

A silent black shadow slips between my legs, Baxter crossing the kitchen to hop nimbly into Grace's lap. Absently she runs her hand through his fur.

"What's she supposed to do now? Just wait for another telegram?" Mattie bites at his fingernails as he watches her.

"I think tonight will be the worst," Helen says. "She just needs someone with her till Mrs. Whitley gets home."

Mattie changes out of Sidney's shirt and drapes it awkwardly over the laundry rack. His is still damp, but they'll all get wet enough outside getting from the house to Helen's car. I watch through the kitchen window as her headlights glow on staccato raindrops cutting through the gloom and sweep the apple trees swaying in the wind, and then it's only Grace and me.

The telegram dangles from Grace's fingers. She seems to be staring at nothing in particular. Seeing old, long-buried stories where there's only an icebox and a counter with a cutting board.

"Do you want more coffee?" I ask, leaning on the back of the chair opposite her. "Tea?"

"You'll stay with me?" She looks up at me without hearing my question.

"Of course. I'm not going anywhere."

Grace shakes her head. "No, I mean—you'll be here when I wake up?"

"Wake up from what?"

She doesn't answer. Baxter, who usually hums like an old engine when she holds him, is quiet in her lap. I turn the radio off.

"I can make you something," I offer, feeling the need to keep busy. "Eggs, toast—"

"I think I'll take a shower." Grace lifts Baxter up and sets him on the floor, and he slinks to the woodstove and presses his back to it. "I've been cold all afternoon, and that'll warm me up."

With some hesitation, she finally sets the telegram on the table and stands. Crossing her arms over her chest, she says, "You don't need to make anything for me, but help yourself to anything you can find. And you know where the books are, and there's last week's Sunday crossword in the living room. I know you like those—of course you've probably already done it."

"Baxter will keep me company. You go on, get warm."

I watch her back as she disappears into the hallway and hear her feet on the stairs. There's the sound of the water moving through old pipes. So we've made it through the first stage of triage.

First I spit the wad of spearmint chewing gum into my hand and then drop it in the wastebasket; no chance tonight of anything coming of that. Then I go to the phone hanging on the wall and lift the receiver. Kitty at the telephone office answers, sounding put out to still be at work on such a dismal evening. I ask her to put me through to the church, because I have a feeling that Dad is sitting at his desk there, watching the rain out his window when he should be working on tomorrow morning's sermon. The war in Europe is more than two months over, but the list of folks to pray for only grows as war in the Pacific slogs on.

I tell Dad about the telegram and that I'll stay here tonight till Mrs. Whitley gets home so Grace isn't alone. The tone of his voice makes me wonder if he had some sense of what I'd intended to say to her today, but he knows as well as I do that this is not the night. I also tell him not to wait up for me, and know he will, anyway.

As soon I replace the receiver, Baxter lets out a yowl from deep in his throat without moving from his spot by the stove. His green eyes glow in the dim kitchen. I turn on the tap and try to start washing the coffee mugs, pouring the dregs down the drain, but he yowls a second time in obvious offense. When I turn and look at him, he stares back. He looks like a night sky with two glittering constellations breaking the velvety surface.

"I don't know what she feeds you. If I get it wrong, then I'm in trouble."

He ducks his face and licks at his paws, and another small rumble escapes him, as if he's prepared to argue.

"Look." I point at him with a spatula I found in the sink. "Sometimes we all have to set aside our own needs to help someone else. Right now Grace doesn't need you to be an ungrateful little curmudgeon. When she comes back down you better do your job, which is to be cuddly and nice to pet."

Baxter stretches his toes out and then his back.

"And it's not as if you're bringing in any income for the household, either," I add.

He sneezes.

When the dishes are done—and I think that ceramic mug with the painted sunflower already had a chip in the handle before it slipped out of my soapy hands—I look around for something else to do. I'm not hungry, and I don't have the presence of mind for a crossword puzzle or a book. Baxter pads around after me as I pace the kitchen with my hands in my pockets, thinking, though none of my thoughts really has a beginning or ending. Only fragments flit past. I avoid looking at the telegram on the table as though the sight of it will turn me to stone.

In the middle of my wandering I hear Grace call from upstairs, "Richard?"

Maybe I take the steps two at a time, I can't remember after, but I am out of breath by the top. Across from the stairs, the bathroom door is open a crack, just enough to reveal a strip of yellow light and nothing else.

"I'm here."

"I forgot a towel, and there're none in the linen closet—would you fetch one from the laundry? That little room right behind the kitchen, they should be folded on the counter."

Back down the stairs, slower this time. I find one clean towel and two others folded that looked to be clean until Baxter's muddy paws marched a trail across them, like Hannibal's elephants crossing the Alps.

Grace's arm is reaching out the door when I come back. "Thanks, I'll only be five minutes." I put the towel in her hand and force myself to turn away from the cracked door.

The rain beats on the roof in a lullaby. In the kitchen, I notice the fire dying in the stove, so I find a pair of what must be Sidney's rain boots in the foyer coat closet and tug them on. Baxter sits behind the screen door and watches as I go out into the yard. From years past, I remember that the woodpile is across the backyard and between a little grove of oak saplings and an old willow tree. It takes longer than it should to find it because the oak saplings have grown up and the willow is weighed down by rain, water running off its weak branches in streams. I lift the blue tarpaulin from the pile just as the back end of a damp brown mole scurries through a crack in the logs.

By some miracle, the logs catch the flame of the match I hold to them as I crouch before the stove. I thought they'd be too wet from the dash back to the house to light. I shake the match out and drop it in the sink and when I turn, Grace has appeared in the kitchen, the white towel wrapped around her hair. She has on a wine-red sweatshirt that's too big for her with "Kappa Delta" on the chest in white letters.

"Richard, you're all wet," she says. She unravels the towel from her head and tosses it to me, and while I shake the rainwater from my hair she stands in front of the stove and holds her hands out over it. "Maybe I'll take you up on that cup of tea now. There's chamomile in the pantry—do you want one?"

"Sure. Oh, and what does Baxter eat for dinner?"

Grace shakes out a match, strikes the flint on the box, and holds the flame to the burner as she turns on the gas. "Just half a can of the tuna in the icebox. I'll get it."

I almost say that I will, but one glance at Grace tells me she needs something to distract her, and feeding a cat is a small accomplishment that's better than nothing. So instead as she peels back the aluminium top of the tuna with the can-opener, I say, "Let me make you something to eat, even if it's just eggs and toast. My mom always says that being hungry makes the bleak things even more bleak."

"Well, all right," she says, scraping the tuna into Baxter's glass dish by the back door. "Only if I don't have to eat alone."

"I'd never make you eat alone."

While Baxter eats in that odd little delicate way that cats do, Grace sets the kettle on the stove and drops chamomile teabags into two of the ceramic mugs I washed. The kitchen is warm, and though I wish the circumstances were different, it feels comfortingly familiar to move through it with her, remembering which cupboard the salt is in and passing ingredients to one another. I drop bread into the chrome toaster and crack the eggs on the edge of the frying pan. Grace goes out to the telephone in the hall while we wait, and I hear her asking Kitty for her great-aunt's house in Bangor. I try not to listen after that—not that there's very much to hear, anyway. When she comes back to the kitchen, pressing the heel of her hand to her tired eyes, she says, "Gran's starting home early."

The teakettle whistles. I take it off the range and set it on the counter. Grace, leaning against the sink, picks at a loose red thread hanging from her sleeve. Baxter has polished off his dinner and slides across the floor to bat his paw at it, standing on his back legs like a beggar dog in a circus act and backhanding the offending thread. Grace turns her head to the side and smiles at him.

"All okay?" I say, pouring the steaming water into the mugs. I know it isn't all okay, but I don't know what else to say. "You can tell me the truth. If you want."

"I..." Grace rubs her eyes. When she raises her head with a resolute deep breath, her expression surprises me. A sort of frustration with the betrayal of her emotions, as though even when it's only me here, she has to chastise herself for letting this part of her be seen. The strange light of a cool, rainy summer evening falls on her cheeks as she stares out the window without seeming to see what lies beyond it. Finally she adds, in a tone that makes me doubt its sincerity, "Yes, of course. So many families have gotten worse news. I'm—I'm okay."

She has so much trouble forcing out those last two words. Her disgust at them is obvious. I wish I hadn't asked, because I know that feeling. I poke at the eggs with the spatula and turn off the gas. When I turn to fetch the plates from the cupboard, Grace is standing between the sink and the table with her arms crossed in the too-big sweatshirt sleeves, staring vacantly at the floorboards and looking lost.

Then she raises her head and looks at me, an expression of alarm passing over her face. "Lena," she says, her mouth falling open. "Richard, what about Lena? What if she doesn't know?"

"She was probably the first to know, as his wife. I'm sure she's gotten a telegram."

Grace picks at the dangling thread, loses her patience with it, and yanks it out of her sleeve. Baxter patters across the floor after it. "I don't know why I haven't heard from her lately. We'd been writing back and forth."

"Maybe a letter was lost in the mail—that's bound to happen between here and Australia."

"What if she's pregnant?" Grace runs her hand through her damp hair, staring at me with wide eyes. "She could be all the way across the ocean, alone, trying to raise a child."

"You don't know that," I say gently, "and it's no use speculating about what may or may not be. Grace, that isn't your responsibility, not tonight. We'll face that tomorrow."

But she isn't listening. She paces in a tight circle between the back door and the table. "If he's—if Sidney's dead, I don't think I can carry another person's grief, Richard. I don't know if I can bear Lena, too, and I hate, I hate this—" She presses her hands to her eyes and laughs in a way that unnerves me a little. "I hate grief, have I ever told you that? We buried our parents three weeks apart and we wore black for months so every moment of every day all I could think about was how cold they must be in that—in the ground in that ugly little cemetery in Ipswich, and that's what Lena will be, the black clothes reminding me how cold Sidney must be. What if they never find his b-body?"

Before I can move to stop her she opens the stove and throws the telegram in and steps back, her breath coming in short little gasps. I stare at the paper as the edges turn black and curl before falling away in ash.

Grace makes a sound in her throat. When I look at her, her curled fists are pressed to her mouth.

"I don't—I don't know why I did that—"

I put my hand on her arm, turning her away from the stove, and hug her. She shakes against me as though anticipating another knock on the door any moment. In ten years of friendship, I've never seen her cry, much less weep, crumpled into it as if fully given over to the grief she hates so much. Her tears dampen Sidney's shirt, and each sob sends a tremor through my chest till my own eyes sting, for her, for Lena, for Sidney. I feel as though I'm crouched again in the aisle of a C-47, holding the gory remnants of a throat together. Helpless to put back together what the flak sliced through, when it unmade what had once been made in love.

Storm clouds roll past the valley. Soft rain falls in the sodden grass and the light changes, slanting through the kitchen windows with that strange, filmy quality of a sun-shower. I opened one of the windows while the eggs cooked, and now the scent of warm rain drifts through the screen into the kitchen, heavy with the fragrance of the apple trees. *Look,* I want to say to Grace, *there are still good things,* but why would she believe me, when I can't put her family back together?

"Richard." Her voice trembles on my name. She won't look at me, turning her face so I can't see its redness. "If you want to go home, it's okay, I'll be okay."

"I'm not going home. I want to be here with you."

She makes no attempt to dry her face, so I say, "Grace?" and I mean to say more, to reassure her that I won't go and that it's okay if she cries. But the words die out when she finally raises her eyes, those light-through-summer-water eyes, rimmed red round the edges, ashamed.

The stove crackles warm at her back. I wipe the trails of tears from her cheeks with my thumb as she makes a pass at her nose with her sweater sleeve. Slowly, a little stilted, she rests her head on my shoulder, and with that same careful movement I touch my hand to her back. There's no flush of romance to it, only her need for someone to hold onto. To be held onto. We stay like this for a minute till the rise and fall of Grace's chest slows.

"I think you should eat something," I murmur. "And you're probably dehydrated."

I guide her to the table, and she sits reluctantly. "You know, during the war, all us medics carried two canteens on our belts," I tell her, "one for ourselves and one for the wounded. So trust me that I know what it looks like when someone's used the last of their strength."

She spreads butter over the cold toast and I reheat the tea water, but she's really not herself when she doesn't dump three spoonfuls of sugar into her tea. After getting up to put the dishes in the sink, I almost sit back down in the chair across from her when she says, "Sit next to me?" So I do, the chairs a little too close, hip to hip.

In the steaming water my tea bag creates a plume of pale green, rising gold up to the surface. Grace lifts her tea bag by the string and bobs it through the water in her mug, like boatlines over a calm harbor.

"I don't know why I thought if we made it this far, we'd make it," she says, absently looping the tea bag string around her finger. She takes a sip and makes a face. "I think this needs something stronger, don't you?"

She goes to the shelf to the left of the sink, where a small collection of bottles crowds together, and takes down a fifth of Hennessy whiskey. It does wake up my senses at first, but its effect in the long run probably isn't so different from the drowsiness of chamomile.

"Things will look better in the morning," I say. "At least, that's always what my dad says, and sometimes he's right."

"Mm." Grace makes the same unsatisfied face again as she swallows her chamomile and whiskey cocktail, and pushes it away. "Chin up and all, that's what Grandma Pitcher would tell me—don't burden the rest of us with yourself, Grace."

She must see the confusion on my face because she waves a hand wearily, just as I say, "I'm sorry, that's not what I meant—"

"I know. I know it's not. That was the voice of Pitcher relatives possessing me. I didn't mean that at you, Richard, I'm sorry."

She looks so tired. I feel as though I'm searching in the dark under a raincoat, knees in the mud and only my hands to guide me, no light, for a spurting artery and a handful of seconds to find it and clamp it off. I don't know what it was that hit Grace before she got to Maine a decade ago, but clearly the veins were never clamped, and the wound is still hemorrhaging, just a years-long trickle instead of all at once. Shrapnel, left in the flesh, because it hit a place she could never reach on her own.

"No one else is listening," I say. She looks up, a thread of curiosity through the weariness. "You're not burdening anyone, Grace, not when it's only me."

"You have enough on your mind, Richard—you think I can't tell, but I can, and I don't want to weigh you down with—"

"You're not weighing me down. I promise." After a hesitation, I add, "They're all in the past, aren't they? Your mother's relatives?"

Grace tilts her head to the side. I can almost see the hundred thoughts that come to rest in the same moment. After a few seconds' deliberation, she says, "Do you believe in ghosts?"

If she'd asked me that in college, I'd have had some Protestant professor's intellectual answer ready to rattle off for her, that there's no margin for undead spirits haunting the earth while waiting to be let into heaven or hell. But that Protestant professor probably never saw a war and never was the transient watcher standing in the presence of those spirits passing. "Yes," I say instead, thinking of sleepless night after sleepless night filled with visits from old friends.

"I always ask God why it couldn't be the ghosts of my parents I see," Grace continues, "or at least hear, just so I could be with them one more time. But it's never them. It's always the ghosts of people who're still alive."

"The Pitchers?"

"The Pitchers and their big awful house in Ipswich that I hope burns to the ground. Of course, even if that happened, all they'd care about is collecting the insurance check and they'd tear each other to shreds for it.

At least that'd do the gene pool a favor, the less of them that are around to reproduce."

I set my mug down. All it took was a light tapping on the chisel positioned over the ice for the vein-like fingers of the fracture to spread. It frightens me, though, that this may be a spurting artery that I don't have any way to clamp, that the blood loss will be too great, that once again I'll be scrambling in the dark to try to hold someone together. Only this time, it isn't mortar shells breaking through the trees. If Grace's expression like she's just bit into a lemon is any indication, these hits are far more precise, more insidious, and able to continue their deadly work long after the first wounds have scarred over. Although by that last measure, maybe it isn't so different from a shell hit to the lungs, after all.

Grace taps her finger on a tear in the cloth, right through the heart of a honeybee. "If you knew them, Richard—the Pitchers—if you could see them in their ivory tower thinking it's the rest of the world that's out to get them but they never face any consequences for what they did..."

I wait for her to go on, but no other details are forthcoming. As carefully as pulling a stitch through a flesh wound that still stings, I ask, "What did they do?"

An agonizing few moments pass as she looks at me, our faces too close to hide any feelings. Then an iron grip releases from around my heart when the scales in her mind weigh in my favor. In this clear instant of understanding, I have a sense of the nature of our relationship immediately and irreversibly shifting. The change is palpable, like the birth of a child or a life extinguishing beneath your hands, and after it there's no going back to how things were before, whether for better or worse.

"I've already said too much about it. I'm sorry," Grace says, as though she was about to tell me everything and then saw one of those ghosts from her past over my shoulder. Just in case, I glance around, but the hallway is dark. "I didn't mean to bring you into this."

"If I'm in, it's because I want to be. Besides, they aren't here." I gesture to the kitchen, empty but for us and our mugs of chamomile whiskey and Baxter purring on Grace's lap. "So this is only your story, and no one can tell you it isn't. But you don't have to tell it if you don't want to."

"Richard, you don't have to do all this for me."

I give her a look that I hope says *Of course I do.*

She takes a deep breath, then rests her elbow on the table and bites at her thumbnail. "Sidney and I, we always looked out for each other, took care of each other." She doesn't meet my eyes. "Mostly he took care of me. He—"

It takes a long time for her to find whatever it is she's looking for. When she does find it, she says in a voice that doesn't sound at all like the girl I know, "Sometimes I'd watch from upstairs. It was a big old mansion with all sorts of places to hide, and I'd be where they couldn't see me. She always liked me better. Claire Pitcher, my mother's mother. She said that Sidney was a—a devil of a child, and that she had to discipline him."

Grace bites her lip as she glances away, this afternoon's tears brimming. "He always protected me, Richard, and I—I couldn't protect him from this. I couldn't help him."

Sidney, a devil of a child, needing the kind of discipline that brings his sister to tears a decade later? Nothing could be more contrary to how I remember him.

"She'd always tell us it was for our own good," Grace goes on. "That our parents would be so disappointed if they'd lived to see how we turned out. And she'd say there was still hope for me, but not for Sidney because he was too bad and he was beyond her saving, so it was up to the Lord what happened to him. And that was true, wasn't it? Because the Lord knows what happened to him, and what if I never do?"

I don't mean for the silence to linger as long as it does, but my mind is trying to comprehend a history for these two that I never once considered, and I can't believe I didn't. The pieces fit themselves together: Sidney's aversion to violence, always leaving me with the sense after fighting with Mattie that it was really Sidney I'd hurt; the way Grace carefully steps out of the light of honesty, like when we'd build fires at the river and tell ghost stories and secrets to each other and she'd cover her ears and refuse to contribute. Her finely tuned awareness of just who to be and what to say in any situation, except the one in which her brother might be dead. More than likely is dead.

"Grace, do you mean that your grandmother hurt Sidney?" I ask after a minute. "Did she ever hurt you, too?"

There's another too-long silence that answers the first question.

"No," she says softly at last, shaking her head, "she never hurt me."

That seems debatable, even if it is true that her grandmother never hit her. Everything I can think of to say in the way of comfort is so trite.

"I'm sorry, Gracie," I say quietly. I want to make it better, but I can't. All I can do is watch as the past and the present bear down on her from both sides.

She nods and gives me a sad little smile. After another spell of silence, she straightens her shoulders and says, "I've never told you how Sidney and I came here. Of course, your dad played a part."

"I know he paid most of the adoption and legal fees your grandmother couldn't afford—this grandmother, Hannah," I add.

"Yes, it never would've happened without that." She rubs the tip of Baxter's ear in her fingers, and then she looks at me with a softness in her eyes and something lifts from her. Not the grief or these memories, but maybe the loneliness of holding them without companionship. "Gran came once to see us a few years after our parents died. She'd been trying for so long to get to us and Claire always kept her away, burned her letters, told us she hated us. It was really the opposite, that Claire hated my father's family, those Maine rednecks." Here she smiles, but it falls away just as quickly. "I don't know why, but finally she let Gran visit us in Ipswich when I was 12. We had maybe fifteen minutes, but we could barely talk to her. We were being watched the whole time."

Grace's eyes are distant. She pauses, builds up her courage, and tiptoes again into the past, leading me along with her.

"As Gran was leaving—well, as Claire's butler escorted her forcefully out the door—she slipped a note to Sidney. It was the name of a minister in Ipswich, a friend of your dad's from seminary, and your dad had already arranged with this minister to help us. He was one of the few people there in a position of influence that the Pitchers didn't have in their pocket. Gran told us to go to him if we were ever in trouble, because he could get us to Maine. She was showing us how to run away. Taking care of us even when she was kept from kissing us goodbye." Grace hesitates, staring at the stove, and her knuckles tighten in Baxter's fur. "So we did. When things became too—um—well, we knew we couldn't stay. And that minister put us on a train for Caspar."

She doesn't say what the catalyst was, but I can guess well enough. I swallow back my growing rage for the people who hurt her because my anger won't do Grace any good, and this isn't about me. When she's quiet, I knock my knee against hers. She's tired and I don't want to force her to dwell on this beyond her ability, so I only say, "Thank you for telling me."

"I'll tell you the rest someday," Grace says as dusk falls outside, washing the kitchen in silvery light. "If you tell me some of yours."

We sit in the kitchen together without talking. Grace absently feeds Baxter a piece of crust. I shake the deck of cards from their packet and ask her if she wants to play, but she shakes her head so I deal a game of solitaire on the table. Baxter hums in contentment while she scratches him. Every so often she silently points to a card I hadn't noticed, and I place it on the stack under a three of spades or a queen of hearts.

Grace's contributions grow fewer and farther between until I feel her cheek on my shoulder. Her hair tickles across my collarbone. If I ask her if she wants to go up to bed, she'll say that she can't because she needs to wait up for her Gran. So I finish this game, gather the cards and shuffle them as best I can without waking her, and deal another round. I feel her breathing and her heartbeat slow till I know she's asleep.

I scratch one finger behind Baxter's ear, and he opens his eyes lazily and regards me with somewhat less disdain than usual. He stretches his legs out as I incline my head to the stove. Then he hops light as a feather from Grace's lap and curls up against the stove's warmth.

The house is dark, but the clouds moved away from the moon, its light glowing through the window at the top of the stairs as I carry Grace up. If she woke when I slipped my arm under her knees and the other beneath her neck, she didn't show it. Moonlight illuminates the oriental rug under my feet and glows on the white walls where silver frames encase photographs of Grace and Sidney as children—taken before their parents died, I'd guess—and some, too, of their father as a boy with his father and mother, a much younger Hannah Whitley.

In Grace's room I lay her on her bed as gently as I can, disentangling her arm from about my neck. I unfold a pink knit blanket from the end of the bed and drape it over her. This room hasn't changed much from the few times I saw it in years past, mostly when we were all spending the night with boys in Sidney's room and girls in Grace's and we'd poke our heads in to bother the girls before they chased us out. The iron bed frame is losing its coat of gold paint in chips, and the walls are still papered in a pattern of blush roses and green leaves. Nailed into the corner is a shelf that holds a collection of old books and dried flowers and cameos. I notice a double-sided picture frame that opens like a book with studio portraits on each leaf of her parents when they were our age. There's even a tiny porcelain cat the size of my pinky finger painted all black, just like Baxter.

Grace is out like a light, curled up on top of the white coverlet and pillows that look like summer clouds. I draw the curtain closed across the big window opposite the bed so the moonlight doesn't wake her. As I listen to the rainwater dripping from the gutters, I look around at the rest of the room. There's a white desk under the window where I imagine she grades French compositions and Latin conjugations during the school year, with more books crowded along the top; I can make out a few titles in French on their spines. In the daylight she must be able to see Mt. Katahdin from this window, maybe even the Alewife River where it cuts out of the trees. Beside the desk is a musty old armchair upholstered in mustard velvet, a book dog-eared on the cushion. I move it enough to see the cover: *Little Women*.

There's a rustle behind me, and Grace whispers, "Richard?"

"It's me."

I sit on the edge of the bed beside her. She doesn't seem to be really awake, her eyes still closed and one hand tucked beneath herself, but with her other hand she reaches across the blanket to touch my fingers. I turn my hand up so that our fingers are clasped.

At the touch she opens her eyes. We look at one another, indistinct in the darkness, quiet for a minute. Then Grace breathes, "Stay with me for a little while?"

"Okay." I brush my thumb along her ring finger, against the soft skin there. And I sit for a long time in the dark, listening to her breathing fall back into sleep, the warmth of her leg against my hip, till at last I ease up with a creak of the mattress and slip out of her room.

In the kitchen, the dusty Bakelite clock reads 9:28. Picking up my mug of cold chamomile whiskey, I go to the living room. Baxter pads after me. He alights on the couch beside me, and after a bracing sip of the tea, I reach for the half-finished Sunday crossword with the pen clipped to it from the coffee table. It's warmer in the kitchen, but I don't want to be in there without Grace. Too many ghosts. So Baxter and I do the crossword, and I ask him for an eight-letter answer for "to ponder deeply" as we wait to hear Mrs. Whitley's key turn in the lock.

PART II

CHARIKLO PRESS

XV.

TRANSIENT

19 August 1944, Quorn, England

Wildflowers wash the canal bank in coverings of blue and gold. Quorn's elusive sunlight spills through rolling clouds as a breeze tickles the translucent petals, delicate as tissue paper. Some float beneath the stone footbridge, an adornment for Ophelia, though I hope there are no drowned lovers in the canal. White wisps reflect on its languid surface. I hold onto all these bits as carefully as if they could disintegrate if I care too much. What a strange microcosm soldiers live in, believing the bloody marshes and dysentery-plagued camps to be the whole world. When you're in them, they *are* the world, or the world stripped to its skivvies, the unmentionables from which anyone else would avert their eyes. And when you've seen that, the stringy meat hanging off the skeleton after the world you thought you knew gets blown to hell, it's everything else that becomes a mirage. I sweep my hand through the wavering cattails and imagine this landscape in desolation, the canal poisoned, the cattails on fire.

But Jenny interlaces her fingers with mine and leans her head on my arm. We talk about growing up under the watchful eyes of the church, the Sunday School pranks and frogs in the offertory plate (I was grounded for two weeks after that one), the Nativity plays and fellowship dinners. But Jenny seems somewhat disinterested when I mention the dusty old copy of St. Augustine's *Confessions* that I found at the bookstore in the village. She hums her recognition when I say I didn't miss a single one of C.S. Lewis's "Beyond Personality" talks broadcast over the winter, which I listened to on a transistor radio in the frigid barracks in Belfast, alone at first and then others clustering around my bunk as the weeks went by. I don't understand her indifference, but it doesn't matter much. There's plenty else for us to talk about. She knows the name of every farmer in the surrounding Leicestershire countryside and the birthdays of their goats and grandchildren, who sprained an ankle in the field day races last spring and which old ladies are allergic to milkweed, which is all a pleasant enough distraction.

We walk along the canal path, Jenny laughing as I try to identify every plant I see. "What's that one?" I point to a patch of tall flowers growing on the bank, a cluster of white trumpets.

"I don't know. They all look the same to me."

"You don't like flowers?"

"They're pretty enough." Jenny shrugs. "But I'm not a botanist or an herbalist, so what are they really good for?"

"Jenny, every girl likes flowers. *I* like flowers."

She lets go of my hand, steps down the bank, and pulls a couple stalks of the white trumpets. Lifting the skirt of her blue sundress as she comes back, she says, "For you to take to your barracks and show to the other fellows so they can all be jealous." Then the wind blows so she has to promptly hold her skirt to her legs again as she holds the bouquet out to me.

"Oh, thank you, I'll be the prettiest bachelor at the Netherfield ball," I say dryly, but I've barely had time to take them—and wonder what to do with them—when Jenny takes my hand and pulls me to the shade of a willow tree whose branches sweep the surface of the water. I drop the flowers in the grass as she wraps her arms around my neck. Reflections of the water move in veiny shadows across the undersides of the green leaves.

"These Sundays are my favorite," she says, looking up at me. Light moves through her hazel eyes and falls across her face. Sometimes this war doesn't feel like a war at all.

"Mine t—"

I can't say the rest because Jenny kisses me with an urgency I wasn't expecting, as if I've just received orders to ship out tomorrow. She pulls me closer till her back is against the tree. I try to enjoy it, though I can't help thinking that what I'd really like is to sit in the grass and talk about more than just the neighborhood gossip.

She lets go of my neck. "What's wrong? You're all tense."

"Nothing, I promise. I'm just stiff from running yesterday. Let's walk some more."

The late summer light fades to copper over the canal. I've spent every Sunday with Jenny since our return from Normandy in July. I listen to her father preach at the Methodist church, and after the service he always insists I eat lunch with them. Each time feels like a feast in Camelot compared to the chow line and what passes for meat back at camp on the Estate. I love walking hand-in-hand with her through the village at twilight as the streetlights flicker on. I love Friday evenings at the Blacksmith Arms', dancing amid a haze of smoke and laughter. I count down the days till I can see her on the weekends, even as I try to convince myself that I don't want or need more in the way of companionship. In the back of my mind is the nagging question of what comes next, but whenever I approach the subject Jenny cuts me off with some playful observation or a kiss, and so the question crawls back into the dark, only growing in its need to be answered as the days pass.

After an evening at the Arms' in early September, Jenny leads me to the house with her after I try to drop her at the gate. I've never been in the rectory at night unless invited over for supper by her father, who, from the sound of it, is asleep upstairs. The snoring carries into the kitchen as Jenny holds her finger to her lips and eases the door shut without a squeak. I had enough to drink at the pub to make me tipsy, that in-between state when the stars seem to glow brighter and touch feels like more than touch. Rumor's been going round the camp that we're jumping this month into Europe. No one for sure knows where. But if it's true, then I have to know where Jenny and I stand.

If we were anywhere else, I might've been the one to pull her in. But Reverend Holbrook is home and I don't care that he's asleep; I still want to check over my shoulder in the dark living room as Jenny presses her mouth to mine and unbuttons my jacket with one hand. I try to ask her what will happen when I have to jump again, but she says, "Mm, I thought we didn't make promises, Richard."

Embers still glow in the fireplace in the warm little rose-wallpapered room. Whether it's the effect of the alcohol or the thought of an imminent jump into enemy territory, I choose to ignore the uncertainty, looming as ghostly in my mind as our shadows reflected on the wall from the gooseneck lamp Jenny turns on.

I don't care. *I don't,* I tell myself, as the moment shifts from innocent kisses to more than that. She backs up against the wall as my mouth brushes her neck that smells of cinnamon and vanilla. And so I guess it's because I don't care that I find myself leaning over her on the couch, lightheaded, telling myself it's just human nature.

But then I hesitate. I don't know why, staring at the curl of dark hair falling across her white throat, the heat of her cheek warming my hand. Before I quite know what's happened she's pushed me back on the sofa and begins undoing my tie, slinging it off with my jacket while she kisses me. She unbuttons my shirt, too, as my hand moves down to the small of her back. Then her yellow blouse floats to the floor and her skirt with it, and she's perched on my lap in only an ivory-hued silk slip.

She touches my chest, soft fingers trailing my collarbone. My head is swimming—is it her or am I more drunk than I thought?—and that touch, holy hell.

I feel her reach into my trouser pockets, and then she whispers, "Where are they?"

"Where are what?"

She laughs, pressing her cheek to mine. "What every GI keeps in his pocket. Condoms."

"...Oh." The thought never crossed my mind.

"You don't have any? ...Is this your first time?" Jenny's hand reaches for my belt before the matter of the lack of protection has even been settled. "How is that possible?"

I try to force the sudden tension out of my shoulders. "Does that make a difference to you?"

"That you're a virgin? Of course not." Jenny kisses my neck, quickening my pulse. "I'm just surprised."

"Shouldn't we—I don't have any, so shouldn't we w—"

"I don't care. It's more fun without."

"But I think I care..."

"Has anyone ever told you that you talk too much, love?"

I try to scoot to the edge of the sofa, but I had just enough to drink that sitting up is too much effort. "You know, I don't think that—"

"It's only one time. It doesn't even matter about the condom, just this once."

"But I think it does, because it only takes...three months from now I could be dead while you're pregnant and alone and I just don't—even if I make it, what then, do we get married—"

Jenny rolls her eyes. "You're not going to get me pregnant. And I'm not marrying you."

"How do you know that?" I take her hand and guide it away from the zipper on my trousers. "I just don't want us to regret anything."

"Does that mean you regret me?"

"No, that's not what I mean, Jenny, you know that."

"Good."

She trails her fingers down my neck, her touch lingering on my ribcage. With her other hand, she tilts my head back and kisses me till I feel all the blood in me rushing to certain places. "There you go," she purrs against me. "That's right."

Three months from now I could be dead, my own voice echoes in my mind. I don't really want to die a virgin, like some pagan sacrifice. As Jenny presses herself into me, I have trouble remembering what I was protesting. One hand on the softness of her hip, mouth moving across her throat, I say, "Let me ask you something."

"Mm."

"Do you love me?"

"Do I love you?" She laughs. "Come on now."

I pull back enough to see her eyes. "...I didn't think it was a complicated question."

"Richard." Jenny sighs. "Is that what this is all about? Heavens, and I thought GIs were sex-hungry, the lot of you."

"So all this doesn't really mean anything to you?"

She touches my cheekbone with her perfect finger and whispers, "I didn't say you don't mean anything to me. You do."

"But you don't love me." I press the heel of my hand to my bleary eyes, feeling suddenly very drunk. "And I don't love you, either."

"It was never about love. Wasn't that what we said?"

"That was what you said. I'm sorry, Jenny, but it means too much to me and I—I can't do it, I'm sorry."

She tugs at the end of a curl in her hair and turns her face toward the hearth. The moment has passed, and my desire recedes with it.

"We're moving out soon. That's the rumor," I say as I try to do my belt buckle, but my fingers might as well be coated in slick oil. I reach for my shirt and tie and jacket. I don't want to be here anymore. In fact, I can't seem to get them on fast enough, desperate to escape this room and go out free into the night air.

"That's it, then?" Jenny looks back at me and for a moment, held by those eyes, a rush of affection almost makes me stay.

But I stand, unsteady on my feet as I do up my buttons and belt and say, "I'm sorry." Then I wait, not sure if I expect an apology or even if she owes me one, but nothing comes.

Instead she sighs and shakes her head. Even that rings of an accusatory nature. "If I'd guessed how serious a personality you really are, I might never have danced with you that first night."

"So you'd give up all the fun we had."

"I don't know. I thought we agreed about no promises."

"And sex isn't a kind of promise?"

She doesn't answer.

"Jenny, you've made Quorn feel like the closest thing to home," I say quietly, realizing that I'll never be able to think of this village without also thinking of her.

She stands and we go into the hall and linger in the doorway for a minute, not quite looking at one another but not quite looking away, either.

"Take care of yourself, Richard Dare," she says at last, raising her head with a resigned smile. "You're sweet. But you might try climbing out of your own mind once in a while."

She kisses my cheek, and I leave her standing in the dark doorway as I cross the garden to the front gate. When I glance over my shoulder, the door is shut.

1 September 1944, Edinburgh, Scotland, 1530 hours

S team rises off the placid surface of the water. I carefully set my uniform jacket on the arms of a hanger and hang it on the towel rod as sunlight cuts through the narrow window high above the porcelain bathtub. The street outside is quiet except for the birds on the roof gables singing. As if we ran to the edge of the world to hide, trying to find eternity in a weekend pass.

I grimace as the scalding water meets my foot. The light falls through it so beautifully that for a moment I don't want to disturb the surface. My hands, I notice when I turn off the hot tap, are not the hands of the kind of man who stays in a hotel on Edinburgh's Royal Mile, even if it is the cheapest of the lot. I turned twenty-two in June but when I lower myself into the tub, my hips feel thirty years older. Despite spending half the summer in dirty trousers and a jump jacket, my arm is brown against the alabaster tub.

With the water pooling around my propped knees, I'm too tired to even move one finger. *It was never about love,* Jenny said. But isn't everything about love? Even when it's missing. Maybe most when it's missing. I stare at the plaster wall and ask myself for the hundredth time what must be wrong with me to turn down a girl like her.

She said it as if I was the idiot, the uncultured American. As if love as a feeling and love as an act are so divorced from one another that only someone with no experience of either could conflate the two. I guess the ending spoiled the rest of it because I don't miss her. But she has left me with a bitter taste in my mouth, wondering if after all this is over, if I'll even be able to love anyone. Or if I'll just be begging for love wherever I can find it, cloaked in its shame and lack.

I rub my eyes with wet hands and try to bring myself back to the light-filled bathroom. For the first time in months, it really is quiet. I don't hear anything within the quiet, which surprises me. The first sentence of *Pilgrim's Progress* comes to mind: "As I walked through the wilderness of this world, I lighted on a certain place where was a den, and laid me down in that place to sleep; and as I slept, I dreamed a dream."

Rumor is we'll celebrate a German surrender by Christmas. I'm not so sure. I don't know why, but every time someone mentions going home, a voice in my mind whispers that it can't be that easy. No respite of three-day passes and steaming baths can alleviate the weight of that doubt.

The water has gone lukewarm by the time I wake up. Seems that what I told Berk in a foxhole in the Bois de Limors was more prophecy than I thought, and after a full day in Edinburgh, his bloodstream's probably a quarter Scotch. I reach a dripping hand out for my watch: just past five o'clock. The light has moved and turned the color of tangerines through the water.

In the bedroom I'm sharing with Peter, Berk, and Fish, so tight that we can't all stand comfortably at the same time, I tuck my trousers into the Corcorans and lace up. We couldn't stretch our jump pay to afford more than two rooms, though it's generous to call the space on the other side of the wall where McNuts, O'Connor, and Skinny are staying a "room."

There's no bathroom attached so they have to come over to use ours, and last night it didn't take more than two seconds after walking in for McNuts to misjudge the water pressure on the shower and flood the tiles. At least he gets his own bed in the broom closet, after Berk refused to share with him "because he kicks in his sleep like a sonuvabitch." I swear I saw McNuts smirk at that.

"This hotel wasn't built for Americans," Peter muttered earlier, lying flat on his back on the bed to lace up his boots so he wouldn't kick Fish, who was on his hands and knees on the floor, hunting a runaway cuff link. "Matter of fact, the proportions of this whole country weren't built for Americans."

"There might be a reason for that," came Fish's voice from beneath the bed.

When we got off the train at Waverley Station last night, barracks bags on our shoulders, the sight of the old jagged skyline made me stop in my tracks. Structures older than time itself, rising to pierce a tumultuous, leaden sky. Mossy green Aston Martins and silver Bentleys idled at the curb as their headlights cut through the gloom. I might've stood transfixed for ages if Peter hadn't called, "Rev, you coming?"

Though the sun has parted the clouds tonight, I know the weather here turns from peace to squall on a dime, so I resolve to enjoy the absence of rain for however long it lasts. The long humming notes of bagpipes fill the evening air as sunlight flickers on the gothic bricks. I walk slowly down the sloped Royal Mile, away from the castle, glancing at storefront windows with my hands in my pockets. Laughter and snippets of Scottish accents drift through the air as I walk by the White Hart pub, its doors open to the evening. The church steeples remind me of the sandcastles Laurie and I used to make at the beach when we visited our grandparents in Boothbay, scooping up handfuls of wet sand and squeezing it out between our fingers in drips.

I squint into the distance at the craggy hill, Arthur's Seat. Spires grow indistinct in the haze, and the gold-handed clock on the weathered façade of a church ticks to six o'clock. All the narrow alleys and tight staircases and pass-throughs connecting one building to the next fascinate me. Who lives behind those white-paned windows and beneath those steep gables? I feel as if I'm walking across the backbone of the world. "Athens of the North," Jenny called it, a name that seems to sum up all the disparate parts of me and stitches them into a whole. Dad wrote me last week that he thinks the Dares come from clan Ross, far north, near Inverness. I wish he was here to see this. I wish I could show it to all of them, this moment exactly as it is, not through a postcard of Edinburgh Castle from a tourist kiosk.

A bell chimes as the door opens from a shop called "Lindsay's Fine Woolens and Cashmeres." Peter comes out carrying a white paper bag.

"Sarge, I don't think fine cashmere is regulation dress code," I call.

Peter turns and grins. "There you are. I was wondering if we'd ever see you again, or if we've lost you to Edinburgh." He fishes out of the bag a cherry-red scarf overlaid with green and gold thread. Looping it around his neck, he says, "It's for Chrissy. Think she'll like it?"

"She'll love it. Is she Scottish?"

"Not that I know. I just picked the nicest plaid." He glances down at the label sewn into the scarf. "Clan Cameron, apparently."

We walk down the Royal Mile, reading the names of shops aloud, pausing to hear bits of conversation between the people who pass by. Peter folds the scarf carefully and tucks it back in the bag. "Do you miss her?"

"Who?"

He bursts out laughing. "I guess not, then. If you've already moved on from Jenny so quick—"

"Oh. Well, I guess that's your answer."

I stop as we draw near to St. Giles' Cathedral. The dark medieval windows are webbed with what appear to be thousands of cracks, but it's just that the angle of the sun hasn't hit perfectly to illuminate the stained glass. Spiked flechès catch the light as they cut like spindles into the fading blue sky, and squat crosses loom above the saints carved in relief over the doorway.

We look up at the spires in silence.

Peter looks at me. "Go on, give me the full history. I know you know it."

"I have read a few things here and there." I slide into the offered conversation opening and make myself comfortable. "It's more than a thousand years old, and—apparently—St. Giles was actually a Greek hermit who lived in France, and his only friend was a deer."

"A Greek hermit whose only friend is a deer? Is that you in twenty years?"

"If I pray hard enough, maybe."

"How'd he get to Scotland, then?"

"I don't think he did; they just named this cathedral after him. He was the patron saint of lepers."

Peter shades his eyes from the lowering sun. "They sure built a pretty church."

"John Knox is buried somewhere around here," I add, glancing behind us at the wide square around the cathedral. "We might be standing on him, as a matter of fact."

"Another saint?"

"No, the opposite. The father of the Protestant Reformation in Scotland. Actually, he converted to Protestantism and escaped to Geneva, where he met John Calvin. Then he came back to Scotland, and on June 29th, my birthday as it happens, he marched right into St. Giles' with all his disciples and hangers-on, and had the gall to just preach here like he owned the place. They elected him the minister, and two weeks later the Reformers started purging the church of everything Roman Catholic. Then a few months later it was back to Catholic, and the next year it was Protestant again..."

I finally stop to catch my breath. Peter, listening graciously, looks at me and laughs.

"You learned all that in college?"

"From my dad, actually. Scottish Reformation history is a specialty area of John Dare's."

"What a character. My dad's specialty areas are insurance sales and fishing in Tichigan Lake." He nods toward the door of St. Giles'. "You want to go in?"

Four boys crouch near us in the shadow of the cathedral, shooting marbles on the crooked cobbles beneath the carnelian-colored glass. Palace Beautiful, steadfast on the backbone of the North. I eye the dark stone crosses. The truth is that I'm afraid to go in, for fear the past year has carved out my prayers into hollow, worthless husks.

"I'll come back tomorrow," I say to Peter, because I don't want to admit that I'd rather not make a spectacle of myself before God.

We find Berk, Fish, and O'Connor playing cards at a café table outside a pub called the Scotsman's Lounge, on Cockburn Street, which curves like the inside of a conch shell. Berk and O'Connor are playing, really, and Fish is tilted back on the legs of his chair, sketchbook on his knee, looking up every so often at the light-ebbed street. A little white terrier with a duster-shaped tail trots up the cobbles, and an old couple ambles after him, hand in hand. At Berk's prompt, Fish puts down a card without looking at it, eyes never leaving the couple as they climb the winding sidewalk.

I thought he was drawing the cityscape, but when I sit beside him, I realize it's a sketch of Berk and O'Connor. Berk's hands in graphite pencil are frozen in the motion of shuffling cards, and O'Connor's elbow is on the tabletop, his face in profile, laughing. I look up at them, the sketch come to life.

"Hey, Fish, that's really good."

He starts as if I gave him an electric shock. "Christ, I didn't even see you guys. Yeah, thanks." He tilts the sketchbook so that it catches the light and then the shadows. "Just a sketch. I got tired of drawing buildings."

"You going to show us those someday?" Peter wonders as Berk gathers up the cards to shuffle and deal us in again.

Fish shrugs. "I might. I'm afraid we'll never see any of those photographs the regimental photographer takes, so I've got to do this instead."

There aren't as many American soldiers in Edinburgh as in London, which gives the city a quieter atmosphere, its local flavor not too dimmed by foreign presence. Three middle-aged women are engaged in intent conversation at the table behind O'Connor's shoulder. There's a young couple two tables over, both no more than sixteen or seventeen, giggling as their forgotten tea grows cold. The boy blushes the color of Peter's scarf as his girl laughs and reaches for his hand, her head tilted as she smiles at him.

"Puppy love," Berk says, dealing out the deck. "That's sweet. Hey, Toothpick, they're almost as old as you. Maybe he'll be a flake, and you can take her dancing."

O'Connor rolls his eyes. "Don't need her. Been going with the same girl since I was fifteen."

"So about a year now?"

"Four years, and you're just jealous of my youth."

Peter puts down a three of hearts and says, "He's right about that, Berk. Kid's still young while you've only got, what, a screwed-up hip to show for all your trouble?"

"Hunk of metal six inches long—ask the Rev, he was there!"

"I heard you woke up from surgery and asked if you could keep it," I put in. "The shrapnel, not your hip. Though that was touch-and-go for a while."

"It's a survivor's limp, thanks very much."

"Tell that to your titanium hip in ten years," O'Connor snorts, grinning and ducking out of the way as Berk tries to elbow him in the ear. "So where is it, that shrapnel?"

"Hell if I know. I don't even remember saying that. I was high off my ass on morphine."

Fish's chair tilts forward and he holds up his hand, the pencil between his fingers. "You two," he says to Berk and O'Connor, "don't move. Berk, can you make that face again? Yeah, perfect."

"So where're Tweedle-dee and Tweedle-dum?" I ask as I consider my cards.

"Skinny said something about sightseeing"—O'Connor's eyes flick toward me as he sits stiffly with his head turned—"which I think means being on the prowl for girls. Fish, can I move? My neck's gettin' sore..."

Berk signals the waiter as he comes out of the restaurant. "There he is, finally. Drinks on me, boys, because I've been married *three* years today."

O'Connor whistles and calls him an old man as Peter and I tell him congratulations, and Fish squints at his sketch before chiming in with his own belated "well done."

"Not sure I deserve that. After all, we've spent more time apart now than we have together. Actually, we've never been together for an anniversary. I left for basic before the first one."

"Poor Emily," Peter says. "Of course, keeping house is probably easier without your sorry ass to clean up after."

"I'll drink to that." Berk takes his Scotch glass as our waiter disperses the rest. "Thanks."

Fish puts his sketch down, and O'Connor lets out a dramatic sigh of relief as he rolls his neck. Peter holds up his glass. "I'd make a toast, but Richard is the poet among us."

"Me? Not really," I protest, but now they're all waiting expectantly. I lift my glass, thinking of the one thing we all want. "To going home—to Emily and Chrissy, and—what's your girl's name, Toothpick?"

"Katherine."

"And Katherine," I add just as footsteps reverberate on the cobbles and Skinny and McNuts run up, out of breath and red-faced.

"Don't interrupt our toast, you Philistines," Berk says to them. They fall exhausted and laughing into chairs around our crowded table—so either they gave up on flirting and climbed to the top of Arthur's Seat instead, or they were a little too successful in their wooing—and raise aloft the extra two drinks Berk ordered. "Richard, you may want to take it from the top."

"Jesus," Fish says.

I wait for Skinny and McNuts to get settled. "As I was saying. To going home—to Emily, Chrissy, Katherine, and Eva—" Skinny nods appreciatively—"and to living the rest of our lives in peace. And to Edinburgh, which I don't think any of us will ever forget."

"And to Grace," Fish adds beside me, smiling helpfully as if I'd forgotten.

"If you were paying attention to the pattern, I was specifically toasting wives and girlfriends—"

"Wives, girlfriends, old flames, fool's hopes..."

McNuts sighs. "Can we drink or not?"

"You know what? Scratch all that. New toast," I say. "To the biggest platoon of idiots in the whole 82nd. You all give me a headache. Happy anniversary, Berk. *Yamas, slainté, l'chaim,* whatever the hell you all say."

"Or just 'down the hatch,' if you're my grandma," Peter remarks.

"What was I thinking? Of course Richard wouldn't be toasting to Grace, not yet." Fish sets his half-empty glass on the tabletop. "First we have to get a few drinks in him to help him get over Jenny."

"Who said I wasn't over Jenny?"

"Hey, we never heard why you told her to take a hike," McNuts says, only one drink in and already rosy-cheeked and gossip-hungry. He's a discredit to Irishmen everywhere.

"This is Richard we're talking about. He probably wrote her a letter of resignation and had it notarized."

"Berk, don't make me reach across this table—"

He grins and stuffs his hands in his pockets as he leans back in his chair. "That a threat or a promise?"

"Listen, I already asked him about her," says Peter, swallowing the last of his drink, "and he's so over her, he forgot he ever had her."

"Again," Berk notes, "this is Richard we're talking about, so who's to say he ever really had her? You know what I mean?" His chair tilts forward, and he points at me and crows triumphantly. "I knew it. I knew I could make you blush, you Puritan!"

"No one in my family was a Puritan! Not everyone who lives in New England is a Puritan! Fish is from New Hampshire, and you never say he's—"

"Fish just sits there and draws his pictures. He doesn't preach to us about, hell, I don't know, the martyrdom of the Early Church."

I point at Berk with one of Fish's pencils. "Next time you get a chunk of smoking metal six inches long in your other thigh, you can find some Jewish medic to stop up your spurting arteries."

Berk slings his arm around the back of his chair and grins. "He'd probably try to charge me first, though."

Fish cups his hand around the lighter flame as Skinny holds it out for him. It flickers blue to match the deepening sky. "British girls are swell," he says, "but sometimes I wish I had a girl waiting at home."

"Well, I'll tell you, there's nothing I look forward to more than Chrissy's letters," Peter answers. "They make me remember why I'm here and doing all this. But having a girl means having more to lose. I'm always thinking about that."

"Me too." Berk nods. Just as the mood begins to feel too somber, the waiter props open the door, and the sound of live music and singing drifts from inside the Scotsman. Berk orders another round and spirits rise again. We're swept into laughter and arguments and I don't realize how late it is till I glance up and notice the moon has risen, a quarter of silver hanging over the city. Inside someone's started a riotous chorus of "The Parting Glass," sung in a thick Scottish brogue, that carries out into the cool night air.

"'Of all the money that e'er I had, I spent it in good company,'" O'Connor sings, and McNuts downs another Scotch and joins in.

"What is this song?" Berk says, humming along.

A drizzle begins to fall and within seconds, it becomes like buckets of water dumped on our heads and cuts the two Irish boys off mid-verse. We scoot back our chairs, and Fish scrambles to tuck his sketchbook inside his uniform jacket as we run into the Scotsman with dripping hair, trying to all squeeze into the front of the smoky, crowded pub. An old man at the bar lifts his beer to us and sings as though we're old friends returned from a long time away:

> *So fill to me the parting glass,*
> *And drink a health whate'er befalls*
> *Then gently rise and softly call*

Goodnight and joy be to you all...

XVI.

SURRENDER

14 August 1945

"And that's why I'm taking such preventative measures to keep the gout from returning."

"Oh," I say, not quite following the trail of Mrs. Moore's family health history, which included unexplained references to her grandmother's dalliance with a Millinocket postman and the possibility that her nephew is defrauding his Boston law firm. I'm sure it would all make sense in connection to the recurring gout in her knees if I wasn't so distracted by my desperation to return to the Red Sox game, which I had to turn down on the radio when she came in.

"The doctor has raised his rates, surely," Mrs. Moore remarks with a testy note to her voice. She glances up at me while writing out her check with the start of a conspiratorial smile. I smile back and fold my arms on the desk. Better to say nothing at all than to contradict a patient.

Warm air from the street wafts through the door as she marches out with the assistance of her umbrella, even though the sun is streaming through the practice's windows enough to make me squint. I wait till the door swings shut behind her, then scoot back in my desk chair so fast I almost roll over my feet. I flick the volume up on the radio that sits atop the steel filing cabinet—just in time, too, to hear Catfish Metkovich's bat make contact with Bill Zuber's curveball. Dr. Linstead was called to the Delfinch paper mill because one of the line workers was having chest pains, which is why I can listen to the game broadcast from New York. That's also why, as I'm kneeling in front of the filing cabinet to reorganize a billing system that hasn't been revised since probably 1912, I don't hear the bell jingle or realize someone came in till a familiar voice says, "Put your shoulder into it, Catfish! You swing like a little girl."

I start up so fast I hit my head on the arm of the desk chair and fall back to my knees, the sound of my swearing followed by Grace saying, "Oh!" and laughing and then, from the sound of it, trying to hold back her laughter.

"Are you okay?" She comes around the desk and crouches beside me. "I'm so sorry, I couldn't resist."

"You too could resist." I do my best to be offended as she presses her lips together, although they tremble. "How did you know that's exactly what I was thinking about Catfish?"

"Because you were talking to yourself."

"I don't talk to myself."

Grace snorts. "Richard, is the pope Catholic?"

I give her a look, but when she grins I can't keep a straight face for long. We're lucky no one else comes in and finds us sitting on the floor behind the desk with my dropped files scattered around, laughing at apparently nothing.

"Okay," Grace says at last. She wipes at her eye and smooths the pleats of her navy skirt over her knees. "Let's pull ourselves together. Look, you aren't even bleeding."

"Would it be funnier if I was?" I bat her hand away as she tries to touch my forehead. "No, don't try to be sweet now."

She touches it anyway. "It'll just be the tiniest little bruise. But if you can see your way to forgiving me, I came to ask if you want to have lunch with me."

The pharmacy is as crowded at noon as Caspar ever gets. Kids sit with their legs dangling from the stools at the counter, sipping on root beer floats and listening to the game. Grace and I slip into the last empty green-and-white booth under the window. I tilt my head toward the magazine rack by the door.

"There's your man Jimmy on the cover of *LIFE*. For a dime, he could be yours."

Grace looks over her shoulder at a black-and-white Colonel James Stewart striking a natty pose in his Air Force uniform. "Oh, I didn't even see him there."

"Right, and the pope isn't Catholic."

Neither of us say it, but I sense we both know that something changed between us the night of the telegram about Sidney. I think of the way she let me hold her in the sunset kitchen with her hair and skin still damp from the shower. How I would've told her that day if the courier hadn't appeared out of the rain, carrying the phantom of someone we can't even be sure is dead. The not telling her in the weeks since then has eaten away at me more significantly than all the last ten years put together. But it'd be real shitty of me to try to fill her grief and confusion with my own feelings, which is why I've promised myself to just let her be for a while.

Grace dips a french fry into her root beer and says maybe she'll sacrifice a dime for Jimmy on our way out. But from her unfocused stare at the apothecary shelves on the back wall, I can tell her mind is already straying. And for a few minutes, at least, I want her to be able to think of something other than Sidney, a subject we'll eventually have to broach. So I steal a fry to get her attention, and as she swats at me I say, "Would you rather step on a porcupine or walk across hot coals?"

"Would I rather...what?"

"Porcupine or hot coals." I snap my fingers at her. "Any day now, Whitley, first thing that pops into your head, before the coals get cold."

"Well—um, hot coals," she says, tapping her fingers together. "No, maybe the por—no, it's the coals, definitely. Because I don't want to squish the porcupine and hurt him."

"That's the right answer. You've earned back one fry." I put one of mine on her plate.

"Is this what you lie awake at night thinking about?"

"You'd be surprised. Okay, your turn."

She considers. "Would you rather...eat your weight in coconuts or drink only orange soda every day for a year?"

I hold my index finger under my nose to mimic a mustache and drawl in my best Groucho Marx impression, "'Me, a man who's eaten his weight in live caterpillars, afraid?'" at which Grace bursts out laughing.

In a disturbingly better Groucho impression than mine, she adds, "'That's fine. Why don't you bore a hole in your head and let the sap run out?'"

The irony of a couple of the highschoolers glaring at us to be quiet only makes it worse, so we turn our faces away and laugh.

Careful not to let high spirits drop, I answer, "You had to pick two flavors I hate, didn't you? Coconut and orange soda."

"Are those the ones you hate?" She shrugs and sets her chin on her hand. "I forgot."

"You never forget anything. I can already feel my organs shutting down, but I guess the orange soda for a year, because 145 pounds of coconuts in one sitting might kill me."

"145 pounds? That's generous."

"Excuse me!"

Grace grins as she reaches for her grilled cheese. "Oh, Dennis put tomato on this. Well. I suppose I need something healthy to counteract the fries. Go on," she waves her free hand at me, "ask me your next challenge so you can eat that BLT and claim even 140 respectably."

I flick a bit of soda at her with my straw. "Let's make this harder. Would you rather sleep alone the whole night in a haunted house or run naked through a graveyard?"

"Richard!"

"You wanted me to ask you."

"Actually," Grace says, "I have done that."

"You've run naked through a graveyard? Why didn't you give me a heads-up?"

She nearly chokes on the root beer and starts coughing. "No, you idiot. I slept in a haunted house. Last summer—you know that old house by the river, technically on our property? My great-grandparents used to live in it, but it's been abandoned for years. Toni and Helen and Mary and I made a bet that whoever chickened out first had to give the other girls five bucks each. But no one paid up because we all made it."

"How do you know it was haunted?"

"How could it not be?" Grace shakes her head. "You lie there with the lantern making shadows on the rotting walls and tell me you don't hear footsteps creaking about upstairs. And," she adds matter-of-factly, "Toni saw a door close."

"Well, I bet there's no glass in the windows. The wind would've blown all the doors shut."

"She saw the lock turn, too."

"Did you or Toni consider the possibility that someone completely human and alive was there, too? And how much wine did you fortify yourselves with before you marched out there?"

"I don't have to listen to the justifications of skeptics," she says, adopting an expression of apparent indifference. That means they were at least tipsy.

"All right, then I'll amend the question—would you rather spend *another* night in that house and this time completely alone, no friends, or run naked through a graveyard?"

"Graveyard."

"I didn't say what time of day it was, or if there might be a parade going on in town."

"Or what graveyard, so I picked that overgrown one out past the train station. You can't even see it from the road anymore."

I point a fry at her but realize I've been outmaneuvered. "Yeah. Okay. You win, Whitley."

Sunlight falls through our drink glasses and on Grace's bare arms in emerald waves. She hasn't cut her hair all summer, and I like how the loose curls fall on her shoulders and how the sun's brought out the freckles across her nose. The volume at the counter rises but when she looks at me it feels as though we're alone, and the kids' voices and even the Sox game cutting in and out on the radio all fall away.

There's a smile playing around her mouth, but she's looking at me with an expression I don't understand.

"...What?"

Grace stirs her root beer with the straw, not taking her eyes off me. "Tell me something about yourself that I don't know."

"Is this a test...?"

"I'm just curious."

I sit back and think. "Oh. I have some freckles on my left wrist that look like the Little Dipper."

"No, you don't. I would know that."

"I do, promise," I say, and I unbuckle my watch and hold my wrist out to her.

"Huh. So you do. Or it could be a mouse—there's his tail. Have you got a cat on the other wrist?"

"I hope not."

She smiles. "Okay, tell me another."

"There's not much more you don't know about me—"

"C'mon, Richard, there has to be something. I'm trying to make up for three years' worth lost time."

"Lost time?"

"You know what I mean."

I've always assumed it was only me carrying regrets, even though those three lost years were completely out of my control. But Grace is more practical than I am. I've never known her to look back like this.

She's still waiting, though, so I reach for the cherry on her plate. She always takes it off the top of the soda and saves it for last. "Can I borrow this? Just the stem."

"You're not doing what I think you're doing," Grace says, sitting up and crossing her arms on the table in rapt attention. "No way."

I pluck the stem off and toss the cherry back to her. "For the prettiest girl in the audience."

"I'm absolutely blushing."

It takes about thirty seconds for me to tie the cherry stem with my tongue; not my best time, but I have to contend with heckling from the peanut gallery across the table. Giving her my best victorious "I told you so face," I say with a lisp, "Excuse me." Grace nods and laughs as I spit the tied stem into my hand, a tenuous knot through the middle.

She shakes her head, looking somewhere between intrigued and repulsed, clapping as I mock bow over the tabletop. "And here I thought

Mattie was the master of party tricks. How did that one never come up before now?"

"Mattie's the master of shots, not much else. And you didn't ask till now."

"Can I ask you something else?"

"Of course."

"You've been home for almost four months, right?"

"Something like that."

"It's just..." Grace pauses, watching me again with that expression I can't place, though I sense that this time she won't be asking me for party tricks. "Well, when you stayed with me after the telegram—I never said thank you."

"You don't have to thank me, Grace."

"I know. But you've done so much for me. And I wanted to know, well, how things are for you, I guess."

"What do you mean?"

Grace twists her mouth in thought. "Being home. Are you all right? That's all I mean—if you're all right."

"Sure," I say, without considering the question. "I've got no reason not to be."

"Well." Grace raises her eyebrows at me. "That's not really what I asked."

"Are you thinking about this because of Sidney?"

"No, I'm thinking about it because of you," she answers. "I'm asking you, Richard, not Sidney."

"Of course I'm all right," I say to satisfy her, though she doesn't look convinced. "I made it home, didn't I? That makes me one of the lucky ones."

"Yes," she says after a moment, with a little sigh that deflates her watchfulness. "I suppose it does. We know that all too well."

"Speaking of, I assume you've had nothing from Lena?"

Grace shakes her head.

"She'll come around. And mail from Australia takes a hell of a long time, especially with a war still on."

"You're right. Yes, of course, you're right." Grace nods. She reaches for the salt and sprinkles it like snow on her fries. Mid-pour, she says, "Do you feel lucky, then?"

"What was that?"

"You said you're one of the lucky ones, but do you feel that way?"

I'd rather not say that no, I feel like a stupid SOB with a crippled body and no direction to my aimless life except when I'm laughing with her, so I only shrug. "Not most days."

"Sometimes I do." Grace twirls her straw, staring at our crumpled napkins on the table, then lifts her head and smiles at me. "Feel lucky, that is." When I tilt my head in a gesture for her to go on, she says, "I don't know if I should say it. It makes me sound cruel."

"You're not cruel. And I was in the Army; I have a pretty thick skin when it comes to honesty."

She drops the straw and folds her hands together. "I think about how if you hadn't gotten wounded, you might've never made it home. I know it almost killed you, but it brought you back, too." After a moment she adds, softer, "That's awful of me. To ever want anything to hurt you."

We're both quiet for a minute. Her words skim a thin surface beneath which is so much more that neither of us has ever said.

"I don't know if I can think of it that way yet," I answer at last. "But that doesn't mean I think you're wrong."

"To our mutual wisdom, then," she says, raising her root beer. We clink our glasses, and then I set mine down. When she's glancing out the window, I take out the straw and stick it in hers. She turns her head back to take a sip and jumps at finding us face to face. "Again! You did it to me again! How much of my rightful soda have you drunk in your life?"

"Mine was all bubbles, and yours is always sweeter."

I'd walk on my hands across the soda counter if I thought it would make her laugh even more. Short of that, as we stand and argue for a moment about who's paying, I fish in my pocket for an extra dime, make it to the counter and the till before her, and tell her to fetch Jimmy from the newsrack on our way out.

I jerk upright, the edges of the sheets caught in my fists.

Moonlight spills onto the tangled covers and for a moment, the white sheets look like the snowy ground in Belgium. I see a river of blood pooling in one of the folds and flinch away from it before I blink and realize there's nothing there. Only the shadows of the trees outside, swaying in the moonlight, and Hen, looking up at me with sleepy eyes. The images of my dream disintegrate as quickly as the bloodied sheets. All that's left is discomfort and disquiet, every breath and heartbeat threaded with unease.

I flip my pillow to the cool side, lie back down, and close my eyes. Every night I go to bed early because I can't keep my eyes open, and then I lie here in darkness for hours watching film-reel memories play on the ceiling, each minute feeling as long as a year, the hands of my watch on the nightstand ticking by interminably. Whenever sleep does finally catch up with me, at midnight or dawn, it's too thin to bring any relief. And there's not been a single night since I came home that the war hasn't visited me in dreams.

There's the sound of a light switch flicking on in the hall. I open my eyes and watch a shadow move across the thin stripe of orange light beneath my door. Lying very still, listening, I wonder if I might've screamed during the nightmare and woken someone. Well, Dad was probably already up.

Then there's a knock. From behind the door I hear his voice, quiet: "Richard, you awake?"

"...Yeah?"

"You might want to come downstairs."

"Are you okay? What is it?"

I hear another door creak open. Hen whines and hops off my bed as I reach for my bathrobe on the end of the bed frame. She scratches at the door with her paw.

"I'm coming. Dad?"

The hallway and stairs are bathed in light that makes me squint. Dad is standing at the top of the stairs, still dressed, so he must never have gone to bed.

"What's wrong?"

He glances up. "Nothing, nothing. I only thought you might be awake and if you were, you might want to hear this live."

Laurie's bedroom door opens. His disembodied voice says, "You having a meeting of the UN out here or what?"

"John, are you coming to b—oh." Mom appears in the door to their room, wrapping her thin cotton robe around herself as a draft rattles the windows. "What are we all doing out here?"

"Well, I didn't mean to wake the whole house, but as long as you're all up now." Dad waves us toward the stairs. "There's something we should all hear."

"What time is it?" I say, pressing my hands to my eyes and seeing gold sparks.

"Past 2:30." Laurie sounds characteristically put-out.

In the living room, Dad fiddles with the signal on the radio as voices cut in and out over one another. "It was working a few minutes ago, one of the Bangor stations was clear as a bell."

I let Hen into the yard so she can inspect the perimeter, as she likes to do whenever she thinks something's wrong. Mom leans on the banister, setting her chin on her hands. Her eyes fall shut. Laurie balances on the arm of the old green armchair and I sit on the bottom step, where I can keep an eye on Hen patrolling outside.

Then the signal catches and Dad says, "There we go."

Whatever's going on in the Bangor newsroom sounds like chaos. I lift my head and listen.

We all wait in hushed silence for the announcer.

And finally: "Just a couple of minutes ago, at 7:35 AM London time, the Swiss Radio in London received the official report of Japan's surrender from Allied officials in Tokyo. Again, we are reporting that the Swiss Radio in London confirms the Japanese surrender from Tokyo..."

Dad's hand is still on the dial. None of us move as the announcer repeats the report, adding information as it arrives in their newsroom. He keeps saying, "The war is over. The war in the Pacific is over."

No one seems to breathe. Even my chest is quiet.

"I'll put coffee on," Dad says.

H en jumps onto my bed and circles the same spot in the tangled sheets three times before curling up and tucking her tail between her legs. She watches me from a swath of moonlight, concern in her eyes only for whether I'm coming back to bed. I lean against the window frame and stare out the pane at the road in the darkness, the streetlamps out, the church steeple barely distinguishable in the black sky.

It's over, a nurse told me in Belgium, when I was delirious with a fever that first night in the field hospital. *You can sleep now.* But I couldn't sleep. It wasn't over, it had never ended, and it still hasn't.

I walk from the window to the bed and sit and stand up and walk back again. My fingers tingle with that falling-asleep feeling, as if in the last year they've done just that. They seem to remember better the sensation of thirty seconds on a trigger in Holland than all the days and nights of wrapping bandages and pressing syringes.

Most of the time I was too late. That time I was also too late, but for half a minute the power to kill quickly and violently was in my hands.

I don't know how anyone else does it, how they live now. Any of them who were really soldiers. Because I was hungry to feel the kickback on the M-1 I lifted off a dead body in a moment of blind rage, but those guys marched with their rifles on their shoulders every day. Empty cartridges fell away in places like Biazza and Nijmegen like wheat chaff, ghoulish relics ground into the dust under Corcoran boots, and unless a guy was a real sicko he didn't count how many. He just followed orders and fired his weapon.

If I'd been in any other branch, if I'd listened to Sam that warm June afternoon three days before my birthday in '42. If I'd joined the line for the Marine recruiter beside him instead of letting the glamorous rumors of the Airborne capture my attention, I might've carried a rifle same as him. Might've died on a tropical atoll like Saipan same as him. And that would've been for the best because I'd have been a monster with a weapon in my hands. I don't mean I'd have been good at being a soldier. Just that I'd have been a menace.

I lower myself onto the floor, breath warm on the palms of my hands as I cover my eyes as if to hide. But that childhood logic doesn't make what happened in Nijmegen come untrue.

XVII.

NIJMEGEN

20 September 1944, Hunnerpark, Nijmegen, the Netherlands, 1620 hours

When you've been fighting for long enough, you start to imagine things. Real horrible, gruesome things that would deeply disturb your minister father a world away if he could see them.

You imagine all the ways you'll die, piecing together scraps of all the deaths you've witnessed, till you have your own Frankenstein's monster of what your body will look like when the machine guns or artillery or fuck-all is through with you. It's wicked, and it's even wickeder to imagine what your folks would think if they could see that body. A twisted thread of pleasure runs through those images. You start to long for it.

Then you think things like, *I've made it this far, but this next step will be it.* And, *Maybe this is the last time I see the sky. Or the last thought I'll have.* And you realize you don't want your last thought to be wishing for a pair of clean skivvies.

You see some poor bastard who never had as much as a hangnail get his legs blown off. Every moment you tell yourself you've come to the end, and you're shocked when it's not you. Then each step feels like struggling upstream in a storm-churned river, the crash of gunfire and artillery slowed till they sound like groaning ghouls, and the battlefield becomes a psychotic maze.

But to my disappointment, on this autumn afternoon in Hunnerpark, I do make it through. Crawling on my stomach through the Lombardy poplars draped in gowns of smoky gold, I see forms hardly more substantial than ghosts ahead of me. .20 millimeter shells rip through a pale fabric sky and through the cover of the trees, blowing shredded tatters of crisp orange leaves over my dirty hands. Bodies lie in inhuman positions throughout the park, draped across one another like ancient sacrifices among the Roman ruins. On the stretch of river west of the bridge, the water is calm and silver under an ashen sky. East of the bridge, the 504th paddle across open water in boats, bombed and strafed by the Germans holding the Lent riverbank. I see a mortar shell detonate in a white geyser on the water and swallow a boat whole.

Enfilade fire sweeps through our lines from snipers hiding in the Valkhof ruins. The park slopes to the river, terraced grassy stretches winding like ribbons through the quivering trees. Two bridges span the Waal River, connecting us in Hunnerpark on Nijmegen's northern bank to Lent's southern, and the battalion's objective is to secure the bridgeheads and sever the krauts' vital supply route along the Rhine. The park is inconsequential, but they're dug in here on the high ground, hiding out in machine-gun nests and artillery emplacements in the crumbling ruins that pepper the woods. In the remains of Charlemagne's palace on the Valkhof hill, they pound us with all the shit that can be stuffed in a gun barrel and fired. But we still need the bridgeheads, and unlucky for the krauts, these paratroopers have lost too many friends today. Like a helpless graveyard witness to a procession of the dead, I watch them in my peripheral vision, fighting savagely, almost animalistically. Any residual mercy in them is not suppressed but crushed.

I stagger to my feet on the unsteady ground as white tracers arc over my head. A shroud of blue smoke hangs in the air, and the poplar and birch trees cast the park in looming shadows. One moment the silver strip of river glimmers in the haze; the next it disappears in the breeze sweeping the smoke along. I want to hold my hands to my ears and scream at God about how the fuck I'm meant to help those I can't even hear or see.

But in listening against the roar, I remember how to feel out the wavering thread of weak humanity all but swept into the roiling, mechanical current. When you find it, clear as a bell on an empty Sunday morning, you tug it and hold on for your fucking life. For his. And so I run.

As I crouch in the haze, stuffing bandages into a private's open chest wound, I see paratroopers flinging grenades into the German foxholes and charging with bayonets. The smoke burns my eyes as I try to see what's become of my platoon—and then I spot Berk's distinctive limp, his mouth open in a perpetual shout as he signals to his riflemen.

"It'll be close quarters fighting, boys," Lieutenant Greer said earlier to the platoon. We'd gathered in the skeletal shadow of the bombed house serving as aid station.

"Fuck it, sir, we'll take 'em hand-to-hand if we have to," Berk answered, and some of the boys have taken that bravado to heart.

This kid would probably still be on his feet with his rifle if he hadn't charged ahead of his squad right into the fire. Wide-eyed replacement with stars in his eyes and a hell of a lot to prove. As I push up his jacket sleeve to insert the catheter needle for the plasma, I happen to look up in time to see another replacement in Berk's squad pull the pin on a grenade and throw it into a kraut slit trench, where two SS grenadiers are scrambling to reload their overheated machine gun. He jumps back and covers his face with his arm—and nothing happens. It's a dud.

"GET OUT, Linitski, get the hell out!" Berk screams, or I think that's what comes out of his mouth. He jumps from one of the terraced ledges and runs toward Linitski and the dud grenade, but he's too late, and I'm close enough to see it all unfold like a horror film from which you can't look away. Before Linitski can escape, one of the SS grenadiers snags his ankle, drags him back, and sinks the end of his bayonet in Linitski's back. He's gotta be dead before the blade even comes out.

I stare at his body face down in the wet grass. Once in Airborne training, I lost my grip on the wooden wall we were ordered to scale in the rain, fell flat on my back, and knocked the wind right out of myself. I feel it again now, and I'm afraid that every last one of them will end up like skewered animals, flesh sodden and bloated in the mud till the grave crews swing the rotting bodies onto the trucks for burial.

My breath returns, jolted back into me, when I see Berk scream orders to destroy that kraut gun. So help me God if they're all as foolish as Linitski. Three of Berk's guys dispatch the gun crew with grenades that aren't duds, and then they drag Linitski's body away, where it will wait until I come to tag it. I want to scream at them all above the artillery to be careful—fuck you, just be fucking smart about this. Don't make me come tag your dead fucking body lying open-mouthed in shock because you couldn't control yourself. Who the fuck cares if the Allies win this shitshow, if we're all lying under white crosses by the end?

A gurgling sound snaps me back to the private on the ground beside me. As I talk to him, Lieutenant Greer shouts from the cover of a brick wall encompassing the park. DeMartino's voice follows, screaming into the radio about support on our right flank. I pass them with my hands hooked beneath the private's arms just as an .88 shell slams into a 2nd platoon officer three feet from us. It blasts half his torso clean away.

2nd's medic Walt Bruning appears through the haze and flings himself down beside the lieutenant. Fox is hemorrhaging officers like an arterial flow; he's the third casualty in minutes. That can't be coincidence. I stop and crouch over the private with the chest wound, angling my body to shield him, and look up into the splintered trees swaying over the wall. That's when I see the barrel of an .88 poking through a hole in the bricks, one of those massive hidden guns that can uproot hundred-year-old oaks. It's targeting individuals. Officers.

"GREER!" I shout, dropping the plasma tubing from my teeth to call his name. The kid in my arms groans in pain as I lower him to the grass. From behind me come the agonized shouts of the 2nd platoon boys whose lieutenant just died in their arms. They run past me, promising to rain holy hell on that ill-judged kraut gun crew, and I scream at them to stop as they make for the wall. No one listens. "Greer!" I shout again, voice cracking, sweat running into my eyes, feeling as if every person who crosses my path is running to his death.

The acrid smoke dissipates enough in the breeze that I catch a glimpse of Greer, crouched at the wall with platoon headquarters and shouting to Sergeant Autry. Just far enough from me that the fire swallows my voice.

I lift the kid again, tubing in my teeth, and drag him behind the jagged stump of a beech tree's remains. "You two," I shout at the riflemen using the stump for cover, "get him to the aid station. That's an order!"

I hand the plasma bag and tubing to one of them and then I make for the wall, screaming Greer's name, pointing, but he doesn't hear me.

"SIR, GET D—"

The machine gun propped through the hole in the bricks opens fire. I drop to my stomach in the grass just as Lieutenant Hastings falls sideways, a shot clean through his neck.

The fire lacerates DeMartino's voice: "L-Lieutenant—Hastings—d-down—"

"Is anyone else hit?" I shout. "Sir, are you—" I crawl to Greer, daring not to lift my head for fear it'll get popped off. He was thrown onto his back, wind knocked out of him, brick dust in his nose. Blood spurts from the side of his left knee like a sieve jammed into tree bark for syrup. "No no no, you're not getting up. Stay down!"

DeMartino screams into the radio that we need mortars on the enfilade wall as I drag Greer away. He winces at every throttle of the artillery guns, fingernails digging grooves into my wrists when I stumble. Tracer fire opens up in front of us. Two dozen rounds weave in a fatal tapestry, so we stop on the slope, the burned-out frames of Nijmegen's buildings wavering like heat mirages in the smoke. I touch the bloody, ragged edges of Greer's wound gently, my fingers brushing bullet fragments. I bind the bandage as tight as I can to stanch the flow. Blood soaks it as though poured on.

"Jesus Christ, I can't believe—" he grunts out, dropping his head back and sucking his breath through his teeth as I try to gingerly navigate the crushed bones protruding from his knee. "—Sonuvabitch. Can't believe I was that stupid—"

"Not your fault, sir."

"Gone and got myself knocked out of this fucking thing..."

"You're not out, sir, just down." I start to break open a morphine syrette, but he shakes his head to stop me. Cries for a medic pierce the air, and I say, "I need to go. Can you get to the aid station?"

He nods and begins the uphill crawl on his elbows. I've never seen fire so close, almost point-blank range from both sides. One of the British tanks blasts the wall where the machine gun strafed us, and brick fragments and dust explode into the trees. The SS grenadiers pull back only momentarily before they stand their ground, planting their guns in the rubble and opening up on the wooded hillside.

I squint through the ash falling like autumn snow. The only way to get to the wounded who are stranded on the descending levels of the terracing is through this fire. Just as I draw in my breath, hoping for some bravery, someone shouts, "Dare!"

Bruning is beside me on his stomach. Blood, probably not his own, cuts dirty trails down his neck. He wipes sweat from his eyes and shouts, "I'm making a run to the aid station. I'm clean out. What do you need?"

"Whatever morphine they can spare, bedsheets if there're no more bandages, and I have a feeling I'm gonna need vein clamps—" Artillery rains on the slope above us, and I have to scream in his ear to be heard. "Vein clamps! Whatever you can get!"

"Got it. Keep an eye on my boys? They're—"

A single, metallic ding cuts him short. Without so much as an inhale, he slumps forward, falling onto his chest on the grass.

"Walt! Walt, hey, are you..."

He doesn't get up, doesn't shake himself off and snort cynically at how lucky he is. *Shit shit shit shit shit.* Maybe it glanced through his helmet and exited without hitting his head. Maybe it was only a ricochet, though I know it wasn't because I saw it. Maybe it just knocked him out. But I know that's not true as I stare at the little tendrils of smoke curling up from the perfect hole right through the back of his helmet.

It's that bit of smoke, so distinct even in this gray landscape, that snaps me out of the reverie. I roll him onto his side. Dead eyes greet me, not even a trace of shock in them. It happened that fast.

"Fucking hell," I mutter. I reach for his hand. Already stiff. With my other hand I shut his eyes. *Sorry, Walt, I'm real fucking sorry.* Could've been me. Should've been me.

And then I just sit here beside him, staring at the soiled brassard on his arm and the bit of red-dyed fabric that pokes out through the dirt. It's as if I'm staring at myself, at the body I've imagined so many times, only it isn't a mangled and torn-apart body. One bullet, straight through. *I'm clean out.*

"Rev, hey, Rev!"

I look up, dropping Walt's hand, and see O'Connor crouching in front of us. He's got two bandoleers of ammo for a light machine gun draped around his neck. From up the slope comes the sound of Peter's squad flushing out the ruins.

"Ah, shit. No way." He stares at Bruning, shoulders dropping till he looks again like a nineteen-year-old far from home, not the hardened soldier I've watched him become. "All right. What do you need?"

I shake my head as I rip off a tag from Walt's booklet and begin writing the details. "Nothing, get back to your gun."

"Richard—"

"You hear that shit?" I shout, nodding to the ruins hidden in the trees and smoke. "Your squad needs you! Branson needs you on the gun!"

When O'Connor doesn't answer, I raise my eyes from my trembling handwriting. His mouth is set in a hard line, and in his eyes I can see he's already made up his mind. I don't have the strength to argue with that stubborn Irish expression. There's no sending him back, not till he's helped me somehow. He'll follow me like a stray dog.

I lean over Bruning's body and reach for his kits. Just as he said, he's out of everything but a couple rolled bandages. I stuff those into the pockets of my field jacket and yell to O'Connor, "You sure you want to help me?"

He offers no change of expression, no hesitancy, only that characteristic bullheadedness I never could've imagined from the jittery kid outside the barracks that night in England when we first talked.

"Go to the aid station, get me as much as you can—bandages, morphine, and see if Doc Ryder can spare any vein clamps. Actually, anything they can give you. As much as you can bring back to me." I loop the straps of Bruning's kits over O'Connor's head. "I'll find you."

"You got it, Rev," he says, and then quick as a shot he's up and gone, jumping like a track-and-field hurdler over the dead. As soon as he disappears, the roar of the battle fills my ears as though I've risen to the surface after too long underwater. I pin the tag for the graves crew on Walt's jacket and try to swallow down the bitter taste in my mouth. A whole life boiled down into that scrawl on a tag. Name and date and means of death, and all that differentiates him from the hundred other casualties rotting in this wet grass is a filthy brassard.

We weren't close, but there was always a dark-humored camaraderie between the three of us Fox medics, me and him and Donny King. No one else could ever fully understand. Two platoons need me now. If it had been me with a bullet through my skull, and Walt were alive instead, there's no doubt what he'd do.

I slither through the soaked grass, looking for wounded. The tracers are thick as a French hedgerow. They sever the fragmented words knocking around my skull—*whatever it takes whatever You ask of me*—sucking all meaning from the syllables till they melt into the siren scream of noise on every side. Twice I hear the whistle of an incoming mortar just in time and roll out of the way, by the grace of God not rolling myself into machine-gun rounds.

"Sonuvabitch, Rev, what the hell are ya doin'? You're gonna get yourself killed!" someone screams. It's Santorini, under the yellow birch trees with his mortar crew. I didn't realize I got that close to the rear. The mortar boys are set up behind some sandbags not far from the traffic circle that 2nd platoon secured, and just beyond them is the street strewn with debris and the pharmacy-turned-aid station for 2nd battalion. Behind me the steep slope of Hunnerpark drops away, riddled with slit trenches and bodies and razor-sharp tree limbs and hidden guns. And at the end of that is the river and the two bridgeheads, the crux of this whole bloody fucking shitshow. If the boys don't get through the park to the bridgeheads, this'll all have been for nothing.

Rodriguez drops a round into the mortar tubing and shouts, "Hanging!" and Skinny answers, "Fire!" All that signals the round's departure is a little puff of air. Skinny's still shouting at me as they load the gun again, but telling me I'm in danger won't get me to them sooner. As I'm pulling myself toward their gun nest on my stomach, a German MG-42—better known to us as Hitler's Buzz Saw—hidden somewhere in the ruins swings around and opens fire on the mortar boys.

I've seen the rounds from this gun cut men in two. The boys hit the deck but not before Skinny fires off the hanging mortar round. Just as he does, his back stiffens. Rodriguez grabs him and pulls him down, shouting for me.

I hit the ground, feeling the rush of air as the rounds ricochet over my back. Then I hear a gun discharging and the Buzz Saw goes abruptly silent, the space it leaves filled with the whoops of British grenadiers as their tank trundles by.

Skinny is on his back beside the mortar tripod as the boys crouch over him. When I'm close enough, Rodriguez grabs me by the shoulders and drags me into their sandbagged mortar nest.

"Rev," Skinny grunts when he catches sight of me. "Rev, c'mon, tell these idiots I'm fine. They're makin' a fuss for nothing."

Under my hand, his heart is going a mile a minute. His skin is pale and clammy, body temperature dropping alarmingly fast. Blood has pooled in the grass beneath him. That can wait. I can't do a blood transfusion, but I have lost boys to shock. It comes so suddenly, so quietly, a thief in the night.

"Skinny, I think this time they might be right," I say as I fish out my last plasma bag and tubing and cut open the sleeve of his jacket to expose his inner elbow. "But you're gonna be just fine. We're gonna see about getting you out of here. I'm giving you some blood plasma, okay?" I unscrew my canteen and reconstitute the plasma with a few drops of water. "It's a beautiful shot; you shoulda seen it from where I was. Million-dollar wound."

"Million-dollar wound?" he repeats, inhaling shakily. "Like the going-home kind?"

"Could be. Eva'll be real happy to see you." As I say her name, I stick a morphine syrette in his shoulder.

"Shit..."

Rodriguez holds the tubing for me, barking out an order for the two privates to resume their places with the gun. I swab the alcohol in Skinny's elbow. The moisture helps illumine the blue veins in his olive skin. As I try to find a vein, he mutters something, twitching his head from side-to-side in the grass.

"What is it?"

"My legs."

"Your legs?"

He swallows hard. "I don't know, they feel...well, I don't know how they feel."

"Okay. I understand." The last thing he needs is to panic that he might have just been paralyzed. "Nothing for you to worry about now. Help me get him back to the aid station," I add to Rodriguez and one of the privates. "Careful of his spine, boys."

The façades of the burnt Nijmegen homes and shops up the street from Hunnerpark loom hauntingly in the gray air. Rain begins to fall, making the smoke feel thick and solid in my lungs. I clutch the plasma bag in one hand, the tubing between my teeth to keep it from snagging on the ground, as Rodriguez and the private fasten together a makeshift stretcher. They lift Skinny onto it. He doesn't make a sound, but his hand squeezes mine so hard I expect to feel a bone crack.

"Holy shit, you seein' that?" Rodriguez shouts, tilting his head.

I glance over my shoulder. Colonel Vandervoort and two other officers are walking toward the battle as casually as if taking a stroll through the park. I watch incredulously as he strides right up to Peter, whose squad is fighting tooth and nail with the SS around the Valkhof. Vandervoort says something to Peter and gestures to a stationary Sherman tank nearby.

Rodriguez laughs humorlessly. "These officers are crazy as shit."

Someone shouts "MEDIC!" near the ruins and Rodriguez tells me to go, promising they'll get Skinny to the aid station. I find one of Peter's replacements with a flesh wound on his arm, not serious, probably not even serious enough to be screaming for a medic. Sometimes it takes a few days for these new kids to figure out what'll kill them and what's just a waste of my time. But his anxiety over a bullet nick in his wrist dropped me in the right place at the right time, because I see Peter break away from Vandervoort, sprint to the British tank through a maelstrom of fire, climb up onto it, and pound on the turret with the butt of his service revolver. The tank commander pops out of the hatch like a rabbit from its hole. They talk for maybe a minute, Peter pointing out targets, all the time completely exposed. Then he hops down and signals to his squad to follow him, or what's left of it. I see blood on Fish's neck and the flash of Branson's grim face as he hoists up the tripod and gun and runs.

It's Branson alone with that gun that reminds me of O'Connor. They're a pair. I haven't seen any trace of him since he left me with Bruning's body. Then Branson stumbles and falls back, dropping the tripod and the gun in the slick covering of leaves. His trousers are soaked in blood when I reach him. It was a tracer into his right femur. If he's in pain he barely shows it, only clenching his jaw when I bandage the wound, a couple of "fucking hells" making it past his teeth. I tell him I've got him as I swivel my head to look for O'Connor. Peter's squad is storming the ruins with no covering fire on the machine gun. Rain drums on my helmet, running into my eyes and cloaking the dark trees in mist so I can't see more than a few feet ahead.

Branson can't move even to drag himself, so I prop him against a tree on the wet leaves, empty his rifle of ammo and switch on the safety just in case, and splint it to his leg using ripped bedsheets. I shout to catch Peter's attention. He and Fish are crouched in the cover of a crumbled stone archway, eyeing what appears to be a barbed wire entanglement protecting a Great War-style trench through the trees. I shout his name again, and when he lifts his head, I angle my chin in the direction of the street beyond the park. "I sent O'Connor for supplies, but I'm out of everything. I'm gonna go find—"

"Rev!"

I turn and come nose-to-nose with O'Connor, who has a white-knuckle grip on the straps of the two kits hanging at his side. Peter signals to him to get the machine gun and follow them to the trench, and O'Connor signals back in the affirmative.

"Rev, I got you the bandages and sheets," he pants, dragging the back of his hand across his eyes. "They didn't have much morphine, but I took what I could..."

"Okay, good, got it. Go, sarge needs you."

Peter and his boys have gotten past the wire and dropped into the trench. O'Connor retrieves the gun, and I crouch beside Branson again. His eyes are shut, head tilted against the tree trunk as rain soaks us. I talk to him as I dump the supplies O'Connor gathered from Walt's kits into mine—a few rolled bandages, some balled-up sheets that don't smell clean, a couple of morphine syrettes. Those won't go far.

Branson says something I don't catch. Peter and the rest of the squad are embroiled in what sounds like hand-to-hand combat with the SS in the trench. "What's that, Scotty?" I say, checking his bandages again. "You just take it easy. I'm gonna get you back to the aid station."

He says the same thing, and again I can't hear him, but on the third time I do: "O'Connor..."

"What?"

He nods, eyes staring past me. I look over my shoulder.

O'Connor is flat out on his stomach above the trench, alone, providing covering fire for Peter and 1st squad in the trench. He feeds ammo into the Browning machine gun with one hand and fires at the Valkhof ruins with the other. I don't know if he misunderstood Peter's order to join them in the trench or if he's disobeying it on purpose. Either way, covering fire in that spot is a suicide mission.

"O'Connor!" I shout. The Brits have gotten off a few good hits on the ruins, but nothing short of death will stop the SS in there. They return O'Connor's fire, tracers gleaming in the steady rain. "O'Connor! You need to get down! Get out of there!"

He shoves a new clip into the gun and pulls the starter. If he hears my shouts, he ignores me. I try to run to the trench, but the tracer fire at hip-level forces me to drop and drag myself through the leaves.

It's almost too easy for an experienced SS soldier.

"Jacob, get out of there, you're gonna get hit! JACOB—"

No sooner do I hear the whine of the Buzz Saw than twin rounds hit him.

I get to my feet and run, reaching the trench just in time to keep him from falling in. One round in his chest, one in his stomach. Maybe the gunner has mercy on me because I find the two of us in a pocket of quiet amidst the horrific, endless noise of fighting.

"It's okay, it's okay, I've got you," I say, words to placate my own thudding heart. Jacob isn't convulsing, isn't panicking or crying for his mother. "You're okay. Let me take a look at these. I'll get you back to the aid station."

His wrist closes around mine. "Richard."

My other arm is under his head, the full weight of his body on me. He doesn't have the strength to hold onto me and drops my wrist. I feel along his chest and then his stomach, my hand instantly soaked in blood.

"It's not so bad," I lie. "Two scratches, that's all. Enough to go home, probably."

I slip off his helmet and set it on the ground beside him, running my hand through his dirty blond hair, praying that the touch is of some comfort. Jacob's skin has lost its flush, his lips bluing at the edges. He starts to tremble in the cold rain. I keep talking, aware of the panic in my voice but unable to control it. Two bullets in him, and he's calmer than I am.

He turns his head to the side, falling against my elbow. "It's okay. You don't have to s-say that. W-whatever it takes. You taught me that, r-remember?"

Fuck. Why'd he hold onto that? Just something I carelessly told him the morning after D-Day when we were marching between hedgerows looking for our company. He said he saw me praying on the plane the night before and asked what prayer it was.

"I did, didn't I? But you don't need to think that way yet, Jacob, I'm going to take care of you and get you home. Get you back to North Carolina. Your folks will be so glad to see you, and your sister, and Katherine—"

"That's okay." His voice weakens with each word. "I kn-know they'll be...upset..."

"No, that's not true. They're so proud of you. They couldn't be more proud."

Jacob takes a deep breath, closes his eyes as his temple brushes my jacket sleeve. "Where's...where's the chaplain?"

"I'll find him."

"I don't want to die—without—without—"

"I know. You won't. I know it's not the same, but I'm here."

"...Okay." He swallows. Blood trickles from both sides of his mouth. He touches his chest, searching for his dog tags, and I guide his hand. He clenches them against his grease-stained jacket. "Just—tell the g-guys—"

Whatever he wanted me to tell the guys is lost forever because another shot rings out. I feel the force of it hitting Jacob's side, throwing me backwards onto the leaves. I don't know how the bullet misses me. When I crawl back to him, his gray eyes flick toward me, his mouth open in shock as blood runs down his chin. And then he's still.

I feel someone watching me and look up through tears clouding my eyes. An SS grenadier in the ruins has the Buzz Saw trained on me. Whether that last shot was meant for me or Jacob, I doubt I'll ever know.

The grenadier stares at me, then slowly pulls back the starter on his gun.

I drop Jacob's body, grab his rifle from the leaves beside his machine gun, raise it, and pull the trigger. Then again and again and again, startled at first by the kickback I haven't felt since target practice in basic.

Cartridge casings fall away. The fourth shot hits the grenadier in the left cheek. I fire again and clip his shoulder, and he drops below the stone wall.

I strip Jacob's body of his ammo and jump into the trench with his rifle and run along the length, jumping over bodies, following the sound of Peter's squad flushing out the last stretch. The trench ends at the dip in the hill that drops to the approach road and the southern bridgehead.

The tattered remnants of 1st platoon have dug the SS soldiers out of their emplacements, and the black uniforms swarm down the hill toward the bridge. A fucking turkey shoot.

Peter and 1st squad are already firing. Climbing from the trench, I reload, then begin picking off as many as I can. One stumbles, falls, gets back on his feet and tries to run, bent almost double and pressing his hands to a wound. I shoot him three times.

A handful make it, sprinting to what they believe is the safety of the bridge, but one remains. It's the one who killed Jacob. I know from the blood caked on his left cheek. He runs in a limping gait. Gritting my teeth and shutting one eye, I take a deep breath, and just as I fire a strong hand grabs my shoulder and a familiar voice yells, "Okay, soldier, that's enough—"

I turn and Peter stares at me. "...Richard?"

Wrenching myself out from his grasp, I look back toward the river. The grassy slope, slick in the rain, is so strewn with bodies it's impossible to tell if I hit my mark or if he got away.

XVIII.
SISTER

10 September 1945

"Hell must be freezing over if you're on your second drink, Richard." Helen clinks her glass against mine. "Is work that bad? I thought you'd like Linstead's."

"Sorry? Oh, no, work's fine," I say absently. Across from the bar, Mattie solemnly presses a bass clef key at the piano. The somber note fills the nearly empty Green Moth, and he pulls a face of mock pity. I roll my eyes. "Most of the time. If they're not calling to yell at me over the telephone when it's not my fault they missed their appointment, then they're coming in to show me the rash on their leg, right there in the waiting room." I shrug. "Sure, I guess I have a kind of medical education, but not like they think."

Mattie tilts back his third scotch and lets his fingers travel an octave on the white keys. "So you're saying I shouldn't come in tomorrow, detach this bastard"—he taps his prosthetic—"and throw it on your desk?"

"No, go ahead. I'd rather that than Walter Adams describe to me again his gastrointestinal troubles."

Helen snorts. "I'll take the drunks I get here."

"You mind very much if I'm your next?"

"Richard Dare, drunk? I've never had the pleasure. But it's never you I'm worried about."

"I resemble that remark," Mattie throws over his shoulder. "And correct me if I'm wrong, Dick, but didn't I hear a rumor you were a medic during the war? How is it some old fellow's irritable bowels are what finally do you in?"

"Yeah, that's just it—during the war. I hung all that up the moment I became the patient."

Craning his head back toward the floral carvings in the plaster ceiling, eyes closed, Mattie plinks out a tune that sounds like "Taps." The restaurant closes at 10 on Friday nights, only a few minutes from now, but there are still a handful of inebriated regulars finishing off their drinks at the other end of the bar. I got here in enough time to listen to the last of Mattie's set, which at the late hour was mostly melancholy jazz songs set to the mood of dusky red lights and forgotten drinks. They feel oddly appropriate as the days shorten and the moon rises earlier and cold air nips down off the mountains, summer's face hidden once again. Eight long months of winter ahead.

Helen, relieved from front-desk duty in the hotel, tops off our whiskey and sodas. "Play us something nice, Mattie."

"You didn't like that?"

"It was a little gloomy."

"Hm." He swallows the last drop in his glass, crunches on the ice, and tries a few chords. The chords turn into "Somewhere Over the Rainbow," and he says, "How's that song for gloomy?"

"Have you seen Grace this week?" Helen asks me.

"Mhm. I brought her lunch at school yesterday."

"She's putting on a brave face."

I tear off the edge of the damp napkin under my glass and watch Helen's ashy blonde head tilt in the mirror behind the bar. "Yeah, she is."

"She told you something, didn't she?" Mattie says. "That night after she got the telegram."

I nod, thinking of the orange glow in the stove when the telegram burned. The ache in Grace's voice when she told me about the black mourning clothes.

"That's why I wanted you to stay," Helen says. "I know there are things she won't tell even me and Toni."

"I don't know." I finish my drink and shake my head when Helen gestures to ask if I want another. "I felt like there was more I could've, or should've, done, and I didn't know how to help her."

Helen smiles consolingly. "I promise you, Richard, you did everything you could, and she knows how much you care."

"I guess I never realized..." I hesitate, careful in holding Grace's story because it isn't mine. "I never realized how much she and Sidney protected each other. And she feels like she's let him down. Anyway, I've probably said en—"

The bells over the door jingle, and I turn around on my stool as Helen calls, "We're closing, actually, but if you need a room, the front desk is on the other side."

A woman in a beige trench coat is standing with one hand on the half-open door and the other holding the handle of a battered suitcase, which looks barely held together by its hinges. Stray bits of dark hair fly out from under her silk scarf in the breeze.

Helen hops off her stool. "I can show you—"

"Sorry, I went in there. No one was at the desk." The stranger steps aside as one of the regulars stumbles out, tipping his cap to her.

"Dad, for Pete's sake. Must've been on his bathroom break. If you need a room, I'll check you in."

"Oh, no, I don't need a room." She crosses her arms and tucks her bare hands beneath them, then glances back over her shoulder, out the open door at the cool September night. The temperature's only in the mid-fifties, but her cheeks are white with cold. "I came from the train station. I'm looking for the Whitleys', thought I was on my way there when I got lost and saw the hotel sign..."

Mattie and I glance at each other. He raises his eyebrows as his hand absently moves across the keys, filling the quiet room with solitary notes. I try not to stare at the woman, but her face is so familiar, and I can't pin down her accent.

"The Whitleys'?" Helen repeats. "Oh, you must know Grace from college. Did you go to BU, too?"

It's when she hesitates that I suddenly know, the certainty of it as familiar as my own name. Of course. Her features begin slotting into place in my mind, based on the one photograph I've seen of her.

But it can't be.

"If I could impose on one of you for a ride, I don't know how far it is..." Before I can rouse myself from the stool and say her name, she tilts her head, watching Mattie at the piano. "You're Mattie, aren't you? The piano player."

He looks at Helen and me and then back to her with a cornered-animal expression, as if expecting the woman to produce a cop with a nightstick from beneath her trench coat. "Who's asking?"

"And you're Helen," she continues, "and of course, you must be Richard. You're all Sidney's friends."

I unhook my feet from the rungs of the barstool and stand. "...Lena?"

"It's Lee-nuh, actually," she answers with a prompt smile. "But if she'll do just as well, then yes."

We stare at her in perfect silence. I'm dimly aware it's not the warmest welcome, but I have no idea what to say. Then Mattie lets out a low whistle.

"I assume Grace has told you about me?" Lena looks between the three of us. She looks exhausted in the harsh shadows from the porch light, but hopeful, too, that second wind when you know the end of the road is close.

I can't see her, but I feel Helen's thousand-yard stare as she says, "Yes, she's told us."

There's a silence that lingers for just a moment too long till Mattie clears his throat and Helen starts to say something, and Lena says instead, "No, it's okay. I don't want to take up more of your time if you're closing, but if one of you wouldn't mind pointing me toward the Whitleys'?"

I can't just let her wander off into the night again, no idea where she's going. Especially not to turn up unexpected at Grace's door. I don't know what good I am to either of them, but for some reason I feel the need to be there, as if my neutral presence might soften the blows that are coming for them both.

"Let me drive you," I say. "I need to be getting home anyway, and it's on my way. It's not far." I reach for my jacket from the stool and take my keys from the pocket. "And I'm not drunk. I promise." Then I wonder if maybe she'd feel more comfortable with another woman than with a man she doesn't know in a town she's never been to—try a *country* she's never been to—and start to say, "But if you'd rather Helen here—"

"Oh, this'll do fine, thank you. I really appreciate it." Lena starts to pick up her suitcase. I tell her to let me take it and that I'll be along in a moment.

"Helen," I say, turning back to the bar with my wallet in hand, but she shakes her head and lets out her breath.

"Drinks are on me tonight. Within reason," she adds with a glance at Mattie. "You sure you don't need another?"

"I think I'd better be sober for whatever's going to happen next."

Mattie pushes back from the piano bench and joins us at the bar. "Two things before you play chauffeur, Dick," he says. "One, do we know if she knows about Sidney? Will you have to tell her? And two, she sure seems to think that Grace is expecting her, so they're both in for a hell of a shock tonight."

"I know." I look over my shoulder at Lena's silhouette beyond the frosted-glass pane of the door. "And if she doesn't know about Sidney, I don't know if I should be the one to break the news to her."

"This is one hell of a pickle."

Helen stares at the door and bites at her thumbnail. Finally she says, "I don't know. It shouldn't have to be you. To tell her, I mean."

"But she'll know if you try to avoid answering," Mattie adds. "Smart gal, she'll see right through you."

"That's reassuring."

"Do you want us to go with you?"

"No...thanks, Helen. I'll figure it out."

I tell them goodnight and go out into the rich, early-autumn air. Lena has her arms wrapped tight around herself as the wind whips back her scarf. We look around the same age, but there's something in her face that reminds me of battle-weary soldiers who've gone days without sleep. On her feet through sheer determination. Beneath that friendly demeanor I sense an undergirding of steel—you don't come all the way from Australia alone if you're an indecisive sort.

"Sorry if I made you uncomfortable, recognizing you," she says as I take her suitcase from the threshold. "It's just that Sidney told me about all of you, so many stories."

"All bad, I hope."

She laughs, looking at the streetlamps shining on the wet pavement and the orange leaves in the gutters. "Even at night, it looks like how he described it."

"Wait till you see it during the day. You might wish for night again."

"You must be a native."

"All my life, except for college and then when the Airborne called. Sorry about this," I say as I open the pickup's passenger door for her. "It probably fulfills all the cliches you've heard about American country folks."

"Oh, I grew up on a ranch. Been driving trucks since I could see over the wheel."

I tuck her suitcase between us in the cab and Lena climbs in. I haven't used the heat in the truck in years, so it takes a minute of fiddling till warm air flows out of the vents.

"Lena, listen," I say as I pull out onto Linden Avenue. "Grace doesn't..."

She watches me, expectant. Mattie sure said it. *This is one hell of a pickle.*

"Grace doesn't know you're coming," I finish. "None of us did."

It's silent in the cab for a few moments. Finally I steal a glance at her. Her lips are pressed together, eyes on the road ahead. Then she pushes the silk scarf off her hair and sighs. "She didn't get my letters?"

"No. I'm sorry."

"You probably think me the world's greatest fool," she says, a hint of self-deprecation in her tone. Maybe even fear.

"Give me a little more time to judge that."

"I'll do it for you. I am a fool. Coming all the way to America on an uncertainty."

"Something tells me you wouldn't have married Sidney if you thought he was an uncertainty," I say without thinking, then kick myself for the lapse. Sidney might be this town's greatest uncertainty right now. What I meant was that I doubt they would've married if either had any reservations about their love or about what a relationship between an American and an Australian means, but if I haven't had enough time to judge whether Lena is a fool for traveling to Caspar, then I also don't have the right to make any assumptions about her marriage. So I add, "I'm sorry, we don't even know each other. Not my place."

"It's okay." Lena props her elbow on the door. I brake for a stoplight and glance at her again out of the corner of my eye. She's as pretty as she was in that photo I saw of her and Sidney, which I assume was taken on their wedding day. Profile fit to print on a postage stamp.

I wish I could reassure her about the Whitleys, that she has no reason to be afraid about what awaits at the farm. She's one of their own now. But I can't speak for them. I'm only the messenger, in the wrong place at the right time. Of all the gin joints in all the world, and Lena Whitley walks into Helen's. Anyway, a woman who was brave enough to make a solo journey across the world probably has little use for reassurances from me.

"So you're from Brisbane?" I say instead.

"Sort of—my parents owned a ranch in—I don't suppose you're very familiar with Australia?"

"Not much, sorry."

"Well, they had a ranch in the bush in Queensland. After they died, I moved to Brisbane when I was seventeen, had some adventures...and that's where I met Sidney, about a year and a half ago." She doesn't seem to mind telling this to a stranger. "You mentioned the Airborne?"

"Yes, I was in Europe throwing myself out of airplanes, so if anyone's the fool here it's me."

"Foolhardy, maybe," Lena says and smiles. She straightens out the folds of her coat, fidgeting in her seat a bit. "I don't know why I'm so anxious to meet them. If they're anything like Sidney, I'm sure there's nothing to be afraid of."

From the way she says his name, I'm sure she doesn't know. As his wife, wouldn't she have gotten a telegram, too? I try to sort through the dates in my mind. Grace says they were married in late May, right before Sidney returned to the Philippines. Lena's crossing alone would've taken five, maybe six weeks, and then she had to get from California to Boston, a week by train at least. That puts her departure from Brisbane in late July. So maybe a telegram meant for her never actually caught up to her.

I turn left down the lane to the farm, shrouded in darkness except for the headlights on the gravel. The lights sweep the valley across the dirt lane and the white house. Beyond are the full apple trees, the river bluffs, and then the mountains.

I glance at Lena in the shadowy dark. "Is this how he described it, too?"

"Yes," she says simply, sitting up straight and pressing her hands together.

We sit at the top of the hill for a minute. Then she nods, and we continue on.

When I pull up in front of the house, we see a light glowing in the kitchen and Baxter curled against the screen door. As I get out, not quick enough to get the passenger door for Lena, Grace appears in the yellow square of light behind the screen. She steps over Baxter and jumps off the stoop into the mud, wearing her black rubber boots.

"Richard!" Grace runs across the dirt lane to me with a folded letter in her hand. I have a vivid recollection of her sitting on my porch steps in the spring, holding the letter that set off this whole perplexing chain of events. She and Lena don't see each other because Lena's gone around the truck and is staring out at the dark fields. "Richard, you won't believe this—this letter came today, it's from Lena in San Diego, she's okay, but listen, she's coming *here,* to Caspar. She doesn't know about Sidney. She could be here any d—wait, what are you doing here so late? Are you okay?"

Grace finally looks past my shoulder and sees Lena, who's watching us. The light from the kitchen falls on her and illuminates her small smile and the apprehension in her eyes.

"What happened?" she says, her voice small in the valley. "What don't I know about Sidney?"

Grace stares at her, then looks back at me, and then drops her eyes to the blue stationery sheet in her hand.

"It's pronounced Lee-nuh, actually," I say, "so we were wrong about that."

"Oh," Grace says. She looks from the letter to Lena, as if not comprehending how the two could coexist. Her eyebrows knit together, and then she stuffs the letter in my hand and crosses the distance to Lena and without hesitation throws her arms around Lena's neck.

I lean against the truck's warm hood and refold the letter without looking at the words on it, pressing my finger along the creases. I hear words murmured between the two of them and see Lena's pale hand on the back of Grace's cherry-red cardigan, her cheek on Grace's shoulder. This is not the night I expected when I went to the Moth to drink off a bad day of memories and listen to Mattie play a few jazz sets.

Grace says something I can't hear, though I catch one word, "Sidney," as they pull apart. I fetch Lena's suitcase from the cab and set it on the stoop by the door. Baxter flicks his tail listlessly against the screen and watches me with a judgmental green eye, though he does stretch out his toes in apparent pleasure when I tickle his chin through the screen.

They're talking still and the tone is serious, but Lena isn't in tears, which doesn't surprise me given that she crossed an ocean and a continent alone. I go back to the truck, thinking to leave quietly because this is their time as a family, but Grace calls, "Richard, wait—stay a moment," just as the porch light turns on.

The screen door creaks, and Mrs. Whitley calls, "Grace, who's this? Oh, hello, Richard. Bit late for you, isn't it?"

Lena drops Grace's hands. The wind blows back the long grasses in the fields, sweeping through them with a singing sound and turning Lena's cheeks red. "Mrs. Whitley—Hannah," she says, and then she's silent, as if rooted to the ground.

"Gran, it's Lena," Grace says, and I hear the little catch in her voice, the unspoken words: *it's Lena without Sidney.*

I watch for a few moments and then glance away as Mrs. Whitley crosses the lane just as Grace did and hugs Lena. She tells her "welcome home," as if they've been waiting up for her arrival, as if showing up on their doorstep all the way from Australia is the most natural thing in the world. Feeling uncomfortably voyeuristic, I go to the stoop again, open the kitchen door, and sit on the threshold beside Baxter. He side-eyes me disdainfully but lets me scratch his neck ruff as the women talk.

"We're not giving up hope," Grace is saying as they come to the steps, and I stand. "Not while there's still a chance."

Lena glances away to the mountains, and in the yellow kitchen glow I see the glisten of a tear in her eye. She doesn't let it fall but only looks back resolutely at Grace and Mrs. Whitley. With a veiled expression, she nods.

"Let's go in and get warm, girls," Mrs. Whitley says softly. "You too, Richard, can't send you home without something hot to drink."

I follow them with the suitcase. Grace says that Lena's luggage, what there is of it, can go in Sidney's bedroom. When I offer to take Lena's satchel from Grace, she says she'll come with me and pulls it onto her shoulder so I can't get it.

She sheds her boots at the foot of the stairs and goes up ahead of me. We put Lena's luggage at the foot of Sidney's bed and then stand in his dark bedroom in the moonlight.

Grace crosses her arms and stares out the window that looks over the apple trees, seeming to see something invisible playing out in the glass. At last she says, "Why doesn't anything ever happen slowly to us? Nothing's ever gradual, just a hard stop ending one part of your life and marking the next." She glances over her shoulder at me and smiles sort of ruefully. "If anyone used to go about things slowly, it was Sidney. Maybe this is him telling me I don't know everything about him."

She stares past me at the faces of Wes Ferrell and Lefty Grove and other Red Sox pitchers from the '30s on newspaper clippings taped above the narrow bed. Sidney was a pitcher, a strategist, a thinker with every movement he made. He was captain of our varsity baseball team his junior and senior years. We won the state championship against Augusta in '39 because he led us there. I was in Tunisia when my mom wrote me that Sidney had graduated from Yale with a second lieutenant's commission in the Army Air Force, and I couldn't have been less surprised.

"He's also decisive," I say, carefully choosing the present tense. "Always has been. Takes his sweet time thinking about things, but when he knows…" I shrug, angling my head toward the staircase and Lena downstairs.

Grace sits on the bed. She picks up a smiling sock monkey from his perch on a couple of stiff pillows and holds him by the paws like a puppet. "I thought she'd collapse in my arms or something when I told her. I don't know if I'm relieved or concerned that she didn't." She sets the monkey back and sighs and looks at her hands in her lap. "Richard, can I ask you something?"

I sit beside her. "Of course."

Her hair falls in front of her eyes as she hunches forward, elbows on her knees, and then she straightens up and looks back to the window and then finally at me. "I never expected it to happen this way. Why is she here and he isn't? Why is it all backwards?"

We stare at Sidney's untouched bookshelves, all meticulously organized by subject and author alphabetically, and at his desk, with the miniature spinning globe on it and a double-framed picture of their parents that matches the one in Grace's room. Bronze bookends in the shape of Scottie dogs bracket a collection of notebooks. It looks more like the desk of a professor than of the college student who left it.

Grace swipes a knuckle under her eye. "I want it to all go back to how it was."

"I know. But this is life now. And you don't have to face it alone, I promise."

She rubs her eyes again, looking out toward the invisible trees where the apples are falling so thick that the grass beneath is carpeted in them.

The bed creaks as I stand. I hold my hand out to her. "Let's go down. They're waiting."

I n the warmth of the dimmed kitchen lights and the coal stove, Lena tells us a story, just as Grace told me her and Sidney's shadowed history the night of the telegram. As the wind rattles the windowpanes, we hang onto every word of the story, which sounds like it came from a James Cagney film. This sort of thing doesn't happen in Caspar.

I only meant to drop her off and then head home, not stay at the Whitleys' for an hour listening to her, but I don't even notice the clock till Mrs. Whitley remarks that it's nearly midnight. The whole story would be hard to swallow if it weren't for her complete earnestness, though she's certainly not a wide-eyed foreign girl in awe of America. She doesn't say anything about the interim of her life, after her parents died and she left the ranch, to late '43 when Sidney came into the bar she owned in Brisbane. Selling that bar is how she paid her passage from Brisbane to Pearl Harbor, from Pearl Harbor to San Diego, from San Diego to Copley Station in Boston, where she got on a Maine-bound train. Coincidence and bureaucracy and a peacetime that's only a month old contrived to delay her letter sent from Honolulu. Her first letter from Brisbane probably never left the port, entrusted to the hand of a little boy with a stamp and a few pennies as she was literally running to the docks to catch a boat.

She came the whole way alone. Before the bar she'd worked at a fishery on the docks, receiving the catch each morning from the early-hours fishermen, so she knew the owners of the fishing boats. Sidney was the one who encouraged her to leave as soon as she could and not wait, because there are apparently hundreds of other Australian women who married GIs and could be waiting for passage for a year or more. He also got her a visa through a friend of a friend at the American consulate. If not for the fishing boats and the embassy friend, Lena could still be cooling her heels behind the counter at her pub on Brisbane's South Bank for years to come.

"You said you met when he came into the bar?" Grace asks. She plucks the tea bag from her third cup of peppermint tea and drops it by the string into my half-finished coffee against my protests.

"Him and his friends," Lena answers. I notice when she reaches for her coffee cup that there are no rings on her left hand. "I didn't know his name that first time, but then he came back alone to introduce himself and I almost threw him out. I just wanted to close and go to bed."

Grace laughs. "Sidney going out of his way to flirt with girls he's barely met? Are you sure we're talking about the same person?"

"Must've been the Air Force uniform," I say. "Trust me, that's a whole different kind of confidence."

"Oh, is it?" Grace tilts back on the legs of her chair and looks at me. "And you'd know, you who told me you didn't raise hell with the girls in London?"

"Never said you had to raise hell to have a good time, or even that you had to be in London," I answer, and reach for my coffee cup when I remember she made it a graveyard for her discarded tea bags. "Ew, Grace, drown these little carcasses somewhere else."

It's only Lena and Mrs. Whitley's presence that keeps me from flinging them at her face. Instead I plop them back in her cup, and she can't decide between laughter or rage that I've ruined her tea with a few drops of coffee, even though she ruined my coffee first.

Mrs. Whitley gets up to put the kettle back on the stove as she says, "These two again. They tend to forget anyone else is in the room."

"Oh!" Lena touches her hand to her chest. "I almost forgot—Hannah, I have something for you."

"Something for me? Oh my."

"I never took it off the whole way. I wanted to keep it safe," Lena says. She lifts a gold necklace chain from around her neck. Hanging on it are two rings, one an engagement ring with jewels, the other a gold wedding band. She undoes the chain's clasp and slips the rings off so that they catch the light as she holds them in the palm of her hand. "Sidney gave the engagement ring to me, but I know where it came from."

Mrs. Whitley sits beside her at the table, her eyebrows drawn together. "Oh, Lena. You brought it all this way for me?"

Her new granddaughter puts the ring in her hand. Mrs. Whitley turns it in the light, and for a moment she seems to be completely alone in the kitchen.

"Your grandfather gave me this," she says, turning to Grace and handing her the ring. "Out there at the top of the cow pasture. He got down on one knee in the snow, and I laughed at him. I didn't think he really meant it. We'd only been seeing each other for a month."

Grace tilts the gold ring so the rectangle-cut diamond glows through the carats, flanked by smaller diamonds glittering in clusters. "I remember it. You used to let me wear it sometimes when I'd play dress-up in your closet. And I remember you giving it to Sidney, but I had no idea he took it with him."

"I never expected a ring, and certainly not something so beautiful or so important to him." Lena runs her finger over the wedding band lying on the table. "We got these to match, and I told him I didn't need an engagement ring, but he had that the whole time."

"You never wore either of them?" Grace looks over the diamonds at her.

"I wore the wedding ring, but then I took it off for the trip and now I—it sounds odd, I know, but I think I want him to put it back on my finger. And your ring," Lena adds, nodding to Mrs. Whitley, "I couldn't bring myself to. It's not mine. I wanted to bring it back for you."

Mrs. Whitley runs a hand through her gray hair and smiles. "I gave that ring to Sidney for this very reason, and he gave it to you, and that boy is nothing if not wise. It's yours now."

Grace holds it out to her. Lena hesitates for a second or two before she takes it and slips it onto her finger.

"Besides," Mrs. Whitley says, "it isn't the ring. It's what he promised you."

Lena reaches for her trench coat hanging on the back of her chair. "Speaking of promises, here's my proof, just so you're sure I'm not telling tales." After fishing in one of the inner pockets, she takes out a water-stained envelope, opens it, and spreads out a creased paper on the table. Grace and I scoot our chairs closer to see it.

Certificate of Marriage, Commonwealth of Australia, the heading reads, and under that a seal of a blue cross with a crown in the center: State of Queensland, 1859.

...Joined in lawful wedlock on this day of 18th May, A.D. 1945...

Beneath, a line for "signature of groom"—Sidney Charles Whitley—and one for "signature of bride"—Madeleine Robinson Argent. Robinson. Wonder if that's a middle name. The others don't ask and Lena doesn't mention it, so I keep quiet.

"Look at that, all official," Grace remarks as the wind changes and the smell of burning leaves blows through the open kitchen window. "As if I needed the proof, though. I know what good taste Sidney has."

Lena laughs, a blush coloring her pale cheeks. I try to ignore the smoky scent of the leaves and listen to them talk.

It's only leaves, I think, a bonfire on one of the farms.

But the more the wind blows through the screen and billows out the white curtain, the more restless I feel, a nauseous sort of dread filling the pit of my stomach. The scent floods my head and nostrils till I feel lightheaded.

I push back my chair and hear myself say, "Sorry, I'll be right back." I don't remember leaving the kitchen, only stumbling through what feels like a dark tunnel and finding the bathroom door with my hand and pushing it shut in the dark, and then I'm on my knees in front of the toilet throwing up a mostly empty stomach.

Fear burns the edges of my vision to blackness like a match taken to paper. "It's not real, it's not real, it's not real," I breathe to myself over and over till the words are meaningless. I'm hunched over the toilet seat with my head on my arms. My heart races, and I feel cold sweat on my chest and face. Nausea still grips my stomach.

You are home. You are in Maine.

I reach out shakily for the handle and flush the toilet and close the lid, as if that'll quell the urge to puke again. Then I rest my forehead on the porcelain lid and hold my hand against my mouth.

You are home.

But I can still smell the burning flesh.

It was the night before we fought through Hunnerpark to take the bridgeheads. The krauts torched dozens of homes and businesses full of sheltering civilians, and gusts of wind off the river dispersed the scent of burning bodies throughout the city and into the bombed buildings we occupied. Guys held shreds of cut parachute canvas to their mouths or vomited in corners. Some folks were too spooked and kept running even as we tried to help them in the streets. But the Dutch people lived under German occupation for four years and most loved us, had greeted us in English and waved orange flags when we first marched down the Groesbeeksweg toward Nijmegen. That night, as their city burned, many of them clung to us and cried. They came all night and into the morning. By the time we mounted the assault on Hunnerpark the next afternoon, I was so tired I could barely walk in a straight line. I held children as they died. And I smelled like death, too.

The burnt flesh was bad but the burnt hair was unbearable, the sulfurous scent lingering on our clothes for days even after we scrubbed them in the river. The death scent was so thick and so heavy that we could all taste it, dream of it, wade through it.

A floorboard creaks behind me.

"Richard?" a voice whispers behind the door.

I still can't open my eyes, though I don't know if that's because of nausea or humiliation now. I could tell her that I drank too much at the Moth, but she'd never believe it.

The door creaks open. I hear Grace hesitate, and then she slips in and shuts it with a click.

I press my hands to my eyes. We sit on the cold tile floor of the bathroom for a long time. The fading scent of the bonfire drifts in through the narrow window high above our heads.

Finally I clear my throat and say, "Could you close the window?"

I hear her get up and wrestle the sash down.

"That better?"

I nod.

She sits again. "It was the burning leaves, wasn't it?"

"I'm sorry, Grace, you don't know how stupid I f—"

"Don't say that. It's okay." She moves a little closer till our knees brush. "Richard, listen. Can you open your eyes, if you're through being sick?"

"I'm through. I hope." I drop my hands to my lap and tilt my head back against the wall.

"I think you should open your eyes," Grace says softly. "You're at home—well, you're at my house. You're in Maine. With me. That's all."

My hands tremble on my knees much as I try to keep them still. I don't want to see her, only to listen to her voice in the darkness.

She says softly, "Memories can't hurt you."

I open my eyes at last. We look at one another. The branches of the oak tree outside the window rustle and catch the moonlight, bathing her face in gray light. She watches me steadily as the shadows dance across her blouse and illuminate and then darken her eyes.

I run a hand through my hair and glance away, counting the black borders delineating the hexagonal tiles. "Grace, I am really sorry about this."

"Richard," she says in a lightly reproachful tone, her voice still soft as if she's afraid of startling me. "I'd be some rotten friend if I only liked you at the best of times."

"There haven't been many of those lately." I glance at her and feel a blush spreading up my neck. "Except for Lena. I'm glad she's here. Just in time for your birthday next week."

Grace smiles, but it doesn't quite reach her eyes. We sit a while longer in the glow of the moon. At last she says, "Should I tell you something reassuring, like how even the longest darkest nights don't last forever?"

Of course they do, I think. It all depends on whom you ask. The living? Sure, a person can be pretty dogged in hoping for dawn. Foxholes taught me that. But the dead don't hope. A few seconds is all it takes for that dark night to become perpetual.

"They don't need to last forever," I say quietly, our eyes locked. "Just long enough."

She doesn't answer. I think of her ghosts—her parents in the cemetery, the black mourning clothes, even Sidney—and mine, too many to name. And too many nameless.

If I were to die right now, what would happen? What would've happened if I'd died in Belgium, when I first got hit or on the gurney they used as a makeshift operating table in the field hospital? I think of the words of the criminal hanged alongside Christ: "Remember me when you come into your kingdom." But that's only comforting when it's got hope attached to it. Without the hope, it's a horror story.

I said comforting words just like Grace's to men to whom I couldn't promise anything else. To mothers whose children were dead in their arms, and who cried out to me for some reassurance, as if they thought the red cross on my arm could raise the dead to life.

"Richard, I meant what I said." Grace watches me with so much earnestness it makes me feel nauseous again. "Dark nights don't last forever."

"You still believe that? Even with Sidney?" As soon as I say it, I know it's too far. "I'm sorry—"

"No, I do. I still believe it," Grace says, holding my gaze. "Even with Sidney."

After a minute of those words hanging between us, she adds, "We sit here too long, rumors might start to go round."

"Right. Yeah. I'm sorry, Grace."

"It's okay."

I steady myself with one hand on the toilet lid and stand. My head is swimming a bit, but at least I can breathe.

"I ought to drive you home," Grace says as she gets to her feet.

"No, I'm okay. I'll make it fine."

She eyes me warily. "And I can't convince you to eat anything first? Throwing up is worse on an empty stomach."

"I'm okay, really," I answer. I turn on the tap and wash my hands, avoiding my own face in the moonlit mirror. "I think it's passed. I'd take Listerine if you have any, though."

"Right in the medicine cabinet there."

She turns the glass doorknob and slips out into the hall, leaving the scent of her rosewater perfume in her wake as I reach for the mouthwash to purge my mouth of a much less appealing taste.

I feel as though I'm pounding on the gates of a medieval city, a pack of hounds on my heels, pounding on an impenetrable barrier and crying, screaming, to be let in. But the gatekeeper doesn't know that there's anyone outside, and I'm not even able to turn around to gauge how close the dogs have come.

All I want is to go home. But I'm not sure I even know what that means anymore.

"Thank goodness she's not some city girl afraid to get dirt under her nails. She's wasted no time, you know. I don't know if she even went to bed last night—I think her body is currently living in about a dozen timezones. This morning she went to the post office and then to church to pray and I told her, 'Lena, you don't need a sanctuary to pray. You can pray while you're feeding the goats.' But she's a little new to this all, still—religion, I mean. And if going to church to pray alone is what helps her feel close to Sidney—and God—then I guess I can't fault that, can I?"

A beat passes, and I realize Grace is waiting. I look up. "Sorry, say again?"

"Are you listening?" she asks playfully. "You asked me about Lena. Not that there's much to tell yet."

"Right, I did. I'm sorry. I am listening; I just didn't sleep much, and my head hurts. It's not you, Grace."

"Did you drink enough last night? Water, I mean." Grace presses her lips together and watches me. She reaches out, at first, I think, to touch my arm, but then she picks up her coffee mug instead and I wonder if I imagined the slight hesitation and her hand changing course.

"No, I guess I didn't."

Neither of us has brought up last night otherwise, and even though we're alone in the kitchen, I know she won't ask.

"Well," Grace says finally, "I only wanted to bring these"—she taps the carton of fresh eggs on the kitchen table, her excuse for stopping by to check on me—"and I'll let you crawl back into bed. Yes, of course you can. It's a rainy Saturday, and it's not as if you have anything else to do. You look exhausted. Please go take care of yourself, all right?"

My mom appears on the stairs, fastening a pin in her hair. "Oh, good morning, Grace! I thought I heard your voice."

"Good morning, Mrs. Dare, brought your eggs."

"Thank you, darling. How much do I owe you?"

"Richard already coughed up the nickel and dime," Grace answers, then with a wry glance at me, she whispers, "Sorry, poor choice of words." She scoots her chair away from the table as Mom wonders if she'll stay for a late breakfast. "Thank you, but we've got pancakes waiting, and then I promised to show Lena around town. Even with the weather being what it is."

I get up and walk her out to the porch, where rain drips from the gutters in a monotonous rhythm. Grace pulls the hood of her green raincoat over her hair and turns back to me. She seems about to remind me again that I need to take better care of myself, so I say, "I will. I'll go back to bed, Gr—"

Before her name is out of my mouth she kisses me on the cheek, so quick that her lips feel like the brush of a butterfly on my skin. Then she trots down the porch steps in her rainboots and runs through the soggy grass to her car at the curb and is gone.

I stand on the porch, watching the rain fall where the Chevy was parked. My head is pounding to beat the band. Did I hallucinate that?

"Don't you start," I say back in the kitchen, closing the door, painfully aware of the blush spreading from my neck up into my cheeks.

Mom, I am sure, saw it through the window above the sink. But she holds up both hands as though she stumbled in on a robbery in progress. "I didn't say a thing. Not a thing."

"You don't have to. I saw that look."

"Whomever Grace kisses is none of my business." She cracks one of the new eggs over the cast-iron skillet. "And what's a kiss on the cheek between friends, after all? Very French. I'm sure all the young people are doing it now."

I shake my head, too tired to come up with something clever. "I've got a headache. I'm gonna go back to bed."

"Okay, darling. You're sure you don't want anything to eat? Wait—come back."

When I turn around, she swipes her thumb across my cheek. "Don't want Hen seeing this lipstick and getting jealous."

"Why would Grace wear lipstick to deliver eggs?" I wipe it off too and look at the rosy tint smeared on the back of my hand.

"Richard. Good lord. For a smart boy, you really have your slow moments. Go on, go sleep the cobwebs out of your head."

XIX.

BREAKTHROUGH

Maybe a hundred years from now, if we make it that long, historians will still spin theories of why Operation Market-Garden failed. It was too ambitious, or it wasn't ambitious enough. Montgomery tried to go too far; Montgomery should've gone farther. Communications broke down. The execution was shoddy workmanship at best. None of the strategists seemed to consider the suicidal nature of staking the whole mission on one road winding through Holland, the route we called Hell's Highway.

We were told that if Market-Garden succeeded, we'd be over the Rhine, avoiding the treacherous and fortified Siegfried Line that guards Germany, and in Berlin before Christmas. Instead the 82nd took almost 4,000 casualties before Canadian troops relieved us the second week of November from our frontline position on the Waal River flatlands. We must've been a sorry sight, retreating back to France to a camp east of Paris, where they're putting us up in some old French army barracks. Tails between our legs.

The 82nd took Nijmegen, but the Brits couldn't secure the bridge at Arnhem. They tried to go "a bridge too far," the line that circulated among us, supposedly from the mouth of one of the British generals. Our victories were worthless, though I can't say that any ground we took in Holland ever felt like a victory, won in the bloodiest fighting any of us have ever seen. But I don't care about dissecting the operation. It doesn't matter to me why it failed, because it was a fuck-up of miserable proportions and because the fucking war will now stretch into 1945. Market-Garden was the child of puffed-chest promises made by egotistical generals who slept in caravans with beds and running water in Holland, while our sentries stood in empty oil drums to keep their feet out of the freezing mud that characterized the Dutch landscape. We all lived with the same fear steadily growing every time we made it through another day, another night: dodging fate now only delays the inevitable, and the leadership has made it clear we're expendable.

Anyway, no more promises or theories can bring back the boys we lost. Jacob O'Connor was 19. The officers call our exhaustion "combat fatigue," a pleasant neutral name to avoid acknowledging that when a guy loses friend after friend after friend and then survives bloody night after bloody night in bitter raw rain with trench foot eating through his boots, each loss, each cold drop of rain down the back of his neck, chips away at his soul. I don't know how many more tourniquets I can tie on the limbs blown off men with whom I ran through the humid Georgia hills, forming bonds we thought could never be broken but were by German steel. Or if the next time I have to hold in the intestines of a kid three months out of high school, I'll fucking lose the scraps of my mind that remain.

And I'm afraid that if I do come to the end of the war, body intact, the tattered remains of what passes for humanity in me will be so weak that when even the faintest wind blows, I'll be ripped apart—like the bodies shredded by Hitler's Buzz Saw, only I won't have the bullet rounds to put me out of my misery.

Still, the war goes on. We take in replacements, rest, train, march. Reach for handfuls of sleep at night through the plague of nightmares. I dream every night that Jacob's life as it hung by a thread would simply not give him the relief of extinguishing itself, his pain multiplied, magnifying my helplessness as I held him—even though, in truth, he died quickly. Sometimes I wake in the cool darkness of the barracks, Peter and Fish and Berk and McNuts asleep around me, and I thank God for that fucking SS grenadier who fired the last round that put an end to Jacob's suffering.

18 December 1944, Suippes, France, 0230 hours

B right light floods behind my closed eyes. Irritated voices and grumbling pierce the peace of the barracks as I pull the wool blanket over my head and press my face to the pillow to block out the light. I try to fall back into a dark dreamlessness, but footsteps pound on the concrete floor and someone shouts, "EVERYONE UP!"

"What the hell?" Fish growls in the cot beside mine. I struggle up to my elbows as he presses the heels of his hands to his eyes. "This better not be a night march."

"It's not a night march, Corporal Fischer," someone answers—Lieutenant Greer, I realize blearily. He made it to camp three nights ago. Rumor is he broke out of the hospital in England and hitched a ride across the Channel. "Get up, boys. Let's go. On your feet."

We all struggle out of bed in various states of dishevelled undress. Fish has a blanket clutched around his shoulders. I don't know what time it is, but no one even looks in need of a shave yet.

Although Greer is a good officer, he always looks as though he's sucking on a lemon whenever he has to attend to any facet of his job connected to unpleasant news. Which is my first clue that whatever he's about to say, we'll wish it was a night march instead. Sergeant Autry is beside him, hands behind his back, his expression equally troubled.

Greer folds the creases of his beret in his hands. Tapping the metal frame of Tony Rodriguez's cot, he says, "The Germans have broken through the American lines somewhere in Belgium."

The room is quiet for a moment. Then someone mutters, "Shit."

"The 82nd has orders to move out, and the trucks will be here at 0800. I don't know where exactly we'll be going, but it will be cold, so dress warm if you've got it."

If we've got it. He knows as well as we do that the Army hasn't supplied us with winter clothing.

"Sir." Peter folds his arms as a bitter draft blows through the cracks in the stone walls. "We don't have any ammo."

"The supply officers will have a fragmentation grenade and a bandoleer for each of you," Greer answers, shaking his head even as he says it. "I know. It's hardly anything. I'm going to see what I can scrounge up for the heavy weapons and machine guns. Right now, focus on getting yourselves together and ready to go."

"Do we know anything else?" Vandenburg asks.

Greer looks more frustrated than I've ever seen him. Not at us, but at being the bearer of news I doubt even he understands. Especially because of our supply deficit. Autry answers, "General Gavin's already left to hook up with First Army in a place called Spa. All we know is that the infantry there is in trouble, so they're sending us in. Guess they figure the toughest jobs are best left to the paratroopers, huh?"

A few of the guys snort sardonically in agreement. We stand at attention as Greer leaves, Autry staying with us, not really feeling like the hardened sons of bitches trusted to mop up whatever this is. Probably not looking the part, either.

Someone lights the kerosene lanterns, casting a glowing arc on the stone walls. We throw back the lids of our footlockers and the barracks come to life with a hum of nervous activity, all of us dressing and talking and packing. I hear similar sounds from the other buildings around us. Hundreds of guys all learning at the same time that we're likely spending Christmas on the front lines.

"Anyone got a half tent?" McNuts calls dismally as he sits on the edge of his cot to pull on long underwear. "Mine got ruined in Holland."

"No, but I have two blankets..."

"Are they really sending us out into Belgium in December without overcoats? Am I the only one without an overcoat?"

"I need extra socks. Who's got extra socks?"

Peter zips up his field jacket and says, "I'm more worried about the ammo."

"One fucking bandoleer," Berk adds from the corner, where he's field-stripping an unauthorized ordnance Luger, one of the German pistols so many guys are desperate to loot as a souvenir. "That'll last us what, ten minutes, when the shit starts flying?"

For two weeks, the supply officers in camp have put me off when I badger them for more medical supplies, telling me I won't need anything till we see action in the spring. That means I have only a half dozen syrettes of morphine—one good shelling could use up all of them—and even fewer rolled bandages. I have no plasma or iodine swabs or field tourniquets and only two wound suturing kits. My two bags, clipped to the shoulder harness and laid out in front of me on the sheets, look alarmingly flat.

But I promised myself all the way back in Sicily that I would never talk with the boys about what I do, or complain of supply shortages, or say anything to them that might cause their faith in me to waver. Thank goodness they don't ask.

"I feel almost naked going without my chute and reserve chute," Fish remarks, shouldering his webbing suspenders and hanging empty ammo pouches from their hooks. "Guess this'll be our tailgate jump."

Al Akins holds up two depressing socks, each with a hole stretching almost the whole length of the foot. "At least we don't have to wear that fucking Mae West. Look at these—I'd be better off without 'em."

Looking around the dim barracks, it hits me how few we are. We jumped into Holland with thirty-nine men in 3rd platoon. Not counting Greer and Autry, there are sixteen of us left. This night, more than any other, I feel the ghosts of all our friends at our shoulders as we suit up, not for a jump but for a ride on the back of a truck to we can only guess where.

Lieutenant Hastings, dead, machine gun round in the neck. Both our messengers, Hunter and Seaward, wounded and evacuated to England. Linitski dead, bayoneted like an animal. Fenton, Pryer, and Moreland wounded, no word on if they'd make it back—and certainly not now that we're moving out. Haley had a recurrence of his North African malaria so bad in Holland he couldn't breathe or bear his own weight. Branson got a left leg full of tracers in Nijmegen. Rafe Takala survived three bullets in his chest but will never return to combat. Paul North was blown up by a Screaming Mimi, Leo Giacometti lost his arm on Hell's Highway, and Dave Tanner was shot and killed on a patrol. Skinny, our magpie, miraculously survived a Buzz Saw round in his spine at Hunnerpark. I got a letter from him a couple weeks back and shared it with all the boys; he wrote that he still can't walk, but some of the feeling is returning to his legs. He thanked me, too, but I didn't read that part aloud.

And then Jacob. I can't think about him now, even though his blood-choked voice echoes in my mind every waking moment: *Whatever it takes, whatever You ask of me.* I think I'm beginning to understand the reasoning in trying to separate medics from everyone else. Forget protecting me from getting attached, but if I'd kept the aloof distance I'm meant to, maybe at least one young idealist would still be alive.

"Remember, boys, even though we're not jumping in, everything we need, we carry on us," Autry says, fetching his musette bag from his footlocker. "Assume the worst and that we won't be resupplied."

Outfitted in two layers—long underwear, then wool shirt and field jacket and trousers and jump boots, with my overcoat waiting folded on the cot—I cinch my cartridge belt around my waist and hook both canteens to it. I'd fill the cartridge pouches with bandages and wound tablets if I had them, same with the rigger pouches that I clip to my webbing after I slip the shoulder harness on over my field jacket, but I just have to hope and pray that the supply officers come through for us. I strap my trench knife in its scabbard above my left boot as Berk wiggles into a shoulder holster he had custom-made in Paris for that Luger. He pulls his field jacket on over it, looking confident that no officer will be any the wiser.

Guys fill their musette bags with toothbrushes and razors, ASE books and diaries, old letters and photos of girlfriends and parents. If this were a jump, we'd have everything out on tarps on the runways for a kit layout, packing and outfitting as the C-47s cast long shadows. But in the cold, damp barracks, every movement carries a sense of unreality. The jumps into Sicily, Italy, Normandy, and Holland were actions rooted in planning, no matter how poor the execution of those plans, but this is reactionary, the sentry literally caught sleeping. It's the first time we're going into combat without jumping. And for once, we're on the defensive.

"Peter, you mind?" I say over my shoulder, angling my head toward one of my webbing straps. "I can't reach."

"Sure thing." He pulls the strap tight, then the other. "You're all set."

"'Preciate it."

Lowering his voice and turning his shoulder so the others can't hear him, he says, "How're you on supplies?"

"I'll make do, scrape things together."

"Richard, I mean it, and you can tell me."

I tuck my extra pair of scissors into the bag under my left arm. "I'm low. And we don't even have personal aid kits that I can beg."

"I know." Peter sighs. "Okay. I'll keep my ear to the ground."

"Don't say anything to them. As far as they're concerned, I'm the aid station with feet, and I don't want them worrying otherwise."

Before Peter can answer, the door of our barracks opens again and we all look back, expecting to see Greer or another officer. Instead, four deer-eyed privates hover in the opening.

"Evening, lads," Peter says.

I hear McNuts mutter, "Who the fuck are they?"

"Is this 3rd platoon, F Company?" one asks, his brow creased in apparent confusion that we're all there is.

"We're, uh, we're your replacements." Another kid, who still hasn't lost all the baby fat from his cheeks, shifts from one jump boot to the other nervously. "They didn't really tell us anything. The depot truck just dropped us here, and one of the sergeants outside said 3rd platoon needs men."

"Well, we certainly do." Autry jerks his head back at the rest of us. "You boys will just have to hang tight while we get ready to move out."

Rodriguez, whose cot is near the door, pokes his head outside. "Holy shit, how many replacements did they drop off?"

When we leave the barracks, the camp is a hotbed of frantic activity, and compounding the supply and ammo problem are two hundred homeless replacements clustered in little rings around oil-drum fires to warm themselves. They barely seem to know their own names, much less their orders. Seems the repple-depple dropped them in our laps with no warning to them or us. The noncoms try to divide them up fairly between platoons, filling out the squads that took the heaviest losses, but they have their hands full enough already. Dozens of replacements still look as lost as children, so they'll just have to squeeze on the trucks wherever they fit.

The trucks, scheduled to arrive at 8, don't lumber into the camp till 10, at which point we're all pissed off and freezing. Dawn dropped in a heavy fog from the white sky, rolling between the stone barracks and obscuring the trucks in shifting mist. Wherever the fuck we're going, I'm just happy to get out of Suippes. As I plant my boot on the tailgate of the open-air eighteen-wheeler and Berk grabs my hand to pull me up, I hear someone call out, "You really think your sorry asses could leave me behind?"

"No fucking way," Peter says, letting out an incongruous laugh into the bitter morning cold. He hops off the tailgate and throws his arm around Scotty Branson's shoulder, clasping his other arm. "You break out of the hospital? What are you doing back here?"

"I just had a feeling I needed to get back, didn't want to get assigned to some other unit." Branson slings his barracks bag onto the truck as we reach for his hands to hoist him. "Careful with the leg, boys." He grimaces, but then he's up, recipient of handshakes and slaps on the back. "I guess I was right, too, huh? Made it by the skin of my teeth."

"No shit," Berk says. "Word is they're dumping us in Belgium to clean up an infantry mess."

"You serious?"

Peter nods. "Krauts broke through in the Ardennes Forest."

"Where the fuck's the Ardennes Forest?"

"Belgium, apparently."

Branson whistles and says, "Well, why not? Little Christmas vacation."

"A front line ticket for us to say 'Merry Christmas, Adolf, up yours,'" says Fish, plucking a packet of cigarettes from his field jacket, which prompts a chorus of "hey, over here!" and held-out hands.

"I'm sure glad to have my machine gunner back, even if he is an idiot, traipsing through France in this cold." Peter knocks Branson's helmet and ducks out of the way of a reciprocating elbow. "Just wish I had ammo for you."

I watch the other trucks loading, hundreds of paratroopers out of their element boarding wheels instead of planes, underdressed and undersupplied and every platoon undermanned. Besides the losses, a lot of 82nd guys are still on R&R passes in Paris. Probably getting rounded up by the MPs this very moment and told as much about the German breakthrough as we were.

Freezing rain falls on us as we wait and wait and wait, standing huddled together, cold and wet on the bed of the truck. An engineer standing at one of the nearby oil drums shakes his head as we pull the tailgate up. "Shit," he says, "I'd hate to be the first German you fellas get your hands on."

XX.

CHRISTMAS

22 November 1945

The morning after Thanksgiving, a ringing wakes me. I make it downstairs to the phone on the last ring. Disoriented from the gloom out the windows and stiff from a night of little sleep and probably too much of Nana's home-brewed wine, I pick up the receiver. Before I can say hello, the voice on the other end is already talking.

"Who—sorry, who is—"

A breathless ramble about missing identities and bureaucratic inefficiency and a hospital in California comes to an abrupt stop. "It's Grace. Wait, is this Richard, or Laur—"

"No, it's me. Grace, why are you calling at—" I crane my sore neck over my shoulder to see the clock above the stove. "It's barely seven a.m."

"I know. I'm sorry, it sounds like I woke you. I know it's early. But Ellie at the post office—she was awake, and she heard the telegram come in and she brought it to us." Grace sounds as though she's been crying.

I tighten my grip around the receiver and loop my finger through the cord, wide awake now. "A telegram from the War Department?"

"Yes, but—" There's a rustling and a voice in the background that I assume must be Lena's. Then Grace says, "Richard, he's alive. He's coming home. Sidney's coming home."

23 December 1945

The three Whitley women have been, to quote Grace, in a "state" all week at the anticipation of Sidney arriving tomorrow afternoon on the 3:10 train from Boston. He might've been home two weeks ago, instead of on Christmas Eve, but for an infection of a wound on his leg while in the Navy hospital in San Diego. In a long-distance telephone call from his hospital bed, he told Lena he'd discharge himself and limp or hitchhike the three thousand miles home if it came to that.

When I came in earlier this afternoon, Lena was tipping precariously over the banister with a length of fresh-cut pine garland in one hand and crimson ribbons in the other. She said hello to me and waved without dropping any needles or stabbing herself with the sewing scissors. Grace was hunched over a wreath on the kitchen table and couldn't say hello at first because she had pins in her mouth as she threaded dried orange slices together. Judging by the scent of wineberries drifting from the oven, Mrs. Whitley and her pies found their way around the sugar rationing.

I'm sure Grace wanted me to believe that she needed distracting from worrying about Sidney when she invited me over to help her decorate. Her frenetic mood is exactly what I'd expect the night before her brother comes home. But there's a note of intentional lightheartedness in her voice that seems tuned especially for my sake. It isn't only her. Lena enlisted my help tacking garland over the doorframes, though I seemed to slow her down because she had to redirect me every few seconds while I wondered silently what an Australian would know about decorating for Christmas in Maine. And then Mrs. Whitley wouldn't hear any excuses when she asked me to stay for supper. More than once I caught Grace's eyes on me when I hadn't said anything.

Christmas festivities are in full swing at the Dares', too—bread loaves and pastries have taken all the real estate on the kitchen counters (I heard Laurie mutter this morning, "What's a guy gotta do to butter a piece of toast around here?"). Sinatra is always singing at a low hum on the living room radio in the evenings and everyone's in good spirits, especially this being my first Christmas back home. At least I think they are. Sometimes I catch Laurie and my mom watching me, like Grace, as if to gauge my mood so they can appropriately adjust their own. Compensate for me.

Baxter slinks into the living room, where I'm sitting on the rug, swishes his tail, then climbs delicately into my lap as though I won't notice if he's careful about it. Across the hall and in the kitchen, I hear Lena trying to explain something called a "Christmas damper" to her grandmother-in-law. It's a kind of bread or a cookie. I can't tell because Baxter yowls right then, a demand for me to scratch his ears.

Grace returns from the bathroom—"because I just drank three cups of peppermint tea"—stops in the center of the rug on a pair of adjoining fern boughs, and turns around in a circle with her hands on her hips, staring at the bare walls. I can almost see the gears in her mind spinning as she turns this room into her own Holiday Inn, only missing Bing Crosby and Fred Astaire and the piano with the tiny Christmas tree atop it.

"I thought your plan was to do this room up," I say, "and we haven't made any prog—"

"Hush." Grace holds her finger up to me like she caught me whispering in her class. "I'm thinking."

Baxter flicks his amber eyes up at me, as if to say, "You see what I have to put up with, living with all these women?" Grace moves from the built-in bookshelves to the mantelpiece, pressing her knuckles to her mouth and squinting. She touches the gold clock that I notice stopped at six who knows when. The dried bunch of petunias in the blue china pot don't seem satisfactory, and neither does the wide empty space to the right of the sofa, between the fireplace and the window with the view up the lane. Something seems off, and then I realize why.

"Are you missing something?" I ask.

She glances at me, arms crossed. "What?"

"You forgot a Christmas tree."

"...Oh my goodness." Grace straightens, tilts her head, and covers her mouth with one hand, although I'm not entirely convinced by her performance. "Richard, I forgot the Christmas tree."

"Mm, so it seems."

She runs a hand through the loose waves of her hair and sighs. "Sidney's coming home tomorrow, and this will be his first real Christmas in three years. I can't believe I forgot the most obvious part."

Lena appears in the doorway, holding a mug of steaming mulled wine. She starts to take a sip, flinches, and shakes her head. Setting the mug on top of the radio, she says, "What's all this?"

"You all may have forgotten to put up a Christmas tree," I tell her.

"Oh dear." Mrs. Whitley is here now, too, wiping her hands on a dishtowel. "How did we forget that?"

"It's not as though anything else important has been on your minds." I set a disgruntled Baxter on the rug and climb to my feet. "Come on, Grace. We'll go find one together. We'll cut it down. Lena, want to come?"

"Bit cold out there for me. You two'll find the perfect one, I'm sure."

In the foyer, Grace throws my coat and scarf and boots at me, and I catch them all at once like a cartoon character.

"Come on now. We've already lost the light," she says, clapping her hands together. "You are the slowest boot-tier I have ever seen. Didn't you have to do that in the Army all the time?"

"I can't tie them with you staring! And if we've already lost the light, what's the rush?" I look up at her and can't keep in a burst of laughter when I see what she's wearing. "What is that on your head?"

She tries to act indignant, but the effect is lost when she grins and pulls at the flaps of what I guess is a deer-hunting cap. Her red plaid coat is at least three sizes too big for her—it must be a hand-me-down from Sidney. "It's called dressing for the weather. I don't intend on being struck down with any pneumonia this winter."

A gust of strong wind blows into us when Grace opens the front door. She clicks on her silver flashlight, and from under her scarf I hear her whistle for me. I dutifully follow.

Misty clouds move fast across the stars as we crunch through the brittle grass and over the twigs scattered at the tree line from the fall wind. A thick layer of dust coats every surface in the toolshed. After some digging, Grace hands me a saw that looks like it hasn't been sharpened since the Civil War. Maybe it took off a few limbs back then. She also takes a pair of gardening shears, holds them up and flexes them with both hands, and says, "To cut more holly. And now, to the tree."

In pursuit of a tree that meets Grace's somewhat unreasonably high Christmas standards, especially on December 23rd, we traipse from the side yard and the kitchen garden through the hibernating grove of apple trees and along the outer edge of one of the old horse pastures. Frost blankets the slopes of the foothills. There's something strangely comforting about being cold in a familiar place.

"Now," Grace calls as the wind whips against our cheeks, and she waves her flashlight so that the beam sweeps the frozen hillside. "We have to be quick and precise about this. No changing our minds once we've chosen a tree."

"You mean no changing your mind after you've chosen a tree."

"What?"

"Nothing."

She leads me up along the ridge, where in winter daylight you can see through the bare oaks and birches to the elbow-curve of the Alewife—its currents frozen solid now—and to the edge of the woods, where we wade through dead blackberry thickets and across a clearing.

"Here they are." The light catches a stand of blue-needled spruce ahead of us as the land begins to slope up into the unkept wildness of the mountains. "Grandpa Whitley planted all these back in the day."

"I remember my mom talking about that," I say, testing the strength of a branch through my glove. It comes away with needles stuck to the wool. "She said she and her siblings called him the Christmas Tree Man."

Grace laughs. "Don't you think it's funny how Christmas trees are one of those magical things from when we were kids that haven't lost their magic? We haven't had a tree since...well, probably not since Sidney left. There didn't seem like a reason to when it was just me and Gran."

I stop beside a tree that looks full and strong to me, but she shines the flashlight on a gap in the back, right through to the trunk. Then she crouches to inspect the lower branches of a tree just tall enough that I'm not confident in my ability to haul it all the way back to the house. But if that's the one she wants, then I'll push it down the hill if I have to. "My dad always took us with him to cut down a tree, when we lived in Massachusetts," she says. "Sometimes we'd walk around for hours. I think growing up on this farm as the son of the Christmas Tree Man made him very picky."

"And you clearly are the next in their long and hallowed line."

"As long as I take after them and not the other side."

I step out of the way as she reaches through the branches and shakes the spruce by its trunk. Only a handful of needles float to the grass.

"Is this the one?"

Grace nods. "I think it is. This one's for you, Grandma Pitcher, and your eggnog that was watery."

She holds the top of the tree while I lie on my stomach with the saw and the flashlight. She offers to take a turn, which I politely refuse because if I can't cut down a tree, what kind of second-rate husband would I make? My knees feel stuck to the grass and my hands through the gloves are numb, but the triumph I feel when the spruce hits the ground with a thump, as Grace jumps backward, must be what hunters feel when they mount the antlers of the prey that taunted them over their mantel.

We walk back over the hills with our prize in tow. Grace tells me about Christmases in Massachusetts when her parents were alive: how her mother always dried orange slices to string into a garland; walking hand-in-hand with her father to church, Sidney on his other side; the memory of her parents laughing in the kitchen on Christmas Eve after she and Sidney were supposed to be asleep.

"Every year it gets harder to remember those things, though," she says as we come up the rise through the pastures. The flashlight illuminates the rows of leafless apple trees. "And I'm afraid I'll forget them all."

"You won't forget them." I can see the white farmhouse in the distance. "You've just had to remember them alone for years, but this time tomorrow you'll have Sidney back to remember them with you."

When the tree is wrestled into submission, the cheap metallic bulbs hung, and the popcorn strung, Grace and I go back out to fetch the holly and pine boughs she left in the driveway. I shift my load of greenery to my left arm so I can open the door and hold it for her. As she steps past me, she bumps into me with her own armful. Something, a scarf string or a zipper, catches between us. Grace moves to break free, but there's a sound like tearing, and I tell her, "Hold still, hold still," and pull off one glove with my teeth, dropping it on top of my branches. As I try to find the caught bit, I feel Grace watching me. When I glance up at her, her cheeks are pale, green eyes bright in her cold face. Wind pushes at our backs, bitter and stinging our eyes. Finally I find it: a strawberry-blonde strand of her hair pulled into the zipper of my jacket.

She winces as I do my best to guide the zipper down gently, trying to release her hair with minimal losses.

"There. You okay?"

When I get it free, our eyes meet again. There was plenty of room when I stood aside to open the door. She didn't need to move close enough to me to get her hair caught.

"Guess you're not the only clumsy one," Grace says with a smile. "Don't drop your glove."

As she goes in, I turn back and look at the dark gray sky proclaiming snow. I should leave now if I want to make it home before that starts coming down. Laurie and I put chains on the truck's wheels about a month back, and it does all right in the snow, but the sensible thing to do is to start home before that becomes a concern.

But I hear Grace dragging the greenery into the living room and feel the warmth of the rebuilt fire from the doorway. Teeth chattering, I wipe my eyes and nose. She's singing along to a jazzy instrumental version of "Have Yourself a Merry Little Christmas." For better or worse, I shut the door and take off my boots and hang up my scarf and coat, gloves in the pocket, and gather my load of pine and holly up again.

Mrs. Whitley is in the kitchen with an iron and a stack of laundry, and Lena, who I expected to be draping the tree in cranberry strings, has mysteriously disappeared, too. I lose track of time as we transform the living room. Grace changes the record to Bing Crosby's Christmas songs and we climb across the furniture—at one point I have to call to her over the music from a crouched position on the jutted-out shelf of the built-in bookcase, and she answers from the precarious back of the velvet armchair that has a spring falling through the bottom. The smell of the fire still burning in the hearth mixes with the pine and spreads throughout the house. Once or twice I nearly trip over myself and bring the whole string of garland down with me, while Grace laughs so much that she has to grab the mantel to steady herself.

After a while, I hear her over at the window, and then she says, "Looks like you're snowed in, Dare."

I look over my shoulder. We were so caught up in our work that we didn't notice the snow falling on the lane and the hills.

"Pity," I say.

Grace, to my surprise, doesn't point out how the snow—by Maine standards—is barely a dusting and how easy it would be for me to still get home. She only watches out the window with an eyebrow raised and then looks at me and shrugs.

After a while I call home from the phone in the hallway to let my family know I'll be staying the night. Biting down on my lip in the hope that Mom or Dad picks up, I conclude that God must be laughing at me when Kitty connects me and the receiver on the other end clicks, and it's Laurie's voice that says, "Dare residence."

With a sigh I say, "Hi, Laur."

"Oh, look who finally decided to call. I was beginning to forget I had a brother. Have I seen you in the last three days?"

"I don't know. It's you who has all the social engagements."

"It's tough to be the most popular graduate of Caspar Senior High School."

"I bet. Listen, I'm stuck here for the night, so—"

Laurie says, "Stuck where?"

"…The Whitleys'," I say, after too long a silence.

From the muffled sounds on the other end, I can only imagine that he's doing a jig in the middle of the kitchen, or at least what he thinks is a jig. The whistling that follows is exactly the kind of junior-high reaction I was expecting. I hold the earpiece away from my ear and wait.

"Who else, may I ask, will be joining you on this sleepover?"

"No one, because her grandma and Lena are both home, and it's not a sleepover."

"You're sleeping there, aren't you? What would you call it?"

Before I can answer, he rattles on, "But here's hoping they go to bed soon, so they don't kill the mood."

"Well, there's no mood."

"Oh," Laurie laughs, "that's an outright lie. I can tell from your voice that there's most definitely a mood."

"I'm going now. I just didn't want you to think I was lying face down in a snowdrift somewhere."

Laurie fires a series of questions at me a mile a minute, the only one of which I really understand being, "Is Grace listening?"

"Um…I don't think so."

"Had any wine?"

"Goodnight, Laurie." I hang up in the middle of his frantic reminding that wine is an aphrodisiac.

Back in the living room, Grace drops her handfuls of holly berries when "White Christmas" begins. She hums along with Bing and dances across the room to the bookshelves, where I'm tying a bunch of holly into the pine boughs. She reaches for me to pull me down. In the middle of the rug I hold her hand above my head, and she twirls out. Each time she laughs like this, it's like I'm thirteen again and she's hitting me in the chest with a sledgehammer.

She comes back to me as the needle scratches and the song changes, a slower instrumental, written for dying fires and empty drink glasses at the end of the night. When we slow to match the tempo of the song, she tentatively puts her head against my chest. My heart is pounding so hard that I imagine the trauma doctors and nurses from the Belgian hospital are going to burst into the room at any moment, barking about tachycardia and high blood pressure. My chin brushes the top of her head, her hair like silk against my skin.

"Grace?" I whisper into her hair.

"Mm."

"...What are we doing?"

"Just dancing like old friends."

"But are all old friends in love with each other?"

She lifts her head and looks up at me, eyes reflecting the firelight glow from the hearth. A couple of moments pass, our eyes fixed on one another. "Oh," she says finally. "That was something, wasn't it?"

"Only about a decade overdue," I answer, surprised that the words even make it out of my throat, which feels more and more constricted as my heart beats harder.

"Maybe all old friends are in love with each other, and most of them just never know."

"I know I should've said it years ago. I should've told you before I left, I should've told you the moment I got home—"

"Richard, hush." Grace pats my cheek. Her hand is beautifully cold on my flushed face. "I wasn't ready years ago. Do you really think it would've been better for you to go off to war and leave me with those words, when I was only nineteen? Even six months ago, if you'd've told me you loved me, I don't know what I'd have thought."

I hesitate. That's not what I was expecting to hear. "So you're saying that I'm not too late?"

"If anyone's late, it's me. I think we both know that."

"What changed? Or when?"

We're still now, her left hand caught in my right, faces close enough to see the irises of each other's eyes as we lean against the mantel. The fire is warm on the backs of my knees, though I don't need any help sweating.

"The night we got the telegram," Grace says, "and you stayed with me and cooked for me and just—when you sat with me—" She glances at the rug and smiles, as if watching that late July evening play out in the brocade. "But there was a moment, when you were playing solitaire at the table, and I was almost asleep beside you, but not quite, and I remember watching you and watching your hands. I just followed the backs of your hands and those cards, and I thought—"

She cuts herself off with a shake of the head. "It sounds so ridiculous."

"I'm sure it's not."

"Well..." She laughs. "I had the clearest thought—'oh, you're in love, aren't you?' And not that I'd really know what being in love is, but I knew I was deep in it. I didn't realize till then how deep it was."

Her heart beats against me. My hand moves down her waist till there's barely a hair's width between us. Her neck smells like rosewater, and my legs all but give out so that I back into the old armchair. Grace laughs, bumping into me, and I fall against the arm, and then she's looking down at me, our faces almost too close to speak. She puts one finger on my mouth.

"Richard," she murmurs, a note of laughter betrayed in her voice, "if you don't get control of your heart, you'll go into cardiac arrest."

"I don't care."

But she moves her hand to cover mine on her hip, and like a spark extinguished, the laughter is instantly gone. So is the energy I felt thrumming through her. Grace looks at the floor and takes a deep breath. Then she steps back, though her hand is still holding mine tight.

"What is it? Grace?" I don't move for fear she'll let go. "Did I do something wrong? I'm sorry—"

"You didn't do anything wrong, Richard. I promise." Still holding my hand, she sinks into the armchair while I sit on the arm. "I'm sorry, I'm so sorry, after I told you all that, too."

"I don't know what you're talking about. Why are you sorry? There must've been something I did, but I don't know what."

Her elbow brushes my thigh. "This isn't you. I tried to ignore it, but I know it isn't you."

My head is pounding now, taking over for my heart, which has finally slowed. "…What does that mean? How is it not me?"

"When I said I knew that night in July, that I was in love, you barely reacted," Grace says with a glance up at me. "That's not the you I know. When you're happy, you don't know how to hold it in. You have this—this joy, it's infectious, and it makes me happier than anything in the world. And I always want to be close to you so I can feel it, too, but I haven't seen you like that in so long. And I know things have been hard for you, so please don't think that I only want to be with you when you're happy, because that's not true, but Richard—you're not yourself, and I don't know why."

The music has stopped, and the record is spinning round and round on the turntable. I run my hand through my hair. That lingering exhaustion I've kept a step ahead of is finally catching up to me, and I feel nothing. Not frustration or humiliation or heartbreak. Just a white and formless nothing.

"Okay," I say. I let go of her hand and stand. "Yeah, okay. I understand."

"Do you?" Grace gets up too and follows as I pace between the sofa and the fireplace, hands in my pockets. "Because I'm not even sure I do. Richard, tell me. Tell me how to help. Tell me what to do. I'll do anything; I just want you to feel like yourself again."

I stop and turn to look at her. "You keep saying that, that I'm not myself, but then what am I? What if this is all I have to work with and it's the best I can do, and you telling me I'm somehow not myself is like someone driving an awl into an open wound? Maybe this is all I have. Maybe there's no going back, not anymore. You have to stop saying that—no, let me finish, please, Grace—because for a second it makes me think that maybe it was someone else who did and saw all those things but that's not true. Nothing else in my life is as real to me as what happened over there—I live it over and over again every fucking night—and when you tell me that this isn't me, you don't know how much that hurts, making me think that there's hope it might all come undone. But it won't. It never will."

Grace crosses her arms over her chest, standing planted in the middle of the rug, as unmoved as an oak tree in a hurricane. I feel her watching me, though I can't bring myself to look her in the eyes. "You'll have to do better than that to turn me away."

"I'm not trying to turn you away! I just don't want you to fool yourself into thinking that if you wait it out, you'll get some better version of me."

"Richard, if you use me as your crutch while you heal, then I don't think you really will. I want to help you because regardless of how either of us feel, you're still my best friend. But I won't be the finger in the dam for you."

"I'm not asking you to be."

"But do you not think, with time and with the right help, that you could—"

"What help?" I jerk my head to the bay window and the snow-drowsy world beyond the panes. "Do you see anyone lining up to help me, or

Mattie or Sidney, or any other guy you know? There's no middle ground. It's just 'get on with things' or check into a psychiatric hospital."

Grace's eyebrows draw together. "No one's suggesting a psychiatric hospital."

"Well, maybe they should. Because do you know what it's like? Everything feels wrong all the time. And then the person I trusted the most is telling me I'm not myself, so what am I supposed to think?" I shake my head and lean against the arm of the sofa. "If you know something about the future that I don't, please, I'd be happy to hear it. But otherwise it just sounds like false hope."

"Was my praying for Sidney to come home false hope, then?"

"No, I didn't mean it like that."

"I don't know, you might've. Maybe when you're too stubborn to have hope, you don't want anyone else to have it, either."

I stare at her. She doesn't seem to regret saying it, and she lets me take the burden of breaking the silence. "You think I'm just being stubborn?"

"I think you have an iron will, and sometimes that's an asset like when you were wounded, but when you're not careful, it just"—she makes two fists and turns them in toward her chest—"suffocates you from the inside. The very thing that helped you survive during the war is what's unraveling you now."

"Great, happy to hear it. I already feel like shit, so it's comforting to know that I can look forward to becoming the village idi—"

"Stop it!" Grace bursts out, curling her hands into fists at her side. "You have to stop talking about yourself this way. Do you get some kind of comfort out of it, this self-pity? You survived for a reason, so—"

I laugh and roll my eyes. "Why does everyone say that? There wasn't any reason for that; it was all random chance. Everything in war is random. Why does your buddy get blown up in the chow line but you don't? No one knows."

"Is...that what happened?" Her voice is softer, gentler, and for some reason that annoys me. "You and a friend, in the...?"

"No, that's not what happened."

"Okay, well, even so. Maybe you've lost some faith. I wouldn't blame you for that." Grace alights on the opposite arm of the couch and we look at one another, with the cushions in between feeling like a chasm. "But that doesn't mean you have to strip away everyone else's faith, too."

"Believe me, I wish I didn't have the chance to. If I'd never come home, you'd never have realized how you feel and you wouldn't have to be heartbroken."

She watches me with a crestfallen expression. "You don't mean that."

"I promise you I do."

"Richard," she says. "All I want is for you to be happy."

"Then maybe you shouldn't start by reminding me how unhappy I am."

And then whatever it was is over, as abruptly as it began. We sit on opposite couch arms and glance from the fire to the window to the tinsel glittering on the tree, anywhere but at one another. I wait for regret to begin eating me up inside for the things I said to her. It doesn't come.

G race says I can sleep in the guest bedroom if I'd like, but neither of us seem intent on actually going to bed. She reheats the mulled wine on the stove, and I sweep the spruce needles from the slate floor in the foyer. Given what just happened, the wine feels less like an aphrodisiac and more like a nightcap to calm our collective nerves. Grace stretches out on the green couch, a blanket draped over her legs, as Bing sings "White Christmas" in a haunting melancholy. I sit down cross-legged on the rug in front of the hearth and lean my back on the couch, my head filled with the ineffable winter scent of cloves and merlot.

After a few minutes, I crane my neck to look up at her. Her eyes are closed, hair falling across her shoulder, clinging to the red threads of her sweater. The wineglass is still in her outstretched hand, and her feet are propped on the armrest at the other end.

I'm dreaming of a White Christmas, with every Christmas card I write...

I gently pry Grace's glass from her fingers before it can fall and shatter on the floor. I drink it myself as I stare at the fire, then set the glass on the floor by the couch.

Grace says something in a mumble and I glance at her again, expecting to see her waking up, but she's still out. I reach for the Scottish tartan blanket on her feet and pull it over her. Then I lean back with my head on the blanket and close my eyes and listen to the whisper of the snow. And with my eyes closed, I stare down into that deep well of ever-widening anger in myself and realize that it's grown far beyond my control.

I fall in and out of a strange half-dream state, aware of the couch shifting under my head as Grace curls up tighter, even of the hum of the old pipes and the house creaking under the weight of snow on the roof. But I'm so tired that I can't fully hold onto any of those things and can't pull myself up to stumble down the hallway to the guest bedroom.

In between wakefulness and sleep, I dream of a series of white doors and my hand turning the crystal knobs, following a distant knocking and never reaching it, opening door after door and finally coming to a space paneled in mirrors. I turn around and see myself stretching out infinitely. The closer I step to my reflection, the farther away I seem. I reach out, but my fingers never meet the glass. The knocking persists. I can't tell where it's coming from.

A shadow falls over my shoulder. When I look back I see it in every direction, although I'm alone, and then a hand touches me—

I jolt upright. My right hand is clutching my left shoulder, but I can't shake the feeling that my hand is only covering someone else's that was there first.

Grace is sitting up, too, the blanket fallen around her ankles. The fire's gone out and the living room is cold, washed in dark blue light. I start to say, "Is there someone at the d—"

A voice from outside, sounding cold and desperate, calls, "Grace!" We look at each other. Though her face is barely visible in the darkness, I feel the alarm in her frozen stillness.

"I'll go see who it is." All I can think of is a disgruntled ex-boyfriend, though what ex-boyfriend could be disgruntled enough to drive from Boston to Maine the night before Christmas Eve, I have no idea. Still, I never met that Andrew fellow, and I don't know what he might be capable of. I also wouldn't put it past Mattie to show up drunk and unannounced in the middle of the night, but he's much more likely to bother Helen before Grace.

She kicks the tartan off (and unfortunately Baxter with it, who yowls and slinks away to the stairs), climbs to her feet, and holds onto my hand. Whoever it is continues to call out for her. There's no sign of a car outside. The porch is one of those covered kinds that's a nice protection from snow and rain and not as helpful for spying the purpose of visitors who arrive at—I glance at my watch as Grace flicks on the foyer light—12:29 in the morning. I might've told her to stay in the living room, but by her grip she has no intention of letting go.

Just as I open the door, the voice calls out again, this time with, "Gracie!" and I feel Grace's hand press even tighter. It's not just anyone who calls her by that nickname.

Chin tucked into the collar of a wool overcoat and scarf that snaps back in the wind, his reddish hair damp with snowmelt, his pale cheeks red, and his tall frame much thinner than I remember, is Sidney Whitley.

Grace drops my hand and starts to cry, as easily as she did when the Western Union boy stood on this porch. Sidney's face changes in a way I don't know if I have words for, though I think it might have been my own expression when I hugged my mom and dad and Laurie that first afternoon.

She jumps from the doorstep to the porch and into her brother's arms, pressing her face to his shoulder, still crying. With some guilt I realize I'll never know what it is to be the one waiting at home, living on prayers that you don't have to hang a gold star in the window.

Sidney wraps his arms round her tight and starts to laugh when she won't let go of him. "I know—I know, Gracie—yes, I love you, too. When did you go and get so grown up?"

"Come inside, what are we doing out here? Come in," she says, making as if to pull his arm from its socket if he doesn't work on getting warm right this moment.

I start to hold my hand out to him, but in something I never would've expected from the old friend I thought I knew, he pulls me into a hug instead. If he's curious what I'm doing here at this time of night, he doesn't ask. I tell him "Welcome home, Sidney," because that's what you say. That's what folks said to me. And the whole of it always meant more than the sum of those two small words.

He's just dropped his only luggage, a duffel bag, inside the door, when there's a creak of footsteps at the top of the stairs. Lena's willowy frame is still for a few seconds as they stare at one another.

Not a word passes between them, but Lena takes the steps as though her feet don't even touch the wood. Sidney stands caught in the shadows between the light of the entryway and the arch that opens to the darkness of the living room, a figure so long alone. The marriage certificate Lena carried all the way from the Brisbane port seems like flimsy proof compared to their embrace. A few subconscious doubts about them that I didn't realize I was holding onto evaporate instantly.

They stand like that for a long time, holding onto one another, and it feels wrong to watch such an intimate moment. Grace and I glance at each other and then quickly look away. We slip back into the light of the entryway.

"I'll kill him," she says softly, then laughs. She slips her hand into mine again. "I'll kill him for not telling us he was early."

But her voice is light, the kind of disbelief you adopt when you're too afraid to believe in the full goodness of something you've longed for. We go into the kitchen together, and Grace fills the kettle and sets it on the stove. I expect her to be a torrent of words, but she doesn't say much, except to wonder if she should wake up her grandmother or let Sidney be a surprise in the morning. He and Lena are talking in the hallway but not loud enough for us to hear what they're saying.

"Grace, I should probably go," I say. "This is private. I shouldn't be h—"

"You would blow away out there, and you know it." Grace turns from where she's pouring the steaming water at the counter and levels a teaspoon at me. "Richard, don't even think about slinking away."

As it turns out, there isn't much to the story of Sidney arriving half a day early. He had a ticket for a train on the 24th, but in the early evening he wandered from his hotel in Back Bay to the station, and found a train to Maine that was set to leave in ten minutes. Some old gentleman who wore his watch on his belt loop and tilted it up to check the time—"I remembered it because it was such an odd place to wear a watch," says Sidney as we sit around the kitchen table with coffee—was adamant in paying for the ticket. Sidney adds, glancing at Lena, "I would've left my bag in that hotel room, I was so desperate to get here. But it had all my paperwork." He made it back to the station just in time, climbing onto the train as it steamed out of Back Bay. When the old man got off at Newburyport, he waved goodbye and shouted good luck and "go on, get home to that pretty wife of yours!"

At that, Sidney fishes in his back pocket, pulls out his wallet, and takes out a snapshot of him and Lena. He places it in the center of the table. She's wearing a white sundress and her hair is falling on her shoulders in curls, and she holds tight to Sidney's hand and smiles as she leans into his shoulder. He's in his dress uniform, just as he is now, looking into the camera with an expression I've never seen on his face before—happiness? No, there were plenty of times growing up here when I saw him happy. Maybe the better word is content. They're standing in bright sunlight before a Greek-columned building, framed with palm trees, and on the façade is a bronze plaque that reads "Federal Circuit Court of Australia—Brisbane Registry."

"Aw," Lena says, taking the picture from him, "that's the one your friend Lester took."

"My crew's bombardier, and best man," Sidney tells us.

Lena sets the picture on the table. "He was annoyed we couldn't keep our eyes open at the same time, but it was so bright. And then you carried me over the threshold of the apartment I already owned," she says to her husband, "and it was both the most and least romantic thing that had ever happened to me."

The three of them talk for a while longer, and I listen, till eventually we all drift off to bed. Early the following morning, I take my coat and scarf from the hangers in the foyer closet. The house is quiet. Eventually

I must've made it to the guest room behind the stairs, though I have only a vague recollection of falling into bed and the touch of the cold sheets. Even the end of the conversation in the kitchen isn't clear in my mind. To be fair, nothing about last night is very clear in my mind, from dancing with Grace in the firelight to feeling as though she'd punched me in the stomach to seeing Sidney blown in out of the snow like a stranger. But I think that might also be because I drank more wine than I thought, and now I've got a splitting headache behind my eyes.

As I reach for the doorknob and fish my keys out of my jacket pocket, Grace says behind me, "Richard?"

I turn. She's got her arms crossed over an old bathrobe. Yesterday's makeup is smudged under her eyes, probably both from tears and a pillow. She comes over and leans against the closet door.

"I need to be getting home," I say. "Thanks for letting me stay, Grace. And for letting me drink your wine and intrude on your reunion with Sidney. I'm glad he's back."

"You know you didn't intrude," Grace whispers. She tilts her head and smiles. "You know you're just as much a part of our family, too. Honestly, after everything you've done for me this year, how could you not be?"

I feel rotten at that. "I haven't done anything for you. All I did last night was ruin something we've both waited so long for."

"You didn't ruin anything." She watches me with a tenderness I don't deserve. "I'd say we call it a draw. We were both acting like asses."

"I guess. But I am sorry, Grace."

"And so am I," she answers. "But can I ask you something?"

I nod.

"What you said last night. About this being all you have. That wasn't the heat of the moment talking, was it? No one says something like that if it hasn't been building."

"No. Probably not."

"So you believe it?"

I shrug.

Grace bites her lip and looks down at the slate.

"Do you believe everything you said, too?" I lean in the doorframe to the kitchen as pale light falls on my back.

She doesn't answer right away, so I say, "Maybe we have to call this a draw in more ways than one."

"I don't want that," she whispers, eyes moving back up to me.

"I don't either, Grace, but I can't be who you deserve. Maybe I could've been, but not now."

"Well, whoever that person is, I don't want him. I fell in love with you after you came home from the war, remember?"

I don't know how to answer that.

"Funny how we keep doing this," she says, "coming so close and then blowing apart."

We stand close to one another but not as close as last night, both of us reluctant for me to go out.

She draws her toe over the slate, and her expression turns playful. "You said you never do anything for me, but you cut me down a Christmas tree."

"About that. You didn't really forget about the tree, did you?"

Grace hesitates, then crosses her arms and drops her head so that her hair falls over her face. "Maybe I just wanted us to go out and find it together."

We're quiet again, and when she looks up, the attempt to be light-hearted fades from her face.

"Merry Christmas, Grace," I say after a moment, feeling no meaning in those words, and she says, "Merry Christmas, Richard, and be careful getting home," and I promise that I will.

At the top of the lane I roll the truck to a stop where I know Grace can't see me from the house. Everything I held in back there presses into me now. I could get through the rest of it when I imagined there was still a chance with her. Now I don't see the point of trying to get through any of it. A decade of muted heartache seems like child's play compared to this pain, the brass-knuckle sucker-punch. All I've ever wanted has just slipped through my hands because I let it. Any faith I had left is disintegrating. My friendship with Grace is on the rocks because I don't know how we can come back from last night's conversation. You can't take back love. And at the heart of it all beats the war.

I sit in the cab of the truck for a long time without the heat on till my nose runs, and I wipe at it with the back of my hand and my head clears enough for me to remember in crystal-clear detail every stupid thing I've said since last night. And then I start home, miserable and in a mood to bring the whole world down with me.

XXI.

MERCY

Mud spatters the Jeep as Peter turns the wheel sharply through a hairpin in the trees. He flips on the headlights, but they do little to cut through the fog. Wet snow bows the limbs of the pines. The forest around us is fragrant with smoke and resonant with the shells pounding the shit outta Easy Company. We ripped the windscreen off the Jeep and I have one knee planted on the hood, the other dangling into the passenger seat, hunched over this E Co trooper with a web of blood plasma tubing caught in my hands.

"Hang on, boys, it's gonna get even bumpier," Peter shouts, flooring the gas.

Our way back to the aid station is riddled with potholes and ice chunks, which send shocks through the vehicle's hood and yank cries and grunts of pain from the throats of the two boys. One is on the hood with me. The other's on the back because he has a leg wound, but at least he's fully conscious and can hang on to the Jeep. The one on the hood has two kraut bullets in his stomach, covered with my blood-sodden field jacket. I can't tell if the plasma is doing anything to counteract his shock. His body trembles in the cold, involuntary spasms jerking against my arms as I try to hold him still on the stretcher. The temperature has been dropping all morning. Snow dusts his eyelids and his open mouth.

"Pete, if you can go any faster—"

Peter shifts into sixth gear, and the Jeep's engine coughs before the clutch catches. Black smoke blossoms above the treetops. I know those boys. They're facing a full armored division. On our side, airborne light infantry, a few bazookas, and one 57-millimeter artillery gun against five tanks, self-propelled artillery, and flak batteries pulled by half-tracks. The krauts outnumber us twenty to one. But unless Colonel Vandervoort gives the order to pull back, E Co will fight to the bloody end.

Below us, the bridge that the engineers spent all night building clings to the banks of the Salm River, connecting the forest where the Panzer fight rages to the village of Trois-Ponts, our main line of resistance. Fox Company was holding that line till Vandervoort sent us out to cover Easy's right flank, but the brunt of the battle falls on their shoulders. When word spread through our columns that one of their medics had just been killed, I told Peter that I needed to get to their line and evacuate whatever wounded I could to the aid station. Greer told us to go and took command of Peter's rifle squad. We found this abandoned Jeep on the road near the Easy CP and made stretchers out of our jackets and the wounded men's rifles, then drove two wounded back to the aid station in the village, alive, where we got hold of a couple real stretchers and went back again to the line.

Peter jerks the wheel and shouts, "HEADS DOWN!"

A shell ruptures the frozen road ahead of us. He brakes hard as black earth and filthy snow plumes ahead of the Jeep. The kid on the back covers his face with his hands. I wrap one arm protectively around the head of the other, feeling every quiver of his muscles. Powder, both gun and snow, fills my nose.

"I'll say this," Peter yells as he accelerates again, "those krauts have got some bad aim if their shells are hitting the road."

On the hood, the trooper's breaths have turned to gasps. Who knows what else that shell might've knocked loose in him? Even with the plasma drip, his blood pressure is plummeting. I palpate his chest and abdomen, and the warmth of fresh blood reawakens my numb fingers. He chokes as my hand brushes across the hole. The blood flow is heavy and fast.

Aortic aneurysm. It has to be.

Fuck.

The aid station is still too far away. We have to do this here, now.

"Pete, stop. Stop!"

The Jeep pitches forward as he brakes, and it's all I can do to keep this kid from rolling off the hood. We're on the incline with the bridge a few yards below and the forest rising at our backs, snow-swept bluffs rushing down to the churning, slate-gray waters of the Salm. The fog has grown thicker and the snowfall heavier.

Peter jumps out of the driver's seat as I kneel on the warm hood and guide the kid's head to the side so he doesn't choke on the blood bubbling in his throat. I reach for my scissors from the bag under my left arm. "Get the vein clamps from my other bag," I tell Peter, "and two bandages, the sheets."

"Morphine?" Peter says, draping his field jacket over the trooper's legs.

"I've already given him a syrette."

I push up the sleeves of my shirt and then cut away the remains of his jacket. Snow falls onto his bloodied stomach as Peter waits with the clamps and two rolls of cut sheets.

"Hold him down!" I shout as the trees on the bluff split from shells. That's half a dozen tree burst wounds in one shot. "Okay, clamp!"

The trooper isn't in enough shock to be numb. When I go in with the clamp he thrashes his legs and arches his back, his whole body resisting me. Peter pins his shoulders to the hood and talks to him. "It's okay, you're gonna be okay, we need you to hang on—you can do this—"

"I don't want to die," he gasps, voice gurgling. "I don't want to die…"

Feeling returns to my frozen fingers as they wade through the warmth of his blood and internal organs. I can't find the damn artery, and I know I'm making it worse. Scarlet arterial blood spurts on my forearms. This is where it should be, where his lower abdomen meets his pelvis, but there's so much damaged, blood-saturated tissue that I can't feel the finely severed artery ends in the wound cavity. His intestines have also taken a hit, and getting past them is like threading the eye of a needle as the Blitz rages over your living room.

"I can't find it." I slide my hand from the wound cavity, still clutching the clamp, feeling as if I've just let go of a handful of raw meat. "I don't think I can do it. We need to get him to Doc Ryder."

The kid's cries have turned to whimpers. Peter, face red with cold and flakes of snow in his stubble, stares at me. "Will he make it there?"

"…I don't know."

My eyes linger on the kid's blood-soaked stomach, then on the freckles dotting his cheeks, the greasy hair falling on Peter's arm. It all feels so far away. This kid will die and there's nothing I can do to stop it, as Walsh did, as Jacob did, all my attempts to intercede in the steady march of death as hopeless as turning back a Panzer division with almost no ammunition.

"Richard, look at me."

I raise my head. I've seen this expression on Peter's face before, heard the steel in his voice—when he shouts at replacements, crouching in ditches clutching their M1s to their chests as bullets spray the road—*get up and fire your weapon, trooper. You stand and fight.*

Eyes steady on me, he says, "You need to do this, and I know you can."

I take a deep breath, shutting my eyes for only a second.

Whatever it takes.

Then I reach back in.

"Tell me his name," I say, trying to keep my touch light.

There's a jingle as Peter reaches for the kid's dog tags. "John Mazza. He's from Seattle."

"Okay, John, I know this hurts, I know it's horrible. But I have to do this so we can stop your bleeding. And then we're gonna take you to the aid station, where the surgeon will help you, and you can rest, and tell the other guys there all about Sea—"

There it is. That fucker. I press the clamp and feel it catch the artery, and the blood flow halts.

"It's on. Pete, bandages." I stuff the wound cavity carefully with the strips of white bedsheets. "Ready. Let's go."

Mazza chokes, a wet gasping sound. I angle his head again. The blood trickles onto my jacket tucked over him.

We roll over the snowy bridge and the churning whitecaps of the river. I rest my hand on Mazza's forehead, brushing my thumb across his temple, telling him things even I can't hear. Trois-Ponts is in ruins, the same story as our whole trail through Europe: houses and shops roofless under the swirling snow, rafters scorched black, windows blown out and heaps of ash and glass pushed like old snowdrifts to the edges of the street.

Peter pulls the Jeep up in front of the Catholic church serving as aid station. I jump off before it comes to a stop, while a couple of battalion medics run out and help the kid on the back with the fractured leg.

"What's the wait time for evacuation?" I call to them.

"Could be fifteen, twenty minutes. We got a line forming—"

Catching the tubing between my teeth, I tuck the plasma bag under my chin and grab the end of the stretcher by Mazza's boots. "Tell Doc Ryder I've got a patient in shock with a severed aortic, whoever can wait needs to w—"

"Richard. Richard!"

I look up. Peter is at Mazza's head, his hand on the kid's cheek.

"Sarge, grab the other end! We have to get him in! He doesn't have—"

"He's gone."

Snow falls below the collar of my shirt, trickling down my sweat-soaked back. I drop the plasma and tubing on the stretcher, then brush two fingers over Mazza's carotid artery. No pulse meets my touch. His brown eyes watch the winter sky. A scrap of snow falls onto his iris and melts, two more flakes landing on his chapped lips.

I step back from the hood of the Jeep. Something in me begins to burn.

"Richard—" Peter starts.

I fling my helmet to the ground and feel a brimming fury pulsing in my chest, and I press my hands to my eyes as I try to swallow it back till I realize the scream that follows is my own, pulled from my throat as though someone beat it out of me.

My helmet lies cock-eyed in the snow at Peter's feet. Out of the corner of my eye, I see the filthy brassard around the sleeve of my jacket on Mazza's chest, the crimson cross creased and stained.

Peter bends to pick up my helmet and sets it on the hood. His hand meets my shoulder. "It isn't your fault."

"The fuck it isn't!" I jerk away from him, dropping my hands, turning my back so he can't see the tears stinging my eyes. "You all say that to me, and you can say it because this isn't your job. Who the fuck am I going to blame it on, a whole Panzer division?"

"You know that O'Connor knew the consequences," Peter says, digging right to the heart of things I don't want to think about. "He made his choice, one we could all learn from, and he was never going to choose otherwise. And this kid didn't, either."

When I don't answer, Peter adds in a tone that makes me think even he doesn't really believe it, "He did his duty."

"I'm sick to hell of duty. I'm fucking sick of doing the right thing only for the shrapnel to blow up in our faces."

He's silent for a moment, but I feel him at my shoulder. Finally he says, "Me too."

I stare at the gray stone façade of the church and the wooden cross hanging above the arched doorframe. No stained glass, no carved saints standing watch on the pediment, no ornamentation—only that cross, unbowed to German artillery. A stretch of the roof has collapsed and a shell hole near the doors lets cold air and snow into the foyer, where a couple walking wounded wait, exhausted, but still the cross hangs brazenly. As if taunting kraut flak to take a bite out of it.

"But we're going to keep doing it, aren't we?" Peter says beside me.

He drapes my jacket over my shoulders. The fabric is stiff with dried blood, but I guess I need it more than Mazza does. It feels so heavy. Almost enough to collapse my unsteady legs, knock me down to the snowy street.

"I'm sorry, Peter." I exhale, hoping to drive out the pulsing pain excavating a path behind my eyes. "I shouldn't have said that."

He draws the toe of his boot through the snow. "You've got nothing to apologize to me for. You're right. We can't see things the way you do."

"We gotta go back up." I turn and look at the white bluff rising above the other bank of the river, just in time to see shell powder and shrapnel burst through the trees.

"Yep."

I fold my arms over my chest and stare at Mazza's cold body on the Jeep. The two aid station medics come out of the church, cover his body in a blanket, and lift him gently from the hood. One of them says to me,

"We're strapped for help and these wounded are piling up. Think you could give us a hand?"

"We've still got wounded to bring d—"

"Richard, you stay," Peter interrupts. He smacks my shoulder and then hops in the driver's side of the Jeep. "I'll go back up."

"It's too much for you to do alone."

"I'll wrangle some privates if I have to. We'll make it fine; you're needed here."

Before I have a chance to protest, he's gone, and I'm left here thinking of what happened the last time I let someone run an errand on my behalf. Then I follow the medics carrying Mazza's body toward the church. They almost drop him when another Jeep comes roaring through the snow from the direction of the CP in the village, forcing us all to jump out of the way.

"Hey, watch where the fuck you're going!" one of them shouts at the driver as he speeds across the bridge, leaving exhaust fumes in his wake.

I watch the Jeep as it climbs the road up the bluffs. "Wasn't that Colonel Vandervoort in the passenger seat?"

"Hell of a day he's having," the other medic says.

"He has to pull them back." His buddy regains his grip on Mazza's ankles as we all duck into the doorway of the church. "Easy's getting slaughtered. They're not gonna have a company left if he leaves them up there."

"Airborne training's starting to feel like a shot in our own asses," I say.

"How do you mean?"

"We don't know how to retreat."

Time passes differently in an aid station. It could be twenty minutes or three hours that I'm in here, dressing and disinfecting wounds and fetching supplies and holding light for the surgeons as they stabilize the worst cases for evacuation. The medics have set up a couple of barracks stoves and gasoline heaters in the center aisle of the sanctuary, around which we try to arrange the stretchers for the wounded who aren't weight-bearing so they can feel some warmth, maybe save some frostbitten toes. The new replacements are especially spooked. I try to calm their nerves, talking quietly as I stitch up small flesh wounds, but I barely hear my own words coming out mechanically as I retrace every step of what happened with Mazza. When I've been through that twice, I turn to Jacob.

W-whatever it takes. You taught me that, r-remember?

It's only when a private yelps and says, "Geez, Doc, what'd I ever do to you?" that I realize I've let anger guide my hands. I apologize for yanking the bandage so tight and undo the knot and retie it.

When I get to my feet, Doc Ryder passes me with fresh-scrubbed hands from the animal trough of heated water by the altar. He kneels beside a sedated lieutenant and says, "Blood pressure okay, Dare?"

"Two minutes, sir, just to get some air."

"Go on."

Back behind the church, I light a cigarette and tip my head against the wall and stuff my bloody hands in my jacket pockets, eyes falling shut, part exhaustion but mostly rage that I know I need to get a hold of. In truth I don't want to get it under control. What I'd really like is to find a rifle and go out and fuck up some Germans. But for the sake of the boys inside who need my clear mind, I blow out smoke and try to think of anything but the snowflakes melting in Mazza's dead eyes. The artillery fire hasn't died down on the bluffs. Maybe Vandervoort's not pulling back, a thought that does nothing to lower my blood pressure.

I hear raised voices and open my eyes. Two 82nd privates and a sergeant are beside the bridgehead diagonal to the church, gathered in a tight circle around something I can't see. The privates all have their rifles drawn, and the noncom holds a side-arm. Even from this distance I can see his gloved finger on the trigger.

"What are you all doing?"

The privates' heads whip around at my voice.

"Thanks, Doc, but we don't need any help. You can scuttle on back inside," the sergeant throws over his shoulder.

I tilt my head as I walk toward them, but I'm afraid I already know what they're doing. I start to call out again when a shot cracks through the air, distinctive despite the nearby fire because it comes from so close. I duck and stop where I am, frozen in my tracks.

A body falls to the ground past their cluster. Ashy blond hair brushes the soldier's forehead, and a single bullet hole drips a slow trickle of blood down his nose onto the snow. His overcoat is black wool. On his left arm is a maroon and white brassard, framing two interlocking black claws.

I stare at the body till the click of the Luger in the sergeant's hand snaps my attention back. He's already forgotten the Nazi on the ground and has the pistol aimed at the head of another POW, probably a Hitler Youth kid no more than sixteen or seventeen, on his knees in the snow. Dried blood is crusted on his neck and forehead. His friend beside him stares at me without blinking.

"Whose orders are you following?" I approach them slowly, eyeing the distance between the barrel of the Luger and the POW's forehead.

One of the privates glances at me suspiciously, wiping at his red nose. "Patton's."

"Last I checked, Patton wasn't our CO." I crouch beside the SS officer's head and feel for his pulse. Nothing. His skin is already tinted blue. "Why are you executing prisoners?"

"What do you want us to do, bring them back to our line and give them our food and medicine and a nice warm bunk on a troopship to the States?" The sergeant gestures with the loaded Luger, and the two wide-eyed German boys flinch away from it as they hold their hands, fingers interlaced, behind their heads. "Waste of space and resources, so when the brass tells us to blow the Nazis' brains out, we blow their fuckin' brains out."

"No one has given that order, and you know that." I stand and hold out my hand. "Give me your sidearm."

The noncom snorts. "What, so you can do it yourself?"

He takes a step closer to me and flashes the pistol a little too close to my stomach. His eyes tell me it wasn't an accident. "They killed our medic."

"Give me the gun," I say in the tone I only use to pull medical rank on obstinate officers.

"What if it was you they killed? Wouldn't you want your buddies to get the Nazi sons of bitches? Figure we're doing the public a favor, putting them out of commission," the sergeant adds, shrugging nonchalantly.

One Nazi stares straight ahead with his chin jutted out. The other stares, too, but then one eye flicks toward me. I see genuine fear there. And I wonder what they did before they came to Trois-Ponts. Which of their neighbors paid the price for their loyalty to the Führer.

Biting hard on my lip, I say, "We don't kill prisoners."

The two American privates drop their eyes as the sergeant jumps on the wavering note in my voice. "Bet you've never fired a weapon in combat, Doc. Hell of a rush."

I don't bother dignifying that with an answer.

"They shot Frank in the head," the sergeant adds. "Our medic. Point-blank, while he was working on our guys. Just murdered him." He gives me a look that makes me think he'll put a bullet through my head, too, if I continue trying to reason with him. "Don't believe me?"

"I believe you, but—"

"Then don't watch."

He fires one round into the sky with a grim smile. The more anxious kraut starts and then drops his head, eyes shut so tight that deep lines crease the edges of his eyelids.

Fucking die, then, you Fascist pig, I think. I imagine my finger on the trigger of that Luger. I would stand in front of him, where he could see the brassard that should signify hope, so that for the last minute of his life he'd know that this cross means not life but death. I would watch him die slowly as he knew I could help him. And then maybe I'd become impatient with how long dying takes when it's a death you're hungry for and not a life you're trying to save and I'd shoot him again, and then I'm afraid I wouldn't be able to stop.

Bet you've never fired a weapon in combat. Hell of a rush.

I know.

I imagine the Luger rounds grinding through this Nazi kid's flesh and rupturing his organs and draining him of blood like a cadaver under the coroner's knife. I know how his lungs would sound, searching for breath, and how his heart would race into tachycardia as his blood pressure plummeted. He'd go same as they've all gone. All the ones I've loved. And that's a slap in the face, to think that these monsters have human bodies.

Fuck it all.

I hold my hand out to the sergeant. "Pistol," I say, and maybe he's grown tired of the game, too, because he just twists his mouth in derision, sort of shrugs, and finally gives it to me.

Gun in hand, I turn and say to them over my shoulder, "Take them to battalion HQ so Captain Frye can interrogate them. If they don't make it, I'll know who's responsible. You're lucky Vandervoort has too much on his mind to worry about court-martialing you."

At the sound of an engine I look up. A familiar Jeep sans windshield bumps over the bridge.

"And bring this body to the aid station for the graves crew," I add, gesturing to the dead SS officer with the nose of the gun and looking at the two krauts as I do. "Go on, pick it up."

Peter comes to a stop outside the church, helps a wounded man off the back and watches him limp inside, and then starts in our direction over the hard-packed snow. At my back, I hear a heavily-accented voice spit, *"Jüdischer feigling."*

I bite my tongue and keep walking. Footsteps crunch in the snow behind me, the privates and prisoners following. I stop beside Peter, who lets out a low whistle at the sight of the Luger.

"That's a beauty, Rev." He looks past me at the Americans and their kraut POWs, or POSs as I'm starting to think of them.

"I told them to take the prisoners back to Captain Frye at HQ for interrogation," I say as I pop out the magazine from the Luger and then snap back the bolt to make sure there are no rounds in the chamber.

Behind me, the same kraut voice that called me a Jew and a coward says, *"Danke schön,* doctor."

"I'm not a doctor." I turn, Luger hanging at my side, and look at the German. Gray eyes stare back at me, unrelenting. One of the American privates has his rifle poked against the guy's back as the sergeant looks on sullenly.

"Hey, what did I say? Pick up your fucking officer"—I angle the gun toward the body once more without breaking eye contact, of half a mind to drop the Luger and wring his neck instead—"or we'll use him as a speedbump. *Heb es auf."*

Peter and I watch as they go back for the officer, the two American privates chaperoning them. They lift the dead man from the icy road and carry him between them. When they come back, the bolder kraut tilts his chin up and stares at me with an eat-shit expression.

"You got something else to say?"

The kraut shrugs, watching me disdainfully. I turn back toward Peter and the aid station just as he says in English, "Sometimes it is for fun, you see. We look for the red cross. And when we find a medic—"

The pistol-whip rings out like a gunshot. I feel the crunch in his cheekbone and see the garnet pools of blood blossoming instantly beneath his eye. As his head lolls back in a daze, I shove the magazine back into the Luger because fuck mercy. I yank his head forward by a fistful of his hair and level the pistol between his eyes and shout, "Look at me!" and though one eye is already swelling shut, he watches me through the slit of the other with blood cutting twin trails down either side of his mouth.

I hope he thinks it's a Jew who killed him, but then a stronger hand jerks me away and the Luger falls unfired into the snow. I feel a hand on my arm pulling me back as the edges of my vision go smoky, fading and strengthening in the thrum of my pulse. And then I'm back in the doorway of the church among the wounded with no memory of how I got here. The prisoners and their handlers are gone.

"Richard. Hey. Look at me."

Peter grips me by the shoulder, as much to steady me as to keep me from getting away, which I guess is what he thinks I'll do if he lets go. He snaps his fingers in my face.

"Richard, snap out of it," he says, and I realize that my hands are trembling so much that at the moment a jackhammer would be more useful for stitching wounds. I clench them into fists, digging my fingernails deep into the palms, as Peter tells me to take a deep breath. The black stars dancing spastically in my vision fizzle out. Slowly I uncurl my fingers.

The Luger without its magazine is tucked into Peter's cartridge belt. Without letting go of my shoulder, he says in the voice he often uses to whip spooked privates into form, the one he used on me earlier, "I'm taking you to battalion HQ, no arguments. You can cool off for a day running messages for the brass." Without waiting for my consent, he jerks me roughly by the arm and pushes me toward the Jeep.

24 December 1944, Rochelinval, Belgium, 1900 hours

Hollow coughs rattle down the length of the chow line. Jump boots stamp the snow, their owners trying to force feeling back into frozen toes. Two replacements join at the end of the line, their faces clean-shaven and cheeks pink and full, uniforms still olive-drab and helmets undented. They stand out like sore thumbs among the Fox Company veterans. We all have a week's worth of stubble because no one cares enough to shave in this cold. Our trousers and jump jackets are sodden and perpetually damp under the constant snowfall, and it'd take three washes through with shampoo to clean our hair. We're all flirting with the beginnings of trench foot. Last night tiny icicles stuck to my eyelashes. We've only spent one night here so far, but we've already learned that we can't sleep for more than a few minutes at a time because we have to get up and move to keep the frostbite away.

I've slept behind mosquito nets in Tunisian sandstorms, in rainwater-filled foxholes in Italy, in bombed-out cellars in Holland that still smelled of the charred bodies of their previous residents. But Belgium is the first place I'm afraid I'll fall asleep and never wake up.

Tired laughter comes from the little clusters of guys gathered around to eat. They stand and lean against trees with their mess kits in hand, or sit on stumps, grimacing at the lukewarm beans that were ladled into their tin cups. No fires for warmth, so we don't break light discipline. Rodriguez jams his bare hands beneath his armpits and says he's too cold to eat. Vandenburg, reaching for his canteen, upturns it with disgust—the water has frozen solid inside. I interlock my fingers over my mouth and breathe into them, steam escaping between the cracks. There's no moon out tonight, though the snow softens the darkness, casting an ethereal glow through the trees.

Yesterday the 505th evacuated Trois-Ponts and the relative comfort of sleeping in cellars there, to the woods outside Rochelinval, placed in division reserve and ordered to wait and rest. So far twenty-four hours have passed without incident or shelling. Our foxholes are spread along a line in the spruce forest between the narrow Salm River and a dirt road that connects to the main thoroughfare, the Moulin de Rochelinval. It isn't much for Christmas, but it beats getting the shit pounded out of us. Though in the painful cold, even that is becoming debatable.

"Hey, Rev."

Berk appears beside me, holding out my mess kit. He must've grabbed it from my foxhole.

"Special treat for the holiday, hard bread with the rancid beans," he says. "Just try not to breathe as you eat it, and it'll go down."

"Isn't this what we eat every night?" I poke at the beans dismally with the fork.

"Ah, but it's Christmas for you Christians, so that makes it festive."

"Wish I had your imagination."

Jerking his head at a fallen tree by one of the 3rd platoon clusters, Berk says, "Do I have to force you to sit, or will you go quietly?"

Even sitting, I can't keep still. My knee bounces incessantly through no will of my own. Al Akins in 3rd and a replacement in 2nd platoon are both in their foxholes coughing up their lungs and nursing fevers climbing to a dangerous pitch, so at mine and Donny King's suggestion, Captain Robinson radioed for an ambulance to take them to the evacuation hospital in Brand, over the German border. But that was two hours ago, and the ambulance never came and their radio is dead. Peter took a few guys out on a patrol, Fish and McNuts among them, to see what's the matter. I've had a bad feeling about it since the moment their backs disappeared into the snow-swept night.

"Sure hope they find 'em," Berk says after a minute or two of quiet. "I hate to hear Akins coughing up his lungs like that all night. Sounds like my wife's cat with a furball."

"Yeah, and Tucker's got a fever of 104, thinks he sees Marlene Dietrich in his foxhole." I stare at the beans sloshing about in my mess kit.

"Sounds pretty nice to me. God, these are some piss-poor beans. You got anything in that kit of yours for scurvy?"

"Hang on, let me just pick a lemon off the tree there..."

For once I'm grateful for Berk's natural ability to talk endlessly as the occasion requires, both to distract me from thinking about the patrol and to keep my mind from turning to darker things. For two days Peter's acted like nothing happened back in Trois-Ponts. If not for the fingernail-shaped cuts in the palms of my hands, I might wonder if I dreamt those events. I wish he would say something just so I could stop reliving it alone. Even last night in his foxhole, Fish asleep and he and I both awake in the bitter cold, he talked about other things without ever acknowledging it. To what end, I can't tell. Maybe he assumes I don't want to dwell on it. Or it could already be inconsequential to him, though I doubt it. What troubles me most is that he might think differently of me now. If he doesn't trust me, then the boys in his squad will pick up on that and follow suit. And in the darkest, coldest hours of the night, I wonder if they might be right to do so.

I give up trying to eat and set the tin of cold beans beside my leg as Berk tells me how he got arrested once on Christmas Eve at the Woolworths in Fresno, supposedly for forgetting to pay for a bottle of perfume that was another in a long litany of attempts to woo Emily. He claims it was accidental, which almost certainly means it wasn't. We sit knee to knee, shoulder to shoulder on the log to keep warm. I keep an eye on Lieutenant Greer across the clearing, his distinctive, gangly figure crouched at Branson and Kelty's hole. He's practically bitten his fingernails down to the cuticles waiting for the patrol. I know he won't sleep till they all come back. In the interest of not working us both into a greater anxiety, I've tried to keep some distance between us. Peter told me to wait here—"It's only a patrol; no use you getting all the way out there for nothing"—although we don't know how far "out there" is. The ambulance could be anywhere between the 2nd battalion lines and the aid station.

"Mind if I ask you something?"

I glance up. Berk is hunched forward with his arms wrapped around himself, watching me.

"Sure."

He deliberates for a moment, then finally says, "Back in Trois-Ponts. Something happened, I don't know what, but you didn't go to battalion for a day just for fun. No, relax, okay—I won't make you tell me. It's just that you and Pete have both been pretty tight-lipped about the whole thing, and you're kinda making me nervous."

I consider bluffing my way out of it, but I know Berk will see right through any bullshit. "Lost my cool with some POWs. If Peter hadn't been there it might've gotten ugly...uglier."

"Oh," he says, straightening a little. "So you okay?"

"Okay enough."

"Yeah, aren't we all. So what's next, you see a POW and just go ballistic?"

For whatever morbid reason, that actually makes me laugh. "Think I got it out of my system. I just—"

"MEDIC!"

That's Peter's voice, no doubt about it. I hear Berk say, "Oh, shit," as I jump up and take off into the trees. There's another cry. Fish's voice this time. From the sound of it, they're not far.

They come out of the white trees like ghosts. Peter and Fish carry a body between them, and behind them are two replacements from the other platoons, running to catch up.

"Oh, hell, Nuts," Berk breathes beside me.

"Down, put him down!" I shout, finally reaching them through the snow up to my shins. "Let me see."

McNuts is incoherent. I know even before I kneel beside him that he's in shock. He's drenched in blood pooling in his throat and chest, bubbling out of his mouth so profusely with each cry of pain that it's as if he gargled with it. Fish pins his shoulders while Peter tries to hold down his legs, telling him to stay still.

"Hold this," I tell Berk, and he takes the penlight and cups his hand around its glow. "In his eye here."

Berk tilts the beam into McNuts's eye as I gently pry his eyelid open. His pupil is dilated so wide that only a thin sliver of blue iris shows. There's no hint of recognition.

"We need to take him back to the CP," I say, glancing up at Peter and Berk through the falling snow. "I can't get a good look at anything out here."

It's awful getting him back to the Fox Company lines. Fish sprints ahead to tell the officers we're coming. After what feels like an eternity, Peter and Berk lower McNuts onto a tarp spread over the ground in the shelter of the battalion XO's tent as a cluster of concerned faces in and out of the tent look on. Berk and Greer help me get his overcoat off him so it can't inhibit chest compressions if things come to that. Peter balls up the coat and puts it under his feet to keep them elevated higher than his head. Captain Robinson orders a couple privates to hang tarps from the tent poles to block the light. Voices murmur and wonder and then begin to rise in volume while McNuts grows more and more distressed.

"Berk," I say, and he looks up at me. "Get them to quiet down. He needs to hear my voice."

Berk stands and sweeps his arm in a commanding gesture away from the tent. "Hey! All of you enlisted! Back up and shut up."

As the peanut gallery shuffles away and disperses, I say, "Okay, Charlie, it's okay. I've got you."

He deserves his real name tonight, not a barracks nickname. I put one hand on his forehead and talk to him softly as I brush my other hand over the carnage of his throat and chest. Lieutenant Greer crouches at his head. Berk is on his other side, hand holding Charlie's tight. I feel Peter hovering at my shoulder and Fish beside him. Charlie convulses beneath my touch, drawing in short, gurgling gasps for air.

"Shh, it's okay. You're going to be okay, Charlie. It's just me," I whisper.

In Normandy I watched him take a friendly fire bullet to the knee and laugh about it as he waved goodbye to us from the passenger seat of a Jeep, his first-class ride to the hospital. In the Belfast pubs he'd take three punches to the face for some perceived grievance on a drunk Irishman's part, and he'd grin as if it was a game. If he's in pain, then the odds are pretty shit.

"Radio for Doc Ryder," I throw over my shoulder to anyone who's listening. I cut his field jacket open. Robinson kneels beside me and switches on his flashlight, bathing Charlie's head and upper body in an arc of light. "We can't move him again, and he needs a surgeon now. Berk, plasma and tubing from my kit."

I soak up as much blood as I can with a bedsheet rag, all the while talking to him, keeping my touch light on his forehead.

"It's okay, Charlie, it's just me," I repeat, "I've got you."

He's watching me. His eyes are half-open, clouded with pain, but he sees me. By the slightest of measures his body relaxes. I know this could have nothing to do with me and everything to do with his falling blood pressure, so it's a fleeting relief when I get the plasma into him to hopefully offset the shock and buy him some precious time as we wait for Doc Ryder.

"There's nothing else you can do?" Berk says.

We look at one another over Charlie on the ground. Conscious of all the eyes on me, I answer, "I'm not a surgeon, and this is a real mess."

Charlie makes a choking sound from his throat, as if he wants to cough but can't. I ease open his jaw and shine the penlight into his mouth but can't see any obstructions. While we watch, his choking turns to gagging. The lack of oxygen casts his face gray. Something occurs to me—a tiny, slippery bit of hope as scrappy as Charlie himself. The worst of the damage is nearer to his jaw, and his trachea has escaped mostly unscathed. There's no telling how long it'll take Doc Ryder to get through. If he'll get through.

"Tracheotomy," I murmur to myself, only realizing I said it aloud when Berk says, "Trach what?"

I look up at the officers, still brushing my thumb across Charlie's forehead. "His upper airways are blocked. I think I can get him breathing again by putting a tube into his trachea. His windpipe."

Before Greer or Robinson can answer, Peter says, "Have you done that before?"

"He's already slipping into shock. I don't think we have a choice."

"Not what I asked."

I turn to look back at him. "Do you have a better idea?"

"What are we waiting for? Let's do it," Berk mutters.

Peter says to Donny King, who's in the doorway of the tent, "Have you done a tracheotomy?"

"No, never," Donny answers, crossing his arms and staring at Charlie without much hope in his face.

"You want to cut a hole in his throat and put a tube in it? Am I the only one who thinks a surgeon should be doing that?"

No one answers. I hear Peter sigh. Charlie gasps for air, eyes wide and mouth mute and his chest heaving as if a hand is pushing him underwater. As far as I'm concerned, that's the decision made. I won't let him suffer if there's a chance I can help him.

"We don't have time for a surgeon." I fish some extra tubing from my kit and cut it to length with the scissors, about six inches. "It might not work, but if we do nothing then it's over anyway." Before Peter has a chance to lodge another protest, I add, "Now somebody give me a trench knife."

On rainy afternoons off in Quorn, when we had classroom time, I read as many books as I could find on anatomy and medical procedures, trying to give myself even a fraction of the education I never got. Airborne tells you you're a medic, hands you some bandages and morphine, ties a red cross to the arm of your jump jacket and orders you to save men's lives with only a modicum of training for how to actually do that. It was during this time I read and reread a description of tracheotomies in an old textbook, memorizing the steps in case the need ever arose. I convinced myself that it wouldn't—after all, that's what the surgeons are for.

I've never had the chance to practice it, and I haven't looked at those illustrations in months. The margin for error is about as wide as Peter's trust in me. Captain Robinson places his trench knife in my hand. My heart drops at the sight of the dull blade in the dim light, knowing I have no way to numb the incision site.

"Charlie, I won't lie to you," I say, crouched by his head. "This'll hurt like hell, but I need you to trust me."

I feel all eyes flicking between him and me—Greer with his hand in Charlie's hair; Fish and Donny in the tent opening holding their breath as half the company waits outside; Berk gripping his foxhole buddy's hand and probably wondering if the confidence in my voice matches my abilities. And Peter, who thinks I lost my marbles in Trois-Ponts, whose expression of doubt feels more substantial than anyone else's hope. Worst of all is that folks listen to him, especially the inexperienced officers. More often than not they take his word as gospel. So as I swipe the blade with an iodine swab, I pray with a half-hearted faith—less than that, a quarter-heart—that Charlie didn't hear that exchange. He's the one person who can't give up.

Everyone is silent as I drop to my elbows on the ground to get as close as possible to his trachea. Inhaling deeply, I feel along Charlie's throat, past his Adam's apple, till I feel the second bulge. Inexplicably, I think, *Cricoid cartilage*. Brushing my index finger between the two bulges, I find the little depression between them. I've got one shot.

Gripping the handle of the knife, I make the cut, half an inch in length and depth.

"Light closer," I say. Robinson shines it just above my incision. Charlie hasn't made a noise, so maybe he's got enough other shit going on that he doesn't feel much. Small mercies.

Through the incision I see the cricothyroid membrane, pale yellow surrounded by cartilage. I make the tiniest cut into the membrane, not certain if it'll be deep enough.

That's the hardest part done. I drop the knife beside me and grab the tubing I cut. All we can do is hope that there isn't too much damage to his throat already to render the tracheotomy useless. My hands are so dirty that I wince as I position the thin tubing into the hole. But I need to keep him alive. Let the surgeons and nurses deal with infections.

The tube slips in, and I secure it with strips of wound tape as Berk whispers to Charlie. I hold the tube between my thumb and forefinger and put my mouth on the opening, for a second sucking on it as on a straw. A vague memory of the tiny black words jammed on the textbook page tells me that I should feel air coming up the tube, but nothing happens. That must mean it's in the wrong place.

Shit, I hope it's just the tubing, not the cut. There's barely anywhere else for the tube to go. I guide it as gently as I can, half a millimeter from where I put it first.

I try again, and this time a wisp of air meets my mouth.

"Almost there, Charlie, you hang on," Greer says.

Turning my face away from the tube to draw breath into my own lungs, I put my mouth on it again and exhale. I think the diagram in that book showed a featureless person administering two breaths through the tube, so I do it again.

Berk tilts his head toward me. "Is that it?"

"Not until he starts breathing on his own." I watch his chest, hold my palm against it, but I don't feel any movement. I breathe twice more into the tube to no effect.

In a calm voice I say, "Okay, Charlie, you gotta fight for me," and breathe into the tube again.

Thank God his carotid artery wasn't severed. I feel along it for his pulse.

Nothing.

Did I jump the gun, assuming a tracheotomy was his only chance? But there's no way he can breathe again without it.

I fish Charlie's dog tags out from beneath his jump jacket and shirt, drape them on his shoulder so they don't press into his skin, and plant my hands one on top of the other over his heart. Desperation flows out of my hands with each compression as I press down, again, again, again, at the end of my ideas if his heart doesn't take the bait.

"Come on, Charlie, come on," I say through gritted teeth, jamming my hands against his chest and then pausing for two seconds to breathe into the tube. "Don't you give up on me now."

Compression after compression—I lose count of how many—followed by breaths into the tube, followed by compression after compression, till the sweat is running down my back. Peter appears beside Berk and kneels, one hand on Charlie's knee.

"You're always showing us how the boys from Queens fight like hell, Charlie," I tell him. "You gotta fight now, harder than ever."

I feel Peter's eyes on me, but I don't meet his gaze.

"Richard," he says.

I look at Charlie's face instead. Bone white, blue-tinted in the shadows of the tent. His eyes are shut.

That irritating doubt edges Peter's voice. "Richard, this might be—"

I take up the compressions again, anger rising in my throat. I will not lose him too. I cannot hold another dying friend and tell myself that God means it for good.

It's that helpless fury, availed of no other outlet, that makes me breathe into the tube yet again even though I know it won't do any good. Then, on the third compression, I feel the unmistakable crunch of a rib beneath my hands. The others who are close enough must hear it, too, because Peter hisses, "Richard, stop, now you're just hurting him for no re—"

"Quiet, quiet!" I hold one hand on Charlie's chest, the other to his carotid.

For a moment all is still.

Then—the weak thrum of a pulse, followed by a stuttered breath, forcing Charlie's chest to rise just barely.

It worked.

"Yes, that's it, Charlie, that's it," I say, relief forcing the anxious words out, "just like that. Easy now. It's okay. We're here with you. I've put a tube in your throat to help you breathe. I know it hurts, but it's for the best. Don't try to talk."

I carefully touch the opening of the tube and feel air sucking in and out. Charlie's eyes flicker open as it reaches his lungs. His face is still ashen, but he's breathing.

I sit back and press my blood- and dirt-stained hands to my face. A hand grips my shoulder. Greer. I hear Robinson say in a low voice, as if disbelieving the scene before us, "Well done, corporal."

Berk exhales. "Could teach the surgeons a thing or two," he remarks, and we look at each other. Then our low laughs of disbelief fill the tent.

"It worked. That's all that matters. That's right, Charlie, you can rest now. The hard part's over," I add as he closes his eyes. Some color has come back to his cheeks. I reach for my scissors and begin cutting away the remnants of his jacket, which stick to his skin like glue. "Now let's see what else we've got here, see if we can't hand Doc Ryder less of a mess."

When dawn comes, a pale light in the east melting over the white hills that sweep down to the Salm, I'm hunched forward in the passenger seat of a Jeep with my arms around myself for some semblance of warmth. The Jeep driver who picked me up outside the aid station, no more than a farmhouse on the Moulin de Rochelinval, glances to his right as we drive along the silent ridge. An ivory landscape is spread beneath us like a sculptor's marble.

"Kinda pretty," he remarks past his cigarette, and I nod. The Jeep bounces over the icy track, snow tamped-down and dirty from wheels and boots, and soon we're among the trees, the valley gone.

He drops me at the F Company lines. A thin strip of dark green canvas is visible a few yards off under a covering of snow, the edge of the XO's tent where McNuts fought for his life last night. By force of habit I feel the kits hanging at my sides. Both frighteningly light. I jam my hands in the pockets of my overcoat and trudge toward Fox's foxholes.

"Richard," a voice says, and I glance to the left.

Peter is coming from the direction of Lieutenant Greer's foxhole. I stop as he makes his way to me through the snow.

"How's Charlie?" he asks first, tucking his gloved hands beneath his arms when he reaches me.

"Surgeons say he's gonna make it." I squint in the oddly bright light falling through the treetops. "He'll never fight again, but they expect him to make a full recovery. Probably get sent back to England next week."

"Pity it takes a shot to the throat to get sent to England," Peter remarks, and I snort. "Long night?"

"Yeah." I mean to elaborate, but exhaustion fills me to my fingertips. I can still feel the warmth of slippery organs. Spend enough consecutive hours in an aid station, and you start to feel as if you're perpetually up to your elbows in blood, even if afterward you scrub like Lady Macbeth. Instead I say, "Last night. Did you find the ambulance?"

Peter's expression sobers. "Yep. They were on the road up there"—he nods to where I just came from—"snipers got them. Both dead. Charlie was the first across to check if they were alive, and there must've been one kraut left in the trees."

"You got him back quickly. That might've saved his life."

"*You* saved his life," Peter counters in a gently reproachful tone. "But as for getting him back, well, it was really Fish who got to him. I don't know how the sniper didn't turn him into a sieve. Maybe they thought he was a medic."

He doesn't say how Fish was able to get to McNuts under sniper fire, which is enough for me to assume that Peter drew the sniper's attention away, making himself the target to give Fish a clear path. It isn't difficult to imagine. Nor is it surprising to me that Peter doesn't say a word about it.

"I should find Greer and Robinson, tell them Charlie's alive," I say.

Peter nods. "And Berk. Poor sap's chewed his fingernails to the limit. Put him out of his misery, for the love of God."

I laugh, short and hollow-sounding in the stillness. We're quiet for a few moments. Then Peter clears his throat and I glance up and he says, earnestness in his expression, "Richard, I owe you an apology."

I start to shake my head and tell him he doesn't, but he puts his hand on my shoulder to silence me.

"Yes, I do. I shouldn't have doubted you. You've never given me a reason to. And I know I'm biased, but I don't care. You are the best medic in the whole fucking 82nd."

"Pete, you don't know every other medic in the whole fucking 82nd."

"Don't need to." He shrugs. "If I'd gotten my head out of my ass last night, maybe I would've paid more attention to how you calmed Charlie down—I still don't know how you did that, but it was something else. Anyway," he adds, smiling probably because my face is beet red, "all that to say, I shouldn't have acted like that in front of the others. They trust you, and I do too."

A weight that sat on my chest all night like a ballast lifts. In its release, I don't even care that we're up to our knees in snow and the temperature's barely in the double digits. Peter throws his arm around my shoulders as if welcoming me home, and I hug him too, relief flooding me. "You're coming with me," he says, "and take a nap in me and Fish's foxhole so I can keep an eye on you, and make sure you actually do it."

"Yes, sarge," I answer without protest, and he raps his knuckles on the back of my helmet and grins.

"And Merry Christmas," he adds as we start through the snow. "Can I tell you something? I don't know if I'll dream of a white Christmas ever again."

XXII.

GHOST

24 December 1945

The candles have been snuffed out. The pews are empty, and the lights in the front of the sanctuary are switched off so the tree-branch shadows play across the white walls in the moonlight and the dark corners look ominously deep. Helen's father played a haunting rendition of "O Come O Come Emmanuel" on his violin while one of the elders struck a match and went down the center aisle, lighting the candle of each person sitting at the end of the pews. The sanctuary grew luminous till each row was filled with its own stars against the darkness.

Dad is always last in the church on Christmas Eve to clean and lock up so Bill Emmons the caretaker can go home with his wife after the service. I offered to help him while Mom and Laurie went home to finish the baking. Traces of wine stain the bottoms of the communion cups that I gather from their holders on the backs of the pews beside the hymnals. Still brooding on this morning's heartbreak, I go downstairs to the dim basement and begin washing out the tiny glasses in the utility sink. Card tables and metal chairs are folded against the cinder-block walls. The tap water down here only has one setting—so cold I don't know how the pipes haven't burst.

I don't look where I'm reaching and knock half a fleet of glasses to the concrete floor, where they smash with a sound like a gunshot. I stare at the shards littered like sparkling snowflakes all around me. Dad's voice calls down the steps from the foyer: "Richard, you okay? What broke?"

"I'm fine."

Without thinking, I crouch and try to gather up the biggest pieces. A little ribbon of blood appears on the tip of my finger. This is stupid; I need a broom. I stand, but when I look around my heart stops for a beat. The stark cinderblock and concrete of the church basement is gone. Did I go upstairs and outside unconsciously?

Everything is covered in snow. It isn't the road outside the church because there are no houses. Just a ragged tree here and there, leafless branches splintered. The blood on my fingertip has frozen. What happened to all the broken glass?

"...Dad?"

The sound of my voice is lost in a familiar ghastly scream of artillery fire.

I turn and run. Images go in and out of focus before my eyes, first a flashing white landscape and then the yellow paint of the church stairwell and the wooden railing. It feels like the church and I just ran up the stairs, but it sounds like the front line in Trois-Ponts. I hear someone calling my name and can't tell from where.

"It isn't real, it isn't real," I say aloud as cartridges click. "It isn't real..."

The sanctuary stretches before me, filled with the scent of smoke. Something touches my shoulder and I spin around, coming face-to-face with a bone-white Jacob O'Connor.

He steps forward as I step back, the sanctuary floorboards creaking beneath his boots. Arms catch me from behind as I stare at the three bullet-holes in Jacob's stomach and the blood blossoming across his jacket. But it doesn't make sense. He never even made it to Belgium.

Two more figures appear at his shoulders. Their faces have the ghostly hue of death left out too long in the cold, cheeks gaunt, eyes empty, staring right at me without seeing me. Walt Cook and John Haley. Their bodies have been made impossibly whole, because there were no bodies to bury after their hole was hit in Rochelinval.

"I'm sorry," I say as Jacob reaches for me. I back up against one of the pews, adding, "I'm sorry, I'm so sorry, Jacob," because maybe that's what he wants to hear—that I would've done anything to take his place if I could have.

The white forest is gone. A congregation of the dead spills from the foyer and the shut windows and the doors that lead to the cemetery. As they close in on me, the sounds of Belgium fall away. I know every face, every name. I remember how they died. Their uniforms are gray with the damp, and their faces are unshaven. Some approach me and others sit in the pews. I glance down, noticing their boots splitting at the seams, then the blood that appears to have no source, pooling on the floor and washing over my feet.

"This isn't real, it isn't real, it isn't real..." I can't back up any farther. Jacob and I are eye-to-eye, so close that I can see each scratch on his cheeks and how paper-thin his skin is. His dirty blond hair is perpetually dripping wet, and he makes no attempt to blink the water out of his eyes that, unlike the eyes of his companions, seem to see deep into me. Pressing my hands to my own eyes, I tell myself again that this isn't real, but that feels less important now than the fact that I don't know how to make it stop. "What do you want?"

Ghostly hands brush at my back, moving toward my throat. Jacob's hand closes on my wrist with a touch so cold it sears my skin. I jerk away, feeling my elbow hit something solid. The hands on my back disappear. Blinking, I notice the crimson seeping over the floor has vanished. I lift my head.

The sanctuary is quiet and empty. I look over my shoulder at the altar, but no one is there. No one is coming in through the wide doors of the foyer. The windows are shut, and snow gathers on the sills outside. There are no figures in the pews and no blood on the seats or in the grain of the floor.

Empty, that is, but for Dad standing in front of me. The sleeves of his white dress shirt are rolled to his elbows. He has a handkerchief pressed to his left eye.

"That's my fault for getting too close." He sort of laughs. "I should know better. Dangerous as waking a sleepwalker."

My breath rattles, the solitary sound in the sanctuary. Only now do I notice how hard my heart is pounding. Something touches my arm, and I jump and then feel like a fool because it's only him.

"It's just me. It's okay." His hand drops from my arm. "Richard, it's okay."

He lowers the handkerchief. I stare at the bruises rimming his swollen eyelid and the bridge of his nose. The skin is wine-red with fresh blood pooling just beneath the surface.

"Well, my nose isn't bleeding, so it can't be too bad," he remarks.

"Did I..." I stare at him, fixated on his swollen eye, and am sure I can see the bruise spreading like the blood on Jacob's stomach. "Did I do that?"

Dad shakes his head. "It was my fault. I shouldn't have scared you." He glances down, then crouches and picks something up off the floor. "There they are, almost stepped on them. Not that it would've mattered, I guess."

The sanctuary is still dark, but enough light shines through the open door from the foyer to see the bruise and now his broken glasses as he holds them. The left lens is cracked and a jagged chunk is missing.

"Oh my god. I could've blinded you—Dad—"

He tucks the broken glasses into the pocket of his shirt and shakes his head again. "But that isn't what happened, so no point in thinking about it."

"I'm sorry, I'm so sorry," I say over and over again as he puts his hand on my shoulder and guides me from the sanctuary. "I'm so sorry, Dad. I didn't mean to..."

"I know you didn't. You were spooked, that's all."

"But I could've hurt you, I mean, I *did* hurt you—"

"Richard." Dad flicks off the switch for the electric lights in the foyer, bathing us in darkness. "It was an accident. And it's just a bruise. It looks worse than it is, I promise."

I stand on the stone steps as he locks the door of the church. "But your glasses—"

"Glasses can be replaced."

"—and I broke the communion cups—and I didn't clean them up, I'm sorry—"

"Good. I've been petitioning the deacons for months to fit a new communion set into the budget. They were old and brittle, anyway. The cups, not the deacons."

He must've put my coat around my shoulders, though I don't remember him doing it. Snow falls in a silent patter around us. I stare into the darkness at the dim forms of my dead friends still watching me, till Dad murmurs, "Come on, son. Let's go home. It's Christmas Eve."

This happened once before, in the field hospital in Liege, after I was wounded. Because my left arm was in a sling for my broken collarbone, the medics bound only my right wrist to the cot frame. They taped my ankles while I screamed at them because they were keeping me from helping my boys, who were dying in the snow all around me. But in truth there were only other occupied cots around me and a hospital ward of men I'd awoken because I thought I was back on the front lines. It was a nurse, finally, who calmed me down, who took a chance that I wouldn't try to hurt her. And I didn't.

But it was only a matter of time.

"I thought—" I look behind me again, still sure that somewhere out here in the endless northern night, they're waiting for me. All the ones I couldn't save. Dad watches me, his eyebrows drawn together. "I saw th-them, in the church—" I point, unnecessarily, as cold and fear bring my words to a stutter. "They were there, c-coming toward me. They tried to touch me."

"Who?" Dad's face is lit by the streetlamp in front of the church.

"All of them." I look at him desperately, wondering if this, too, is just another hallucination. Or maybe what I saw in the church was real and this is the shadow. "My friends, and I couldn't help them. I was supposed to help them and I didn't—"

"It's okay. It is. You did help them. I know you—I raised you—I know that's the kind of person you are." Dad steps closer, and thank God this time I don't try to knock out his other eye. "I don't know what they wanted, but they can't hurt you now. You're home. It's all okay."

"No, it's not! It's n-not okay!" Angry tears fill my throat. "Stop saying that. It's not, and I'm—I'm so tired of pretending that! You wouldn't say that if you were there—if I'd been able to save them—"

"So you think that's why they're back?" Dad says quietly, a sharp contrast to the climbing pitch of my voice. "Because they're angry and vengeful you couldn't save them?"

I swallow hard. "No, I...no, I don't know. But if you'd been there..."

And then I don't know how to go on, unsure if Dad is really here beside me, if I ever really did come back.

"Let's go home." His hand rests on my shoulder, gentle and determined, as if to pull me back from the depths of the night and the snow where I know, if I wandered, I would find them again. "Let's go home and get warm. It's almost Christmas."

T he more I think about the way Dad looked at me with that quiet patience in the church, the farther I want to run. He has an apparently endless capacity of understanding that irritates me all evening till the irrational desire burns in me to do something that will truly anger him. He told Mom that an icicle falling off the church roof nailed him in the eye. She didn't believe him, but she didn't ask about it again. She sat him at the kitchen table and gave him a dish towel wrapped around ice and he said no, don't bother Linstead on Christmas Eve.

Mom still said she'd feel better if I'd take a look at it because I'm the closest thing we have to a doctor, which would be funny if I didn't feel like shit. Feeling like the thief returned to the scene of the crime, I looked at it, shining a penlight into his pupil. I asked him the questions I used to ask guys who took a blow to the head: Does your head hurt? Are you dizzy? Is your vision blurry?

He said no, no, and no. He was kind not to note that my hand was shaking as I held the light. In his expression I saw the shared secret between us, his defense of me at his own expense. It took everything I had not to say "I'm sorry" like a broken record.

I hurt him, so who else could I hurt, and worse? What if that had happened last night at Grace's house instead?

If only he was angry with me.

A contented snore sounds from beneath the sheets. Hen settles her head on my feet as howling wind whips the house, shaking the windowpanes in their casements. Laurie, who drew the short straw in giving up his bedroom for our grandparents, stretches out on the cot we brought down from the attic. He half-folds his pillow beneath his arm and stares out the window above my bed.

"I forgot you can see the church steeple from here," he whispers. "You're the night watchman of Holland Road."

I follow a twin trail of headlights moving through the trees past the church and wonder who it is and where they're going so late. The lights catch the falling snowflakes in their path. Then I roll onto my back, tired but restless. "It's too bad Faye couldn't come for Christmas. When are you gonna marry her?"

"Tomorrow, if she'd let me." Laurie flops down on the pillow. "But realistically not till after she graduates in the spring. She always says she wants to get married in the fall, so we'll see if I can wait that long."

"Mm."

"I don't care when, really. But it would be nice to have enough money saved for a house."

"In Caspar?"

Laurie shrugs. "Not necessarily. Places like New York don't matter to me, but I wouldn't mind a beat where the most interesting story isn't the new freezer Chip Crane bought for his store."

The radiator clangs, and a puff of steam hisses out. We lie here silently for a long time, long enough that I think he must be asleep. Hen's chest rises and falls against my shins. My own chest is tight, breath like a dry-bone rattle when I exhale, verging into wheezing territory. I wrap my arms around my pillow and count the dark grains of wood in the bedframe and try to breathe out evenly to fend off the closed-in feeling, which has begun to creep in like a soft hand pinning my throat. I drop my head on my arms, wondering for the hundredth time if I'll wake Laurie tonight with my nightmares.

He whispers, "Hell of a wheeze."

"Sorry. I can't help it."

"It's okay."

I think of the nights when we were children and Laurie, afraid of the dark, crept into my bed, and we slept spine to spine, feeling the quiet breathing of the other all night long. I wonder how old we were when that last happened. If we had any inkling it was the last time. We'd laugh in the dark together about little things no one else understood till Dad's voice in the doorway told us to hush and "go to sleep, boys."

Laurie's breathing slows after a while, so he must really be asleep this time. I lie still and listen to the mountain wind. For a bit I flit just beneath the surface of sleep and dream of a hand in my ribcage dismantling all my ribs from the inside, setting them one atop of another like a rock cairn. I touch one and it disintegrates like ash on my fingers, like gunpowder.

Something catches in my chest and jerks me out of the half-dream state. I sit up and hold my hand to my mouth to keep from coughing, then as carefully as I can I untangle myself from Hen.

I hold in the coughing till I'm in the bathroom with my eyes watering. When it's over, I fold my arms on the porcelain sink basin and rest my head on them, sigh, and stay hunched here for a minute. If I woke anyone with that episode, they were gracious enough to pretend I didn't. I hear my grandfather snoring from Laurie's room. The upstairs hallway when I leave the bathroom is dark and quiet except for the dim glow at the bottom step. A light on in the kitchen.

Some nights I hear footsteps outside my bedroom door, and then they'll move away again. I wonder how many times he's come that close and in the end let me be. Only for me to creep closer when his back is to me, a moth drunk on the porch light.

At the bottom of the stairs I watch him sitting in the kitchen under the single lightbulb. He's stoked the embers till they glow in the stove. For someone born with scoliosis, he's not helping himself sitting hunched like that. I cross my arms over my chest. The thought of lying in bed while Laurie and Hen are asleep and I count every breath, wait through the darkest hours till dawn, is too much to bear.

The old wooden stairs creak as I step off the bottom. That's when I see Mom at the table too, at Dad's right where I couldn't see her from the staircase. They both look at me, Dad craning his neck around.

"Sorry, I didn't realize." I start to turn back. It's been a long time since I've heard her down here at night with him. I used to hear the hum of their voices through the heating grates, never clear enough to make out words.

A chair scrapes back across the floor. "No, it's okay, Richard. I was just going up. Come sit with your father." Mom draws her bathrobe around herself as she moves away from the stove.

She stops at the stairs and hesitates a moment before putting her hand on my cheek and kissing my forehead, tilting up on her toes to do so. Then she goes up the stairs in a rustle of fabric, and I hear their bedroom door latch shut.

"Couldn't sleep?" Dad says.

A shadow of bare branches silhouetted by the porch light moves across the back door. Into the light, out of it, in again, just like my conflicting desires to tell him everything so that he can help me understand it, and to never say a word of it aloud because then it's out of my control. Besides, he has enough burdens to carry. No one with a peaceful mind sits awake reading in a cold kitchen at one o'clock in the morning. And only someone else restless with anxiety would come down to sit with him at such an hour. Which I suppose bonds my mother and I tonight.

"Not really," I answer, coming to the table and dropping into the chair closest the stove.

There's a book lying dog-eared on the table. *The Salt-Cellars* by Spurgeon. I nod to it and say, "Some light reading?"

"Figured I'd save the likes of Calvin for a clearer mind."

The harsh bulb leaves half his face obscured. He's not a big man and Laurie and I both grew taller than him in high school, but his broad shoulders and firm-set jaw give a weight to his presence that I didn't inherit. The backs of his hands are nicked with old scars from hard labor or fights or whatever his life held before he came to Caspar. Some are from woodworking. He made this table when we were little and likes to walk around it and point out its flaws, saying he could do better now, but Mom won't let him cut it down to rebuild it. Says too many birthdays happened at it.

"I'm sorry I passed my insomnia down to you." He smiles apologetically. "Why is it always us two, this time of night?"

To my relief he doesn't seem to expect an answer. He picks up the Spurgeon, bends it open to see the words hiding in the margins beside the narrow spine, and continues to read. We sit in silence. He looks to be content just reading with me beside him. But I feel increasingly more uncomfortable, as if someone took a corkscrew and snaked it down my throat and twisted up my organs. It doesn't take long for the corkscrew to reach my lungs and for my lungs to decide it's time to work a little less. Dad, in his graciousness, makes no comment about the wheeze every time I inhale. I cross my arms over my chest and try to force down the welling up of anxiety and paranoia and doubt, but it's no use.

"How are you always so sure?" There's a note of desperation in my voice that disgusts me. I hesitate a beat before continuing. "How do you...know?"

Letting the book fall closed over his finger in the middle, he watches me. He deliberates for a long time. He seems to have expected the question, as if he's only been waiting for me to ask. "I've had unbelief, just as I think you're experiencing now."

"Unbelief?" I don't know why I ask, because I know what he means by it.

"That lingering little doubt in the back of your mind that you've been trying to press down every time you come up for communion, wondering if the body and the blood are meant for you too, or if you're the only person in the church they *aren't* meant for," Dad says. "If I can recognize that in my neighbors, then of course I can see it in my son."

I know my cheeks are burning. I shouldn't have come down.

"Richard," Dad says, and him saying my name is even more repulsive to me than my voice was, not because it's him saying it but because it means he sees me and is thinking of me and, the worst of all, praying for me. He sets Spurgeon on the table, props his elbows on his knees, and watches me.

This makes my face burn even more. Finally I look away to the embers.

He goes on, "I could give you a dozen verses about the assurance of faith—from Psalms, Hebrews, 1st Peter, the Gospel of John—and I will if you want me to. But I expect you already know them all, and me trying to convince you wouldn't get you very far."

I am not ashamed, for I know whom I have believed. I could recite that whole chapter of 2nd Timothy back to him. But the words appear to me strangely meaningless. Severed from their original significance that I once blindly trusted. I think of Christ's warning to the disciples after he washed their feet, before they went and fell asleep in Gethsemane: *I am not speaking of all of you; I know whom I have chosen.*

The lines on Dad's face are deeper now than the day I came home. He watches me intently while I stare at the bittersweet orange glow in the stove. Then he says, "You look cold," and he shrugs off his old green-and-white plaid flannel, stands, and drapes the shirt across my shoulders like a cape.

How could I ever say to him that the light I've been following all my life has been snuffed out? I know I couldn't dispute the truth of what he preaches. Somehow it is true; it's just not true for me—and this is the most frightening thought. Once it occurs to me, I can't think of anything else.

Maybe death is only death and some miseries are beyond redemption. Maybe there's nothing more than that. No golden morning or house with many rooms. For others, maybe. But not me.

Standing over me still, I feel Dad's light touch on my shoulder blade. I know it isn't only for my sake that he winnows away the night reading and praying. But I've just laid a lifetime's worth of sleeplessness at his feet.

"After all these years," he says, "I've learned that the morning always comes."

Even the longest, darkest nights don't last forever.

"Okay."

"It does, Richard."

They don't need to last forever. Just long enough.

He says, "Would you let me pray for you?"

A moment passes.

"Sure. Fine."

So he does, hand on my shoulder. I hate every second of it. I dig my fingernails into the palms of my hands to keep from jerking out from his touch. And I almost make it. But as he says "amen" I angle away, pulling my shoulders in, and I feel him hesitate for a long, painful couple of seconds. Then he moves away, sits and crosses his ankles, and picks up Spurgeon.

XXIII.

COUNTDOWN

31 December 1945

I move my champagne from one hand to the other as I slip my arm through the sleeve of my coat and step out the kitchen door onto the porch. The announcer's voice on the radio, live from New York, is all but drowned out by half the neighborhood in our living room. My watch says 11:37. Twenty-three minutes till 1946.

The stars blink in a slick, oil-black sky. Distracted, I accidentally kick a forgotten champagne flute, half-full, off the edge of the porch. Alcohol the color of goldenrods spills onto the icy step. As I right the flute, a voice from the other side of the porch says, "Sorry, that was mine."

A half-arc of porch light falls on Sidney, who leans on the ice-crusted railing. A cigarette is between his bare fingers. Smoke wafts out over the still, dark yard, where the white snow glistens in the moonlight.

"Didn't know you smoked."

He snuffs the cigarette out in the gathered snow on the railing as I come over. "I don't."

That's exactly what I said when I picked up the habit in Sicily. Sidney looks out at the streetlamp quavering yellow on Holland, and I stare at the lit windows of the kitchen, thinking of the tangled myriad of events it took for the two of us to be standing here together on the eve of a new year. A year without war.

Out of the corner of my eye, I notice Sidney fiddling with his packet of Lucky Strikes, tapping the bottom with one finger and then sliding the cigarettes back in. I'm not sure he hears the tap of his foot on the porch slats.

"Hey, listen, if you—"

He glances at me with that look of his I'd forgotten, one of honest intensity, his complete attention on me. It used to make me stutter because it reminded me of the way my dad looked when he was preaching. I don't think Sidney's ever really been aware of it.

After a brief hesitation, I finish, "I only wanted to say that if you need somewhere warmer to wait out the party, you're welcome to go upstairs."

The lines in Sidney's face soften. "Yeah, thank you. I'm okay here. Appreciate it, though."

"Your wife's made quite the impression on Caspar," I say. "Everyone who meets her loves her."

"You can see how I had no chance, then." He watches the windows, as if expecting to see Lena's shadow floating past, and smiles at some memory. Her natural popularity while he's out here hiding from the party hasn't seemed to stir up any resentment in him. Pocketing the Lucky Strikes, he adds, "Maybe I should keep you around all the time, and you'll help me kick this smoking habit."

He crosses his arms and burrows his chin into the collar of his coat. The soft light from the kitchen illuminates the nicks and faint scars on his face from the part of his story I haven't heard. But come to think of it, the war's not the only part of his story I don't know.

"So why are you hiding?" he asks. "I thought you loved New Year's—all your family's Greek traditions."

"I'm sure my mom will make us hang an onion over the front door tomorrow." One of the old country traditions I'm not convinced we really need to keep alive anymore. But no matter what becomes of the onions, the gambling is a part of New Year's Eve that will have to be pried from the dead hands of the Kalikredes for them to give it up. "And didn't you see my nana fleecing the church deacons at blackjack in the living room?"

"I did, and I thought it was very gracious of a minister's wife not to collect." He laughs. "The spirit of auld lang syne and all."

"Somehow she's never so gracious when she beats me."

Our breath lingers like the smoke as icy wind stirs the tops of the pines. Sidney says, "You didn't answer my question."

I swallow the last of my champagne, wishing for something stronger. "You didn't answer it, either."

"It's too warm in there." He takes his lighter from his pocket and flicks the flint. A white-fringed flame catches, snapping back in the cold air. "You know I never really was one for big gatherings."

"I know." Conscious of how close this is to crossing into matters that are none of my business, I add, "But Lena's in there. At least you're not alone."

"Grace is in there, too," Sidney says, eyeing me with his usual perceptiveness. "And you're still out here with me, freezing your ass off."

"Is that you encouraging me to go inside and woo your sister?"

He flicks off the lighter and shrugs. "I've always known how you feel. And now I know how Grace feels, too. It wouldn't take much wooing on your part."

"Sidney, the night you came home—"

"You don't have to explain anything to me."

"I know I don't, but I want to. Nothing happened. Nothing's going to happen, not if I can't get out of my own head."

"Oh." Sidney frowns. "She said that?"

I spin the stem of the champagne flute between my fingers. "No, I said that."

The screen door bangs shut. When I glance around, Mattie has appeared behind us, carrying three drinks like a bartender. "Gentlemen," he says, dispensing one glass to me and one to Sidney without a word. He adds, in a rare conscientious moment, "Okay if I join you out here?"

"Of course. But *you* want to leave the pretty girls and the free drinks and hang around with us?"

"Guess I'm not much in the mood for New Year's this time. Should we toast to something?"

"I think toasts are what we came out here to get away from," Sidney says.

"Yeah." Mattie looks down into his drink. "Yeah, you're right. Fuck it," and he swallows half of it like a shot.

"Chip Crane said hello to Lena and Grace when we came in and didn't recognize me at first." Sidney says this not quite to either of us. He adds, a note of humor in his voice, "And then when he realized who I was, he told me how much I have to be thankful for."

"I guess he means well," I put in half-heartedly. "They all do."

"I know. And he's right." He takes a sip of the scotch. "So why can't I make myself feel that way? You said it, Richard. Lena's in there and I still can't believe my luck, marrying a woman like her. So what am I doing out here, shooting the shit with you two?"

Mattie sits stiffly in one of the snow-dusted rocking chairs, stretching his prosthetic leg in front of him. "My mother thinks I should be satisfied with just making it back alive. But then what happens?"

"What do you mean?"

"Well, if we're lucky enough to come home, mostly in one piece, then folks who weren't there seem to think that scraps should satisfy

us. That's how it's been for me, anyway, I don't know about you two."
Mattie leans out of the arc of the porch light, but I can see his gray eyes
reflecting in the darkness. Something tells me this drink on the porch
was his first. I've never heard him speak with such clarity, especially not
on New Year's Eve, when he's usually sloshed. "Thank you for your
service and all that, and oh you're a hero and we love you, and here's your
disability check every month, and now go be good and quiet and do your
work so we never have to imagine you got your hands dirty in a war."

For the first time I can remember, I finish my drink before Mattie
finishes his.

"You ever meet a guy who really thought of himself as a hero?" Sidney
looks between us, and we both shake our heads. "Sometimes I wonder if
that word's just a made-up comfort for gold-star mothers."

I think of the number of times I've seen Sam's mother sitting in the
second pew on the right side in the church, the life gone out of her
because she couldn't even bury her baby. If that word, "hero," has any
meaning still attached to it, then it should be given to the bereaved.

Mattie looks out toward the road and the white plaster houses huddled together. "I want to scream at old Wagner, you know, my boss at
the garage—just let him have it. Here's what I did over there while you
were getting fat and rich scamming your neighbors to use all their savings
to buy pieces of shit cars—but I was a fucking Ranger, you know? I
was a Ranger and I worked for you in high school, and I come home
and you dock my salary fifteen cents a week because of this"—he raps
his knuckles on his pants leg over the prosthetic—"because you knew
about that stupid disability check. Because you have a new high schooler
working for you who's the prodigy with two legs."

"I hate that disability check," I say, desperately wanting a cigarette
about now. "I can't even look at it. Every month when it comes I want
to burn it."

"Real swell of the government to remind us, 'Hey, you disposable grunt, you're crippled.'"

Sidney brushes his hand across the snow on the railing, cascading it off into the frozen bushes. "Sometimes I'll think to myself how I can't stand it if I don't tell them—my family—and then I think about how I wouldn't be able to stand it if they did know."

"I guess I'd rather hold onto it all myself than have my sisters know," Mattie says. "Just like they don't need to know that our mother spends the check on booze, not food."

I feel a twinge of guilt at everything I have that they don't. An unbroken family, both my parents still alive. A mother who's not an alcoholic, relatives who never abused and gaslighted me. What would they do if they were me, if my father was theirs, and he asked about what they'd done during the war—would they open up to him?

"There's a reason we can talk about it with each other and not with them," says Sidney. "Whatever it is that binds every guy who fought, no matter what branch or where." He inspects his fingernails under the light, and none of us look at one another, as if even in this bond there are still some things that can't be acknowledged. Maybe especially in this bond.

Not paying attention, I nearly knock my empty scotch glass into the snow and catch it just in time. "But if we don't ask for help...whose responsibility does it become?"

Sidney shakes his head. "What kind of help is there, though? When you think of how many thousands of guys are coming home and stepping back into the current and swimming, you just..."

"Tell yourself you're the odd one, that you'll get over it eventually," I finish for him.

"I think there are some things we'll never get over," Mattie says.

"Yeah." Sidney lets out a breath, the steam hanging in the air. "I know."

He's always been tall and thin; now, though, something in his bearing has changed, not only the aura of the war that also lingers around Mattie and, I assume, myself, but...an exhaustion. One that can't be slept away. Each time I've seen him in the last week, his eyes, even when laughing, seem to be keeping watch.

Mattie tips the bottom rim of his glass in a slow arc on the arm of the rocking chair. "Japan surrendered beginning of August, Sid."

The porch shakes with the movement of dancing feet inside. Home, at last, and Benny Goodman on the Victrola competing with the NBC radio broadcast from New York. Our families just inside the door. And we're still out here, trading war stories.

"You want to know where I was," Sidney says.

"You said we were talking about things amongst ourselves." Mattie gestures to the empty porch. "It's just us."

"Well, I don't want to bore you..."

"Not a chance."

Sidney hesitates. I can tell he's sifting through the memories to test which are fit for the light. "You know, I guess the best way to tell you is this."

He takes a couple steps closer to Mattie and me, lowers his head, and pushes some of his hair back from behind his right ear. The light is just bright enough to see a white scar, raised and still red at the edges, about three inches long across his skull. It must've taken twenty stitches.

When he straightens up and speaks it's in short bursts, like the stutter of a machine gun, as if attaching clarifications such as "I" or "we" would render the still-fresh memories too personal to be said aloud. This way, they might as well've happened to any guy.

"Plane went down near Borneo—5th Air Force was supporting the Australian ground troops there. Two of our engines were hit; she never had a chance." Sidney's cheeks are pale, though from the cold or the story, I'm not sure. "No one else made it, just me. Cracked my skull." He taps the spot above his ear. "Don't remember much about getting out, just seeing the fuselage burning and my plane sinking. I must've found something to hold onto because apparently the Australian Navy picked me up around sunset, and they brought me to the Aussie field hospital in Morotai, one of the islands near Borneo."

Mattie and I are quiet for a few moments. He seems to be mentally calculating the time, too.

"And that was in...July?" I venture. "Before we dropped the bombs?"

Sidney reaches inside his coat and below the collar of his shirt. In his hand are his silver dog tags on their chain. "You still wear yours?"

I fish mine out, and so does Mattie. The metal is warm from my chest.

"These aren't the tags I started the war with," Sidney says. "I was issued these in the hospital, after they found out who I was. In November."

"And your old ones are at the bottom of the Pacific." I try to imagine the shock and force of the water rising as unforgiving as concrete to meet the nose of the bomber. What it would feel like to survive that.

"But your uniform—?" Mattie begins.

"They said I had no jacket or boots, just an undershirt and trousers. I don't know, maybe I used the jacket to try to stop the blood...I remember there was a lot of blood."

I shake my head. "So you were in a coma for three months? In M—where?"

"Morotai," he supplies. Then he laughs, unexpectedly. "No, pretty soon they moved me to a field hospital in Australia—Sydney, of all places. I couldn't talk the first day or two after I woke up, but when I could, I asked the nurses to tell me where I was, and they said 'You're in Sydney,' and I said, 'I *am* Sidney.' I already knew where I was; I heard them talking. I just wanted to make that joke. But it was the first bit of personal information they had about me, my name."

I can't help grinning, and Mattie snorts. I did my fair share of antagonizing the nurses in Belgium to combat my homesickness and how much I missed my guys, but at least I didn't spend the end of my war in anonymity, three months of my life erased from memory.

"Actually," Sidney adds, and he holds his hand up to the porch light, knuckles facing us, so that the light catches the gold of his wedding ring. "This was the first thing they knew about me, before I woke up. My dog tags didn't survive the crash, but the ring did."

Mattie is still holding onto his tags, as if touching them takes him back. I think of the nurse in Belgium who found me outside the hospital on the bloody stretcher. Her name was Evelyn, and she heard me calling out for a nurse when no one else did. She'd gotten an oxygen mask over my nose and sealed off the sucking chest wound in my ribs with a dressing on three sides, and then while waiting for the medics she picked up my dog tags, read out "R. Dare," and said that she'd always wanted to go to Maine.

Most of the time they're a comfort, these stamped pieces of metal with our blood types and religions designated by a single letter each—*P* for Sidney and me, *C* for Mattie. But I wonder if for Sidney, these fresh tags, untempered by battle, are just a millstone about his neck to remind him of every man who went down with that plane.

"Well, it's a good thing," I say, as Sidney absently twists his ring 'round his finger. "The government doesn't reissue wedding rings."

He glances up, then smiles. "I'd rather be court-martialed than explain to Lena that I just flung this into the ocean."

Inside, the radio crackles with the euphoria and desperation of every American to make the past four years a footnote in our lives. We don't have a piano, but someone has begun to sing "Auld Lang Syne" a couple minutes early. I used to love this song. But now I hear its strains in the voices of cold, pneumatic paratroopers, the eerie notes weaving off-key through the broken trees above me as I lay in the warm, wet snow, with blood running out of my mouth.

Sidney tilts his head, listening. I wonder if he can pick Lena's voice out of the crowd of neighbors. He finishes his drink and says, "I was in Brisbane last New Year's. With Lena. Where were you two?"

"Already on a hospital ship in the Atlantic, trying to wheedle Hershey bars out of the nurses." Mattie glances at me. "Not as eventful as your New Year's Eve, Dick."

I was hoping to worm my way out of answering, but Sidney's attention has been caught. "No," I say. "I was in Liege—Belgium. But that wasn't till well past midnight."

"You were wounded on New Year's Eve?" Sidney says.

"Mhm."

"In Belgium?"

I nod.

"Richard was a medic; I bet you anything he was stitching up some poor fellow's ass when his luck caught up to him. If anyone was heroic out there," Mattie adds in a reflective tone, "it was you medics."

Sidney says, "I'll drink to that," and a sick feeling grips the pit of my stomach. I'm wondering what to say when a series of shots bursts from across Holland. We all jump, and Mattie knocks his glass off the chair's arm. It shatters on the porch. The three of us lift our heads at the same time, and I realize we all covered them instinctively.

I go down the steps, almost slipping on the ice, and stare at the black sky. A rain of silver sparks falls over the treetops. I flinch as another bang rattles the night, and plumes of silver and green spread out in mushroom clouds above snow-covered roofs. Someone inside turns up the volume on the radio. Ben Grauer is nearly shouting into his microphone to be heard from the balcony of the Astor Hotel over the multitude in Times Square.

"Rockets are flying—yes!" Even from the yard, I hear his excited voice rushing over itself. "One of the youngsters has dared to send up a rocket out on 40th Street, and it just launched in the sky with forty seconds to go..."

One of the not-so-youngsters on Queen Street has also dared to send up a bouquet of bottle rockets and cherry bombs. The porch door opens and Laurie and Faye appear. Faye calls back inside, "Come outside! Come see!"

Folks trickle out onto the porch and into the yard, exclaiming at the falling colors, and I find myself somehow at the back behind all the other heads. My parents are a few feet away, hand-in-hand. Dad says something in Mom's ear and she glances at him and laughs. Then he looks over his shoulder at me. I try not to react as another one goes off, but I meet his eyes, and even though he doesn't say a word, I know what he's asking. So I nod. *I'm all right.*

Someone's started the countdown: "Ten! Nine! Eight!..." I glance back at the porch. Mattie is still sitting in the rocking chair, though leaning forward now, carefully gathering up the glass shards and placing them in a row like toy soldiers on the table between the chairs. Sidney's come down into the yard with Lena and has his arms around her shoulders while she laughs.

I squint, looking up at the after-haze of gold sparks, the falling colors like a Whistler painting. How has it been one year already since that night? My chest feels cavernous at the boom of the fireworks, as though to remind me that those deadly nights in Belgium are still part of my body, sunk deep into my skin, like the 82nd tattoos some of the guys got on leave in London.

"Three! Two!...ONE!"

As a chorus of "Happy New Year!" and "Good riddance, 1945!" rings out through the neighborhood and champagne flutes are lifted high in chilly hands, a brilliant gold firework explodes in the sky like a meteor shower.

I feel a touch on my arm and turn to see Grace, also rosy-cheeked, wearing nothing but a green velvet dress and black pumps that have no business walking through snow and ice. She's holding champagne and slips her free arm through mine. "Happy New Year, Richard," she says, her voice buoyant as though we haven't been avoiding each other for a week. "Shall we kiss like everyone else?"

"Who's asking, Grace or the champagne?"

She smiles as the fireworks reflect in her eyes. Her hair is done up in waves on her head, but a couple of loose golden strands have fallen out. "I am, maybe, a little tipsy."

"It happens to the best of us." I extricate my arm from hers and shrug off my coat. "Put this on, won't you?"

"Oh, you need it more than I do—"

"I doubt that."

I hold her champagne for her as I guide my coat over her shoulders with my other hand. She looks very small inside it. I take a sip of her drink while she tries to find her hands through the sleeves, and she says, "You thief, that's mine—"

"I'm only looking out for you. Any tipsier, and you'll be tipping right over in the snow." I hand the flute back to her. She swallows the last drop while watching me.

"It *is* New Year's," she whispers, nodding to our families and friends, all watching the fireworks and absorbed in one another, no one taking any notice of us. "Maybe we call it a truce, just for tonight?"

The empty flute dangles upside-down from her fingers. It's too tempting an offer to refuse and maybe it will never come my way again, so without giving it much thought I do kiss her. It's quick, the champagne-flavored New Year's kiss of the tipsy, the "just friends" caught up in the rush and sparkle of a fresh year. Grace pulls away first.

"You taste like scotch," she whispers, patting my cheek. "That was nice. Now we've gotten that out of the way, we'll be experienced at this for whenever you decide you're ready to sweep me off my feet."

And then she lets go of my hand and wanders back toward the house, falling in step with Helen and Toni, talking about dancing.

I move the toe of my boot in a shallow half-moon through the snow gathered by the porch steps. Footprints traverse the empty yard, which still echoes with the bursts of the fireworks and the collective breath of relief that we made it to 1946. And I'm still echoing with the phantom touch of Grace's mouth, the tingling, golden taste of prosecco and her smile as she slipped away, as if she hadn't just felled me.

It took me a couple minutes to pick my jaw up off the frozen ground, and I was mostly useless for the rest of the night. The last of the guests trickled home an hour ago. My grandparents have migrated to my room so that Faye can stay in Laurie's room, sans Laurie, whom Dad says can "act as he sees fit" away from home but under this roof is bound to the laws of propriety. Laurie fell asleep the moment he curled up on the couch in the living room under Nana's patchwork quilt, but I lay on the too-short loveseat with my knees drawn up uncomfortably and stared at the ghostly form of the Christmas tree, half its needles dropped. Dad's insomnia must be giving him a rest because the kitchen was empty, and there was no one to see me slip out the door onto the porch in just my shirtsleeves. I was too tired to change out of this evening's clothes.

Sidney pulled me aside before they left, saying he wanted to give me something. Afterwards I took it up to my bedroom and put it behind a stack of theology books on my desk. I couldn't bring myself to look at it. When I came back downstairs, Grace was laughing with Mattie as she tied her red scarf around her neck. I thought about how maybe Sidney has it all wrong—maybe we've all had it all wrong—and how sometimes for no discernable reason, whatever expected thing doesn't turn out the way everyone was so sure it would.

Sleet begins to fall with a whisper over the snow. I don't want to sleep because I know what I'll see there. Will I keep a sentinel over this night every year of my life? Each hour I've tried to reconstruct where I was a year ago at that minute. I glance at my watch—*2:21*. I'd have been in surgery, not even in a surgical ward. Awake on a gurney in the tent corridor and the thoracic trauma doctor bent over me with the scalpel in his hand to cut into my chest so they could place the chest tube. "Tension pneumothorax!" I remember one of the nurses shouting, minutes before that, as my heart went into tachycardia.

I never should've been there. I wasn't the one who should've made it to the hospital with a scrap of air still left in me. And to remember every moment of that night when death hovered around me—every nurse's touch, every IV needle under my skin, every breath wheezed through an oxygen mask—is a promise that I know what each of those things meant. How each one was more than it was. The resuscitation of a ghost.

There's someone else, I tried to tell the nurses, but no one knew who I meant or where he was.

I hunch forward, arms crossed. Wind blows down Holland from the north. I close my eyes as sleet falls in my hair and eyelashes and turns my hands numb. It snowed that night, too, soaking through the back of my uniform and covering over the black powder on the ground.

The cold troubles my breathing more than usual. Something rattles around in my chest as I stare out past the streetlamp at the sleeping houses. Behind me our house is asleep, too, and warm, a couch and a gray wool blanket and Hen curled up in the blanket awaiting me. But I don't know why I can't get up and go in.

Once when I was seven or eight, we got home late at night from my grandparents'. It was summer so I could smell the warm air through the station wagon's cracked windows. My dad was wearing that old worn green flannel that smelled like woodsmoke and coffee and a hint of sweat. His stubble scratched my forehead when he kissed my hair, and my cheek rested on his shoulder as he lifted me carefully from the backseat because he thought I was asleep. He carried me up the porch steps and I closed my eyes, afraid he'd put me down if he saw them open.

But now I know he wouldn't have. He'd have done anything to hold me as long as he could.

XXIV.

FEVER

My bedroom is in a perpetual dusk, just like the world outside deep in winter.

A hand moves across my back. "Are you cold, *yiannaki?*"

The mattress rises back into place as she stands and a minute later returns with another blanket. It won't do any good.

Dr. Linstead came yesterday. He listened to my lungs while I lay on my side, and was not satisfied when the best I could give him was those wheezy half-breaths. The drum of the stethoscope was so cold on my back. He knew I had never called the veterans hospital in Augusta, although he didn't say a word about it to me. He went out of the room with my parents. I could hear them through the door. The surgery is my choice but if he were them, he'd call Augusta as soon as possible. He diagnosed me with a lung infection and wrote a prescription for antibiotics.

I don't know what time I stumbled back in the house the morning of New Year's, and I don't remember falling asleep on the couch. It was the smell of bacon cooking on the stove that woke me. Everyone looked up at me at the breakfast table when I coughed hard enough to drown out the conversation. The fever came on by degrees, draining the last of my energy till finally I was in bed, wheezing like a chimney bellows.

After Linstead left yesterday, I croaked out "no" three separate times to my parents, when they asked on the hour three hours in a row about Augusta. I'll have to be dead or at least not sentient for them to drag me into that hospital, at which point it won't matter anyway. I don't need surgeons and nurses and IVs and a hospital bed. I just need to sleep and let the antibiotics get a foothold, and then I'm sure tomorrow will be better.

I hear the mercury of the thermometer shaking, and a moment later Mom tells me to open. She sticks the thermometer under my tongue. As she counts off the seconds under her breath, her hand on my forehead, I think how luxurious it is to be sick at home and not in a barracks or foxhole. I open my eyes and watch her when she takes the thermometer out. She squints in the twilight falling through the window.

"What is it?" I say, my voice somewhere between a croak and a wheeze.

"101." She sets it back on the white handkerchief spread out on my nightstand. "Are you sure you won't eat something, darling—just some soup?"

I shake my head. The soup I did have earlier came up again almost immediately, and I'm still fighting off nausea by trying to lie perfectly still.

"You'll need to eat something soon so you can take the antibiotic. If you take it on an empty stomach, it'll just make you sick again."

"In a little while."

She says, "Okay, in a little while," with an intentional lightness in her voice that isn't quite enough to mask her concern. "Do you want to try to sleep?"

I nod, though I'm not sure how perceptible the head-shaking and nodding are from the chills.

"There's a clean handkerchief if you cough—and a water glass here—and aspirin." She shakes the little bottle of capsules. "I'll be just downstairs if you need anything."

She leaves the door open, where the fading light falls in patches on the white rug by the stairs. I hear Nana puttering around the kitchen, probably cooking something, though I can't smell it. When I still had the strength, earlier, I lay propped on my elbows on my bed and watched Pop out my window as he dug a trail in last night's snow between the front porch and the sidewalk. He saw me and waved, his teeth shining like pearls in his face that's still golden-brown despite the temperature. He loves winter storms, becoming like a child again at the mention of a bad forecast. Snow seems to bring him back to his youth—even though his real youth was spent in sunny cyprus and olive groves, swimming in the warm Ionian sea—because he knelt and gathered up a handful of the wet snow, drew his arm back like Lefty Grove, and pitched it up at my window, seventy-year-old joints be damned. Even through the glass pane, I could hear him laugh, which made me smile.

7 January 1946

I turn from one side of the pillow to the other, but the coolness is gone. Heat pulses under my skin. Each breath is like staring up at an icy mountain pass, knowing I have to cross it, knowing that each time it will hurt more.

For two days the antibiotics kicked in and although I was still coughing and tired, the fever crept quietly down. On Mom's thermometer read-outs that she conducted hourly with the timed precision of an orchestra conductor, the degrees decreased: 100.5, 100, 99...

Until at some point yesterday when I awoke from my deepest sleep in months with blood in my mouth, choking as I coughed it up on the clean new pillowcase stitched with bluebells.

102, 103...

"104." Dad touches my forehead, moving back my tangled hair.

"That's the highest it's been," Mom murmurs. "Why aren't the antibiotics working?"

His hand settles on my leg, over the sheet. "I have no idea."

There are bottles of aspirin on the nightstand, cups of turmeric and peppermint tea that have gone cold, a forgotten jar of honey from mixing honey and water to gargle, which didn't give me any lasting relief. Nor did holding my face over a basin of steaming hot water with a towel over my head. The curtains are drawn against the chill that creeps through the windowpanes. Day and night have become one, the only light the candles flickering on the nightstand that Mom snuffs out and replaces when the wicks burn low, because the wind this afternoon blew the power out. I stare blearily at the flames as my parents talk quietly. Wax drips down the side of one, my bedframe in miniature reflected in the liquid drop. I imagine the wick snuffed out and smoke trails lingering like the crooked currents of a dark river, the wax drops cooling at the base of the candle. My lungs don't feel so different, each breath hardening them more. I cough hard and roll onto my back, and then my other side, and then my back again, trying to find any way to lie that doesn't make my joints ache.

"All right, darling, it's all right." A hand on my cheek. "John, his face is on fire..."

The floor creaks. Dad takes his hand from my restless legs as I roll onto my side again. "I'll fetch some ice and washcloths."

"Maybe if we can get this fever down," says Mom as she kneels beside the bed and touches my back, "then you can eat a little something." But she doesn't sound hopeful.

I stare at the edge of the pillow and try to think of anywhere but the dark ward in the hospital in Liege. Mom is whispering something in Greek, maybe a prayer. Hen, curled up on the rug by the bed, raises her head and thumps her tail when she sees me watching her. She tried to climb onto the bed before but she was too warm, ducking her tail sadly between her legs when Mom shooed her off.

Dad's footsteps sound on the stairs. The damp, cold edge of a wash-cloth touches my forehead, then another on my chest.

"Why don't you take a break, Lizzie?" he says. "Your mother's making moussaka."

"John..."

"We'll be okay. I'll call if anything changes."

Silence for a few moments. Then I hear the crack in her knees as she stands. Out in the hallway, her footsteps stop and she murmurs something, muffled; Laurie must've been waiting by the door.

Dad is quiet. He rolls up his shirtsleeves and wrings out the washcloth in the ceramic basin. I watch as he lifts the pitcher to pour fresh cool water on it, the stream turning orange in the candlelight. His hand moves through my hair as I drift in and out of painful sleep. Gray darkness floats behind my eyelids, the ragged ache of my lungs amplified in my ears.

I awake with the taste of blood pooling in my mouth. My elbows give out beneath me as I cough, but Dad's arm is around my shoulders. He drums his fist between my shoulderblades. I see the red stain of bloody mucus in the basin that he holds in his other hand.

"It's okay. It's okay, I've got you." He sets the basin on my nightstand and wipes the blood from my mouth with a handkerchief. Then he moves my pillow and sits on the bed, his back against the frame. His arm is still around my shoulders as he holds me against him.

I feel my chest heaving against Dad's as chills begin to shake me all over. He reaches for the blankets kicked to the foot of the bed and draws them up around me. Moonlight glows through a gap in the curtains. Dad sets his new glasses by the washbasin and then hands me a water glass. I drink a little to get rid of the bloody taste that burns in my throat, but swallowing is agony. He takes my temperature. He must know that I'll reach for the thermometer myself and look if he doesn't tell me, because he says, in the voice of a man who sees the enemy riding toward his gates, "105."

Without a voice all I have in the way of resistance is my body. I look up at him, and he looks from the thermometer to me. The lines of his shoulders seem indistinct and not just because of the candlelight. My eyes have trouble focusing, so I stop trying and shut them.

"I don't know who, or what, you're holding out for," he says quietly. "I don't know if you're trying to prove something to me...I don't know if you think you deserve to be in misery, and if that's true then I don't know how to convince you otherwise. But"—and here he shifts slightly to let me lie against his hip—"I don't have to convince you of that. What I have to do now is take care of you. And the best way I can do that is by taking you to Augusta."

I shake my head without opening my eyes, silently begging him to listen to me. *Please, please just let it end here,* I try to say to him, but I can't say a thing. And even if I did have a voice, it would make no difference.

Dad draws the blankets closer around my shoulders and says, "You're in a tremendous amount of pain with no hope at the end, only there is still some hope—a chance—and I don't know why you won't reach for it." He sighs. "Maybe someday you'll tell me what all this means."

I listen to the steady thump of his heart till the beat of my own fills my ears like the rush of the Alewife in spring rains. Past it, I hear him praying—no, not praying, reciting, the same Psalm hanging heavy in his mouth: *I wait for the Lord...and in his word do I hope.*

My soul waiteth for the Lord, more than they that watch for the morning.

Some time later, I don't know how long, Dad shifts again. He says softly, "If I can't convince you, then maybe there's someone else who can."

He climbs off the bed. I turn onto my back, pushing the tangled, sweaty sheets off my chest. He slips out the door and I hear him talking to someone in the hallway. Then I hear his footsteps on the stairs.

The door creaks, and a little breeze stirs the room. A new voice whispers, "It's only me."

Grace.

The fever has distorted her face into wavy brushstrokes. As I stare at her sitting on the edge of the bed, she reaches out and touches her hand to my forehead. "I'm not a dream. I'm really here."

Sounds like something a dream would say. I wish she was one. I twist away from her hand, draw the blanket back around my shoulders, and turn to face the wall.

That doesn't seem to put her off. She wrings out a washcloth in the basin and presses it to the back of my neck. "Let me just sit with you for a little while," she whispers. "Please."

I cough, which makes the wheezing worse. Grace touches her hand to my back over my lungs.

"Sounds like murder," she says.

Using the voice I really don't have, I choke out, "I don't want you to be here."

"I know, but I am."

She lifts her hand as I roll back to face her, only because I want her to see how much I want her to go. I don't want to see her. I don't want her here.

Her touch is light as she holds the damp washcloth to my forehead and says, "Lung infection turned to pneumonia, your dad said."

I don't answer.

"You know, someday," Grace continues, pushing back my hair, "you're going to need to let people love you."

We're bathed in a wash of reddish light. The silver buttons on her blouse look as if they're falling like raindrops. She slips her fingers through mine, watching me with a tenderness that makes me feel nauseous. I turn my head to the other side of the pillow, but it's all damp from sweat and the tepid water.

Grace rubs her thumb against my forefinger. "I know it's real, the infection, the pneumonia. But...it seems like there might be another part to it. In your mind."

I grunt in reply. In the steamy room with her sitting so close, it's getting even harder to breathe.

"Richard, I think you're torturing yourself for someone else," she whispers, "but none of us know who."

I weakly push her hands away.

"Can't you tell even just me? Because it doesn't seem like this is just your body; it's like your mind working against you, too."

The wheezing turns to coughing. Grace tries to give me the washcloth, but I push her back again. She touches my leg. I feel her stand. "I'll get your dad," she says softly, and then finally she's gone.

When he comes back, he leans on the windowsill and folds his arms. "Not even for Grace?"

Cheap trick, I want to say but can't. He knows what I'm thinking, anyway.

"Short of lifting you out of that bed and putting you in the car and driving us to Augusta, that was my only idea." Dad's voice is tired but resolute. The window casement creaks as he straightens. "So I guess that's what we're going to do."

15 January 1946

"Okay, slowly now," Dad says, his shadow flickering on the wall behind him from the living room lamp. "One step at a time, that's all there is to it."

One hand on the banister, the other on his arm, I look up the endless staircase that never seemed so long before.

"Okay?" he says again. My left arm is around his shoulder, his right arm around my waist. "All right. That's good."

The first three steps aren't too bad, but they become increasingly painful, and by halfway up, my fingernails are digging into his sweater. "Can you go one more?" he asks.

But I can't take the next step, so Dad says, "We can rest here. You let me know when you're ready again."

I open my eyes. My knuckles are white on the banister.

After a minute we make it two more. On the third, the pain throbbing in my back steals what breath I had left. If I had the strength I would scream in frustration. I lose my grip on Dad's shoulder and end up on the step, hunched over, feeling as if my anger is about to burst through my ribcage.

Dad, a dark figure leaning over me in the faintly lit staircase, says, "That's okay, we'll w—"

I push his hands away. Shallow gasps echo off the wall and through the living room below us, where I know Mom and Laurie are waiting, listening.

I wish I could say it wasn't like this. But any courage I might've once had is gone. Everything's gone, drained out of me like the fluid from my lungs.

The shadow shifts, and the stair creaks beside me as Dad sits.

"If you'd rather sleep on the stairs," he says, without mockery, "then I'll certainly stay here, too. But your bed might be a little more comfortable."

The top of the staircase tilts alarmingly in the wrong direction. It was his help that got me here, but I never wanted to come this far. My body at least understood what I wanted even though none of them do. His hand on me feels sharp through my sweater.

I can't stand it. I can't stand any of it. When I arch my back, his hand lifts.

He slides it under my arm instead and says, "Let's get you upstairs so you can rest."

Somehow we make it up, and Dad turns the glass knob of my bedroom door. All evidence of the sick room has been cleared away, the basin and washcloths and aspirin bottles gone from the nightstand, fresh sheets turned down on the bed. They crease as I sit, gathering the ends of the blanket in my fists. It's not quite four o'clock in the afternoon but all I want is to sleep, without an IV and cannula and whatever other shit they attached me to in the hospital.

I don't remember anything before the surgery, not even how we got to Augusta. Mom said the nurses there got the fever down enough for the surgeon to operate safely. They did the lobectomy, and now the lower lobe and part of the upper lobe of my left lung are gone. They also drained fluid from my lungs with a chest tube just as the surgeon in

Belgium did last winter. When I woke from the surgery a week ago, in a bright white thoracic ward, they had me on oxygen to help me breathe. My right lung still collapsed twice. Dad stayed up with me every night while I coughed and tried not to cry from the pain of it. He and Mom got a hotel room in Augusta that I know they couldn't afford, but I don't know if he ever left the hospital. Every time I woke out of a medicated haze, he was there, reading or praying or just watching me.

And now I feel crushed with guilt for hating him. But it would've been so much easier if he'd listened to me. If I wasn't here to burden him, all of them, it would all be easier.

"Laurie's going to the pharmacy to fill your prescriptions," Dad says from over by the bureau. "Where do you keep your pajamas?"

"Top drawer."

A few seconds pass, and then he says, "Aha."

I struggle to keep my eyes open even to watch him. He shuffles things about, and he starts to say something else, then stops.

"Aren't they there?" I say, glancing over.

"Yes, they are. I just…" He takes the folded pajamas from the drawer and comes to the bed. Already dusk has fallen outside and the streetlamps are lit, shining through the window to hollow out the darkness under his eyes. "I didn't know you kept it in there. I didn't know you'd kept it at all, actually."

"Kept what?"

He helps me slip one sleeve off, then the other. "The whole catalyst for all this, you might say. That medal."

Oh. The Purple Heart, presented to me at the English hospital. I wanted to burn it the moment it was placed in my hands. To be honest, I'm not sure why I haven't yet, or why it's been hiding in my drawer for months when nothing would give me more pleasure than to watch it melt in the stove.

"Purple Hearts were a dime a dozen in the Airborne," I say. I'm sure one of his editions of the *Caspar Sentinel* that he so carefully saved has an article with a headline reading something like, "Minister's Son Wounded in Europe, Awarded Military Honor," when the fact was that no guy I knew really considered these medals an honor. At best, they were an annoying symbol of whatever wound was keeping a trooper from rejoining his company. And at worst, as I consider it, it's a talisman of death.

Dad doesn't say anything more about it. He folds the sweater I was wearing and sets it on the chair by my bed. In the mirror over the bureau, my reflection is watery, as if the image might wash away any moment. I touch the bandages taped to the left side of my ribs, stretching to my back. Linstead spoke on the telephone with the doctor in Augusta and said he'll take out the stitches this week.

I drop my hand but can't seem to look away from that ghost in the mirror, the lines of my body all sharp, bone-skinny. "How much was it, again?"

"Thirteen pounds." He says it as casually as if we were settling an insignificant debt between us, as he guides my arm through the sleeve of the pajama shirt. "So you have your work cut out for you. You're not quite back in the land of the living, not yet."

Or I could let nature take its course as it would've done a week ago had he not intervened against my will, but before I can say that I notice in the mirror that something is missing. I touch my hand to my chest, but the mirror isn't playing tricks on me. Nothing is there.

"Where is it?" I twist around to look behind me on the bed and feel my stitches jerk, pulling a gasp of pain from me.

Dad catches my shoulder and says, "All right, careful, careful—I knew that would happen sooner or later." He gently guides me to sit straight again.

"They're gone," I say, looking up at him as he stands beside me. I haven't taken them off in three and a half years. That Purple Heart is worthless to me, just another generic medal fished from the drawer of some desk-bound colonel, but these—these went through the whole war with me, these are all I have left of Fox Company, of the boys, a memorial that has become as much a part of my body as any organ, beating every moment of every day against my heart. I can't believe I didn't notice they were gone till now. "Did the nurses take them? Did they get lost?"

By way of answer he reaches into his shirt pocket, beside his glasses folded there, and takes out my dog tags on their coiled chain. "It's okay," he says, draping them over my head. "One of the nurses took them off before the surgery, and I held onto them for safekeeping. Didn't want them getting lost in the shuffle."

I close my hand around them, the beat of my heart steadying.

"Richard." He kneels beside the bed, puts his hand on my knee. "You can be angry at me if you need to be. I can take it. But everything's going to look bleakest tonight, so how about for now, we just get you to bed?"

XXV.

INTERCESSION

16 January 1946

L aurie built up a fire in the living room fireplace before he left for work this morning. He was already gone, the fire already crackling behind the grate by the time I made my way downstairs at a tortoise pace. Now it's nearly four o'clock, and the flames have dwindled to a tame blue glow under the logs. Hen has spent the day flitting between hearth and couch, stretching out before the fire to warm her tummy, then panting back to me and jumping up to stretch out on my feet and dangle half off the couch. Her tail flicks listlessly as she dreams.

"Would you like to go to a party of dwarves, Hen?" I say, glancing up from *The Hobbit* open on my bent knees to watch her nose twitch. "Maybe you're dreaming of raspberry jam and apple tarts and mince pies."

I've read the first stanza of the dwarves' song of smashing the bottles and burning the corks three times without really seeing it, and my mind fills in "that's what Bilbo Baggins hates" from memory even as my eyes fall closed. Only a minute has gone by when there's a knock from the porch door in the kitchen. Gandalf?

"It's open," I call.

The door creaks and there's a stamp of snowy boots on the mat. I can tell it's Grace by her footsteps before she says, "Richard?"

"Living room."

Hen pops up, uses my legs as a springboard to leap from the couch, and skids into the kitchen, her claws clattering on the wood. She and Grace exchange greetings, and I hear Grace setting something on the table.

"I just brought some bread. And maybe a few eggs and some goat cheese. And Lena might've snuck in a couple jars of apple preserves."

"You're the opposite of a party of hungry dwarves raiding my pantry," I say as Grace appears in the doorway to the living room, unwinding her wine-red scarf from her neck.

"Ah." She nods to my book, then tries to drop her voice a couple octaves. "'Do you wish me a good morning, or mean that it is a good morning whether I want it or not?'" Taking off her wool gloves, she laughs, the rosy tint of cold still in her cheeks and nose. She drapes her green coat over the back of the armchair and smooths the tuck of her silk blouse. "But it's long past morning—I'm sorry I couldn't come earlier. Of course, I had a whole gaggle of students lining up with questions about Latin subordinate con..."

Her words trail off as I kick away the blanket gathered at my feet and stand slowly—thinking to stretch my legs, which are beginning to tingle with pins-and-needles—and then I realize we haven't seen one another since New Year's Eve. Well, that's not quite true. But she hasn't seen me on my feet since then.

"Sorry." I cross my arms. "I should've warned you I look like the walking dead."

She seems uncertain what to say. After an awkward couple moments of silence, she hugs me. She stands on her tiptoes to wrap her arms around my neck, though gently as if I might break. I don't know how long we stand this way. Dusk gathers at the windows.

There was hope in that kiss on New Year's, brief as it was. I know she felt it, too. But this doesn't feel like that. More desperate, maybe. A last-ditch effort to hold onto something slipping away.

"Richard," she whispers.

"Hm?"

Quiet again till she says, "I don't think I know how to do this."

"Hugging? I think you're pretty g—"

I feel her smile. "No. I mean that I don't know how to not love you. I'm trying, but it's not working."

We stand completely still, my hand frozen on her back. The gloam outside seems to have seeped into the house.

"Because it took so long," she continues, "and it's finally here, and it's as if my heart is trying to make up for ten years' worth of what you already knew and I didn't. It's so much to hold. And I just wish…"

I think I know what she doesn't say: *I just wish you could hold it with me.* But if I could, none of this would be happening to begin with.

She presses the back of her hand to her eyes. "I've made your shoulder wet. Sorry."

"It's okay."

I don't know what else to say. I don't know how to comfort her or where my own heart is in all of this. It should devastate me like it does her, but I feel so hollowed out, excavated, as if the surgeon opened me up with a trowel and scooped out everything in me capable of loving and stitched me back up empty.

Grace wipes at her eyes again and says, "How're you feeling?"

"Not swell."

"I meant physically."

I shrug. "Okay. The painkillers are pretty strong, so I'm mostly just tired."

"Let's sit, then. I shouldn't be keeping you on your feet."

We go into the kitchen and sit at the table, and Grace shows me the apple preserves that her grandmother canned last summer. She tells me about the two weeks I've missed, like drawing a sheet over the discomfort of what just happened in the living room. I smile at the story of Baxter still refusing to acknowledge Sidney after Sidney forgot to feed him the other night, and then Grace says, "I don't know if you remember, but I came over a couple of times when you were sick."

"I remember."

"That was some fever."

I fiddle with the ends of my sleeves, wishing she hadn't brought it up. I don't want to think about what she said that day—that I was making myself sick for someone else's sake. "Sorry you had to see that."

"It was because your dad called me," she says, glancing down at her lap, "and I...well, I had to come."

"Oh."

"Because—"

"No, I understand."

She nods resolutely. "Don't scare me like that again, okay? You try anything, and I'll hunt you down and kill you myself just to teach you a lesson."

"With what, a butter knife?"

"Now there's an idea."

We sort of laugh. Then Grace draws her thumbnail over the apple-blossom pattern on the glass jar of preserves. "New Year's Eve was the anniversary of when you were wounded, wasn't it?"

"I'd really rather not talk about that."

"Richard." Grace leans forward, and the little golden cross she wears on a chain around her neck slips out from behind her blackbird blouse. "I know there's more to it than that; I know there's something you haven't told me. Or anyone. Do you think...maybe it would help if you did tell me just a little...?"

Her voice falls away at what I assume is the answer written on my face. She sighs, then shakes her head. "Obviously it's no use for any of us to tell you to be more careful."

"No, go ahead. Tell me off for not taking care of myself. Make me promise to do better—"

"I'm not going to ask for any such promises because I know you would never keep them," she says quietly. "Even though you've gotten your second chance. Third chance, even."

"I never wanted them."

"Don't say that."

"I thought you wanted me to be honest. That's all I have, Grace. That's me being honest."

She looks undeterred. "What I want is to know what happened, because if you could tell me a little, I might understand."

We didn't turn on the lights. In the darkness, I can't make out much of her face.

"No, you wouldn't," I say at last. "I don't even know how to tell it to myself." After a moment, I add, "And you don't really want to know."

"Yes, I do. You can't be sure of that—"

"What you want is for me to say that it's all okay and I'm okay and it's behind me and we can move on and have a wonderful life with each other. Right?"

We're both quiet for a long minute. Finally Grace straightens, exhales through her nose.

"If you wanted me to leave," she says, "why didn't you just say so?"

She stands so I do too, and then she slips past me to retrieve her coat from the living room.

"I suppose I'll see you at church." She lingers in the kitchen door, wrapping her scarf around her neck. "Oh. One more thing. Sidney and Lena are adamant they don't want any kind of wedding or party, but they thought they'd have some friends over for dinner Saturday night—just something to mark the occasion. You should come. We needn't sit beside each other, if that's a concern."

And then she turns and bumps into Laurie, who's just come in from the porch. I didn't even hear the truck pull into the driveway.

"Hi Grace," he says. "Sorry, wasn't looking where I was going. You off?"

"No, that's okay, sorry Laurie—uh, yes, I should go."

"I'll walk out with you," I say.

But she says, "No thank you, I'm fine." Then she's gone, as if she couldn't get out fast enough. Through the window I see her walk, straight-backed as though she knows I'm watching, to her Chevy at the curb.

Laurie kicks off his boots and slings his bag over the arm of one of the kitchen chairs. Without looking at me, he says, "Want to tell me why Grace just ran out of here looking like someone broke her heart? What did you say to her?"

"I really don't want to talk about it."

"Yeah, well." He peels off his gloves, shrugs off his coat, and drapes it over his arm. After a moment, he turns to me, just close enough that I can see his irritated expression. "Maybe the rest of us do. Maybe we're tired of walking on eggshells around you, wondering when you'll go off and for the love of God why."

He pushes past me and goes up the stairs. A minute later I hear the water running in the bathroom.

23 January 1946

I set my chin on my hand and watch the new snow falling on the old snow outside on the sidewalk. From behind the closed door to the surgery, I hear Dr. Linstead say, "Cough for me."

I look back listlessly at the invoices I'm supposed to be stamping. Linstead was skeptical when I wanted to come in on Monday, saying that his old secretary Mrs. Carr wouldn't mind filling in a couple more days while I got my sea legs, but I more or less begged him to let me work. Even promised him he could listen to my lungs if he didn't believe I was ready. He couldn't argue that thoracically speaking, my recovery is proceeding better than was expected, although like every other person in my life he's paranoid about my diet. Between 11:30 and noon for the past three days, he's stuck his head out the surgery door to call for some favor or assistance, to cover his curiosity about whether I've brought lunch. I made it a point today to crunch a carrot within earshot, and he seemed satisfied.

Now that I'm back, though, the phone calls and appointment reminders and invoices all feel so meaningless. But what else would I do in Caspar, take tickets at the cinema window or sweep the aisles of the general store? The Airborne isn't much concerned with transferable skills.

Thank goodness the phone rings before I can explore that thought further. "Dr. Linstead's practice. Richard speaking, is it an emergency?"

"Richard, yes, it is an emergency," a breathless voice answers, and I hold the receiver away from my ear as our chronic hypochondriac

Eleanor Hartman rattles off a graphic description of the phlegm she just coughed up. Seems like everyone in Caspar is coughing something up these days.

"...and I'm having chest pains..."

For the hundredth time I try to explain to her that the chest pains are almost certainly a product of her diagnosed anxiety disorder and not, as she is desperate to believe, a heart attack, "—because as you might remember Dr. Linstead explaining on Monday, chest pains are very rarely a symptom of heart attacks in women—" and she snaps that how would I know anything of the anatomies of women? Then because the waiting room is empty, I set the receiver on the desk and resume stamping the invoices while she works herself up into a good sweat.

Eleanor has only been going about a minute when the bell over the door chimes and a timid-faced young woman enters, carrying a red-faced toddler on her hip, shushing him in French while he weeps and tries to burrow into her snow-covered shoulder. She pleads with him to be quiet as a man behind her catches the closing door with the toe of his boot. It's Harlan Wagner, Mattie's boss—dammit, I forgot he had an appointment today—and then the Franco mother and crusty old Wagner and Eleanor Hartman are all fighting for my attention. The mother and her son seem to have the most urgent claim because Eleanor calls at least once a day with "emergencies," and Wagner believes that any person at any moment should wait on him hand and foot.

"—and you know I trust your medical opinion," Eleanor is telling me, "so if you really think I should come by and let the doctor—"

The rest of her rambling is lost in a wail from the little boy. Wagner not so subtly huffs at the disturbance, turning away to examine Dr. Linstead's framed certificates on the wall. He's clearly put out at having to breathe the same air as two Francos. By the time Eleanor has made up her own mind to take some aspirin and go to bed, the child's wails have reached a pitch and fervor that can probably be heard in the pharmacy next door.

Wagner sniffs when I come out from behind the desk and tell the mother I'll be gentle. Franco families keep so strictly to themselves that only the most serious circumstances could induce them to bring a child to an American doctor. I don't blame her skepticism, but after a couple moments' eyeing me warily, she puts her son in my arms. His warm tears dampen the shoulder of my shirt as I gently hold my hand to his forehead—dry, hot—and try to talk to him in a few of the local dialect Quebecois words I've picked up from Mattie.

He clutches at his left ear and doesn't seem to hear my voice. I treated enough ear infections in Fox Company to recognize it now, even though this child doesn't seem to have the words to put to his pain and my boys were more than capable of bemoaning their every ache. I tell his mother that Dr. Linstead will be out to see him soon and am about to give the little boy back to her when the surgery door opens. Linstead and his patient appear, the latter waving goodbye as he goes out.

"Now, what's the trouble here?" Linstead wonders as the child's cries turn to a whimper. The woman says something in French to him. I hear the name Jules. "Oh my. It can't be your lungs ailing you, young man."

"I think it's probably an ear infection," I tell him. "Low-grade fever, too."

"I reckon you're right." He takes the child from me and asks the mother to follow him into the surgery. "We'll have you right as rain in no time, little one."

When they're gone, Wagner ambles back to my desk. "You're wasting your time on those Francos, Dare. She'll come out of there crying that she can't afford the bill, mark my words."

"I think whether or not she can afford the bill is beside the point when there's a sick child," I answer. Wait till he catches wind that Linstead runs a clinic free of charge once a month in the Catholic church in Petit Canada. Luckily he didn't seem to hear me, so I take the chance to soften my tone and add, "Is it your ulcer acting up again, Mr. Wagner?"

"I'll say. Son of a bitch kept me up all night."

That accounts for the cheery mood. He sits in one of the chairs beneath the window, stretches out his legs, and actually whips out a cigar and lighter from his jacket. I sit and watch him with my fingers frozen above my typewriter keys, trying to resist the urge to stuff the cigar down his throat so its ashes can line his peptic ulcers. Only after he's lit up, flicked the lighter off, and returned it to the pocket of his suit jacket do I point to the sign over the door and say, "We have a no-smoking policy, as a matter of fact."

He grunts disinterestedly. "And who enforces that?"

This paratrooper who could kill you nine ways with his letter-opener, I think, though Mattie has first dibs when it comes to putting Wagner in the ground.

I stand and swipe the ashtray I keep on my desk for just such occasions. You'd be surprised how many people come through this door with a glowing cigarette between their fingers, then lie to Linstead's face that they've never smoked a day in their lives. I hold it out to him. "Or you're welcome to smoke outside."

A white fog of snow has enveloped Main Street, cold wind creeping through the crack under the door. Wagner mutters something about uptight dagos, snuffs out the Cuban cigar, and says as I return to my desk, "You're buddy-buddy with Faucheux, aren't you?"

"Mm."

I'd hoped that the clatter of my typewriter might dissuade him, but he presses on. "Next time you see him, tell him he's hanging onto his job by the skin of his teeth. I've had about all I can take with that drunk."

This is the sort of thing I'd rather stay out of—Mattie would blow a fuse if he hears I've been checking up on him. But Wagner doesn't give me a choice because he says, "Shows up late and hungover, leaves the garage a filthy mess..."

"And you'd like me to talk to him?"

"I wouldn't like you to do anything. I'm just making conversation."

After only about eight minutes of waiting, during which the pale winter sun sets and the snow finally stops falling, Wagner is on the verge of storming out. I wouldn't mind seeing him explode; I only wish it wasn't in such close proximity to me to threaten the scattering of all my papers. But Linstead and the mother and child emerge at last, the little boy somewhat quieter now. Linstead says something to her in French and she answers, *"Merci, merci,"* and bundles her boy's head in a scarf before stepping out into the deep snow.

"What sort of establishment are you running, Jim, a free handout for the riff-raff?" Wagner trails Dr. Linstead into the surgery, leaving behind the scent of black pepper and cigar smoke.

With him gone and the waiting room empty again, there's nothing to keep my mind from straying to Grace. She acted as though nothing was wrong when we sat across the table from one another on Saturday night, toasting to Sidney and Lena, but I know how she is. Someone could pay her the most egregious insult, and she'd still act the perfect hostess. I don't want to be another of the people she watches from a safe distance, far enough to keep herself from getting hurt, the rest of our lives spent in polite acquaintance. I can't bear that thought. But I also can't bear her knowing, and she can't know, even if I wanted her to.

The bell chimes again and a tall, sharp-boned figure ducks in, shaking snow off himself like a dog. Mattie kicks a bit of snow back out the door and limps in, eyes watering from the cold. "Afternoon, Dick."

"...Mattie." In the excitement, I never checked the afternoon appointment book. He's early. "I forgot you were coming in."

"Fourth Wednesday of every month I'm here. You know that." He swings one of the waiting room chairs over, plants it backwards in front of my desk, and sits, draping his arms across the back. "Mind if I wait here with you?"

"It's at your own risk. Guess who's in there." I tilt my head toward the surgery. "Your boss and his ulcer have a date with Linstead."

"Shit," he says with a start, staring at the white door as if he expects Wagner to break it down. Then he mutters, *"Trou de cul,"* which I know, having been on the receiving end of that insult, means "asshole." "That's so much worse. Say, you have anything to drink?"

"Just rubbing alcohol," I joke.

His eyebrows go up. He stuffs his gloves in the pockets of his threadbare raglan coat he's worn since before the war. "That'll do fine."

"Yeah, I thought it might. Forget it."

As a general rule I'm reluctant to ever offer Mattie alcohol, but straddling the chair restlessly, tapping at the curved wooden back as though it's an octave of piano keys, he sure looks like he could use a drink. If I wasn't working and he wasn't here to see the doctor, I'd even suggest going to the Green Moth. He turns his head to watch the street as headlight beams sweep past. His gray eyes are bloodshot, angular cheeks more sunken than usual, but there's no slur to his words or whiskey on his breath.

"Out of curiosity," I say, cranking the wheel on my Royal Arrow to wind a new sheet of paper in, "and you can tell me to fuck off if it's none of my business, but any chance you're trying on purpose to lose your job at the garage?"

Mattie glances up from biting at his ragged fingernails. "He said something to you."

"Wanted me to give you a warning. I didn't bother telling him I've spent half my life running after you, trying to warn you not to do most of what you do."

He grins and says, "But we've had a pretty good time of it."

"Except neither of us are much for running anymore."

"Yeah, well." Mattie lets out his breath in a long exhale, tapping a pattern into the floorboards with his foot. "I don't know if it's been on purpose. But I guess you might not be wrong."

"Could you make ends meet if you were only playing for Helen?"

"I doubt it. Her dad's barely scraping together a budget for live music as it is."

We both fall silent. Mattie bites his nails while I stare at the white paper, trying to remember the recipient of this invoice. I never turned on the electric lights overhead, so the only light is from my desk lamp, weak like the glow of a firefly at summer's end. We sit in grainy dimness, and though I could get up to turn on the overhead lights, I don't—perhaps because I know better than to shine a light, literally or figuratively, on Mattie.

A soft, all-but-imperceptible intake of breath catches my attention. Mattie's face is turned in profile. His knuckles are white on the back of the chair, and he's biting down on the side of his thumb on his other hand, so hard, in fact, that I see a red drop appear and trickle down his nail.

"Mattie?" I stand, watching him. "Mattie."

He finally turns to meet my eyes.

"Is everything okay?"

He glances at his thumb, not seeming to notice the blood. "What?"

I sit again and say, as gently as I can, "I just asked if everything is okay."

Raised voices sound from the surgery. Well, one raised voice, followed by Linstead's, much quieter. Mattie watches the door, looking as though he'll bolt for the street if Wagner comes out right now. I wait for him to say yes, of course, everything is okay, as he always does even when he knows I know better.

But he doesn't. He pulls his coat in tighter, jaw tensing, one nostril twitching. His eyes drop to his lap.

This time I do come around the side of the desk. I sit on the edge, one leg dangling down. We can sit here as long as it takes, till Wagner comes barreling out of the surgery and wrings Mattie's neck himself, though he'll have to get past me first. Not that it'd take much to do that, these days. But I know that if Mattie wanted to divert attention from himself, he'd have brushed off my question, telling me I don't look so good myself or making some crack about me and Grace and a lovers' quarrel. He never lets eyes linger on him unless he's making a spectacle of himself on purpose.

"I guess your standing appointment fell on a day you really need it," I say at last.

Mattie doesn't look at me as he says, "I can't lose my job." He puts his forehead against his hand, propped up by the back of the chair, and his jaw tenses again like he's swallowing down pain. "I can't lose this fucking job because it's the only thing I've got. Sure, it's hell, but at least it's a different kind of hell. I can't be in that house with her...you want to know why I'm such a drunk? Learned everything I know from her. We're exactly what folks say we are, aren't we? Dirty Francos boozing up, beating on each other till they bury us in some of those unmarked graves behind St. Vincent's." He sighs and mutters, *"D'osti d'calvère du saint,"* and I don't need the exact translation to know that must be a string of Quebecois vulgarities.

We sit facing one another in silence for a minute.

Then Mattie grimaces as he stretches out his prosthetic and says, "You don't have to listen to this, Richard. You need to work."

"Forget the invoices. It's not as if folks will empty their pockets out tonight to pay their debts," I say. "Did you forget I had two years of keeping an eye on guys trying to hide their wounds?"

He shuts his eyes, deepening the pain lines in his face. "I have some nerve damage in my leg. It never healed right. Linstead wants me to go to a physical therapist in Bangor, but I don't even have a car, so how'm I gonna get to Bangor? Fucking ironic, isn't it? I work for that skinflint"—he flips up his middle finger at the surgery door—"and I can't even afford a car."

"Mattie, I'll drive you to Bangor. You should've said."

"Yeah, well...thanks." He meets my eyes, then just as quickly glances away. "That's just it, how all this goes in one big circle, like some kinda demon carousel off its tracks, and I can't seem to hang on."

"What do you mean?"

He shakes his head. "Don't make me talk about money."

The only way he'd be able to afford physical therapy is with his disability check, but he told Sidney and me on New Year's Eve how that check turns to booze in his mother's hands before he even sees it. I don't say anything else.

"I can't leave them there with her," he says. "My sisters. Adrienne's old enough to be on her own if she wanted but she won't leave, either, and the younger two...you know, she'd even forget to feed them if I didn't buy food."

The room has grown so dark I can only see his face when a car passes on Main Street. He sits with his head bowed.

"I don't even know why I'm here," he says at last. "There's nothing more Linstead can do. I need a specialist now."

"Seems like that's only one small part of it, though."

"If I pull at one string, they all come undone. Everything's balanced just so. Wagner wears me down all day, I go home and drink, but home's *home,* y'know? So I drink more. So he smells the whiskey on me when I come in hungover. I don't know what to do. Who the fuck else would hire me?"

He doesn't say it, but I know what he's thinking: Franco, cripple, delinquent. To which I'd add, veteran. And all those together are a hell of a cocktail when you're trying to land an interview, no matter how much weight they actually carry to anyone else.

"It's so stupid, all this," he mutters. "God, it is so fucking stupid. Sometimes you sit and think, 'Jesus Christ, I watched Europe eat itself alive. How could anything back home ever make up for that?' And then you realize it can't, but not till you're back in Hicksville, Maine begging for scraps." He rubs at his face with one hand and laughs, hollow and yet still aching. "Sorry about all this. I don't know where it's coming from. I should be asking you how you are. You're the one who just had surgery."

"That's okay. I don't have much to say about it, anyway."

He turns back in the chair to face me, though we both look anywhere but at the other. In the glass door, I see a memory of two boys circa 1938, leaning together against the streetlamp in a mist of snow. Both dark-haired, kicking at each other's ankles, elbowing ribs, mouths open in laughter and taunts. Bound together by, well, I'm still not sure what. More than baseball and detention. One of us knew at fifteen he wanted to go to seminary; the other smoked Camels in the tall grass behind St. Vincent's during Holy Communion. But glancing at Mattie now, his chin on the back of the chair and his eyes a little glassy, a whole litany of schoolyard fights and scrubbing one another's faces with mud and dragging each other underwater at the river suddenly seems to me to exist not in spite of our friendship as I always assumed, but—couldn't it be that we were desperate not to lose one another? So afraid that we would because our lives and personalities diverged so drastically, that our way of holding on was to beat the living daylights out of each other? We were only boys. No language existed in our vocabularies to say, "I care about you." And even if it did, we would've gagged to avoid saying it.

"Your leg," I say quietly so my voice can't carry through the wall. "Was it a shell hit, clean off?"

He stands, disentangles his legs from the chair, and stuffs his hands into his coat pockets. "It was Hill 400," he answers. He chews at his nails, walking in his stuttered gait in little revolutions between the door and the desk. "Hürtgen. Three years to the day since the Japs bombed Pearl Harbor, as it happened."

The Hürtgen Forest campaign. I was still in Suippes then, no way of knowing that the Battle of the Bulge was coming. But a month later, convalescing in a hospital in England, I read about that infamous hill in the January issue of *LIFE*, about the Rangers who held it without reinforcements for three days through bloody German counterattacks after a half dozen other units had tried and failed.

"We took a few casualties, but mostly we made it to the top okay. I made it up. Then the second day the krauts started raining fire down on us, artillery like you've never seen—" Mattie stops and catches himself. "Forgot who I was talking to; of course you've seen it. Anyway. We were even fixing bayonets, fighting hand-to-hand, you know. Real bloody stuff."

I nod, careful to keep quiet.

"So we were at the top of the hill, and the woods—it was so tangled, the kind of trees you imagine in fairytales, or like fighting your way through one of those hedgerows in Normandy—the kraut infantry used all that for cover. Then they'd rush us, flinging potato-mashers into our foxholes. And during all that..."

He stops. Runs his hand through his hair. I know how it is to be back there. How every time you do go back, you go alone.

"I was buddies with my platoon's machine-gunners," Mattie says, angling his neck and his shoulders with a sort of nervous jitter, as if he's having withdrawals. Maybe he is. "And I was near their gun nest when the shit started flying, you know, wondering what good are my rifle and some fragmentation grenades against .75s. There were a couple privates just flat on their stomachs, scared out of their minds, and I was trying to get them to move, to get up..."

It's all too easy to imagine. Change the name and it becomes the Bois de Limors in France, or wooded Hunnerpark.

Mattie flexes his fingers and then curls them into a fist. "I don't know. Maybe you don't want to hear all this, Richard."

I don't say anything, but I hope he can tell that I'll listen for as long as it takes. Whatever brings him some measure of peace.

"But I've got this far," he adds, after a few moments, "so what the hell? .75 mortar hit the gun nest dead-on. I guess they never felt a thing; they were dead instantly. So was one of those privates. The mortar hit brought down tree shrapnel, these real heavy limbs that were just impenetrable. Pinned me like a ragdoll. I couldn't get my leg free."

No sooner is the last word out of his mouth than the door to the surgery slams open, banging back against the wall and making us both jump. Wagner makes a "to hell with you" gesture at Dr. Linstead behind him as Linstead for about the hundredth time reiterates that the first step in treating peptic ulcers is to stop smoking two packs a day.

"I don't believe in merely medicating a problem, Harlan, and I'm sorry, but I won't write another prescription for your ulcers until you take some corrective measures for yourself."

"The hell do I pay you for, Linstead? Those pills you gave me last year—"

"—are a patch that will do nothing to treat the root cause, and the more tobacco and alcohol you pour in there—"

"I didn't come here for a lecture on morality. First your fucking amateur of a secretary—couldn't you even get one of those pretty agency girls?—now you refusing to do your damn job as a physician, and..."

He stops abruptly when he notices Mattie, standing with his hands in his coat pockets beside my desk.

Wagner laughs. "You little fucking Canuck rat. You've got some nerve, showing up here. Do I pay you to laze around and gossip with your buddy here like a couple of women?"

"Matthieu is a regular patient of mine, Harlan," Dr. Linstead says firmly.

"You're probably drunk off your ass again," Wagner continues, ignoring the doctor and crossing the waiting room with a startling swiftness for a man of his size, "and I swear to God if you try and come to my garage tomorrow stumbling around like yesterday—"

Mattie backs away, his face white. Dr. Linstead and I exchange a glance, and I move to block Wagner's path to Mattie, just in case.

Linstead says, "How you treat your employees at the garage is your business, Harlan, but I won't have you threatening my patient inside my practice."

A few excruciating moments pass. In the glass door's reflection, I see Mattie staring at his boss. This time it isn't nerve pain forcing the twitch of his nostril and the clenched jaw.

Wagner raises his smooth, lily-white hands as if surrendering in a shoot-out, shaking his head and laughing in a sickening way. "Sure, Jim, I'll go quietly. This is hardly worth my time." He steps over to me and leans in, close enough that I have to hold my breath to keep from coughing at the reeking scent of cigar smoke, ground into the fabric of his clothes and coming out on his breath. "Hey, dago, do me a little favor, won't you? Tell your Canuck friend"—he says this loud enough to echo throughout the empty waiting room—"that this is his last warning. One more time clocking in hungover or smelling like whiskey around my customers, and I'll make him wish the war had knocked his lights out before I got a chance."

He sidles over to the door, reaching for his coat and hat from the rack, and takes his sweet time putting his arms through the cashmere sleeves. In the open doorway, he looks back at the three of us. "I thought you knew better, Jim. You know you'll never get the Franco stink out of this place, no matter how hard you scrub." He slams the door as the bell rings above it. We watch him go to his Cadillac parked at the curb.

"What an afternoon," Linstead remarks. His voice is gentle, but resolute. "Matthieu, how about you come on back and we'll talk? I believe you're the last appointment of the day."

Mattie swallows, staring out the door at the clear patch of asphalt where the Cadillac was parked. He wipes at his nose with the heel of his hand and then looks at me. "I should've stood up to him."

Linstead holds his arm out, wordlessly guiding Mattie to the surgery door, and he goes through as if in a trance.

I stare at the door long after it's closed. Their voices within are hushed, the words indiscernable—not that I want to listen in, but—well, I guess I do want to listen in. Just to make sure Mattie is okay, even though I know he can't be.

Finally I sit at my desk and look at the blank paper resting in my typewriter's carousel and feel the warmth of the space heater on my feet. How am I supposed to type invoices now? I put my head down on my arms.

We were so sure—I was so sure—that what we gave during the war meant something. But come home, and the currency of service is worthless. You're still just a dirty Franco, an uptight dago. A cripple. I don't want a handout from anyone, a parade, any glory or fuss. I only thought, however naïvely, that everything I did was to preserve everything I loved back home. Only to come home and watch those loves sift, fine as dust, through fists I don't have the strength to clench.

25 January 1946

The olive oil dish slips out of my hand and clatters on the porcelain sink basin. "Sorry," I say, reaching for it with soapy fingers. At least it isn't broken. I still feel guilty over the fleet of communion cups shattered on the floor of the church basement on Christmas Eve, whenever I happen to think of that night, which I try not to.

"Where do we keep the teaspoons, Lizzie?" Dad moves through the kitchen, opening drawers and saying, "That doesn't look right..."

"Drawer to the right of the stove," Mom answers without looking up from her cookbook open on the table.

"...Aha."

Laurie's typewriter keys pause, a reprieve from his furious typing of yet another obituary. Winters always do a number on Caspar's elderly population. Through the muffle of the running tap water, a commercial drifts from the speakers of the Philco on the windowsill, some bright-voiced girl gushing about how much her teeth gleam after switching to Ipana toothpaste. "Ipana for the smile of beauty," she says dreamily, and then the band takes up to play the Camels cigarettes jingle that announces the Abbott & Costello Show.

"So how's Grace these days? I haven't seen her around much," Dad says as I pass him a wet plate.

I scrub at the cast-iron skillet, where a bit of chicken skin is trying to make a last stand. I still don't know if I've forgiven him for asking

Grace to come when I was sick. "Fine, I guess." I overcome the chicken skin at last, setting the skillet on the draining rack. "Would you mind, my sleeve...?" I say to Dad, angling my head toward my sweater sleeve slipping close to my wet hands.

He rolls it back up for me as Laurie says from the table, "Quick, someone, a synonym for cheerful."

Mom circles something in pencil in her cookbook. "Sunny."

"Lighthearted," I answer.

Dad suggests, "Good-natured? No, that's a can of theological worms."

"You win, *Mána* ... 'Edith's sunny personality was a delight to all who loved her, reflecting the sunflowers with which she filled the church every summer...'" He returns to typing furiously, muttering, "Yes, that's good."

Dad takes a pair of drinking glasses from me and says, "How about Mattie?"

"What about Mattie?"

"Haven't seen him in a while, either." He dries the glasses with a fruit-patterned dish rag that's about disintegrated.

"He's having a rough go of it at the garage, with Harlan Wagner behaving like Harlan does," I answer. "And things are hard at home, too...you know." I hesitate to say anything else. Mattie is already wary enough of my dad, sure that imminent judgment will rain on his head if he crosses paths with the Reverend, which thankfully doesn't happen often. Mattie has probably never set foot in our church.

"I wish there was more I could do for his family. For so many of the French-Canadian families," Dad adds, "but we know how they are about charity."

"Ay-uh. Well, he needs physical therapy for his leg in Bangor, but he can't afford it. I'd give him my disability check for it if I didn't think that would end our friendship on the spot."

I reach for a coffee mug in the sink. A sharp pain stabs my back, under my left shoulder blade, right where Dr. Linstead removed my stitches earlier this week. With an inhale, I grip the edge of the sink and count in my head the way we'd count at parachute school when we jumped from the blocks before doing the real thing out of planes: *one one-thousand, two one-thousand, three one-thousand...*

"You okay?" Dad says, his voice quiet, though I notice out of the corner of my eye Mom glancing up.

Before, I could tuck it away most of the time, out of sight and out of mind, but now it seems to wait for me around every corner. Every movement, every conversation trails back to it, pulling my body ever closer back to the past while the world before me narrows.

In answer I reach for the coffee mug again and say, "Yes, fine."

"You look a little white, if you'd like to sit—"

"I said I'm fine."

It comes out louder than I meant it to. Laurie's typewriter keys are silent, the rustle of Mom's cookbook pages still. Dad stands with dishrag and plate in hand, his eyes on me.

Don't say it, I warn myself. *Don't—*

Turning from the sink, I say, "Why did you force me through that when you knew it wasn't what I wanted?"

No one says anything. Dad crosses his arms over his chest and leans against the refrigerator. I look from him to Mom and Laurie, both of whom make a point of dropping their eyes.

"I don't know how none of you understand that. Why won't you listen to me? Why are you afraid even to look at me?"

For a moment Dad looks much older in the lines of his face than he is. "You were in no condition to make life or death decisions."

"That's not true. I'd never been more sure of anything."

"Sure you wanted to die?" he says. "Think about what you really mean by that."

"Oh, I do." I raise my eyes to meet his. "It's all I think of. You could've spared me that, too."

"Last summer you came to me so afraid that you'd do something unintentionally to hurt Grace—wouldn't this be the pinnacle of hurting h—"

"Why do you keep bringing her up? This isn't about her!"

"Yes, I forgot," Dad says. "It's only about you. Of course."

The kitchen is silent but for the trickling tap water, till I reach out and turn the faucet. Dad watches me with an expression I can't place. It isn't anger or even irritation. When I realize what it is, I feel the same rage that filled my throat outside the church in Trois-Ponts.

He watches me with grief. As if I'm too far gone.

"I know you wish you could've been left to give up. But what kind of father would I be, to let that happen?"

"You're not the one who has to live with this the rest of your life."

He considers this and then nods. "With your lungs?"

"No, it isn't only about that. I shouldn't have had a second chance, or a third, because he never got that. He'll never..."

"Who?"

"No one. Forget it."

"Richard. You have to know that everything I've done, whether or not it was the right thing to do, I did out of love. That's all. Love and following God's will, as best I know how, which is broken and human. Sometimes I've been wrong. But I would do it again. I will intercede on your behalf a thousand times if that's what it takes for you to see"—a more gentle note tinges his voice—"that I will not give up on you."

My heart stumbles at that word. *Intercede.* Only a minister would use it. It's forever bound in my mind to a body I reached too late under the blue smoke in Nijmegen, Jacob in my arms asking for the Catholic chaplain, Jacob for whom there was no intercession and who died because of the words he heard me pray on D-Day. *Whatever it takes, whatever You ask of me.* I was so caught up in my grief even while there was still breath in his body that I never thought to carry him out of the German grenadier's sights. He might've made it till the chaplain came if I had taken care of him the way he needed me to. If I'd acted the medic and not his friend.

"If you really loved me, you would listen to me. That's all I've been trying to tell you. None of you listen to me."

"I am listening," Dad answers. "I haven't done it well lately. But here I am. What do you need me to hear?"

I drop my hand from my face, vaguely aware that Mom and Laurie are still watching. "I don't know. I said forget it."

"I know you do know. Otherwise it wouldn't be eating you up so much."

"No." I shake my head as if the movement might keep back the ghosts, especially the one lingering behind Jacob. "No, I don't. I don't know."

I flinch when Dad touches my arm. He doesn't take away his hand.

"Okay," he says, "we won't—"

But my voice cuts him off, seeming to come from outside myself, "No" and "I don't know," over and over again.

He puts his hand on my shoulder and I pull away from him, my voice rising and breaking. "No, stop, *stop* trying to make me feel like this doesn't matter! It should have been my choice! You took away all I had left of him!"

"Who?"

"I don't—I don't know—"

"He must be some—"

"Stop!" I shout, burying my face in my hands, breaths coming short and fast, the kitchen tilting. "I don't know, stop asking me, I don't know!"

"Okay, it's okay, you don't have to tell me. I'm sorry."

"I don't know, I don't want to go back there—"

"You're not."

I feel myself shaking. "I don't want to go back there."

"What can I do to help—"

"I've had enough of your help! You're the one who made all this happen. It wouldn't have happened if you'd just listened to me to begin with!"

I stand for a long time against the sink, hands to my face and heart pounding. *No, no, no, no, no, no.* I can't go back. It's taken a year to get far enough away.

When I lift my head, Dad is beside me, but now it's not him I see. And now I can't think of anything—or anyone—else.

It was always going to come to this, wandering through my memories. It was always going to end here, with him, which is also where it began.

XXVI.
PHILIA

L ieutenant Forrest lifts his hand. All us Protestants tilt back the little glass cups he carries in his portable communion kit, swallowing the cold drop of wine. I wish there was more. We're huddled like pack animals shoulder to shoulder for warmth, on our feet instead of our knees because of the snow. Across the clearing, Captain Odell and the Catholics drink and then make the sign of the cross. The night is uncharacteristically clear, a thumbnail moon trying to hide in the cloudless black sky past the treetops.

"Lord, I commend each man here to thy care," Forrest prays, "and I pray thee to guide their footsteps tonight, as we hope for a warmer dawn."

I keep my eyes on my boots throughout the prayer, wondering how many more footsteps I have left before the leather truly splits from its seams. Lieutenant Forrest lifts his head and says, in a verse from Ephesians that sounds as though it could've come from the mouth of our CO, "Keep alert with all perserverance." I glance at the men around me, Peter on my left, Fish on my right, a few of the other F Company boys mixed in with strangers from different companies in our regiment. When

Forrest gives the benediction, his voice borders on the weary. He, too, must be praying for the day when he doesn't close the stiff eyelids of dead boys. "Grace be with all who love our Lord Jesus Christ with love incorruptible. Go in peace."

The groups disperse and the Protestants and Catholics mingle again, tramping off into the woods together, men's voices rising and fading out in the cold night.

Peter holds his gloved hands to his mouth and breathes into them. They were full gloves when we set out from Suippes, but they're mostly fingerless now. "You should take these, Richard. For an hour, at least, we'll trade off."

Yesterday I gave my gloves to a replacement private when his got blown to high heaven—a shell hit his foxhole when he happened to be off taking a leak. "You know I work better without them," I tell Peter. "And when I'm not working, and you two better not give me a reason to"—I cast a glance at Fish, who shrugs as if to say, "who, me?"—"I'll just try not to pick up handfuls of snow with my bare hands."

"And what happens if you lose a finger?" Peter wonders. "Do you expect us to stitch our own flesh wounds?"

"Well, just don't get any flesh wounds."

Fish swings his rifle off his shoulder. "I'm off to find Bill and then we're taking our turn on the line. Don't wait up, fellas."

"Write if you get work," Peter calls, and Fish waves in reply as his back disappears into the gray gloom under the trees.

We turn to go the other way. Peter says, "You bunking with us tonight?"

"If there's room. I'd go to Berk's, but that replacement in his foxhole wouldn't shut up last night. Talked for two hours straight about how it's seventy degrees in Florida this time of year." Of course, I could've left and gone back to my own foxhole, but even if I didn't hate being in there alone, the cold has now made isolation downright dangerous. Two to a foxhole, at least, for warmth—Captain Watson was adamant about that this morning, after we hit record lows during the night. The thermometer in his tent at the CP read -7 when I wandered over there at dawn.

Peter tucks his hands beneath his armpits and hunches into his wool scarf. "I sure miss McNuts. So does Berk, I bet."

"Maybe I'll send his replacement to look for morphine for me, spell Berk a little from listening to stories about hunting alligators in swamps."

"I know it's apples to oranges, but what I'd give to be in the south Pacific right now…"

"Just think about Tunisia and the mosquitoes as you curl up in your igloo."

We tramp through the deep snow, each step like walking over a bed of needles. All the hell I give the guys about trench foot and keeping their feet dry, and now it's come for me.

"I should check on the guys," I say, eyes watering as wind stirs up the snow.

"No way. You're asleep on your feet." Peter slings his arm around my shoulder and guides me toward his and Fish's foxhole, through trees that all look the same. "Come rest for a bit, then you can check on them. You're no good to us half-alive."

We're all half-alive at best, but I follow him anyway. Pine boughs, hacked from the trees with axes or gathered off the ground after a shelling, cover the tops of foxholes filled with exhausted paratroopers. We left the Rochelinval woods after Christmas, and now we're camped on the northwestern side of the highway between the villages of Renardmont and Stavelot in the Amblève River valley, blocking the German approach to Trois-Ponts and any possible counterattack. Rumors began swirling last night that we'll be used for an offensive this week to drive them back to their lines. In Captain Robinson's tent this morning, I heard *Noirfontaine* and *Volksgrenadier* and one of the officers saying we won't move till the second or third of January. Three more days in plummeting temperatures, half the guys without overcoats or long underwear, nothing hot to eat or drink. What's more, we're on the high ground and can see the shingled and thatched rooftops of Stavelot in daylight, though no smoke rises from the chimneys. At first the thought of spending a night in a damp root cellar—paradise, in other words—was tortoruous to us out here, till we learned what Joachim Peiper and his 1st Panzer divsion did in that village. A hundred civilians dead, the stories went round, women and children murdered, too. For a little while, anyway, that thought sobers you up as you shiver in your ready-made grave.

Peter and Fish's foxhole is a nice piece of real estate near the edge of the woods, where on a clear day you can see white fields rolling down the hillsides to the road. The rest of 3rd platoon is dug in all around, although we're hemorrhaging more men than we are taking in replacements. Peter lifts the tarp covering their hole and hops down, and I follow. His and Fish's musette bags and bedrolls are at the bottom and not much else. A couple ammo cases to make coffee in, a pack of saltines and a razor falling out of one of the bags. Some guys are souvenir magpies, like Skinny was, but the rest of us seem to be shedding belongings the longer this drags on. I don't know if that makes me feel as if our identities have been whittled down to only what really matters, or if it's just another reminder of losing ourselves.

Peter sets aside a dirty mess kit from the chow line earlier, then unzips his sleeping bag and drapes it like a blanket over his shoulders. I sit back against the dirt wall and close my eyes. My body feels like it's fusing with the frozen earth. "How're your feet?" I ask.

"Still got two of them and ten toes, so I figure that's as many as I came to Belgium with."

I open my eyes. "If I find you've been hiding a frostbitten toe—"

"Cross my heart."

"You better."

Peter nods at my feet. "Yours?"

"I'm fine."

"You were limping away just now. I meant it—we need a medic who isn't falling apart himself."

I sit up and prop my left boot on the other knee, undoing the laces as best I can with numb fingers. "Well, if you really want to see my feet, just remember you asked for it. But I guess I oughta dry out my socks anyway."

It takes a bit of wriggling to get my Corcorans off, not only because the leather is so warped and brittle but because trench foot has caused the bottoms of my feet to swell. That accounts for the constant pins and needles.

"Mm, that's trench foot, all right." Peter leans forward and flicks my big toe, and I flinch. "Ah, there you go. At least you can still feel that."

"For how much longer?" I drape the damp socks around my neck. "The more this goes on, sleeping in the snow, the more..."

"What?"

I make a spinning motion with my index finger at my temple. "You know."

"Yeah," Peter says. "Yesterday I caught one of those replacements in 2nd platoon walking around without his boots on. Asked him about his boots, he didn't know. I brought him to Lieutenant Perry. Don't know what happened."

The Germans have shelled our position each night we've been here. Every rustle of clothing or clatter of a mess kit makes me jump. Nervous in the service, as we say.

Blood breaks through the cracks in my knuckles. We huddle beside each other for warmth, beneath the thin cover of the sleeping bags, my bare feet propped on my boots. Peter's coughs rise up into the darkness.

"Remember how hot we were in Sicily?" he whispers, laughing, coughing again.

I wrap my arms around my middle, but despite the long underwear and wool shirt and jump jacket and overcoat and Fish's sleeping bag, I might as well be bare-chested. "I wish it had been under different circumstances."

"Wish what had been?"

"I mean I wish we'd all grown up together."

"Yeah." He pulls the blanket up to his chin. "Me too."

"Stars are out," I murmur, staring up into the black wash as light glows through the wispy clouds. I risk taking my bare hand out and point to a pattern rearing its head, though half the stars are hidden in the trees. "There's Leo, the lion."

"You know anything about astrology?"

"Not really. My grandfather just taught my brother and me all the constellations. He loves the stories. Used to watch the sky back home, said when he came to America it was the only thing that seemed familiar."

We fall quiet for a couple minutes as low voices from the neighboring foxholes sing "Auld Lang Syne," shaky and pneumatic. Then Peter says, "Say, you still got that picture of you and Grace?"

I take off my helmet and slide the snapshot out from the lining. I haven't looked at it in a long time. It hurts to see Grace's smile, her shoulders drenched in summer sunlight and her face out of focus because she was moving and laughing as we lay on our stomachs in the grass. Whenever I take out that perfect late summer day, August of '39, I hear the frogs sing in the marsh grass and see the shadows of the white hydrangeas move on the side of the house. And she's at the center of it. Smiling as though she was the one pulling the strings to make the breeze blow.

"You almost feel warm," Peter says. "Geez, feel like I know this photo as well as any of mine."

I know Fish's mother's blueberry pie recipe by heart, and every stop on the train McNuts took from Queens to The Bronx to see his cousins. Drop me in the middle of Fresno, and I could find my way to the courthouse where Berk and Emily were married in '41. The melodies of the old bluegrass songs Jacob used to sing on marches in Normandy still flit through my mind at the oddest times, his North Carolina voice filling the night: *The darkest hour is just before dawn, the narrow way leads home...*

I know this photograph of Peter and Chrissy, too, as Peter takes it from the lining of his overcoat and holds it, the edges quivering. We found shelter in one another's lives, homes carved out of memories belonging to other men. It's a phenomenon of combat I don't believe could ever be replicated anywhere else.

"Don't know why I think if I stare at it long enough, it'll just come to life again." Peter bites at his thumbnail poking through his threadbare glove. "That day was perfect."

The photo has a bluish cast to it. I know the inscription on the back: *Peter & Chrissy at Tichigan Lake, Summer 1941.* It was taken before their sophomore year at the University of Wisconsin. They're standing in the shallows of the lake, or Peter is, and he's holding Chrissy bridal style, arm under her knees as he kisses her. Her light hair blows into his face. It's obvious he's smiling.

"You better marry her the instant you get home," I say. "Do it right there on the station platform."

Peter laughs. "I think she might want some time to find a dress."

"If she's a smart girl, she'll come to the station in her wedding dress already. All you have to do is call the minister out, pick some wildflowers." I shrug my shoulder against his. "Plus, the train will be right there..."

"So she can whisk me off on a honeymoon before I've even set foot on home soil?" Peter grins. "You may have a point there, actually."

"Of course I do. Sweep her off her feet before she has a chance to reconsider marrying you."

He coughs, head bent to his knees, but I hear the laughter through it. "Not sure I need to take advice from someone who can't even bring himself to take his girl—the one he's been mooning over for so long—to the pictures."

"Make a deal with you, then." Our breaths have fallen into a rhythm. "Propose to Chrissy on the train platform, and I'll ask Grace out, first day I'm home."

"Yeah?" Peter glances at me, tucking the photo back into his overcoat. "Okay, Rev, you've got yourself a deal. Write me when you've done it."

"I'll do you one better—a wedding invitation."

"Now that's confidence."

We're quiet for a while, feeling the temperature tick down by degrees as the night deepens. I should put my boots on, go out and check on Fish and Bill on the line, make my rounds and see who needs something. But the idea of moving hurts as much as moving itself. And I'd like to linger in the glow of these photographs for a little longer.

Peter stirs, turning his head on his musette bag, and says, "When you get home—besides going out with Grace—what's the first thing you'll do? The very first thing."

"Hug my mother, I guess. My dad'll probably be at the church. Tell him I missed him. I don't know what else I'd tell him."

"Yeah," Peter says after a few moments, "I don't know how to tell it, either."

"What about you?"

"Probably jump from the train and kiss the ground." He laughs. "But it wouldn't do to kiss Chrissy with a dirty mouth."

I smile. "I doubt she'll care."

Silence falls between us again for a minute till Peter says, his words stuttered in the cold, "You know th-hat old saying, there's no atheists in a f-foxhole?"

"Mm."

"I guess it's true. I keep thinking about how it all has to mean something."

"Then you have more faith than I do."

"How do you figure?"

I wince as I turn my stiff neck to look at his profile. "You still believe we're here for a reason?"

"I d-don't know. Maybe all I need's a reason to keep getting up."

"You have your reason. The boys. That's what you've always said."

"Not only that. I mean, if we're just pawns out here, why should I care if I died right now? Why not just get it over with?"

I shake my head weakly against Fish's musette bag. "I don't know."

"Do you think this is it?"

His eyes glow a faint green in the darkness. I drop my chin to my chest and sigh. "You mean, do I think we'll both die before this is over?"

"Just that if we do...do you think it's all darkness, nothing after?"

I don't know what to say.

"We know that combat strips every last thing from a man, starting with his dignity," Peter says softly. "And then finally you're left with a lot of guys who've given up hope. So you start to think maybe they're right."

"But maybe they're not," I say, wondering when we traded places and he came out of the equation with more faith.

I've lost hope of making it out of this alive. But maybe Peter is right, after all. Who's to say that hope doesn't grow in the dark, up among the thorns where it has no right to be?

I awake with a start, not knowing what jolted me out of sleep, not even aware I did fall asleep. Someone is crouched at the edge of the foxhole and is whispering to me. I squint, unable to make out the guy's features.

"Corporal Dare?" he whispers. Must be a replacement if he's calling me that. "Corporal Dare—"

"What is it? Is anyone hit?"

The guy shakes his head, his helmet so big that it moves with him. "No one's hit. But it's Lieutenant Perry. 2nd platoon, we were on a patrol, and he must've stepped in a hole or something because we think his ankle's broken. Captain Robinson told me to come get you."

I sigh. "I'm coming."

Peter lifts his head from my shoulder, blinking. "About time I checked on the boys, anyway," he says. He glances at me as I loosen the laces on my boots. "Good luck."

He scrambles up the edge of the hole and disappears. Finally I just jam the boots on, wincing at my feet on fire, and I fumble with the laces till they're knotted so at least I won't trip. I climb out and follow the private past the 3rd platoon foxholes, guided by faint moonlight.

Lieutenant Perry is in Captain Robinson's tent, his ankle propped on a stack of empty crates, arguing with Robinson that he doesn't need to go to the aid station as 2nd platoon's new medic tries to wrap the busted ankle. Perry grimaces and snaps at him not to touch it. The kid, barely out of jump school by the looks of him, flushes red and sits back. He got here two days ago after Donny King was wounded and evacuated in a shelling. If I had to guess, I'd say this kid had about two hours of classroom instruction on being a medic.

"Gillan, if you'd stop poking at it," the lieutenant says through gritted teeth, and poor Gillan takes off his helmet and pushes back his sweaty hair.

"You step in a gopher's hole, lieutenant?" I joke, kneeling beside Gillan and taking out my penlight. I cup the light with my other hand and sweep it across the lieutenant's bare ankle, where his skin is purple and swollen. After checking for sensation and movement in his foot, I say, "I can splint it, sir, but we can't set the bone here. A surgeon needs to do that. Doc Ryder's at the aid station, just down the hill in Stavelot."

He tries to protest, so I counter him. "Not setting it, or having me set it wrong—it might never heal right. Unless you want to walk with a limp the rest of your life, you need a surgeon to take a look, sir."

Perry finally gives in. Gillan watches as I show him how to splint the ankle, using one of my last bedsheets from Trois-Ponts and some strips of wood another private pulled from the empty crates.

"His whole foot and ankle need to be kept steady during the transfer to the aid station," I say, knotting the ends of the bedsheet around the splint and over Perry's shin, "so the fracture doesn't get worse if the ride is bumpy. If we just wrapped it"—he blushes again because that's what he'd been about to do when I came—"that wouldn't keep anything in place, see?"

He nods and says, "Yes sir," and I say, "You don't have to call me sir," and he says, "Sorry, si—sorry."

Robinson's radioman calls for a Jeep. Gillan and I help Lieutenant Perry out of the tent when it arrives, his arms slung between our shoulders. Once he's gone, Gillan snaps his medical bag closed and looks at me. He looks like a baby deer lost in the snow. "How do you learn these things? They barely taught us anything at Bragg."

"I've been here a while."

He falls in step with me as I head back toward the CP. "Is it okay to be scared?"

I glance at him, surprised at such an easy admission of fear. Most replacements puff out their chests till the shit starts flying.

"Yeah," I answer. We stop at the CP to part ways. "As long as you don't let them see it. Trust me: when a guy gets hit, he'll be afraid enough to cover you both."

"Got it," he answers, a grim smile flickering across his face. "Thanks, Doc." I watch him move off toward his platoon's foxholes.

Coughing and arguing rise from the tarp- and tree-limb covered holes as I trudge toward 3rd platoon. What a New Year's Eve. I wonder where Grace is tonight. Dancing, I hope.

I scoot onto the end of a snow-dusted log beside the hole Tony Rodriguez and Chuck Regan share. Chuck's flossing and at the same time trying to tell Tony about some Greta Garbo film he clearly can't remember the plot of, and Tony's got out his entrenching tool, trying to deepen their shallow hole. A fool's errand in this weather.

"Evening, boys," I say, and they answer, "Happy New Year's, Rev." Chuck drops his used floss on his pack.

"Lookin' cute tonight, Rev," Tony grunts, throwing his shoulder into it as he tries to break the frozen ground. He leads the mortar squad now, though he hasn't been quite the same since Skinny was wounded in Nijmegen. Sobered up, which always seems to happen to a guy who loses his partner-in-crime. "Got a date?"

"Yeah, with your sister."

"She's too good for you!"

I knock on Chuck's helmet and say, "Heard you got sewn up nice, Chuckles."

"Real nice. Whaddya think?" He pulls the scarf from his neck and shows off the six stitches from a shrapnel fragment that took a bite out of him two nights ago.

"It's a beauty."

"Hey, I got an extra bandage for you," he says, taking a rolled bandage out of his aid kit and tossing it to me. "Sorry it ain't much."

"Thanks. You guys need anything? Any toes turning black?"

They assure me they're okay. A few yards away in the moonlight, I see Peter crouched at another hole, the butt of his rifle propped in the snow beside him, a couple of our new guys looking up at him and laughing. I move along, stopping to pass the time, hear snippets of letters from home that I've already heard three times over, listen to coughs and check for fevers. Two riflemen in Berk's squad can't even stand because of the trench foot rotting their feet. I tell them that at first light, they're off to the aid station.

There's a shuffle of snow behind me as I leave their hole, and I glance around. Fish and Bill Hullman tramp through the pine trees carrying their rifles, just relieved from line duty, their heads together as they talk in low voices. Bill says goodnight and breaks off to his own foxhole.

"You find any champagne on the line?" I say to Fish.

He grins, his cheeks blue. "Oh, there's a whole shindig out there, the most gorgeous girls, Benny Goodman with a five-piece band. Wait, no...that must've been all in my head."

"Geez, real sorry I missed your corker of an imaginary party."

"When we're back home," he says, "we'll meet up in Boston for a real corker, huh? I've got a cousin in Charlestown, he knows all the best clubs."

"Yeah? Okay, why not. It's a deal. December 31st, 1945."

Fish and I stop at other foxholes to shoot the shit with guys who're still awake. We may live in the woods, but New Year's Eve is New Year's Eve, and Herb Heslett, who's been collecting souvenir watches off dead krauts, announces that it's thirteen minutes to midnight. Berk comes out of the trees near his foxhole, zipping up the fly of his jump trousers and doing the buttons of his overcoat.

"Swear to God," he announces, "my pee freezes the moment it hits the air."

Fish makes a face as I say, "You sure know how to paint a picture."

He touches the tips of his gloved fingers to his helmet. "Happy to be of service."

"I wonder what Times Square looks like tonight," Tom Maslow says, hanging on the edge of his hole with a creased letter in his hands. "My ma says Brooklyn's swarming with sailors. They're gonna marry the best girls before we even get a chance."

"I don't care about Times Square. It's Berlin I give a shit about." Berk flexes his fingers and exhales slowly. "Give us the fucking order; I'm ready to jump. Want that fifth star on my jump wings. Because the sooner we get to Berlin—"

"—the sooner you get home to Emily," Fish and I say together, and Berk snorts.

"Well, it's true," he says. "We're gonna get out of Fresno, I was sick of it there the moment I was born. Go up the coast to 'Frisco or maybe down to Santa Barbara. Build a big house with enough bedrooms for all the little Berkowiczes."

"You might be onto something there." Fish stamps out his cigarette butt in the snow. "Have to find me a girl first, though."

Lieutenant Greer comes through the splintered tree trunks, wishing the guys a happy new year. "Don't want to interrupt anything, just wanted to say Happy New Year, boys," he tells us, slapping Fish's shoulder as Peter comes over, too. "Next year'll be better."

"It'd be hard-pressed to be worse," Berk remarks, and Fish says, "Don't tempt fate."

"Get some rest if you can. Word from division is that we're not moving out till the 2nd, but you know how plans change. And I—" Greer breaks off abruptly, then says, "Dare, aren't you a little underdressed?"

I look up. He's watching me with his brows drawn together, and it takes a moment for my mind to catch up. "Oh. Yes, sir, I guess so."

"Where's your overcoat?"

"Oliver needed it more than I did, sir. His got blown up last night."

"But you're the one wandering around in nothing but a jump jacket and trousers. What happens to us if you catch your death from cold?" Greer starts to unbutton his own overcoat, but I hold up both hands.

"Sir, really, I can move faster without it."

"Did you give Oliver your gloves, too?"

Peter laughs under his breath. "Believe me, sir, I've tried to reason with him. There's no stopping him from stripping when he's in a charitable mood."

"You have taken at least a year off my life, Dare," Greer remarks. "Let me give this to you, just for tonight. You can return it in the morning."

"I can't, sir, really. I'll just end up taking it off if I need to move. But I promise I won't spend the night in my hole alone."

I can't tell if he's going to relent, but then Sergeant Autry calls for him from a few foxholes away and Greer shakes his head. "I'm keeping an eye on you. Don't make me regret this."

When he's gone, Berk laughs. "If anyone had any doubts that you're from Maine, this clears them up. And now, I'm gonna go lie down and shiver all night. Fishy, you're comin' with me. Give me a break listening to Stevens chatter."

"Aye-aye, sarge."

"Night Rev, Pete," Berk says. "Sleep tight. Don't let the frost-bite...well, bite, eh?"

"I need to talk to Captain Robinson about some trench foot cases," I say to Peter, hooking my thumb in the direction of the CP. "Grady and Brenner, they've got it bad."

He pulls his scarf up around his mouth and says, "I'll join you. Maybe he has hot coffee."

We walk, and Peter wonders if we'll get mail before the rumored attack. The trees open into a clearing where the holes are spread a bit farther apart, whispers and snores breaking the stillness. I start to say, "If we do make the attack tomorrow, I—"

It happens in an instant, a succession of movements so fast that my mind can hardly separate them: Peter's hands shoving me back, his shout in my ears, then black powder like rain filling my nose, a mouthful of ashes, and finally the burning sensation of fire biting into my chest.

We all know that if you hear the whistle of a mortar shell, you're safe. Out of its path. It's the whistles you never hear that swallow guys whole.

And I didn't hear a thing.

I feel the explosion bursting through my eardrums. Then I'm falling backwards, the snow breaking my fall, though someone—it must be Peter—is on top of me. The force of his fall and his weight knocks the wind out of me, or rather, yanks the breath from my lungs like a heavyweight punch to the solar plexus.

Sometimes a dud shell will hit, land in the snow with a fizzle, as harmless as an Easter egg. You call the fellows in that foxhole some lucky SOBs and laugh and try not to think about it.

But what do you call the guys who get hit twice?

Twice cursed?

Before we can move, a second stormcloud envelops us. I feel us at its center like we're caught in the eye of a hurricane, and then the force of it spreading past us, and then the sudden stillness.

...

That should have been it. But I don't think we're dead.

The ringing is so close it sounds as if it's coming from inside me.

Three things occur to me in the same instant: I still can't move; my chest is soaked and warm; and past the ringing, I hear more shells exploding in the forest. I lift my head and force open my eyes into a cloud of black smoke.

"DARE, ADLER, STAY DOWN!" a tinny voice calls from a long way off. "We're coming! Stay where you are!"

I try to feel my chest, but the only part of me not pinned down is my right arm. "Pete," I choke, but I barely get his name out. With my free arm I shove his shoulder, thinking the force of the second shell must've rattled his skull and knocked him out. "Peter! You have to...get up..."

He's well over six feet, and he was a linebacker on his high school football team while I wasted my time running cross-country. But I can't breathe, so there's nothing for it. I push against him with all my strength and at last shift him just enough to wrench my body free. And when I do, through the smoke watering my eyes, I see the bloody river pooled in the impression left by my body—and the blood seeping into the snow from beneath Peter as he lies motionless facedown.

Shit. Someone calls our names again as bright white light illuminates the skeleton trees. For a few seconds at a time I'm able to see Peter before the light flashes out, the cycle repeating itself as the krauts shell us to high heaven. My helmet and my kits are gone. I pull myself up onto my elbows and immediately collapse again in the snow when pain bursts through my chest. I try a second time and almost throw up because of the intensity of it. *Oh, God.* I hold my hand to my mouth and will my body not to give in to the comforting temptation of blacking out. I have to get to him.

At last, trembling and with an involuntary gasp of pain, I haul myself up and drag myself back through the blood to Peter's side.

"Hey, Pete," I say. My voice is slurred, and the words taste metallic. I spit blood into the snow, not wanting to know where in me it came from. I reach out to shake him awake. "Pete, listen, we gotta...we have to get to a f-foxhole..."

Then the light flashes once more through the trees, and that's when I see what the shell did.

The side of his face is bloody, so it must've knocked him out like I thought. But it's the open wounds across his back that turn my stomach. Not because I haven't seen worse. But because it's Peter. Torn flesh and muscle stick to his blood-soaked overcoat, tendrils of smoke wafting from the holes.

He'll suffocate facedown in the snow. I don't want to turn him onto his back, so I slip my right arm beneath his shoulders to get him on his side. Pain stabs the center of my chest again, as if the hands of a giant are prying apart my ribcage.

I can't. I can't do it, I think, shutting my eyes and drawing in desperate breaths but no air. Cold tears trickle down my neck into the sticky mess of blood.

Whatever it takes, whatever You ask of me.

With a primal sound from my throat that sounds as if it came from a dying animal, I get Peter onto his side.

"Hang on, Pete, I've got you." I put one hand on his forehead to brush the bloodied hair away, the other over his carotid artery. A weak pulse meets my fingertips. "Okay, Pete, hang on for me, okay? Help's c-coming..."

I crane my neck over my shoulder and gather just enough breath to scream into the smoky, shell-rattled darkness, "MEDIC!"

Black spots dance before my eyes. One elbow collapses. Instead I put my arm across Peter's chest, as if that will keep him safe if we get hit again. His eyes move beneath his lids. When they flutter open I can tell he sees me. He opens his mouth, but blood comes before words. I wipe it from his chin with the sodden edge of my jacket.

"You're hit, too," he slurs. His lips are bluish, pupils dilated so much his irises are only slivers.

"I'm fine, Pete. It's nothing."

He moves his head weakly. "It's more than that..."

I feel a rush of air behind me and look up. Though my eyes have trouble focusing, I make out the forms of Fish and Lieutenant Greer. Fish drops to his knees and slips his arm beneath Peter's head just as I feel someone else catching me from beneath the arms and gently drawing me back. It's Berk, I realize, when he shouts for a medic. He guides me gently to lie on his overcoat spread over the snow. I turn my head to my left and see Fish and Greer crouched by Peter, and then a handful of other 3rd platoon guys appear. One takes off in search of a medic, but the other three cluster around Peter, too, and I can't see him anymore.

"Berk, wait." My head is on his knee. "Just let me see Pete..."

"We'll take care of him. Of both of you," Berk answers. "Just try to relax now, okay?" I hear him mutter under his breath, "Where's that goddamn medic..."

I try to look at Peter again, but Berk guides my face away with a hand on my cheek. "Let's just worry about you for now," he says.

"Is he okay?"

Another figure comes tearing through the snow into the clearing. A couple feet from us, he stops and stares.

"Hey, pal!" Berk snaps. "You a medic or not?"

"I, uh—yeah, sorry, sarge."

When Gillan can't seem to decide which of us to go to, Berk says, "Him first," and he must mean me because Gillan kneels beside me.

"No, Pete first. Peter's hit w-worse," I say, angling my head to the cluster of troopers around him. "I can wait..."

"I don't know about that." Berk nods to Gillan. "Stay."

I want to protest, but I haven't got much breath in me. Come to think of it, I can't breathe too well at all.

Gillan fumbles with the scissors and my jacket sleeve, then with the plasma tubing, and pokes my elbow like a pincushion a half dozen times before he gets a vein. He seems to remember what he should do only after he's begun to do something else, first trying to soak up the blood, then retracing his steps back to the sulfa powder that he sprinkles on my chest, then remembering to shine the penlight into my eyes and look into my mouth.

"That wheeze sounds like hell, Doc," murmurs Berk, and I glance up at him to answer when I realize he's talking to Gillan.

"I know. But all this, I don't know if I should touch it..."

Uncertainty, always comforting to hear in a medic's voice. Be faster if I did it myself.

"You know what, screw it." He begins pulling cut-up bedsheets from his kit to stuff me with. "Gotta stop the bleeding."

I drop my head to the side again as Berk pushes back my hair and talks in a soft monotone to me, the way I always do with wounded men. But as I'm watching the cluster gathered around Peter, I see Greer at his head turn to one of the privates.

What I hear is "forest," but what I know he must've said was "Send for Lieutenant Forrest."

Though Berk has his hand on my right shoulder, he isn't holding me down, and when I jerk away from him and Gillan, he's too caught off-guard to pull me back in time. The plasma tubing drags along the ground for a moment beside me, and then the needle breaks off in my arm as I crawl, still on my elbows, toward Peter and the opening beside Greer left by the private who was sent for the chaplain.

My words come out choked, thick with blood but clear enough: "Why aren't you helping him?!"

Voices carry over one another and someone tells me to stay back, but no one answers me. The privates just huddle closer together to block me from getting in, all sitting there uselessly while Peter loses more blood and sinks deeper into shock.

"You need to let us take care of him and you." Greer raises his voice above everyone else. My vision is still out of focus so that all the figures triple before me like a kaleidoscope. The other faces are washed-out, featureless. Greer's voice adds, "Let Gillan do his job, Dare. Let him help you."

"He's not doing his job!" I shout, "Peter's alive, he needs a medic, not a chaplain—"

Berk holds onto me by the shoulders. Then I'm on my back, feeling like a dog taken out back to be shot.

"Let me go, you have to let me go!" I plead. "Stop, please stop—let me go, let me go!"

I arch my back and push against them as incoherent words pour from my mouth. Red faces and shouting mouths float above me. It feels as if someone is squeezing my lungs in a tight fist, wringing every last breath out of me like water from a rag. A paroxysm of coughing brings up more blood and silences me for a few moments. Out of the corner of my eye, I see a pile of soaked red cloths growing beside Gillan's leg.

And that's also when I see the lone figure of the chaplain appearing out of the night.

He goes to Peter's side. Kneels beside Greer and Fish, touches his hand to Peter's forehead as his other hand clutches his New Testament.

I could save him. They're just letting him die, and he can't die. He has to go home to Milwaukee and marry Chrissy on the train platform and kiss his parents and swim in Tichigan Lake again, and they've all just given up.

"PETER!" I scream, though it doesn't sound like his name at all. I raise my head to see Forrest's mouth move. With horror I understand the words from Philippians: *This will turn out for my deliverance...*

Their arms draw me back once more, creating a barrier between Peter and me.

"I'm going to give him some morphine as a sedative. Should help with his pain, too."

My eyes move from Forrest and Peter to Gillan's white hands glowing in the moonlight and the syrette between his fingers sucking up the morphine dose from the little metal tube. Shit. He doesn't know what he's doing. He's going to kill me in the name of comfort.

And if I black out, give in to the morphine dampening my lungs, then I won't be with Peter when he goes, too.

"No—no, s-stop, you d-don't—no," I choke out, trying to reach for Gillan's hand, but my fingers only brush Berk's arm. "Stop..."

I fling my head to the side, try to gather any remnants of strength in me to scream at him to stop, maybe ask him if he'd like to fill out my tag for the graves crew while he's at it. But they seem to think that I'm thrashing in pain. I look for Peter one last time and see only his dark head on Greer's knee. Lieutenant Forrest has his hand on Peter's chest as he prays.

In that moment of distraction, Gillan stabs the needle into my left bicep.

"Richard, hang on," Berk says. "The ambulance is coming..."

I tell myself to stay awake, to not let go. To be Peter's witness till the end. But I can't breathe, and the blood drenching my chest is so strangely warm. I wonder if Gillan knew after all that morphine is a respiratory depressant, and administered it on purpose as a last comfort.

The last thing I hear before I sink into the darkness is Forrest murmuring "and the glory forever" to Peter.

XXVII.
PRODIGAL

1 February 1946

Yellow lamplight casts my looming shadow on the white wall of the surgery. I arrange the bottles and tins how Linstead likes in the glass-fronted cabinet that stretches from the floor to the ceiling. From the radio on the windowsill that looks out onto the back alley, Edward R. Murrow gravely reports on the ongoing labor strike of more than half a million steel workers in the Middle West. I wonder what a labor strike would look like in Caspar's textile mills, if the Francos and poor Americans could ever get themselves organized. Most evenings I can't stomach listening to the news, but Linstead turned it on, and in an unexpected way Murrow's voice is almost comforting.

"Richard," says Linstead from his desk across the room, rustling some papers, "why don't you head on home? Finish that up on Monday."

I shut the cabinet with a click. "If you're sure."

"Of course, it's a Friday night. Shouldn't you be at the hotel with your friends?"

"I guess none of us have really felt like dancing lately."

The wheels of his rolling desk chair clatter over the wood floor. I glance back at him. His white head is bent before the dark-stained bookcase, where he keeps tight rows of medical volumes, all leather-bound and thick with dust. He pops back up holding the glass neck of a bottle of White Label scotch.

"Then have a drink with me." He reaches into his desk drawer and produces two drinking glasses. I hesitate, and he laughs. "It's all right. I promise not to tell your doctor."

I guess I wouldn't mind an excuse to put off going home. So I sit across from Linstead in one of the oak chairs meant for patients, and say thanks when he passes me a glass, filled a quarter of the way with amber scotch.

He pours out one for himself and says, "I wouldn't consider this a habit of mine, but sometimes, in this line of work, a little nightcap takes the edge off the nerves. Yes, even I have my irritations. And then there's you—if anyone could use a sedative."

"Is that a diagnosis?"

"Call it a prescription." He takes a sip and tilts his head, listening to Murrow move on to news from the White House. "How are you sleeping?"

I roll the bottom rim of the glass on the arm of my chair. "Actually, it's strange...you know I was barely sleeping at all last year, but since the surgery..."

Linstead raises an eyebrow, a gentle reassurance for me to continue, so I do.

"Since the surgery I've slept more than I ever have, and I'm more exhausted than I've ever been." I swallow most of the scotch in one go—the corner of Linstead's mouth lifts—and add, "It isn't like last year's exhaustion. I don't know how to explain it. Heavier. Sometimes I feel I haven't woken up at all, and all day I can't wait to crawl back into bed."

"So you sleep, say, ten or eleven hours, without nightmares?"

Caught off guard, I glance up and say, "No. Not without nightmares."

"I expected not." He leans back in his chair. "Do you know how often you wake up?"

"I don't know. Couple times an hour."

"That must be exhausting."

Feeling a red flush in my cheeks, I just shake my head. "It's okay."

"Well, you can't go on like that forever. But it sounds to me like good old-fashioned insomnia wearing a mask. Insomnia runs in your family, on both sides, if I recall correctly?"

"My dad, which you know. And my grandmother talks about how my uncle Laurence never slept, either. God rest his soul," I add.

"Yes." Linstead spins the scotch glass between his fingers. "What's it, now, almost...twenty-three, twenty-four years since he died? Hard to believe. Such a tragedy."

I frown, mid-swallow. "Twenty-four? No, he died in 1918. At the Somme. That's not quite twenty-eight years."

A strange, fleeting expression passes over Linstead's face. He takes a sip and says, "Yes, of course, I must be misremembering—it's been even longer than I thought."

"Oh. Okay."

We're both silent. Linstead watches his glass as though it's a mirror to the past and something is there only he can see. I know the inscription on Uncle Laurence's gravestone in the church cemetery by heart: "Laurence Anatolios Kalikredes, beloved son and brother, eternally at rest in the Lord, 1897-1918."

No, that's not right. There are no birth and death dates on his grave. My mind tries to fill them in, but I know they aren't there. The inscription ends with "LORD" in carved capitals.

The clink of my glass on the desk catches Linstead's attention. "Thanks for the drink, but I—I need to get home," I say, standing up quickly. "I'll see you Monday."

"Yes," he says, and looks up at me with that same strange expression I can't place. "Yes, I'll see you then. Goodnight, Richard."

Twilight clouds outlined in gold hang over Main Street, though an ominous sky is swift at their heels. I pull my coat collar up around my neck and walk home, hopping over patches of ice in the road. I don't try to catch my fragmented thoughts. This is irrational. Linstead misremembered the years; he said it himself. But what was that expression and the silence that followed it, a silence heavy with something he knows and I don't?

The screen door on the porch is swinging shut when I reach Queen Street and see our house. I stand for a moment in the empty road and stare at it. Pillar of the community, that's what my grandfather calls it. The Kalikredes and the Dares are respectable folks. Nothing ever to gossip about, no skeletons in the closets of the pretty white house on the corner of Holland Road—only what a shame about that poor dear boy Laurence.

I run across the street, up the porch steps, and open the screen door. The kitchen is warm and smells like fresh bread. My eyes sting in the yellow light. Hen barks at me, momentarily distracted from watching for scraps from Mom chopping something at the counter. Dad is at the table, the household accounts spread out before him, and Laurie is hanging his coat and scarf on the hooks by the door and saying something about the high school baseball team starting spring training—

Standing in the doorway, I say, "Did you lie to us?"

Dad looks up at me, his glasses in his hand, as Laurie glances at me with a look of annoyance at being cut off.

"Come again?" Dad says.

"Hello to you, too, and what are you talking about, *yiannaki?*" Mom says as she dumps the cutting board of chopped carrots into a pot on the stove.

"Uncle Laurence. Did you lie to us? Did he die in 1918 at the Somme?"

Mom's shoulders stiffen, though I can't see her face. So I look to Dad. His eyes drop to the table, closing for a second. Then he and Mom look at one another, and I feel Laurie glancing in confusion from me to them. Something unspoken seems to pass between them, a signal, as if they've already rehearsed this moment.

Mom leaves the pot simmering on the stove. Dad stands and holds out a chair for her and she sits, pressing her hands to her face, then letting them fall as she stares out the window over the table.

Dad says, "Why don't you both sit down?"

But I say "I'm fine here," and Laurie doesn't move, either.

I cross my arms, waiting. Finally, Dad says, "You wouldn't have understood if we'd told you when you were younger. But we shouldn't have waited so long."

I bite my tongue to keep from asking if they were ever going to tell us.

"Laurence did serve in the Great War," Dad continues, "and he was wounded at the Somme in 1918. But he came home to Caspar. Alive. We had four more years with him, or you did, Lizzie—I didn't meet him until I came here in 1920. Your grandfather would probably say a clean break might've been easier, in the long run—if he'd died in France. At least they wouldn't have had their hope taken away a second time."

Hen curls up on Mom's feet and thumps her tail once on the floor. Mom sets her elbow on the table and rests her chin on it, appearing to watch me, but her eyes are staring into nothing.

"How?" I say.

Dad glances up, his face holding the same expression Dr. Linstead's did. Watching the past play out before him. "What's that?"

"How was it taken away?" The kitchen is quiet, only the broth bubbling on the stove. When neither of them answers, I add, "If you're going to finally tell us the truth, you might as well tell all of it. How'd he do it? Did he string himself up from the porch rafters with his belt? Jump off the Alewife bridge? Did you drag the river for him, or is there even a body beneath that gravestone?"

Mom presses her hands to her face again. Dad brushes her hair from her neck and says quietly, "Maybe we should talk about this another time, Lizzie."

"No," she says, dropping her hands. A tear has cut a narrow track down her left cheek. "No, the boys have a right to know."

For all his life revolving around words, Dad seems at a loss to find any now. He starts and hesitates and goes quiet.

"You can tell us," I say. "That he killed himself. They would've called it shell shock back then. That's what it was, wasn't it? How'd he d—"

"He shot himself in the head with a revolver, out there in the yard at midnight. Three months before you were born. March of '22."

Dad and I stare at one another.

"Where'd he get the revolver?"

"I don't know. We've never known."

"Were you there?"

His silence is enough of a confirmation. I laugh, which is the worst thing I could do. I don't really care. "And in the last year, you never once thought that might be something I'd like to know? Why did you lie about this for so long?"

"It was wrong to keep it from you, from both of you," Dad says, glancing from me to Laurie, "and if you can forgive—"

"Did Nana and Pop ask you to lie? Because him dying in the war, that's the story they've always told. Maybe they even believe it now."

Mom takes a deep breath and looks at me. "The Laurence we knew—the brother I loved—as far as I'm concerned, he did die in France. He never really did come home after that."

"No wonder he shot himself, then, if you treated him like that!" My voice rises. "Were you waiting for him to just be himself again, so things could go back to how they were before?"

She closes her eyes, bites her lip. Her face is creased with worry lines. Good. I want to be vicious, so the two of them feel what I feel: a helpless fury with no place to go.

"So he felt like he was a burden."

"Richard," Dad says, his tone a warning bell.

"What if I have the same bad blood as him?"

The words linger in the kitchen for a long time. Too long. Laurie bites at his fingernail, glancing from them to me.

"It was never our intention to hurt you, although I know intentions don't matter now because we did hurt you. And I'm sorry for that." Dad takes a step toward me, but I step back, angling away from him. "Laurence was the best man I ever knew, and we never wanted you two to know him as anything else."

"Better a dead war hero than a suicidal veteran," I say.

"You know that's not true." Mom straightens her shoulders. "Laurence was a hero, and so are you."

"Have you even been listening?"

"Richard, you and Laurence both—"

"Don't call me a fucking hero!" I shout, and no sooner have the words left my mouth than a stinging backhand meets my cheek, so hard that white stars dance in my vision. I stagger back and press my hand to it.

"I will do it again if you ever so much as think of speaking to your mother that way." Dad's voice is low and perfectly measured. "We raised you better than this."

Slowly, the touch of his hand still smarting, I lift my head to look at him. He watches me inscrutably. I can't make out any hint of anger, or even disappointment, the one thing I've been so afraid of for so long. But that disappointment might be easier to bear than this nothingness.

I turn my back to them, swipe the keys to the truck from the hook, and go out, expecting the screen door to fall shut behind me. But of course it doesn't. I hear him on the porch as I trudge across the yard.

"Richard—"

"Don't try to pin this on me." I stop, consider, and then turn to face him. "You're the one who lied to me my whole life."

"I think tempers are running high," he says, crossing his arms over his chest more from the cold than to make a bodily point, it seems. "Why don't you come back in and we'll talk? Calmly, this time."

I laugh, my breath going out before me as I answer, "Not a fucking chance."

F irst I went to the covered bridge that joins the banks of the Alewife, where the open gap between the roof and the railing is big enough that Laurence could've jumped if he hadn't been able to get his hands on a revolver. People have jumped. Mill workers, men during the Depression who lost all hope. The summer I was fourteen they fished the bodies of three Franco men out, once a month like clockwork, June, July, August. But then I thought that if Dad comes after me, the bridge is the first place he'll look. And if any car's headlights happened to cut through the evening gloom to cross the bridge, from the mill on the other side back to Caspar, they would've seen the minister's son leaning a little too far over the railing, shoulders hunched, watching the churning black water below. Well, a person wouldn't have known it was me at first. But then the headlights would've swept my face and whoever it was would have a second or two of shock, because no one comes to the bridge in winter but for two reasons—to cross it, and the other.

So I got back into the truck, turned off the headlights, and pulled off the road not far from the bridge, in a patch of muddy grass. I sit here now thinking that if I'd really meant to do anything at the bridge, I'd have done it, not driven away. I couldn't even go through with that.

I tilt my head back against the headrest and close my eyes, though the night is impenetrably dark for miles around.

What if I have the same bad blood as him?

They didn't answer. It's a wonder they didn't try to hold me down the day I went to the recruiting office, though a memory comes to mind now I'd long since forgotten: Dad, in the kitchen that evening, the color draining from his face when I came in from the porch with my enlistment papers in hand. As if he felt a ghost at his back.

Why didn't he reassure me no, of course not—you're not Laurence, there's no need to be afraid? I still would be, but I'd have liked to hear him say it. For him to tell me I'm not a burden, that he isn't exhausted because of me.

But he is. They all are. They're sick of the nightmares, the screaming in the middle of the night, the knife's edge my moods balance on, the unjustified anger at the smallest of irritations, the bitterness I can't stop dredging up. It can't go on this way. They lied to me, but that's beginning to seem insignificant held up against the misery I bring into that house. For almost a year I've haunted it, moving through it unalive and yet not dead as I should be.

I wish I'd died on the ground in the snow in the woods above Stavelot. And by wish, I mean that I'm suddenly so desperate for that alternative that the thought makes my stomach hurt. I was the one who never heard the whistle of the shell as it arced over us. It should've been me.

"Guess I have to do everything myself, huh?" I say into the darkness. "Same as Laurence."

God could've at least shown me that one mercy. Letting me die there so no one who loves me could see me this way.

Something sharp brushes my chest beneath my jacket when I move my arm from the window. I forgot I'm still carrying those. And all of a sudden—lacing those sharp little objects together with the thought that if God refuses to have mercy on me, at least I could have mercy on myself—I turn the keys in the ignition, spin the tires in the slush, and turn the wheel, the gables of the covered bridge receding in my rearview mirror in the taillight glow.

The streets are empty. Lights, lemon and sea green and rose, emanate from the windows of white houses cold in the winter darkness. I turn down Main Street so as to avoid driving past the house. *Nothing will happen,* I tell myself, losing the steely nerves that gripped me near the bridge. *You just need to talk to Him. You're not Laurence. You're not going to blow your brains out in the front yard.* And these, in my pocket—I won't use them. I'll bury them by his headstone. No, the ground's too frozen. Well, I'll get rid of them, somehow.

I pull up to the curb in front of the church and stare out the window. There are no lights on inside. No one else is around. This might be the last place he'd think to look for me.

Sleet has begun to fall as I get out and hold my coat over my head. I run up the stone steps to the big double doors. Cold drops fall past the neck of my sweater. Three times I check over my shoulder while I search by feel for the key on my ring, expecting to see Dad's figure walking down Holland, or the headlights of the station wagon flickering on the slick pavement. But no one appears and I turn the key, and the door on the right gives, groaning open as if welcoming me into a tomb.

Foxholes and graves, I think.

The sanctuary is cool and silent. My wet boots leave a trail across the wood as I walk slowly down the center aisle, touching the edge of each pew on the left. Each footstep echoes up into the rafters of the vaulted ceiling.

I raised you better than this, he said, and I wanted to cry, *Yes, you did. If you only had any idea what you mean by that.* I know what he meant. He raised me on that hard, white-painted pew, on his right when he looked out over the congregation, and he taught me to fear God. I could try to make myself believe that I lost my faith in the blue rain at Hunnerpark, or on the river bluffs above Trois-Ponts, or any of the other hundred places that broke me. But that wouldn't be the truth. Because I can still hear Forrest's words as I lay on my back in a pool of my own blood in the Stavelot woods: *and the glory forever,* the tail end of the Lord's prayer.

Lord remember us. Those were the last words in my mind before the morphine sucked me under.

Had I expected to make it home, I would've never prayed that. *God, remember me.* God, please stop remembering me. *Lift your hand from me.* If you had remembered and loved me.

"But you don't." I climb the three steps up to the pulpit and fish out the box of matches Dad keeps there. I go back down and strike the flint, holding the flame to one of the votives on the communion table where the silver cup and the dish sit empty. I light two more and shake the match out, leaving a little ribbon of curling smoke in the air, then continue, "I don't know why I'm talking to you. There's no reason you should listen to me. But do you find it as ironic as I do—? That I believe you're here. I'm not an atheist. I know you hear me."

I drop the spent match on the floor and stamp my wet boot on it just in case. Stuffing my hands in my jacket pockets, I stare up at the white cross in the stained glass above the altar. On clear Sunday mornings, the sun shines so bright through that glass you have to look away. Sleet pelts against it. I close my eyes and try to hear the hymns that resonate in this big room on those mornings. But all I hear is silence.

"Why did you bring me home?" I crane my neck to stare into the ceiling vaults, as if I might see the Lord up there watching me. "That was the one mercy you could've given me. The one." My voice cracks at the end. "How many hundreds of thousands of people died in this war, people who wanted their lives, and you couldn't let me be one of them?"

I sit on the steps to the pulpit and stare out across the sanctuary, all grainy shadows except for the wavering tangerine light of the votives on the communion table just below me. "That's all I'm asking you. You don't even have to give me any hope. Did Laurence pray the same thing? Is it a curse of ministers' sons in this town to go to war and then kill themselves?"

Sudden resolve runs through me. Before it can recede, I say, "I'll do it myself if you won't. I'll do it, and then they can find my fucking body here tomorrow on the floor, and then what'll you do about their grief? Would it change your mind?"

I reach inside my jacket and pull out the fistful of razor blades I've carried with me ever since the night I returned home from the hospital in Augusta.

Offering them up, palm open, like Dad at the communion table blessing the bread sacrament, I say, "I don't want you to love me. Just so as we're clear on that. I think I've had enough of that kind of love."

I upend my palm and let three of the blades slide to the floor, where they fall heavy as ball bearings. One remains in my hand.

Then I back into the aisle, before the altar, before the stained-glass cross and the lamb beside it and the shepherd's hook and the olive branch. I hold up my left wrist, as if God has moved from the rafters to the window and is having a good laugh at this whole spectacle.

Blood bright as scarlet poppies trickles out of the slit in my skin. Not deep enough, though. It'll stop bleeding on its own, leave little more than a white thread of scar tissue.

Deeper.

I hold my fist out before me as the thin trickle drips into my jacket and sweater sleeves, reclutantly, and not very much of it. Why the fuck can't it go any faster?

"None of you have listened to me," I whisper. I mean it at God first and then at the others, seeing their faces flicker in and out. My parents and Laurie and Grace. Berk holding me down while the medic Gillan—the only one who ever gave me a chance at death—stabbed morphine into my shoulder. "I've begged for one thing, and none of you have understood that..." Then the other wrist, again not enough, producing only enough blood to fill a thimble. I make a sound of frustration and say, "Why can't you even let me do this?"

The anger overrides whatever lingering fear held me back. I will not be a coward about it. Touching the flat blade to the pathetic cut on my left wrist, I think about the cleansing feeling of that pain when it finally snags deep enough to put a stopper on this misery.

Then I hear the creak of the doors opening. Glancing over my shoulder, I see the figure silhouetted in the arched doorframe.

"Richard," he says softly.

My name echoes in the empty sanctuary.

"Come any closer, and I will do it." I stare at him, feeling no fear. "I promise I will."

He holds up both hands. For a moment there's no sound, till he gingerly puts one foot before the other and advances a step. I grit my teeth as he says, hands still in the air like I have Laurence's revolver in my hand, "Richard, I know you're angry with me. So take that anger out on me, not on yourself."

"It's not about that."

"What is it about, then?"

I look back at the silver glint of the blade against my skin.

"Funny," I say, eyes going back to him. "How many veins I clamped during the war."

"If you put that down, we could talk. We could talk about anything you want," Dad says. His voice carries across the sanctuary. "Or we could just sit, and you don't have to say a word. I won't make you."

I wonder if this is the speech he used on Laurence. Does he think it'll work this time? I think of how I felt in Nijmegen, the strange hunger to make my parents grieve.

Dad takes another step and another. And I see it's no use trying to keep him away because he'll come anyway, so instead of trying to stop him, I press the blade deeper.

It makes no difference how close he is if the job gets done.

He doesn't shout my name or tell me not to do it. In fact, it's that lack of distraction from him that surprises me in the end. Because as I stare at the confluence of the razor blade with the thin trail of ruby-red blood against my skin, a beautiful stillness resonates through the church, almost as if bells had been ringing and then suddenly went silent. I hesitate, lifting my face to the rafters. And in that moment, he appears beside me and grabs me by both wrists.

"Stop, Dad, listen to me—"

"I am not letting you do this," he says without raising his voice.

"Stop, let me go!" I twist in his grasp and try to yank myself away from him, but he's too strong. "I'm so fucking sick of you thinking you know what I need!"

"Richard—"

"Stop, Dad, just stop. Just let me fucking go!"

In one deft motion he gets the razor blade from me, drops it to the floor, and kicks it and the others away. And when he does so I feel a swelling rage bursting up through my chest, undoing all the surgeries and sutures, splitting the healed bones that were fractured, a ripping apart of every thread that sewed me back together. I don't even know what the words are that are pouring from my mouth except that I'm shouting at him till there aren't any words, and the church and him are drenched in a crimson film like the bloody river my body left in the snow. And still he grips my wrists like he means to manacle them.

"I will not let you go. Richard. Listen to me."

His voice is full of something I don't understand. Despite my attempts to wrench myself from his hands, he doesn't shout. He doesn't jerk me away from the altar to drag me home.

"Richard," he says again, and I realize that the stillness in his voice is the same note I heard moments ago, still lingering lightly in the church like the after-scent of perfume. "Richard, I'm not letting go."

I don't know what compels me to meet his eyes. But I do. Those steadfast gray eyes that followed me across continents, that welcomed me home, holding me now in their stillness as I stop struggling.

And I hear a voice—no, not hear—I feel the words resonate through the rage-swept places in me:

Get up, child.

I look from Dad to the stained-glass cross. And I hear my own voice, humiliatingly small.

"I can't..."

"Yes, you can," Dad murmurs. "Whatever it is, you still can."

On your feet, soldier.

You stand and fight.

But what was the war for me, if not always dropping on my knees beside the helpless?

I should've died when Gillan gave me morphine, but somehow I didn't. Somehow I made it for hours more to the triage station of a field hospital in Liege, where a nurse screamed for oxygen and fit the mask over my face as I gasped.

You took me away to die in the wilderness. And then you didn't let me.

The fight goes out of my wrists. I look again at Dad, watching me in all earnestness, his fingers gentle in the cut places where blood dries on my skin.

A weight falls in on me, a weight so unbearable in its lightness that it feels like the breath beaten out of me. The same splitting rage that broke through me moments ago returns. This time it feels like grief. But there in the midst of it, in the deep snow and the blood, is a light.

And again: *Get up, child.*

Which I suddenly understand really means, *On your knees.*

He catches me under the arms as I collapse into him. He backs against the edge of the pew and holds me as I press my face to his shoulder, chest shaking as it did at the field hospital, only it isn't oxygen deficiency wringing out my lungs but crying like I've never felt before. Sobbing silently till his shirt is wet beneath my cheek.

We sink to the cold floor, his arms still around me. His hand moves through my hair. I don't know how long the purging lasts, only that I can't stop. To be someone's child and then to go to war are two things that can never be reconciled. And the war I saw, the war I had my hands in, is something for which I can never atone.

But then I have a thought so painful that I try to twist away from Dad's arms as though to hide from it: *Maybe there is nothing to be atoned for.*

Maybe it's already finished.

I have to give up something. The ones who gave up everything had no choice which parts of themselves to parcel out. Where did death take them? To the house with the lit windows and the open door and the full table, the many rooms? Or somewhere that would make burned-out Nijmegen look like a luxurious paradise?

I raise my head. "I'm sorry," I whisper, meeting his eyes as I draw the sleeve of my jacket across my nose. "I'm so sorry about what I said, to you and to Mom, but more than that, for being...this way."

The sound of his voice makes me cry more. "First," he answers, "all's forgiven about what was said, if you can forgive me, too. And second, I'm not accepting that other apology because there's no need for it. I am sorry for making you feel that you're a burden." After a moment, he adds, "I love you. I haven't told you that enough."

All I've wanted for ten months has been to come home. And now I know I never will, not in the way I longed for. This is the closest I'll ever come. I don't want to ever forget how it feels to sit here with him, his undivided attention on me, his arms around me the strongest protection in the world. No fuss, no glory. *Just to be with you.* So we sit for a long time, the blood dried on my wrists, watching the candlelight waver in the darkness.

Emmanuel, I think. God with us. God sitting in the pew behind Dad's shoulder. God on his stomach in the prickly dead grass with us on Biazza. God on the other side of Jacob in the rain, crying too. God weeping at the paratroopers hanged in the trees in Ste.-Mere-Eglise. I suppose you could ask why he didn't stop it. But I've spent so long wandering those miserable circuituous questions. What if I came in out of the rain, instead? And left behind these altars to a bitterness I no longer want to call home?

After a long time has passed in quiet between us, I say, "There was something I'd always repeat to myself before a jump, or an attack."

When I hesitate, Dad nods at me to go on.

"Whatever it takes," I say, "whatever You ask of me. A sort of prayer, I guess. And I thought I knew what I meant by it. That if things came down to it, I'd die for any one of them."

Dad listens silently as he watches me. His arm is around me still. I don't want him to let go, especially not now, knowing what's coming.

"But I think I was wrong," I say, eyes falling to my lap. "It wasn't me promising God that I'd give myself up if that's what he asked. It was him asking me to give up everyone else. Lieutenant Walsh, Jacob...Peter."

I haven't spoken his name in more than a year. I've run out of tears, feeling only the scab of the latent grief scratched open to bleed.

He lets a couple moments pass before he says, "I've known for a few weeks that this was about Peter. You've been sleepwalking since the surgery, sometimes for hours at a time. Finally my insomnia is good for something, following you around and making sure you don't wander outside or fall down the stairs."

I glance up at him. "Really? Every night?"

"Most nights. At first I tried to guide you back to bed, but you know what they say about waking sleepwalkers, and you'd always find your way back out of your room again," Dad says. "And sometimes you talk. Different names come up, some of them I remember. But Peter is the one you say the most."

"So you already knew."

"You always seem to be looking for him. As if to put something right, was my impression."

To put something right. To pay a debt Peter never meant for me to owe but that I owe him anyway. Especially because in the last year, I've let his memory wither alone in me, instead of bringing it out into the light where everyone else can see it, too. I've let him die a second time.

"It was so sudden," I say. "The first—it was the first shell that hit me. And he..."

I stop, heart pounding so hard I can't breathe and talk at the same time. Dad guides my head back to his shoulder. I'm afraid that if I don't take this chance now, the window will close and I'll never be brave enough. So I force out the rest through a trembling voice. "Peter must've heard the whistle of the shell and I didn't, so I caught some of that first one before he pushed me down. He landed on me. I couldn't breathe at all. I don't know for sure, but I think it was his fall that broke my sternum. He was a football player. I never stood a chance."

I feel Dad nod.

"And then he..." I falter, feeling myself shaking, cold all over and yet flushed, too.

Dad says, "It's okay if you don't want to tell me."

"No, I—I do—I do want to tell you," I say, looking at him. Why did I ever think there would be judgment in those eyes if I told him the truth? It's as though I'm finally seeing him for the first time. And I don't see any of the things I feared so much, that I built up in my mind, the disappointment, the anger, the mistrust. It seems so ridiculous to have ever been afraid of those possibilties.

At last I say, "Peter would still be alive if he hadn't done it. That second shell would've killed me. And he put himself there instead. It didn't touch me at all."

Dad listens in silence. I feel his fingers curl a bit on my back.

"And I feel like I'll never know why he did it." My voice breaks, filling again with tears, making me angry because I don't want to cry anymore. "He's going to make me wonder that for the rest of my life."

"I think you already know," Dad says.

He's right, of course. But what do you do with all that love when it has nowhere to go, when it floods out? I know it's too much for me to bear. The past year of suppressing Peter's memory so deeply that not even my dreams could dredge up images of his face has taught me that.

Dad shifts his back against the hard wooden side of the pew. We're still sitting on the floor, the boards around us damp with the rainwater from our jackets and boots. "Thank you for telling me," he says. "I know it wasn't easy. But I also don't think that you want Peter to be forgotten, however much it hurts. So any time you'd like to talk, I'll listen."

"But how do people just...go on? After things like this?"

"I don't know if they do." Dad sighs. "I don't know if, after anything so painful, anyone does go on. Or if that part of ourselves dies in that moment and another part splits off and takes up the mantel, keeps going. Always to leave some piece of who we were behind with whatever we lost."

I turn my head to look at him, wondering how long he's let that thought simmer. But instead I see myself lying on the ground, cheek turned onto the bloody clumps of snow beside Berk's boots, throat raw from screaming at all of them, watching the shadow of the chaplain appearing beside Peter's shoulder. And I realize that part of me never got up out of that bloody snow. Part of me will always be crying out for Peter in those woods above Stavelot.

After a minute, I say, "Can I ask you something?"

"Of course."

"You said you were there when Uncle Laurence died?"

"I was."

"But you...saw it?"

He tilts his head in the slightest of nods, perhaps not wanting to give me any room to imagine that scene. I think I understand how he and Mom and our whole family could keep that secret for twenty-three years.

"When I left the veterans hospital in Massachusetts and came here," Dad says, "I really thought that part of my life was over, that closeness with the Great War veterans. But then I met the Kalikredes, and Laurence, and it was as if nothing had changed. I married into their family, and suddenly I was closer to the war than I had ever been at the hospital."

"And then I brought it all back." I wrap my arms around my knees, meet his eyes with a feeling of shame. "I knew I could break Mom's and Nana's hearts all over again and I still did it. But I never thought about you."

Dad shakes his head. "There was no point in me making that choice any more difficult for you."

We sit quietly, listening to the rain on the roof of the church. The single votive flame burns on. Its glow reflects on the white cross in the window.

"After he died," Dad says, "we planned on naming you Laurence, if you were a boy. But then when you were born your mother wouldn't even consider that. The wound was too fresh, I guess. Saved it for a year and then she got worried she'd never get to honor her brother, so we gave it to Laurie and christened him with that nickname the same day he was born." He straightens his shoulders and sighs. "I suppose it's a good thing we didn't name you that. You're not him, Richard. And you don't have any bad blood—and neither did he."

I still think it's true that he'll never fully understand what I tell him of my war. None of them will. But in the end, the grief all seems to look the same.

"Maybe not," I answer. "But it doesn't feel that way."

"I know. But it's true. You'll have to trust me on that."

And then he wraps both arms around my shoulders and reminds me that spring will come again and the open windows will let in the fresh wind through the house, and Caspar will be green, the foothills smelling so sweet it will be as if God soaked the grass and the wildflowers in perfume. He talks about how the church will look in the summer when the red trillium sprawls over Uncle Laurence's grave. We even talk about the truth, hard as it is for me to say, that coming home is never really coming home again. "Because I'm old enough to know that all true beauty has some ache," he murmurs, "and this isn't home, but someday we'll get there."

Before dawn, I awake, lying on the first pew before the altar with my head on his lap and his coat over my shoulders. Inexplicably, the sanctuary is warm. His eyes are closed and his cheek is resting on his hand, leaning on the arm of the pew. I reach up and take off his glasses and tuck them into the pocket of his shirt. Then, before the pale morning light makes its way to us from the eastern coast, I lay my head back down on his knee and fall asleep.

XXVIII.

GRACE

D awn hasn't yet washed the eastern sky when I come down to the docks and sit with my legs dangling over the steel-gray water lapping at the pilings. I tuck my chin into my coat as wind tosses the whitecaps, watching the lobster trawlers putting out, rusty hulls making for open water to haul in their bug traps. Fog shrouds the moon and stars. Over the past few days here I've found myself drawn to these morning preludes, when only the fishermen are awake. I watch the light come on in shades of dusty silver across the water, first awakening McFarland Island out in the harbor, then the other bank of Boothbay, where a white church steeple emerges through the mist.

When the sun rises I'll go back to the house and eat something. And then I'll write another letter. One letter for every day I'm here, though the last one won't arrive in Caspar till after I get home. After breakfast I'll take it to the post office on Oak Street, where the clerk might glance at the recipient and think, *Another to her.* My grandparents' house is full of books and magazines, and Pop told me he expected me to have worked halfway through his library by the time they return from visiting friends in Boston at the end of the week, but I haven't read anything for days except the New Testament I carried through Europe, carefully prying apart the pages stuck together with dried blood.

Their neighbors know me, so no one seems alarmed that I walk sometimes for hours on the quiet, hilly streets above the harbor. I wonder if they know I'm praying. At night I'll lie awake continuing the day's endless litany of thoughts as the scent of saltwater drifts through the crack between window and frame. I think of Peter and Fish and Berk and McNuts and Skinny and Greer and Jacob and Walsh, fastening memories for the times I saw each one happiest. I also think about how life goes on, all things considered. And boy, do I consider them. It's no one else's responsibility to make peace with my war.

What that means, I don't yet know. On the surface, little has changed since the night in the church. I finally have some color back in my cheeks, and when I see myself in the bathroom mirror I look a little less bony. But every night in Boothbay, I've woken up screaming, sometimes half a dozen times before dawn, the sheets tangled and sweaty around me. I know that God could take it away from me in a moment if he wanted, but he hasn't. So what if that's not punishment but grace?

If I'd never signed my life away to the Airborne, I'd most likely be a disillusioned academic picking apart his childhood faith piece by piece till any truth had been worn away. So I try to thank God for his severe mercy and the bandages he put in my hands. Besides, every morning I tell myself that I can't let Peter down. So I watch, walk, write, eat, pray, read the passages I've known by heart since childhood. The more I think about grace, the less I understand it. And so the more enamored with it I become.

Dad blamed himself that I came as close as I did that night, said he was wrong for not following me immediately. By the time he got to the bridge I was already gone. We must've been ships in the night. He said he didn't know what possessed him to go to the church—"well, I do, of course," he added. As far as I know, he hasn't said a word to my mom about what really happened.

But in the morning, after Mom all too easily forgave me, the four of us sat in the kitchen and they told Laurie and me everything. The story trails off in unresolved grief. Laurence killed himself three months before I was born. I'll never know how he really felt, or what he saw at the Somme. I suppose I can imagine it. Most people in Caspar didn't know it was suicide, except Dr. Linstead and Bill Withers, the sheriff at the time. And over the years, the stories obscured the truth, so from one person to another no one could agree if Laurence Kalikredes died in an automobile accident or fell from a ladder, or maybe he really did die in the Great War. The best-kept secret, Dad said, is the one you've forgotten isn't really the truth.

I swing my legs over the water and watch the white cross. At the table, as my parents talked of the past, I hoped it wasn't disrespectful to my uncle that when I looked out at the melting snow, I felt something split away from the sadness. The bad blood draining out, as if a curse was disintegrating before my eyes.

It was Dad's idea I come here. "Watch the house while your grandparents are away, and anyway, you could use a little time to yourself," he said. I was surprised he trusted me to be alone. But he seemed to understand that the few drops of blood I produced with the razor are something I'll never try again. There's light in the periphery now.

For that reason, someone in Caspar deserves to know that I'm also thinking about beginnings.

9 February 1946, Caspar, Maine

The tall pines on Queen Street stand like a company at attention as Hen runs ahead of me through the snowmelt. When we cross the bridge over the creek, she looks back at me with her wet tail swishing.

"Not today," I tell her, "but we'll play in the creek as soon as it's a little warmer."

I told myself that I would walk like a gentleman and be patient, but when I see the lane dipping into the valley and the white house at the bottom, with orange light filling its windows like dabs of paint, I can't hold it in. I run with Hen, feeling like a child as the wind cuts my cheeks. My scarf blows right off and I have to go back for it, a stripe of green plaid spilled in the slush, and I realize that I'm laughing with no one else around. Chunks of snow stick to the fur hanging down from Hen's tummy as she bounds along at my heels.

"Come on, Hen! She's waited long enough!"

As we run past the fence posts and under the bare arms of the willow tree, I rehearse everything I mean to say, most of which I came up with on the drive home from Boothbay last night. She might see me coming and tell Sidney or Lena to turn me away at the door—but it's not called a fool's hope for nothing.

When Hen and I are at the crest of the hill, the kitchen door opens. I slow to a stop. Grace appears on the porch. She shields her eyes with her hand to temper the glint of the pale sunlight off the bits of snow and watches me. Then she comes into the lane, and I run the rest of the way to her. A couple feet of cold mud separates us. She smells like rosewater but is wearing an old plaid coat, too big for her, over a dress and rubber boots. Her hair is loose, caught in the coat collar. She sticks her hands in the big pockets and says, "I was about to come out to feed the goats when we saw you. What're you doing running around like a headless chicken?"

"Before you feed the goats," I say as Hen sits dutifully beside me like a junior attorney and smacks her tail against the backs of my legs, "there's something I need to tell you. Well, a few things. Whether I tell you the others will depend on how you feel about the first. Which—that's up to you. You can send me on my way if you'd rather, Grace. I won't take it hard. But at least let me tell you this first one because it's the most important. And if you want me to go after, I'll g—"

"Richard Dare, one of these days you'll drive me all the way to the insane asylum," Grace interrupts, raising her eyebrows and giving me her "quit your nonsense" expression.

"Yes, I know, sorry." A deep breath. Hen's tail thumps me encouragingly. And, of course, I've forgotten every single thing I planned to say. But it might be more authentic this way, so I launch into it before I can think better of myself. "Grace, I never should've treated you how I did, and I am so sorry. I know I don't deserve it, but that's the thing I'm learning about forgiveness, that if I tried to earn it from you, you'd probably want even less to do with me. So if you're able to forgive me, I hope we can be friends again, because it depresses me too much to think about what my life would be otherwise. Without you."

I don't really know what I say after that. Grace listens with a polite and serious expression to the coherent half. At some point I realize she's been trying to get a word in, and finally she puts her hand on my shoulder and says, "Richard! Richard, stop."

She reaches into her coat pocket and takes out a bundle of envelopes tied with a red ribbon. "Did you forget you already told me all that?" Without untying the ribbon or opening any of the letters, she says, "February 3rd, 1946—did you put the year for posterity's sake, so our grandchildren will know when you wrote these?—February 3rd, you wrote, 'If you can forgive me, I'd love nothing more than to be friends as we were.' But that's not quite the truth, is it?"

Did she memorize all my letters? I don't even know what to say first. "...Grandchildren? Does that mean—" I shake my head. "Wait. Of course it's the truth. I wouldn't—"

"No, it's not." Grace tucks the bundle back in her pocket and looks at me with a smile playing at her mouth. "Be honest with me, Richard. You want so much more than friendship alone." She takes a step closer till there isn't much room between us. "Yes—grandchildren. Have you caught up yet?" Her fingers catch mine, tangling together. "Of course I forgive you. You know I already have."

We stand in the cold mud of the lane, beneath opaque clouds and the weak winter sun, and I say, around the rapid-fire beat of my heart, "Then you don't mind if I tell you the other things, too? You were right; you're always right. There is more, and I..."

I meant to say something about how long I've loved her, how I'll love her for the rest of my life, but my mind goes empty as she watches me, laughter in her green eyes, sunlight tinging her face. Instead I put one hand on the small of her back, the other on her cheek, and kiss her as I've always meant to.

She presses deeper into me, her mouth tasting inexplicably of apples. A flush rises in my cheeks. When I pull back just enough to breathe, she rests her forehead on mine and kisses me quick, the brush of a feather on my mouth.

"Was that the second thing you wanted to tell me?" she whispers.

I gather the ends of her hair from beneath the coat collar as she loops her arms around my neck. Hand in her hair, it takes a few moments to gather myself from the wind-knocked-out feeling. "Yes, and you seemed to take it well"—she laughs into my neck, just as I was getting my breath back—"so I'll take that as encouragement for this last one."

Wind whips against our chapped hands and cheeks as I untangle myself from her embrace, reach into the inner pocket of my coat for what

Sidney gave me on New Year's Eve, and drop to one knee right here in the slush.

"Oh," Grace says, staring at me in apparent shock. "Are you—I mean—I didn't know you were, that you meant to…"

"…Were we not just talking about our grandchildren?"

"Yes, but you—I didn't realize you actually—"

"Maybe I could just say everything first, and then we could hash out the details?"

She looks down at me as the light changes across her face. Without a word, she nods, then presses her knotted hands to her mouth.

"Anyway. Sorry to spring this on you when we've only just met," I say, and she rolls her eyes, "but I've already waited too long to do this, and I love you, Grace, so I don't see the point of waiting any longer." *You better not drop it,* I say to myself as I hold up the gold ring, an agate the color of her eyes perched on the peak. "Will you mar—"

In the middle of the sentence I come to an abrupt stop and hold up a finger, the ring still pinched in the fingers of my other hand. Grace raises one eyebrow, her expression hidden behind her hands. And then I sneeze. Twice.

Something between a squeak and a snort escapes from her.

We wait a few moments in suspended silence. Then I tumble out in a rush, "Gracewillyoumarryme?"

Without any hesitation, she kneels in the mud, too, and says, "We must look pretty silly to anyone watching." She kisses me again, and I feel her mouth smiling through it. "You know the answer. Yes. A thousand yeses. You know I want to be ridiculous with you for the rest of our lives."

She begins to laugh and I laugh, too. Hen is delighted, running in anxious, happy circles around us, fanning her tail through the mud so that it spatters in our eyes. "Hen!" Grace laughs as she fishes a handkerchief from her coat pocket and wipes my cheekbone with it. "We ought to get up before we're really in a sorry state."

We climb to our feet, steadied by one another's hands, and I slide the ring onto her finger even as we're both laughing.

"Yes?" I say, just to be sure.

"Yes, yes, yes. I don't want to wait, either." A grin lights her whole face, but it fades as she holds her hand out to catch the sunlight through the angles of the agate. She's quiet for a moment, then she says, "Richard, this looks just like my mother's engagement ring."

"It is hers." I take her other hand and intertwine our fingers as she stares at the ring, then up at me. "Sidney gave it to me on New Year's. At first I told him I didn't like him that way, and besides he's already married..."

She rolls her eyes again and smiles, although I see the glisten of tears. I add, "He kept it all this time, waiting for you."

"I thought they'd taken it." Grace draws her finger across the agate. She wipes the back of her hand beneath her eye and draws in her breath. "Our relatives. I thought it was gone forever."

"They didn't get quite everything."

Though it's still only February and there's nothing but mud in these pastures, I'm sure I can smell the honeysuckle on the breeze—or maybe it's just Grace's rosewater. I wrap my arms around her shoulders and set my chin on top of her head. When she relaxes into me, I feel her knuckles against my ribs; her fingers are still on the ring.

I want to hold her forever this way, afraid that if I let go, the dream will be lost. But it isn't a dream anymore, and I know that clenched fists are far more likely to lose the very thing they try to hold. She said yes. Neither of us are carrying our love for the other alone.

"Do you think our children will love the farm as much we have?" Grace says softly.

"I think I have to marry you first before you can say things like that."
I look at the half-frozen cow pond, folded like a silver dollar into the side
of the hill. "I hope so, but maybe we should let ourselves see some other
places before we settle back on Caspar."

"Not enough nightlife for you?"

"Just a few too many people who know us too well."

Grace laughs. "I can see us in a little shoebox apartment in Boston. On
Comm Ave, so we can have cherry blossoms blooming in our windows
in May."

"So the bees will walk right off the flowers and into our room," I add,
and she laughs again. "I probably have a better chance of finishing my
degree in Boston than I do here."

"Something to think about," Grace says, turning to look out at the
farm, too.

I do—I think about the summers we'll have together, wherever we
live, and our children playing in the cow pond like we did. Finding our
own place to call home and laughing with her till I have new lines by my
eyes to show for it.

But old fears still lurk, even in a light-filled future. Maybe because
they're neither strong nor brave enough to show themselves in the open.
Maybe because they know that at the end of the story, they're beat.
Whatever their reason, I know those fears are still part of me, waiting for
their moment when my footing isn't as sure as it is here.

"Grace."

"Mhm?"

"When you asked me to tell you about it, about everything, and I said
all that about you not understanding?"

"I know. It's okay."

"No, I just—I still don't know what to tell you, or if I'll...ever be able
to, but I..."

She doesn't say a word, lifting her head and meeting my eyes as I fumble for the right words. Starts and stops, like learning to breathe again. I think of that evening in the kitchen last summer, when she told me about the relatives who raised her and Sidney. She opened a window into the truth even though her voice shook. And I didn't see everything through that reflection, but I saw enough to understand how much more was behind the glass. Everything I hope she'll tell me someday.

"I might've told you how I feel sooner if I hadn't been afraid to let you see into this," I say. "And my instinct, still, is to shield you from it, from me, but that's not fair to you because you have just as much choice in this as I do. But there's—I'm still..."

When I don't know how to go on, Grace takes my hand and begins walking toward the orchard. I follow, letting her lead me. We walk beneath the tangled arms of the apple trees and out the other side to the lower pastures. A thin skein of ice floats over the pond. Her hand is warm in mine as the wind blows, brushing her hair back, turning her cheeks pink. She looks at me, squinting a bit as the sun behind my head casts opalescent patterns across the ice.

"Richard, whether you told me the whole war or never said a word of it, I could never love you less," she says in a soft voice almost lost to the wind. "Do you ever wonder what would've happened if you hadn't gone? If we'd ever be together?" She smiles. "I meant what I said. That I fell in love with you after you came home. So all the memories, everything you don't have answers for...everything you never asked for. Those aren't annoyances to me. They're part of you, and I think love is a choice, and I'm choosing all of that. All of you."

Holding both my hands, she tips up on her toes and kisses me, light as a summer morning and heavy as a marriage vow. I stumble a step forward and she stumbles one back to keep us from falling and breaking through the ice, and then we're laughing again. We steady one another's arms and Grace, still smiling, puts her head on my shoulder. Suddenly I think of Peter and me in his foxhole in Stavelot that last night, huddled for warmth and looking at photos of our girls. He never got to propose to Chrissy on the train platform. And for a moment the grief of that is so heavy that my grip on Grace loosens.

"Are you okay?"

"Yes, I..."

Grace tightens her hand in mine. Peter and Chrissy will never get to have this. For that reason, I know what a waste he would consider it if I continued to punish myself.

"Just thinking about a friend," I answer.

Grace nods, and then we begin to walk slowly past the pond and across the pasture, just wandering so that we don't have to let go. "Tell me about him someday?"

"I will." I press her hand, and this time I mean it.

XXIX.

GLORY

12 February 1946

The waitress comes round to fill my coffee a second time. She empties the pot into my mug and says "sure" when I tell her thank you, which is an improvement over the thousand-yard stare she gave me when I came in. I chew the eraser on the end of my pencil and try to think of a fifteen-letter answer to forty-three across, *Cooper's 1932 turn in a Hemingway classic,* though my attention is caught by the people passing on the sidewalk, watching for a raglan coat and a distinctive limp. Light snow has dusted the Rue des Châtaignes, a grand name for the dingy main road that runs through Petit Canada on the northwestern end of Caspar. I haven't ordered anything yet because I counted on him being late, and diner food loses its already-weak appeal when cold.

A Farewell to Arms, that shouldn't have taken so long. I move on to nineteen down, which is the first I've heard that Winston Churchill was born in a palace. Buckingham is two letters too long, and why would he have been born in Buckingham Palace, anyway?

"Blenheim," a voice says at my right shoulder. "Anyone ever tell you that you talk to yourself, Dick?"

"As a matter of fact, yes." I look up as Mattie shakes the snow from himself like a dog and slides in across the booth. "Spell that for me?"

"B-L-E-N-H-E-I-M. Don't tell me you were stationed in England and never heard the legend about how the prime minister was born in a lady's boudoir in Blenheim Palace."

I frown at him mid-*N*. "No, he wasn't."

"God's honest truth. Call him and ask if you don't believe me."

"You want me to call Winston Churchill and ask him if he was born in a lady's boudoir in Blenheim Palace?"

Mattie shrugs, stashes his coat in the corner of the booth, and reaches for my coffee before I even have a chance to protest. He drinks half the mug while I stare at him and reconsider the reason behind why I asked him to meet me for lunch. "You're the skeptic. Ew, is this black coffee, Dick? How do you drink this?" He finishes it off.

Unfortunately the word fits, so he might not be as full of shit as I assumed. At least not on that front. "You want anything?" I say. "It's on me."

"Awful kind. Why'd you choose this place? I've never seen an American in here. Has Chantal taken a shine to you?" He nods toward the grim-mouthed waitress. "She's an acquired taste."

"Jesus, Mattie, you didn't—"

"Oh," he says, and laughs. "No, not her. But I do like older women."

"That's as much as I need to know about that."

"Mm!" He makes a surprised noise. "What am I going on about? It's you we're celebrating, I should be buying you lunch! You've finally done it—you got the girl! I think you dashed quite a few dreams of Caspar Senior High's class of 1940, '41, whatever." He reaches across the formica tabletop, removes the pencil from my hand, and gives my hand a firm shake, while at the same time gesturing to Chantal. "Here's to playing the long game. Guess you knew what you were doing, after all."

"I wouldn't say that. It's more that Grace has an abundance of patience." I pause while Mattie orders for us both, I have no idea what, in French. Chantal must've been paying attention behind her newspaper because she silently takes away my mug and gives us two fresh ones. "But I appreciate the confidence."

"No, listen," Mattie says, dropping a sugar cube from the dish into his coffee, "I mean it. I really am happy for you and Grace. Can't think of two people I like more. Well, I like Grace, that's for sure. And I'll give you a free pass this time."

"We've come a long way since high school, then. But thanks, Mattie, means a lot."

"So what're we doing here?" He's still adding sugar, good God. He and Grace have alarmingly similar coffee habits. "Sorry I'm late, by the way, I guess I don't have to tell you what it's like getting out from under Wagner's nose at lunchtime. He eats early just so he can spy on us and make sure we don't take our breaks."

"Actually, that's sort of what I wanted to talk to you about."

He eyes me over the raised mug. "You've arranged for old Harlan to have an unexpected visit from the IRS?"

"Well, there's an idea—but not this time, sorry."

"Pity."

I cross my arms on the tabletop and say, "I can't solve that problem; I wish I could. But I might have the answer to another of your troubles. You know that apartment on Main Street, above the pharmacy? Don Harrels put it back up for rent yesterday. Apparently the two secretaries who lived there got better jobs in Portland, so they're out next week."

"Aw, isn't that nice for you and Grace? Your first apartment together. But aren't you worried about living in sin?"

I snort, unable to follow up on that comment as Chantal returns with toast and bacon and eggs.

"I don't care that it's twelve-thirty in the afternoon, we're eating breakfast," Mattie says.

After she's gone I finally say, "No, actually—Grace and I have decided that we're going to Boston after the wedding."

"And when's that?"

"June, if we can wait that long."

I expect him to have a strong opinion about us getting married so soon, even though it doesn't feel soon enough to me, but instead he just nods thoughtfully. "Well, I guess when you know, you know. Why Boston?"

"Seems like the right place to start a life together," I answer. "And I want to finish my degree, but I don't want to go back to Brown. So I'm thinking BU, like Grace. And in a few years we'll probably come back to Maine, you know, when we have too many kids to fit into a city apartment."

Mattie whistles and clinks his mug into mine as he says, "That's the spirit. Confidence!"

"Anyways." I press my hands flat to the tabletop, hoping to steer us back toward my original intention with this conversation. "I've been thinking that I need a place to live before getting married that isn't my parents' house. And you," I add, pointing at him with my fork, "are in need of a living situation that doesn't make you want to drink more after you're already drunk because of your shitty boss."

"A proposal?" Mattie says, raising his eyebrows. He eyes me with some suspicion, as if he's the outlaw at one end of Main Street and I'm the sheriff at the other. "You're on a roll with those, Dick. What's your angle? To keep an eye on me?"

"Yes. That *is* my angle. Because I think you need someone looking out for you. How's it going, looking out for yourself?"

He stares at me, opens his mouth, then is silent. That's what I thought. When he doesn't say anything, I continue, "It's only for three months, but I think it's enough time for you to get away from your mother, breathe a little, and decide where to go next. You're always saying how you should've gotten out of Caspar years ago." I lean forward on my elbows as Mattie leans further back. He looks as if he'd like to slither under the table. "Give yourself the chance to do that."

"The timing of it..." He works on shredding a paper napkin. At least he hasn't stormed out, so I'll consider that a win. "It's interesting, you know. Your boss and his wife just hired my sister Adrienne as their housekeeper. She's going to live with them."

"Linstead mentioned that. I think she'll be happy there; they're good people."

"I hope so. That's one of them taken care of. But the younger two, Félicité and Romy, I don't know..." He sets his elbow on the tabletop and bites at his fingernails, looking a little queasy at having to talk about his family. "Well, they already know how to take care of themselves. We all did. So maybe they don't really need me."

"Of course they need you. But maybe you'd be more help to them if you put a little distance between yourself and home. Keep your disability checks, save those up to get all three of them out of Caspar, if that's what you want."

"I guess I haven't thought that far ahead." Mattie empties the last of the coffee between our mugs.

"All I know is it's not going to get better just by hoping."

He takes a deep breath, drops his shoulders, and says, "I know. But sometimes I still can't believe I enlisted, because it felt like abandoning them, and since getting home I..." He shrugs again and smiles, though it isn't enough to cover the lines in his face that for a moment make him seem much older than twenty-four. "I guess I feel I owe it to them to be here for them now. Because I wasn't for three years. But, wonders never ceasing, I think you're right. The girls do deserve better. In Caspar, none of us will ever be more than dirty Francos. But if we could start somewhere fresh, they might at least have a chance in life."

"You've got to give yourself that chance, too."

Mattie runs a hand through his hair, glances out the window. "I could stay in Caspar for a few months anyway and keep an eye on Adrienne and the younger two. Knuckle under at the garage and keep working till Adri and I both have enough money to spit in Wagner's face and shake this town off us."

He runs a finger around the rim of his mug. The light coming through the window behind his head is so bright I have to squint to see his expression. For the first time since coming home, he doesn't look as if he's trying to hold gaping wounds closed with a single stitch. And that's enough to placate my anxiety for the time being.

"Think about what I said," I say, hoping he hears the understanding I want to convey. "If you think it would work."

"I will." Mattie nods. "Yeah, I will. You sure about this, us living together?"

"No, and don't make me regret offering."

He grins and finishes his coffee, then stretches out in the booth. "I'd say let's raise hell, but this is only Caspar."

Chantal brings the check to us, and Mattie snatches the slip before I can even retrieve my wallet. "Nuh-uh, Dick, you need to start saving those pennies for your wedding. And maybe," he adds, almost mumbling now, "sometimes you're smart, and I might owe you for all the wisdom..."

"Sorry, I didn't hear that last part." I lean forward on my elbows and give him the sort of pleasant smile I know makes him want to puke.

"You make me sick to my stomach. Get that shit-eating grin off your face before I knock it off."

"Don't you just want me around all the time?"

He snorts. "Oh, sure, you think you can be more annoying than me—I'd like to see you try, Dicky, old boy."

"I'm really beginning to love that nickname. Maybe I'll have Grace work it into her wedding vows."

"No!" Everyone else in the diner looks our way as Mattie hauls himself to his feet, pointing at me with his coffee spoon. "Nuh-uh, don't pretend to like something I've specifically crafted to irritate you! You can't just reclaim my hard work—"

"I can if you can't catch me."

He rolls his eyes and says, "Jesus Christ, what is this, fifth grade all over again?"

But when I make a dash for the diner door, he's on my tail, shouting that when we live together he'll answer my calls with, "Sorry, Dick can't come to the phone. He's recovering from his vasectomy. Can I take a message?"

23 February 1946

The porch door opens as I come down the stairs, carrying another cardboard box to add to the growing cluster in the kitchen. Mom shakes the snow from her coat and flips through the mail, saying, "Bill, bill, bill—oh, here's something from Mama, probably that dolmades recipe I asked her for..." She sets the envelopes on the table. "Aha, and one for you, *yiannaki*. Speaking of, don't forget to change your address with the post office."

"For me?"

"Better yet, don't change it at all, and your mail will come here." She sets a rectangular orange envelope on the box in my arms, something stiff inside, maybe to keep paper flat. "Then you'll have an excuse to come see us."

"The only excuse I need to come here is the baklava. And you, and you!" I add, jumping out of the way of her fly-swatter. Where'd that come from?

"That's right. I want you and Grace here for dinner at least once a week, before you up and leave us for Boston."

She disappears in the direction of Dad's study with the rest of the mail as I set the box on the kitchen floor and pick up the orange envelope. My name is scrawled on the front in a careless hand, as if whoever wrote it wasn't paying much attention to legibility.

I make out the return address first, *44 Islington St., Portsmouth, New Hampshire,* and then the messy name comes into focus.

Jack Fischer.

I stare at it so long all the letters begin to melt together. When I was in the English hospital I had a couple letters from him and Berk, even one from Lieutenant Greer, but the correspondence dropped off on all ends and I guess I've been afraid to pick it up. Afraid that out of the war, we're all such different people that we could never know one another as we did then. But now I feel a sweep of guilt for not being a better friend, for making Fish be the one to chase me down.

No one else is around, but I still go out to the porch. I kick snow off the top step and sit, envelope on my knees. Will opening it unravel all I've done these last few weeks? Because it's one thing to know that I'll always carry the war with me, but it's something else to consciously wade back into the past where the mortars still fall.

But Fish, quieter than the rest of us—who spent most of the crossing from the Brooklyn Navy Yard to the port in England on the deck of the troopship, sketching the smoke billows and the sailors and the clouds whose edges glowed gold on the horizon—wouldn't go to this trouble if it didn't matter to him.

So I break the seal and tilt the envelope to the side, carefully drawing out yet two more envelopes, one not much smaller than the outer packaging and one letter-sized. I open the letter first.

He writes that he hadn't looked at his drawings since he arrived home in July of last year. The Purple Hearts and all his combat jumps earned him the necessary points to be discharged while the regiment was in Austria as an occupying force after Germany surrendered, and once he made it back to Portsmouth—

well, Rev, I just didn't have the heart to look back at all this and remember it. It meant too much.

But I guess over the winter, the one-year anniversary of when we got dumped in the Ardennes without ammo (can you believe that? I still can't), I got to missing you all. So looking back was the best I could do. There are too many white crosses in the European cemeteries for Fox Company, 2nd battalion, 505th PIR, 82d Airborne. Graves I might never have the chance to visit, although I hope someday I'll see Europe when hell isn't raining down on her.

I was right—never did see any of those photographs the regimental photographer supposedly took. I spent a whole weekend spreading these out on the floor of my folks' attic, and boy did the memories come flooding back. Some made me real sad. But what I didn't expect was how much I laughed to myself, too.

No other friendships in my life will ever be what I found with you all in our third platoon. War is hell, but damn if it doesn't make for some strange bedfellows I sure do miss.

When I found this one I knew I had to send it to you. I hope instead of stirring up old wounds, it might give you a little peace.

Remember the good times. You all were the best men I've ever known.

At the bottom of the letter beneath his name—signed *Fish*—is a telephone number. He drew a little arrow pointing to the last digit and wrote, *Ring me.* I read the letter over three times before I have the courage to open the bigger envelope.

Into my hands falls a torn sketchbook page. I instantly look away from it and stare out at the white yard. *No, I can't. I'm sorry, Fish. I can't do it.*

But then I think of how I felt in the church when I decided to tell Dad, the thought that almost consumed me with guilt: *I've let him die twice.*

So I know that the least I can do is tell him I remember.

I look back at the drawing.

It's the two of us. The inscription at the bottom says, *Peter & Richard ("Addy & Rev"), August '43, Kairouan, Tunisia.* We're standing in front of one of the mosquito-netting tents, laughing, each detail in our faces rendered so vividly that I almost remember that moment and feel the sting of the sand and the trickle of sweat down my spine. *82d Airborne,* our t-shirts read, *US Paratroops.* I have my arms crossed, turned three-quarters toward Peter, white teeth gleaming in a sun-darkened face. He's got his hands on his hips, grinning and looking at Fish, presumably, who has a photographic memory and sketched so many of these scenes hours and days later.

Fish captured our laughter in charcoal better than any photograph ever could. And it does hurt. Because the two boys in this sketch have no idea what's coming.

Or maybe one of them does. Maybe Peter always knew.

I sit on the step for a long time, staring at them. Wishing I could go back to them and remember who they really were before their identities were swallowed by a war they didn't understand.

For one lighthearted moment, immortalized by Fish and showing all that ease of comfort between us, we're still just kids, and in the end things will be all right. Not yet, not for a while, but someday—that's what Peter would say.

I take a deep breath of cold air, and for the first time, I realize that not all my memories need to be caged in by barbed wire. Like a river undammed, a rush of images floods my mind. Moments when we were all laughing, when even the war—our collective reason for being—didn't matter to us. It feels like a remembrance and rekindling of old love, older than any of us, unbound by time or bodies or life or even death.

The hum of an engine catches my attention. I glance up to see the station wagon pulling into our driveway. Dad gets out, sees me, and smiles, tramping up the snowy walk. Hen noses open the screen door and runs out, slapping me with her tail as she trips down the steps and careens into Dad's legs, as if it's been three days and not three hours since she last saw him.

He scratches her behind the ears, and after she runs off through the snow to the treeline, he comes over to the porch. The drawing is still on my knees. Dad sits beside me.

I tilt the drawing for him to see and say, "From Fish—my artist friend."

My voice catches after that, and I don't know what else to say. I see him smile out of the corner of my eye.

"What a gift," he says. "That's beautiful."

I wipe at my eyes with the back of my hand. Dad puts his arm around me and I set my head on his shoulder, where the wool of his coat soaks up the stray tears. He puts his hand on my hair. His other hand touches the sketchbook page. "I think there's something on the back. Did you look at it?"

I shake my head and lift my eyes. Carefully so as not to smear the charcoal, Dad turns the page over. In Fish's scrawl are the words:

So fill to me the parting glass
And drink a health whate'er befalls...
But since it fell unto my lot
That I should rise and you should not
I'll gently rise and softly call
Goodnight, and joy be to you all.

I stare at it for a long time without speaking. Fish wrote the words, but they are Jacob's and Peter's voices. Sung out with abandon in an Edinburgh pub, come what may, and joy be to you all.

Dad stands up slowly, muttering something about his knees under his breath, and for a moment his hand lingers on my shoulder. But I sit for a while longer, staring at the words. Then I turn the drawing over again and look at Peter and me smiling. Beside my leg is Fish's letter. *Ring me.*

In the kitchen I drag a chair to where the telephone hangs on the wall, sit, and ask Kitty for a long-distance call to Portsmouth. I read her the number Fish wrote. While I wait, I prop the sketch between the back of the chair and the wall. I can't help thinking that Peter's expression is almost admonishing me for not having reached out to Fish sooner.

The line clicks. "Hello?"

I hesitate. Nothing will be as it was.

But God knows I've lost enough friends already.

"Fish?" I say. "It's Rev—Richard." As if he has any other friends with the nickname "Rev."

There's a rustle on the other end. "Hey, Richard," Fish says, sounding a little tinny, but it's his voice, all right. "I was hoping you'd call."

"Well, I just got your letter." It feels so stilted, like we don't know each other anymore, and I guess we don't. Uncomfortably formal, and for arbitrary reasons, considering we suffered dysentery and sandfly fever and a hundred other ailments together. "Thank you. I should've written. I'm sorry for the radio silence."

"No, don't beat yourself up. That signal works two ways." He laughs with a note of anxiety. "This is strange, isn't it?"

"I'll say. So how are you?"

"I'm good, yeah, I'm real good. Doing some drafting for one of the shipyards here in Portsmouth. Not glamorous artist's work, but it pays rent."

"Speaking of art, Fish—the drawing—" I don't know how to finish. The other end is quiet, unnerving at first till I remember Fish was rarely one to interrupt as the others were. Finally I say, "It means a lot, y'know, after everything. I never—well, I never thought I'd see us again like that."

"Yeah. Of course." His voice crackles for a few seconds, the connection dipping out. It cuts back in with, "—and so it didn't feel right going through all my drawings and just keeping them for myself. I sent some to the others, actually, one to Berk of him and McNuts at that pub we loved in Quorn, one to McNuts of him and O'Connor in Edinburgh...oh, and one I didn't even remember, to Skinny, him winning a craps game. And I've still got a couple hundred more."

"So you've talked to them?"

"Sure have. And they're all still idiots."

Fish tells me what he knows, snatches of stories and lives so disparate that it's surreal to think we ever shared foxholes. As we talk, our voices become looser, and I find myself laughing again.

Turns out McNuts is a courier in Manhattan, and every lawyer in the city knows the story of how a medic "'filleted his throat with a trench knife,' his words, not mine," Fish adds with a snort. Skinny married Eva and works in his parents' restaurant, which is what I'm sure he'd tell me a good Greek son does, never mind that my parents don't own a restaurant. I jokingly ask if Berk's made good on his threat to fill his and Emily's house with little Berks, defying the laws of nature since he hasn't been home a year yet, and it turns out the first Berk Jr. is set to make his or her appearance in the spring.

"Actually, it was his idea for us to get together, all of us," Fish says.

"Like a reunion?"

"Yeah, just F Company fellows, not some whole battalion affair. I wrote Lieutenant Greer, and you know if anyone can rally the troops, it's him." He pauses. "I know we're all scattered so it'll take some travel for everyone, but I think it'll be good for us to see each other. No one at home really understands, not like you guys do."

I wrap my finger around the telephone cord. "Tell me when and where, I'll be there. Oh, speaking of get-togethers, Fish, I have a big favor to ask." And I tell him about my engagement, which receives a whoop in reply.

"The fool's hope comes true!" he laughs triumphantly. "Now I get to call Berk and tell him he owes me five bucks."

"Of course you bet on that."

"You can't blame us; you know how hard entertainment was to come by back then! In France he said he was sure you wouldn't last a month without telling Grace, and I said it would take at least six, knowing you, so we shook on it. Gee, it feels swell to beat him."

"You make me feel like some racehorse with 20-1 odds. Anyway," I add, losing count of how many people at this point have placed bets on Grace and me, "I told you that because I want you to stand up with me. At my wedding."

"Rev, you want me to walk you down the aisle?"

Between him and Mattie, I'll give myself a migraine at this wedding from all the eye-rolling. "Yes, Fish, that's all I've ever wanted, for you to give me away."

He laughs and makes a crack about me upstaging Grace. Then he says, "Of course I will. Stand up with you, I mean, not the other stuff. With one caveat. You have to promise to do the same for me."

"...Is this one of those vague, open-ended promises for when you trick a girl into marrying you, or...?"

"Your faith in me is overwhelming," Fish answers dryly, "but no. Her name's Diana and she said yes, fully sober."

"Fishy, no kidding? Imagine that!" I shake my head. "Congratulations. I'm happy for you. Boy, you put me to shame, meet a girl and propose to her all in one year."

"She's an old friend from school. We lost touch, but she looked me up again when I got back to Portsmouth, and things just sort of...worked out."

"I'll say they did."

Though I can't see him, I can picture Fish's smile when he says, "Richard, I'm real glad you called. I guess it's been tough for us all in different ways."

"I know," I say, overwhelmed at the thought that each of them has a story as heavy to bear as mine. "But you get all the credit for this, Fish. I think I'm finally ready to remember the good things."

We trade stories for the next hour, my moving boxes forgotten, and once in a while I glance at the drawing of Peter and me.

I hope it might give you a little peace.
You all were the best men I've ever known.

14 April 1946

L ast night it was winter. The sky was made of slate, and the mountain wind chilled me to the bone as I walked home from spending the evening with Grace at the farm. Whatever bits of hardy grass that had survived the snow were frosted over in the brown ground, and I reached that point of the interminable winter when I stopped hoping for spring to come and forgot that it ever would.

But morning is a brand new country. I wake before dawn and watch the light come on over the hills. Even before it comes, when the sky is soft and gray like sleep itself, I feel the change. The wind has stopped blowing. The trees in the valley are still. Everything is still, not the quiet of winter's trance but the hush before the burst of song. And then light tinted like a painter's wash of silver and rose sweeps the frozen mountain, and I know I have only moments before it comes to life.

I force open the sticky window with my shoulder and dress and open the door so that the cool air and its scent of muddy earth drifts down the narrow hallway in our apartment above the pharmacy. Though we're on Main Street, the smell of wildness always lingers wherever you go in Caspar. Mattie, who usually goes to bed around this time, is still asleep. I tug on a pair of rainboots—by the standing puddles in the street below, it rained during the night—and run out into the cool morning.

Grace, also outfitted in boots, is already standing at the top of the farm road when I come around the bend. She calls, "I thought you'd be up," and she smiles because she knows. It doesn't look like much yet, no verdant green, no white petals, no overrun river banks; but we both know. We run through the mud puddles, breathing in the awakening, that cocktail of fresh wind and wonder.

Whatever the opposite of an Indian summer is called, a spring day before it should really be spring, this is it—a fluke, no certainty that there won't be more snow tomorrow or that we can go outside in bare feet and shirtsleeves after tonight. But when you live this far north, you take whatever you can get, and enjoy it.

So that's exactly what Grace and I do. It's my mom's idea; I never would've even thought of doing this on her and Dad's twenty-fifth anniversary today. "But your grandparents are here, and Faye's in from Bangor, so why don't we have a party?" she says when Grace and I come to the house. "Just a little get-together with our closest, before the wedding, where we'll probably barely see you both."

I'm hesitant, but she assures me it can be both an anniversary and engagement party, if I make a toast to them. Grace jumps at the idea, because how many more chances like this will there be, she reasons, everyone gathered in the same place, without the pressure of a wedding day and drunk neighbors to distract us from being together? So at the farm, Sidney and I carry their grandmother's dining room table out into the orchard by the house, after Grace dusts it off because they never eat in the dining room, and we cart out a mismatched assortment of chairs and even a wooden bench we found in their gardening shed. Lena arranges some stalks of last summer's dried wildflowers and handfuls of thistles in Mrs. Whitley's blue ginger jars. I very carefully bring out stacks of china plates. Grace calls Antonia and Helen, who both cancel their Saturday night dates in Bangor for us. I tell Mattie not to drink anything because my grandmother's bringing a whole case of her home-brewed ouzo, which can burn the barnacles off the hull of your boat and will get you drunker than a skunk in no time. I'll have to carry him up the stairs tonight.

The late-afternoon sun blankets the valley in a golden slant. There are no buds on the trees, but Sidney hung a couple of lanterns from the bare branches so that as they sway in the breeze, half-crowns of light sweep over the table and illuminate faces—glowing eyes, mouths open in laughter. Red wine and ouzo sparkle in Grace's mother's champagne flutes, but even if there was none, I think I'd still feel a little drunk. The hazy flames of green-and-white Christmas candles, all we could find, snap back and forth without blowing out.

Not even the candles are brighter than Grace. After the sun sets behind Mt. Katahdin and the wind forces us all to drape our coats over our shoulders, she seems lit up, somehow everywhere around the table at once and still right beside me. All day I've barely let go of her hand. She knocks her knee against mine, not to ask if I'm okay but as if to say, *Can you believe it?* And I knock back, *Of course I can't.* I love how she leans in when someone speaks, all her attention devoted to their story. I love when her inhibitions fall away and that silly light comes into her eyes. I love her self-deprecating jokes, never taking herself too seriously, and how she has to slap her hand over her mouth to keep from snorting champagne when I tell Berk's tuna fish can on the subway joke. And I love that beside her, knees touching, I feel peace.

The clink of silverware on glass turns everyone's attention toward the end of the table, where Dad is sitting between Mom and Sidney. He glances at me first for confirmation and I nod, so he stands. He puts one hand on the back of his chair and looks at Grace and me. He looked at me with the same expression the evening I knocked on his office door in the church, right after I got home, and if only I'd been paying better attention, maybe I would've seen in it what I see now. Or maybe I wouldn't have. I spent so long running after a love that never left me, only to come back to the beginning and find it still there, waiting for me. *And bring the fattened calf and kill it, and let us eat and celebrate.*

"I'd like to say a blessing," he says, his voice sounding as full in the amplification of the valley as it does in the pulpit. "For the sake of the hot food, I'll do my best not to ramble, which my family can tell you is not my strength when it comes to praying."

"I could've told you that," Sidney remarks, at which Dad points the butter knife at him and tells Sidney not to make him come over there, which of course makes Grace laugh.

Dad closes his eyes, and everyone else bows their heads, even Mattie.

"Lord, we come before you in thankfulness, not least all of for this community and the love in these families and these friendships." I reach for Grace's hand in her lap, and she entwines her fingers in mine. "We know that *'where two or three are gathered in My name, there I am among them,'* and though we're beginning to come out of these past years of deep darkness, we know You never forsook us during that—here in Maine, or in Boston, or Belgium or Australia or the South Pacific. By your grace you brought Mattie, Sidney, Lena, and Richard home to us, but we remember the friends we lost...and we trust in your grace for them, too. Bless our gathering tonight, Lord, and bless the laughter. You know our hearts, and You know that I am..."

I feel someone watching me and open one eye, raising my head slightly. He smiles at me.

"...I am more thankful than I can say for Richard and for Grace," Dad says, "and for what they mean together. I pray for many years of peace and happiness for them."

A chorus of *Amen* goes around the table.

"Well," Laurie says after a couple of seconds, raising his wine glass, "here's to an engagement that came as a surprise to absolutely no one." He takes an expert swallow of his wine while the non-Greek members of our party receive their first jarring introduction to Eirene Kalikredes' home-brewing.

The agate on Grace's ring glows faintly in the candlelight as she tells a story from when we were kids about a hockey game and a fox and hand-me-down ice skates. My grandfather, at the head of the table, is trying to teach Faye and Helen how to flag down the waiters at Greek sidewalk cafes, for "whenever you go to Santorini next, girls," and when Faye says she's not sure she can go to Santorini any time soon, he tells her that she must—a life without seeing Greece is no life at all.

Mattie says that Helen won't need to flag down the waiters, that "her siren beauty will just attract them to her like magnets," and she looks at Laurie on her other side appealingly. He's no help because he's fielding questions about his new job at the *Bangor Daily News,* where he'll be moving at the end of the month, and where he'll no doubt propose to Faye before he's even unpacked one box. Pop calls all the way down the table to Sidney to ask about seminary, which is still in the cards for him. Lena is warm and supportive but is more immediately concerned with buying a house. Then suddenly the whole table is roaring with laughter as Toni retells the time I ruined her baptism by letting a biblical swarm of frogs loose in the sanctuary.

"It was one frog!" I protest, but an Exodus plague is far funnier, as is Toni's completely false claim that a frog swan-dived down the back of her dress as Dad sprinkled the baptismal water on her head. Mattie leans across Helen and Laurie to pry stories out of Nana and Mrs. Whitley, who are seated together at one end of the table—that may've been a mistake—and who laugh so hard about a missionary society meeting gone wrong when they were both young women (pistachio cake on the ceiling, frosting in Edith Delfinch's hair) that they dab their eyes with their napkins. Hen, nosing around beneath the table for scraps, eats both napkins and crumbs without discrimination. Baxter watches lazily from behind the screen door to the Whitleys' kitchen, eyes flicking up every so often.

The last light from the sun fills the valley and backlights the clouds the color of our wine. It isn't Santorini, but it doesn't need to be. It's our little forgotten pocket of the world, witness to our ordinary magic of river-wading and ice hockey games and caught frogs and secrets whispered in haunted houses at midnight. As the dusk deepens I nearly forget to eat, trying to notice everything, to live in this night forever—beauty within the memory of beauty, old love like the scent of flowers even though the trees haven't bloomed yet. My parents' hands on the table beside each other, and Dad's voice saying "Lizzie."

It's that last one that prompts me to stand, knowing that I can't let tonight slip away without saying this. Conversations trail off as everyone looks up at me and I say, "This is for my parents, who wouldn't say a word about it themselves, but who've been more than gracious to let Grace and me do this tonight, on their twenty-fifth anniversary"—cheers and raised glasses—"and I..."

Looking at them, their eyes bright on the other side of the candle flames, I know that whatever I say will only be circling around the edge of the truth without fully capturing it. Their favorite song is Billie Holiday's "The Very Thought of You," and sometimes at night after Laurie and I had gone to bed, I'd hear them downstairs dancing to it on the radio: *The very thought of you, and I forget to do those little ordinary things that everyone ought to do...*

"I wanted to say thank you," I go on, "for everything, you know, and especially for saying 'I love you' in earshot of Laurie and me as often as you do. And one more thing, then I promise I'll let you drink." I glance down at Grace and can't keep from smiling. Her outfit is a perfect summary of the dichotomy between her romanticism and her practicality: the same green velvet dress she wore on New Year's Eve, topped with an overcoat on her shoulders. "To Grace and Sidney's parents, too, who should be here, but who still have a place at this table."

Grace still has her hand in mine. It feels as though we're all drawing up extra seats and setting out plates for our dead, hoping that there's enough food to go around like the loaves and the fish, scooting closer together so that more can gather: *I love you, I miss you, I'll see you at the marriage feast.* The very thought of you.

"Well, I don't know if we can say *yamas* after that," Laurie says.

Grace shrugs off the overcoat, makes a pass at her eyes with the back of her hand, and then stands up beside me with her wine glass held aloft. "Of course we can. My parents would've loved saying that. *Yamas!*"

A fter the wine glasses are emptied, the ouzo is locked in Mrs. Whitley's pantry, where it can't do any more damage. The table is cleared and the baklava sent with our friends. I bring out the portable Philco from the kitchen and set it on the tablecloth, beside the blown-out candles and crumpled napkins. Nana tutted when Grace and I assured her we'd clean everything up, but Mom hooked her arm through her mother's and said, "Maybe we ought to let the young ones be alone now." She kissed my cheek, and the Dare delegation trickled back home. Mrs. Whitley told us it was the best evening she'd spent in a long while and went in to bed, and Sidney and Lena disappeared inside, too, hand-in-hand.

But the kitchen lights are still on, emitting a crescent glow into the lane and the garden. I catch a signal on the radio and the crackly notes of Ella Fitzgerald's voice float through the dark night: *You say it's only a paper moon, sailing over a cardboard sea, but it wouldn't be make-believe if you believed in me...*

I reach for Grace's hand and spin her round as she laughs and swallows a last bit of wine, setting the glass on the table. She shed her overcoat on the back of a chair and seems to have forgotten it, because she's shivering a bit as the wind blows. Despite the sun having long since set, I feel warm, and I drape my suit jacket over her shoulders.

"Nice that it smells like you," she says, "only the real thing is better."

I take her by the waist and draw her in. She slings one arm around my neck, and we dance in the quiet yard as Ella fades out and a slow instrumental takes her place. Grace's green skirt fans out in a twirl and the kitchen lights catch her hair, and I think how I could watch her forever. How I will.

"We get to do this for the rest of our lives." I press my hand to the small of her back. "And no one can stop us."

She smiles against my neck. "Only the county clerk if they decline to give us a marriage license."

"Don't even kid about that."

"I would never," she says, trying to look serious. She touches my cheekbone. "You look so cute. And no, I'm not drunk. I didn't even have any of the ouzo, just the champagne."

"Me too. I didn't want to end up under the table singing."

"Save it for the wedding."

I don't know if it's the champagne buzz or "Moonlight Serenade" on the radio or the pale stars shining through the watery clouds, but a soft haze seems to fall around us, as though we're reflections looking up out of a lake. But it's her, of course. Everything else is just a footnote.

Grace's arm is light on my shoulder. "Richard," she says, "remember how I always tagged you out when we played pickup games, just as you almost made it to home?"

"Mhm."

"Sweet of you to let me. It made me feel good about myself till I realized, how in the world was I tagging out a cross-country runner?" She smiles, and the early moonlight shines across her cheek. "Most fellas try to show off for the girls, but you let yourself look silly for me."

"I think I'm just good at looking silly, Gracie, even on my own behalf," I answer. "Maybe that's my fatal flaw."

"I won't tell anyone. Want to know one of mine?" She slows with the tempo of the song till we're barely moving. Out of the circle of orange light, all I can see of her are the shadowy lines of her face. "I always get so caught up in worrying I'll lose something that I forget to love it. And then I get so upset that I didn't notice it better when I had it."

"I know."

"But you won't let me do that this time, will you?"

"Not a chance." I kiss her, holding her so close against me that I feel every beat of her heart as if it were my own. She holds on tighter when I try to draw back. So I kiss her again because once is never enough, and then she presses her cheek to my shoulder and smiles against my neck.

"I said welcome home to you the day you got back," she whispers, "a year ago. It didn't feel real then."

"But it does now?"

"Yes." Grace tilts her head back to look up at me, just a glint of green eyes in the moonlight. "Welcome home, and I promise not to tag you out this time."

"That's sweet, but I can't promise I won't keep making a fool of my—"

God's honest truth, I didn't mean to back up into the table just at this moment and knock three of the wine glasses into the grass and send two snuffed-out candles careening across the tablecloth, though I don't need to tell that to Grace, who laughs so hard she doesn't make a sound as my jacket slips off her shoulders to the ground. She knows all too well that any comedic timing I have is all providence. God does enjoy humbling me.

"Well, that wasn't entirely unexpected, was it?" I draw her back into my arms. "At some point I should let you go to bed."

"Not just yet," Grace whispers, taking my hand again. "Let's dance."

And so we do dance, just outside the crescent of kitchen light beside the white farmhouse, as the rustling woods and the river and the singing frogs ease Caspar into early night.

Home, I think, and what a world to come home to.

The End

Peter & Richard (Addy & Rev),
August '43, Kairouan, Tunisia

ACKNOWLEDGMENTS

Seven years of my life have gone into this story so far, but it wasn't created in isolation. A huge thank you to Elaine DeBohun, my friend, fellow writer, and visionary behind Chariklo Press, who encouraged me toward indie publishing and welcomed me into her author collective. Thank you to my copy editor, Brianna De Man, for patiently trawling through dozens of repetitions of the dialogue tag "murmur," and gently guiding me into better comma usage. Many thanks to Shelby Nicole McFadden for bringing Fish's sketch of Richard and Peter to life so perfectly. And thank you to my friend Leah Carrere, who made my "I want to feel like a character in my own novel" dreams come true with her film photos of me.

This story has friendship at its heart, and so does its creation. I am grateful to every friend who has been part of its origin and who inspired the friendships found within. To my oldest friend (my Mattie, although a little better-behaved), Molly Maggi: Thank you for coming into my life fifteen years ago with the kind of friendship I thought only existed in books. To Noelle Chow, who has cheered me on with so much joy and enthusiasm. To Sky Walden, who was the first person to read this novel in its entirety, and who has been at my side for so long—witnessing every writer I've been. And to Audrey Chapman, foxhole buddy for life: There wouldn't be a story without you (and Evie). Your influence is woven into every page.

To my sister, Paige Kelly, who not only designed the beautiful cover art, but was the first person—years ago—to read *Holland Road* in its early drafts, and loved it instantly. You have always been my biggest encourager, and I love walking our intertwining paths together, in search of our "true country."

Although my grandparents have all passed, their presence echoes throughout this story. My grandmother, Shirley H. Schwab ("Nana"), was a born-and-bred Mainer and a talented artist who painted countless renderings of her home state, including the watercolor image on the cover. It is for her that this novel is set in Maine, and it has brought me so much joy to have this collaboration with her even after her passing.

To my parents, Douglas and Laura Kelly, who gave me the kind of wonderful, peaceful childhood that everyone wants and that no one writes novels about. My dad is also a writer, and a wonderful source of publishing wisdom—I'm sure it's from him that I inherited my need to tell stories. My mom listened to every plot hole and character frustration on our many pandemic walks, and talked with me through knots I thought I'd never untangle. Thank you for guiding me into who I am with love and patience.

While I've never been to war, and I don't usually set out to write autobiographically, much of Richard's journey with his faith mirrors my own life. I have been saved by Christ, and welcomed home—again and again—by a good and gracious Father.

ABOUT THE AUTHOR

Caroline Kelly credits watching the Battle of Helm's Deep at age 10 as the beginning of her obsession with war stories. A graduate of the University of North Carolina at Greensboro, her essays have been published in *Ekstasis* magazine, and her nonfiction articles in *Our State* magazine. *Holland Road* is her debut novel. She lives in New England.